PRAISE FOR ANNIHILATION ARIA

"[A] bright and exciting space opera [...] Underwood's prose is brisk and funny without ever sacrificing his skilled sf world building. Highly recommended for fans of action-packed space opera and anyone else looking for a fun and fast-paced read."

—Booklist, Starred Review

"This fantastically fun series launch harkens back to Marvel's Guardians of the Galaxy[...] The interpersonal dynamics are delightful, however familiar they may be, and the tightly constructed world, cinematic fight scenes, and ambitious scope combine to evoke a sense of wonder. This is a rollicking good time."

—Publishers Weekly

"This is pure space opera, wild and wacky and silly and strange, high-stakes and deeply personal all at once. I could not be happier to have read this book. Recommended for fans of AXIOM by Tim Pratt, TEENAGERS FROM OUTER SPACE (the RPG) published by R. Talsorian Games, GUARDIANS OF THE GALAXY (Marvel Studios), and KILLJOYS (SYFY Channel)."

—Seanan McGuire, author of the
October Daye and InCryptid series

OTHER BOOKS BY MICHAEL R. UNDERWOOD

THE REE REYES SERIES

Geekomancy
Celebromancy
Attack the Geek
Hexomancy

The Younger Gods

Shield & Crocus

GENRENAUTS

The Data Disruption
The Shootout Solution
The Absconded Ambassador
The Cupid Reconciliation
The Substitute Sleuth
The Failed Fellowship
Genrenauts: The Complete Season One

Born to the Blade (with Marie Brennan, Cassandra Khaw, and Malka Older)

ANNIHILATION ARIA
THE SPACE OPERAS, VOL. I
BY MICHAEL R. UNDERWOOD

PARVUS
science fiction + fantasy

Parvus Press, LLC
PO Box 711232
Herndon, VA 20171
ParvusPress.com
Annihilation Aria
Copyright © 2019 by Michael R. Underwood

Preposterous ass, that never read so far; To know the cause why music was ordain'd! Was it not to refresh the mind of man; After his studies or his usual pain? bit.ly/EpicAria

Print ISBN: 978-1-7338119-5-8
Digital ISBN: 978-1-7338119-4-1

Cover art by Tom Edwards
Designed and typeset by Catspaw DTP Services
Author photo by Meghan Underwood

To all of the families of choice
I've found along the way.

CHAPTER ONE

MAX

MAX WALKER WAS VERY good at running for his life. He had plenty of motivation, given the ravenous horde of purple space locusts nipping at his heels. He cradled the mapping device in his arms, shielding it from the locusts. Dying would be bad. Coming out empty-handed wouldn't be much better.

It was that kind of day. A "you really should have come up with a better plan, but hindsight is 20/20, and hey, you've got a kickass wife with a giant sword beside you, so it's not all bad" day. Unfortunately for Max, those days were pretty common. But hey, he hadn't died yet.

Lahra Kevain, said kickass wife, ran beside him, keeping stride, though she could have easily lapped him any time she wanted. Lucky for him, she'd decided that she liked him enough to save him from the aforementioned horde of space locusts. Even wearing a twenty-kilo set of EVA-capable armor, Lahra moved with impeccable grace. It made sense though, since she spent more time in her armor than out of it. A soldier-caste Genae, Lahra was made for battle. Even when she was running for her life, she wasn't really worried.

As far as he could tell.

They fled the tomb so fast that Max could barely maintain his mental record of the turns and doorways and puzzles that had taken them hours to work through on their way in.

But now, there was only running. And holding onto the mapping device, which would maybe, possibly, hopefully give Max and Lahra the information they needed to finally make real progress on their respective missions.

One of the locust beasties ripped a chunk off the heel of his space suit. Air bled out like a whoopee cushion, and his O_2 gauge started sagging.

"We need to run faster!" Lahra said, still calm despite the odds.

"This is me running faster!" Max replied through huffs and puffs.

Max kept his eyes forward even as he felt the beasts scraping at his heels and crunching beneath his feet. They were gaining.

None of this would have happened if the tomb had been properly sealed. But no, some grave robbers had gotten to the site before them and screwed everything up. Great job, assholes. He'd refrained from kicking their skeletons. It wouldn't help.

"Keep going!" Lahra said, and he felt her drop back.

"Lahra, no!" The vid feed from Lahra's suit showed the horde of locust beasts swarming her, the screen filling with the purple creatures and their black teeth.

"Die, beasts!" she shouted, her scattergun barking death in every direction. "Wheel is just around the corner! I will catch up."

More gunshots. More dead locusts. But the next sound was different—a cry of pain from Lahra.

Max hailed their pilot, Wheel, on the ship. "We got swarmers here. Need a hot extraction."

"No atmo, no flamethrower, kid," came Wheel's reply.

On easier days, Max would describe Wheel as terse.

He could see more of Lahra in the diminished cloud of locusts, her armor gouged and slashed in dozens of places. But the smile on her blue-hued face told him she'd be fine.

"Hit the wall!" she called. Max dove to the side. It'd only taken a few months to accept that in a fight, Lahra knew best.

A blast from the scattergun disintegrated another chunk of the swarm, and Lahra burst free, the creatures fading into the shadows.

She staggered forward, swatting away a few stragglers. "Get us out of here, now!"

They took the final corner and ran down the rest of the hallway. Max's O₂ gauge was tickling the red.

The *Kettle*'s forward lights flashed through the small passageway Lahra had dug through the rubble. It had only been a few hours, though it felt like days.

"Standing by. One of these days, you kids are going to walk leisurely out of a tomb, arms full of loot and not pursued by anything."

Max chuckled. "We wouldn't want to give you a heart attack."

Wheel grumbled.

"I mean, if that did happen, those nanites would just jump-start you, right?"

"Better to nail the jump than count on the net, kid."

Lahra's feet pounded on the floor of the temple foyer as they approached the rubble. "There was never real doubt that we would succeed."

Max crawled through the tunnel, still babying the mapping device. The hold of the *Kettle* opened like the maw of a friendly fish, Wheel holding the ship steady. Lahra followed shortly after, sword-first since she wouldn't fit with the blade locked onto the back of her suit. He offered her a hand as she emerged from the tunnel. She took it and squeezed, letting him "help" even though she was fine on her own. It was one of the many ways they showed one another that they were a team, always looking out for one another. Like when she'd sit up with him as he was studying even though his research could literally put her to sleep.

Max took one last look at the tomb as the ship pulled away, the ramp rising to close. Another brush with death, another run-and-gun engagement, and, if they were lucky, another step closer to home.

But whose home? And what did that mean for him and Lahra?

CHAPTER TWO

LAHRA

LAHRA SANG "SAHVO'S EMBRACE" to her armor in the sun-soaked cargo hold. The embrace was an aria of resilience and rebirth from the epic of Zhore, sung originally by a love-struck guardian to the princess who was her charge.

The song awakened the suit, allowing her armor to repair itself using the sun's energy. The coral-steel resonated with her voice, stitching itself back together, scalloped ridges and joints sealing and smoothing over. Once by one, traces of her and Max's last misadventure faded, and the suit returned to its optimal form.

Lahra stood in underclothes, the cargo hold baking as mostly-filtered sunlight streamed through the starboard portal. The portal nearly filled an entire side of the cargo bay, eight meters high and ten meters long. The radiation of the nearby star was reduced such that it would not harm her but would still power the suit's regenerative capacity, guided by her song. And it might help restore the lustrous azure tone her skin had gained that summer working sentry on the grain farms of Ikerr.

Her voice was low, solid, like packed earth. Her mother's

voice had been richer, like fresh-tilled soil. Halra Kevain had sung to Lahra all her life, taught her all the songs needed to operate the suit and to fight as a royal guardian. All of the greatest power of the Genae was conveyed through song, from the marches of the royal guards to the songs of restoration, as well as the snippets Lahra had picked up from other Genae.

Lahra's repertoire was a mere shadow of the full power of the soldier caste, so much of their legacy lost.

Lahra lifted the heel of one of the suit's legs and watched the puncture hole close over. More warmth slid into her tone as she continued, diving into the chorus. "Sahvo's Embrace" was meant to be sung in call-and-response, sergeant to her squad. She'd taught it to Max, but with the way he fought (mostly through stealth and hiding behind solid objects), it failed to serve its original purpose. The Embrace sang strength into a squad's suits and their limbs, recalling the rebirth brought with the sun's return in the spring.

Max stood on the other side of the cargo hold, bent over his laboratory and research desk, where he had hooked their just-liberated device into his terminal. Up a ladder from the hold were the gunner's turret, the living quarters, and the hatch to the engine room. Above that, at the top and front of the ship, was the cockpit—Wheel's domain.

Max all but lived at his desk. In the seven years Lahra had known him, he'd always been driven, focused, but also kind, charming. He remembered names as easily as textual citations. But not songs. Singing was hard for him, his voice thin. He had an ear for language but not music. A cosmic joke, one of many.

The suit was whole, her song complete. She left it in the sun to absorb energy, her greatsword locked in place on the suit's back.

"How goes the decryption?" Lahra took her customary place to Max's left, looking on as he worked.

"Mostly there. Anything I can't crack, Uwen can take

care of. Anyway, he likes it when I go to him for help. Think he enjoys feeling useful."

"Or that you still have more to learn."

Max nodded, the wall lamps illuminating his brown skin. "Which is true. This section here still makes absolutely no sense to me. And without that, I can't tell if the chart is telling us to go into the center of the Forbidden Sectors or if it wants us to go beyond warp space."

"Surely it is the former."

Warp space delineated the known galaxies. Beyond those bounds, ships crawled along at a fraction of the speed of warp travel. The Forbidden Sectors were so-dubbed because they held the core of the Old Atlan Empire, destroyed by the Vsenk in their usurpation. But since those broken or abandoned planets contained forgotten Old Atlan technology, they were an ideal place to hunt for artifacts.

"I sure hope so. Not sure we could convince Wheel to take a three-month trip on burners only."

"You want me to take the ship where now?" Wheel called down the echoing halls of their ship. The *Kettle* was small enough that it was hard to ever be truly out of earshot.

"Nowhere yet!" Max shouted back.

Lahra laid a kiss on his temple, her fingers trailing along his shoulder and neck as a reminder and a promise. "Let me know if you need any help." She relished in his happy shudder and hauled herself up the ladder by door to the engine room. She walked by her shared quarters with Max, Wheel's quarters, the bathroom, the gunnery station, the ship's meager galley, and then up another short ladder to the cockpit.

Cruji snored in one corner, curled up in his straw-laden cage. The Molja was a mass of tentacles and feathers and had no practical use aside from boosting morale.

Wheel was elbow-deep in the *Kettle's* control console. The Atlan's skin was the color of faded moonstone, arms and much of her back replaced by cybernetic implants. When she plugged in all the way, the console grew to meet her, screen connecting to a cybernetic eye, panels and switches sprouting cables to interface directly with Wheel via ports from head to hip.

The Atlan were the only species fully adapted to cybernetic enhancements, allowing them to control spaceships through a neural link. Lahra or Max could pilot the *Kettle*, but only Wheel could truly inhabit it. Atlan's cybernetics spanned a wide range of technologies, none more fiercely guarded than those allowing direct connection with ships' computers and warp drives.

Lahra and Max had been working with Wheel (and as a result, living on the *Kettle*) for several years. Wheel was taciturn, mostly liked being left to herself and the ship's business, but she had unparalleled contacts—including fences who would take nearly any Old Atlan artifact Lahra and Max could find.

The Atlan had once ruled warp space, but when the Vsenk took over, the Atlan homeworld was destroyed and the survivors scattered to the winds. They survived by adapting and through their monopoly on the capacity to interface with warp drives. What took a day's travel via warp space would take months otherwise.

Now the Atlan were pilots, mechanics, and engineers. They'd made themselves essential but rarely held power beyond their lock on transportation. The Vsenk resented the Atlan's adaptation and continued to scapegoat them at every turn.

"How's the imperial traffic?" Lahra looked out the viewscreen into the black. Sensors would pick anything up before her eyes could, but she couldn't break the habit. And any system could fail. "Always trust yourself more than your gear," her mother had sung to her time and time again. That line was one of dozens from a song she'd composed to a traditional tune, an amalgamation of half-remembered lessons from her own youth.

Wheel's arm twisted, and a map with dozens of red dots popped up on the screen next to Lahra, showing their weaving path through the gaps left between the imperial sensors. "No patrols within range. Just the buoys they've littered around the system like Drell droppings."

To hear them tell the tale, the Vsenk Imperium had ruled for ten thousand years. They created the universe and loved their creation so much that they chose to live among their children as benevolent god-emperors.

Lies, all of it. The Vsenk had overthrown the Old Atlan and made warp space their own a thousand years ago. Since then, they'd tried to erase every bit of history they could. Controlling schools, outlawing texts, enforcing an imperial monopoly on comm relays, the Vsenk kept a tight grip. But the Vsenk had destroyed a half-dozen inhabited worlds along the way, eliminating most of the Atlan's greatest technology.

The Empire could keep the real histories in the margins, but people remembered the truth of the Vsenk's rise and the Atlan's fall. Most were just smart enough not to say so where the Vsenk could hear them.

The last people to challenge the Vsenk had been the Genae, Lahra's people. The Genae gave the Vsenk their greatest challenge, but in the end, even the battle songs of her sisters were powerless against the Vsenk's super-weapon, the Devastation. The Vsenk cracked the entire planet of Genos into several pieces, ending the war in one stroke. The surviving Genae, including Lahra's great-great-grandmother, scattered on the solar winds, swearing vengeance and pledging themselves to restoring the crown.

The Vsenk were many things—cruel, arrogant, aggressive; but above all else, they were absolutists. They prized decisive victories.

With more than two dozen systems to patrol, however, even the Vsenk couldn't be everywhere at all times. By best estimates, there were only a few thousand Vsenk, even after centuries of aggressive breeding programs to counteract their low fertility. They leaned heavily on a vassal-driven military, which meant that Lahra and Max could operate at the edges, keep off the radar, and be about their missions without running afoul of Imperial forces for more than a bribe here or there coming or going from docking stations.

Most of the time.

"How long until we're back at the Wreck?" Lahra asked.

"Without attracting Imperial attention? Better part of two days."

Max walked into the cockpit on the comms. "That should be plenty of time to figure this thing out and be ready to chat with Uwen."

"Two days it is," Lahra said. "I'm going to check our supplies, see how much of our payment we'll need to end up pouring back into the ship."

Wheel cocked her head to the side the way she did when she was analyzing data. "The *Kettle*'s plenty hungry, but she can last a while if need be. As long as you two are fine eating algae paste."

Max made a sound of mock delight. "Just like momma used to make."

"Why not?" Lahra asked. "It's incredibly efficient food." Growing up, efficient food wasn't available. You took what you could get.

Max had come from Earth, an industrialized, non-spacefaring culture. But at least they too had music, so they were odd, not barbaric.

Lahra slipped into a song of memory as she began her rounds, tallying spare parts, rations, and more. The song helped her hold the numbers and details in her mind, a musical memory palace.

They'd survived another adventure, and now the song of battle and exploration gave way to the daily work songs of maintenance and travel.

Until the next explosion. Which would inevitably come sooner than they expected.

CHAPTER THREE

WHEEL

"OKAY, I'VE GOT GOOD news and shit news!" Wheel called down to the lovebirds.

"Shit first, dessert second!" Max called back.

"The shit news is that the there's an Imperial patrol boat parked just outside the Wreck. Probably trawling for bribes. Good news is, we made it. Hurray."

Max's frustration echoed through the halls and up into the cockpit. "Fucking greedy assholes. Bet you the entire Empire would collapse in on itself if they couldn't get people coming and going. Base tax rate's already highway robbery." His footsteps echoed through the halls as he approached, Lahra alongside him. The Imperium didn't just suppress historical truth and tax citizens within a centimeter of their life, they also aggressively conscripted troops from vassal planets and encouraged infighting through scapegoating and competition for appointed political positions.

And worse.

Wheel pulled her gaze from the comms to scowl at Max. "Play it cool, okay? I don't want the *Kettle* flagged in every imperial system for the rest of eternity."

Lahra shrugged. "It's only a matter of time before we end up on some list or another of theirs. They have as many lists as there are imperial citizens. Suspected dissidents, information smugglers, heretical historians, draft dodgers . . ."

Wheel tuned Lahra out as the *Kettle* took its place in line. Half an hour later, when they finally pulled by into range of the bribe boat, Wheel took the call.

The voice was melodious, probably a Rellix. "Vessel, you are required by Imperial law to transmit your information and submit to search."

It was a constant struggle trying to make a living on the edge. Imperial patrols at every port requiring licenses and bribes, taxes pushing most everything into gray and black markets, and the humiliation of keeping up their ring-kissing supplication skills.

Wheel sighed, then switched her comms to broadcast. "This is freighter designate the '*Kettle*.' Captain and proprietor Wheel speaking. I am transmitting my license and registration codes." She sent with it a notice of an unclassified credit packet transfer that could be assigned anywhere by the recipient. Cleanest, simplest way to send a bribe. Flunkies could even send it up the chain to their bosses. If you were being extorted at the end of a barrel, making the transaction as easy as possible tended to get you out of the line of fire faster.

"Yes, confirming receipt of your transmission, *Kettle*, thank you for your prompt reply." She could practically hear the Rellix measuring the bribe and weighing their response.

A few moments later. "Freighter *Kettle*, your data are in order. You may proceed. For the Empire."

"For the Empire," Wheel said through only mostly gritted teeth. It wasn't enough to bleed them dry at every port; the Imperium also demanded that they speak their words, bow to their flag, and salute their god-warriors on sight. For the rulers of a galaxy-spanning empire, the Vsenk's egos were terribly fragile.

Wheel had spent the past decade out on the periphery and had no interest in going back into the core planets, where the Imperials had squads in every neighborhood, overbearing propaganda posters, and vid-screens looping their official histories. The dangers and uncertainties of the edge were far more comforting.

The *Kettle*'s comms pinged again. Jesvin.

Wheel's whole body went tense. *Voiddamnit.*

They were getting it from all sides today. Her nostrils flared as the message played through her comms implant.

My dearest Wheel,

I've received word that you're returning to our glorious home, and I look forward to hosting you in one of my fabulous garages. I know how you like to pamper the Kettle *after your little adventures, and I want only the best for you. While my finest engineers are seeing to your ship's needs, I hope you'll do me the courtesy of coming over for Vrial so that we can discuss your recent ventures and that little matter of your outstanding debt.*

I remain dutifully yours,
Jesvin Ker

Wheel steadied herself and sent a confirmation receipt, red creeping in at the edges of her vision. Without an immediate response, Jesvin would just repeat the message every five minutes until Wheel replied or until the Rellix's goons could track her down.

"Get up here, you two. Jesvin's on our ass again."

CHAPTER FOUR

LAHRA

JESVIN KER WAS A monster wrapped in silks. She presented herself as a pillar of the community, shield to the helpless, friend to all.

But no matter how delicately she wrapped herself in finery, she could not change her feathers. She was a tyrant perched upon the Wreck like a shaky roost.

Years ago, when Lahra and Max were stuck on the Wreck, behind on everything and completely adrift, Lahra had taken a bodyguarding job for the Ker family. All she knew about them was that they were widely beloved on the Wreck.

Jesvin hired Lahra to look after her nibling, Xifo Ker. Xifo was a delight. They loved music more than anything, and though Lahra found their compositions to be fairly intolerable—Max referred to it as "catchy but toothless noise-funk," whatever that meant—Xifo was a caring youth who saw the worth of every being they met. Listening to their music was honestly the most trying part of the assignment for the first six weeks.

That changed when the Iugi brothers hit the apartment in a kidnapping attempt.

When the Illhari gang struck, Xifo had been in their apartment, mixing a new track to share on data drives built into lunch containers.

Two grenades crashed through the window, trailing gas. One large form leapt through after the grenades. Lahra batted one grenade back through the hole it had formed, then grabbed the other between her boots and jumped, kicking her legs forward to toss it right into the chest of one of the masked Illhari. The Iugi brothers were large for Illhari, nearly a meter and a half tall and so muscular they were nearly square.

"Get to the bathroom, put on the mask, and lock the door!" Lahra shouted as the other Illhari knocked down the door and barreled into the room, shock guns at the ready.

Lahra heard Xifo scrambling behind her as she began singing.

"Guard's Duty" was a repetitive song with quick crescendos and de-crescendos. Like many of her caste's songs, it served several purposes, primarily that of reminding the guard of their priority. But each Genae song tapped into the chorus of the universe, granting amazing power to her favored daughters. "Guard's Duty" granted clarity and fortitude as long as she hewed to her mission.

Max called her people's songs Terran terms like "magic" and "scientifically impossible." For all his knowledge, there were still some things he did not understand.

As she sang, the universe matched her, harmonizing with her single voice. Each song had its own feeling—some felt like a hot shower after a long, cold EVA walk, others had the taste of fresh-baked bread. And when she sang in harmony with her sisters, what few of them remained, the sensation was all the stronger.

In that moment, her mission was clear—all she had to do was keep Xifo safe and the attackers away from the bathroom.

That was all she *had* to do. But there were many ways of

achieving an objective. And unfortunately for the Illhari, the apartment was not that large. Xifo refused Jesvin's extravagance, so the Illhari were within measure of Lahra's sword as soon as they stepped into the room. She slapped the gun out of one brother's hands, then shot another with a light bolt. Just enough to stun.

The Illhari attacked in a non-lethal stance, so she'd match them unless the situation called for escalation.

The other two fired, but Lahra's armor was hardened against electricity. Anything less would be self-destructive, given her sword.

She watched fear blossom in the Illhari's eyes as their blasts did nothing.

"Surrender, and you may live," she said. "Flee, and Jesvin will hunt you down. Continue, and you will be throwing away your lives."

They didn't need to know that she wasn't planning on killing them. Her people had a fearsome reputation, after all.

The Illhari fled.

As promised, Jesvin did hunt them. They were humiliated in public, hands tied to a news pole on a busy cross street. Every three-minute cycle of news and updates, the Illharis' crimes were repeated to passers-by on three-hundred-sixty-degree screens above their heads. A minor punishment given the attempted crime, but that had been part of what endeared Jesvin to Lahra.

That impression faded quickly.

Jesvin brought Lahra in-house after the attack on Xifo, saying that "her talents would be better applied closer to home."

It was there that Lahra came to see the cruelty beneath the surface. A cutting word here, an infectious lie there. Jesvin sprinkled manipulation and abuse into her honeyed rhetoric. She positioned herself as the mother of her family, but just like some mothers, Jesvin wielded guilt like a bludgeon.

Lahra had misjudged the intent behind the punishment. At first, Lahra thought it mercy that Jesvin merely humiliated the Illhari mercenaries. She only learned later that after the humiliation, Jesvin had spaced the four. The public display had not been punishment for Xifo's sake, but a deterrent to others. If you crossed Jesvin, death was not the only punishment. You would face humiliation and shame, a total destruction of your reputation. Only after that pain soaked in would death come.

Jesvin was as cruel an abuser as Lahra had seen in her years on the fringe. That she interspersed praise and plenty between the abuse did not make it any better.

Lahra quit as soon as she could, taking two months' pay and chartering a ship to get her and Max off of the Wreck long enough for Jesvin to forget them.

Lahra had broken free of Jesvin's gravity, but she never forgot the Rellix's cruelty.

But Wheel was deep in debt to the gangster. Jesvin had bought up so much of the maintenance and engineering business on the Wreck that it was nearly impossible to get a ship repaired or supplied there without doing business with her in some way.

Every time the *Kettle* limped home to the Wreck, they could choose to add to their bill by trading at one of Jesvin's shops or try to throw together some kind of deal to afford one of the other garages' fees. Rock and a hard place, as Max put it.

As Jesvin put it, "Her love for Wheel was so abundant that she simply could not tolerate the thought of anyone else working on the *Kettle.*"

This meant that every trip to the Wreck was fraught, no matter how joyful it was to see Eihra and her girls or watch Max chatter with Uwen. But that was their life.

***

"We need to take these to Uwen," Max said as the three of

them spoke on the bridge. "We've been dry on leads for months, and if we can't get something else from these finds, we've got nothing. And that's guaranteed to keep us from being able to pay Jesvin."

"None of that is wrong, but there's only so many times you can put Jesvin off," Wheel added. "She gets her hooks in you, plays people like puppets. And she's not above coming at you from the angles. We take this meeting, say the right thing, promise her the lion's share of whatever we find next, and maybe we can get her off our asses."

Lahra stood with her arms crossed, weight back on her heels. She'd been here before. "We can't let ourselves get trapped in her orbit. No future favors, no long-term tasks. If she needs a favor right now, and if it's not too distasteful, it might be best to deliver. A shallow orbit, nothing more."

The words hung there in the cockpit, echoing in her mind. She only hoped that they could make them real. That they could avoid getting wrapped up with Jesvin again like far too many times before.

CHAPTER FIVE

MAX

WORKING WITH WHEEL THESE past few years, the *Kettle* had come to feel like home. He'd gotten over the name pretty quick, especially since it came from Wheel, and Atlan didn't even have that saying about pots and kettles. It was a good ship, all in all. Not that he'd lived in many others.

Now, the Wreck? The Wreck would always feel like his neighborhood. Short of getting home to Earth, if he had to settle down somewhere, it'd be the Wreck.

But just like his neighborhood back on Earth, there were predators along with friends. As a Black man from Baltimore, he knew very well that home didn't always mean safe.

Home to dozens of species and over a hundred distinct cultural and religious groups, the Wreck was the closest Max ever came to feeling like he was back home, walking through Little Italy on the way downtown, then to West Baltimore, and all the way back into the neighborhood he grew up in. Moving through the slices of life all stacked up next to one another like a block of row homes.

The Wreck had once been the *Aspirant-1*, a colony ship

sent into deep space with thousands of families from a half-dozen species, bound for a new future beyond the limits of warp space.

They never made it that far.

Now, the Wreck was a rent-open hulk grounded into a moon-sized asteroid at the edge of a belt. The survivors had thrown a dome up over the wreckage but never made their ship space-worthy again. Hundreds of stories tall, the former colony ship was first a refuge, then a stopover point, and was now a well-known, but out of the way, trade hub, favored by those who wanted to avoid the eye of the Imperium. Jesvin Ker was not the only power on the Wreck, just the biggest and the one they most needed to avoid.

The *Kettle* came in to dock, and fuzzy shapes resolved as they approached, figures and ships, vehicles and cargo containers, markets on every floor, open-air living spaces stacked one atop the other. Lahra and Max had spent hundreds of hours walking halls of the Wreck (mostly at Max's insistence), and they'd seen maybe one-third of the ship and its inhabitants.

But where Baltimore was spread out around the bay, not nearly as built up as New York or Chicago, the Wreck was taller than it was long. That'll happen when your wide spaceship crashes on its side and gets most of its matter refactors cannibalized to create a protective dome to hold in atmosphere.

The Wreck's story was not a common one. But it was what the people here had to live with. And that was the thing most remarkable about the Wreck. The adaptation, the flexibility, the ingenuity. Centuries later, the Wreck was a thriving metropolis.

They'd decided to visit Uwen first, try to get what leads they could on their findings while Wheel placated Jesvin.

On the way to Uwen's shop, Max and Lahra turned the corner into Ruku's bazaar. Ruku was a Yoosh, a rare species of three-meter-tall malleable blobs with googly eyes and the ability to form a mouth anywhere on their body. Max had only met three Yoosh and had no interest in ever meeting the other two again—they were assholes.

But Ruku was cool. They and their friends kept the bazaar safe, edging out the small-time gangs that ran protection rackets elsewhere on the Wreck where official security forces couldn't keep up with the pace of life. Jesvin had made several attempts to buy into the bazaar, but the locals had kept her at bay so far.

Ruku's head poked out from above the sea of canvas drapes, waddling back and forth.

"Care for a drink?"

Lahra pretended to be annoyed, but she liked Ruku as much as Max did. Well, almost as much. Ruku tended to go on.

Max and Lahra shared a round of shike with Ruku, the moss liquor burning as always as they caught up on gossip and heard about Jesvin's latest acquisitions—more manufacturing shops, more labor agencies. She'd even been buying candidates in the Ombuds elections, increasing her influence with the Wreck's government.

Just great, all around.

Once they'd checked in with Ruku, Max set to work. He wove through the bazaar shaking hands, bowing, signing, trading jokes, shifting between a dozen different languages as he re-connected with the regulars. Max and Lahra had lived in a flat on the other side of the bazaar for several months when they were between pilots and ships, and Max did his best to keep up ties with the people here and throughout the Wreck.

Max's official specialty was archaeology. But here, with the living traditions and mélange of cultures in the Wreck, he reminded himself why it all mattered. Archaeology was for sense-making using material remnants within the broader discipline of anthropology. Knowing where someone came from, how their stories shaped their view of the world, made it possible to see the galaxy from someone else's perspective. And the more perspectives you could understand, the more complete a picture of life and its meanings.

Also, the food was amazing.

Max had passed on eating lunch on the *Kettle* and instead spread a few chits around to assemble a fabulous meal in a series of fabricated not-wax bags. A falafel-ish dish in a moss-based pocket, wall-grown root vegetables fried and seasoned with spices his tongue couldn't pronounce, and a drink made from the microscopic krill-like things that the massive Drell ate as they rode the solar waves across space.

In the middle of the bazaar, there was a stall that sold Genae food. One of only two in the whole Wreck. It was a big part of why Max had pitched Lahra on living in the neighborhood.

"Cousin!" sang Eihra, the older Genae woman who ran the stall with her daughters, Vlera and Yldri.

Eihra waved Lahra over, filling a cup with a thick purple liquid that looked to Max like a neon version of boba tea. As Lahra accepted the cup, Eihra and her daughters sang "Returning Hero." They always sang this when Lahra came to visit, and it always drew a crowd.

Genae were rare, their songs even rarer.

Max had studied the songs of his wife's world as best he could, but he learned best from text. Even as a kid he'd memorized songs from worn album booklets when he couldn't pick them up just by listening on repeat. He'd never been much of a singer, and so he felt embarrassed every time he sang along with Lahra, even though he knew she liked it. He just kept sucking. Max couldn't get over how out of tune he was or how his voice never felt like it fit the songs, always shifting the melody down to his register.

And the fact that his natural voice part belonged to the

Genae servant class, which always rubbed him the wrong way.

But that was love sometimes. Inexpertly participating in your partner's passions and culture even though you felt like a doofus.

Lahra drank the first cup down in one long gulp, trading it for a refill with a smooth motion. This one she'd nurse. Lahra sang her thanks, harmonizing with Eihra and her daughters. The daughters swarmed Lahra, the older almost to adulthood, the younger knee-high to Max. Eihra's family were all from the merchant caste, and Lahra was the only soldier-caste Genae they knew, so as far as they were concerned, she was basically a superhero. Harmony in Genae songs was all done by caste—a song could only reach its fullness when performed by members of all five castes—noble, priest, soldier, merchant, and servant.

Lahra took a knee and sang them the story of their latest adventure between sips, until Eihra called them back to the stall to make another batch of the juice. As always, Lahra overpaid for the drinks.

"I cannot take this, it's too much," Eihra protested.

"We are one blood, one people," Lahra said.

Eihra sighed. This was a ritual with them. They sang for her, she told stories and overpaid for the drinks. That money paid for the girls' school, so that they would have options beyond inheriting the stall. Eihra always took the money, but her pride demanded that she make a show of refusing. Lahra could barely spare the money, but it was an investment in the future of her people, so neither Max nor Wheel ever complained.

The Genae were a shattered people, hounded near to extinction, but their pride remained. That pride had led the Genae to attempt an insurrection a hundred years ago, mounted by the generation before Lahra's mother's. Several hundred Genae had scraped together the money for a warship and picked a fight with a Vsenk fleet.

They'd killed five times their number before the ship went down, but after that, Genae were forbidden from assembling in groups larger than five. Like most Imperial edicts, it was enforced unevenly, but it meant that her people were always being watched. Max had seen firsthand the power of just a small selection of the Genae's song magic, and then only performed as a solo. The Genae sagas told of great battleships with weapons powered by a chorus of hundreds, of a squadron of guard-caste warriors raising an entire mountain from a flat plain to cut off their enemy and protect their charges.

The songs of the Genae were real actual space magic, and the Vsenk had good reason to be afraid.

Max checked in with a few more old friends while Lahra finished her story.

"I think you could make a heroic ballad out of fetching groceries from the hydro levels," Max said as they walked away from Eihra's stand.

"I did that, actually. Before we met."

"But did that story feature a dashing archaeologist from the other end of the universe?"

"No. A glaring omission. Every hero needs their chatty sidekick." Lahra leaned over and kissed Max on the top of his head. It was Lahra's way of saying "Yes dear, of course. That's totally not silly," without being patronizing. It was a rare talent. Max had never been in a relationship where he had less in common with his partner, not in the least because he'd never dated anyone not human before he met his wife.

Lahra didn't lord her prowess over him, nor did she hide her light to spare his feelings. She let him be himself, and he did the same for her. Pretty good basis for a marriage, as it turned out. And if he learned to be a bit less useless during a fight, and she saw the utility of looking before leaping now and again, all the better.

***

Some aliens were weird-looking.

Some were scary.

But it turned out that the type of aliens Max had the

hardest time with were the aliens that were unrelentingly *adorable*.

That was the case with the Illhari, who resembled nothing so much as one to one-and-a-half-meter-tall hamster-people.

Every time Max saw Uwen or another Illhari, the same part of his brain that melted at the sight of a puppy or kitten spiked out, and he had to restrain himself. Illhari came from a trade-focused planet that had recently been classified a Special Economic Zone—granted more autonomy in exchange for a substantial tax on trade. The results, so far, had been good for the Illhari and good for the Empire. It was, legitimately, good policy. Or at least less bad policy.

Uwen's shop was even more a hodgepodge than the 'no scrap wasted' aesthetic of the Wreck, but Uwen's mess was deliberate. The building was old plasteel juxtaposed with freshly-carved stone, a hominid-sized door at the center. And beside it, a garage door fit for a Vsenk or a transport ship. The building was tucked up against an elevator shaft that had long since lost its original machinery, replaced by pneumatic pulleys. The shop's sign read "Odds and Ends" in New Atlan, displaying an equivalent phrase in a half-dozen languages.

The Illhari opened the door to receive them.

Lit from behind, Uwen was a matted furry oval, long claw fingers always moving, fiddling, or just twitching from their strong flight instincts. Illhar had once been filled with massive predators, the Illhari their favorite meal. Then the Illhari created poisons, traps, and weapons. After dealing with their predators, the Illhari never developed a proper military—their people were deeply communal. They'd had fights, even skirmishes. Cold wars, economic sabotage, sure. But never sustained warfare.

That pacifism had not served them well in resisting the Vsenk.

"Uwen!" Max said, voice only a bit higher than he intended. "We've got some new weirdness for you to poke at!" He pulled the artifact from his satchel and handed it over.

The Illhari's fingers twitched in excitement, and he turned it over in his hands, tongue flicking back and forth. When Illhari were excited, their sense of smell heightened, hence the flicking to taste the air. Probably a survival response.

"Where did you get this, and what was it doing when you found it?"

"Atlan tomb in Baeu Sector. It'd been raided before, but whoever hit it left this thing sitting under a shattered urn. If the narrative in the tomb is correct, this should point to several other major tombs from before the Devastation."

Uwen studied the artifact, picking through a ring of data jacks. He tried to plug the jack into the artifact, then reversed it, tried again. Finally, he picked up a spanner.

Max's eyes went wide. "What are you doing?"

"It'll be fine. Atlan built things to last." Then he hammered the data jack into place, though Max winced at the impact.

Max treated things gently, hands trained by years of archaeological digs. Uwen's style of repair and investigation was rather more . . . percussive.

He peeked through the cracks between his fingers. "What do you think?"

Uwen wobbled his head back and forth the way he did when he was working.

"I'll give you three thousand for this and the best sites listed for an extra 10% commission on whatever you find there."

"Make it five," Lahra negotiated. "Jesvin is on our flanks again. If you're excited about the sites this device will point us to, then it's in your best interest to make us just as excited."

Uwen flicked his whiskers. "It can be five thousand now, if you give me an extra fifteen percent of everything you find from the best three stakes." Uwen had always been most interested in Atlan artifacts and finds, thanks to his network of buyers looking to reclaim their people's history lost in the margins or scattered to the solar winds by the rise of the Vsenk. In this part of the universe, Max could traipse around tombs, retrieve artifacts, and end up *helping* the living members of the civilization that built the tombs. Preferable to playing Indiana Jones back home. And it meant that whenever they found Atlan tech, Max knew they'd hit a solid payday.

Max thought for a moment, reading Uwen's expression for tells on how far he could push. "Five thousand now, and an extra 15% of the lower three of five stakes. Instead of an extra 15%, it's 12% on the top two." Lahra played hardball, and Max did the haggling. It was a practiced play of theirs, and Uwen knew to expect it.

"Fine, fine. Let me get to work. Go have yourselves some dinner, stay off of Jesvin's radar, and I'll call you when I have your first site."

Max turned to Lahra with a smile. "Mneep's & Mneep's?" he asked, naming their favorite diner in the neighborhood.

Lahra offered her hand, which he took, and they were off for a dinner date while the Illhari pummeled the mapping cube into submission.

Some days, it was an okay life.

CHAPTER SIX

WHEEL

MOST NEIGHBORHOODS IN THE Wreck were about three kilometers in any direction. Some were bigger, some smaller, some built layer on layer within a tall section of the overturned ship, transit achieved through pulleys and chains and ropes.

Jesvin Ker's compound was larger than most neighborhoods and surrounded by a buffer zone of several blocks, crawling with guards and toughs. It was as much fortress as palace. Wheel walked by dozens of guards in the compound's shadow, then another three checkpoints inside, finally arriving in Jesvin's receiving room. It was covered in tapestries and appointed with a dozen different perches that Jesvin would flit between while speaking with visitors.

As Wheel walked into the room, Jesvin swooped down from the highest perch, buffeting the Atlan with the flapping of her wings as she came to a delicate landing.

Jesvin was just under two meters tall, positively towering for a Rellix. She was all graceful lines and resplendent feathers. Her plumage was mostly blue with green and red accents, plus a knife-slash of gold at the top of her head like a crown. As if she needed more reasons to be full of herself. She wore a black robe with lush geometric patterns embroidered throughout in bronze and silver thread.

"Wheel, my darling, it's been too long. I'm so glad that you've come to settle your debt. It's no good having something like that hanging over you. I can see the stress in the bags under your eyes." Her voice was a soothing trill, and already Wheel could feel the hooks probing her heart for places to catch and pull.

There were a few ways of dealing with Jesvin. If you brushed her off, were curt, or turned the screws on her, she escalated. If you just let her go on, she'd talk you into giving her a whole galaxy.

Wheel shot for the middle ground.

"I'm here to talk. My crew just brought in a score, so I can give you as much of that as we can spare and still fuel up the *Kettle*."

Jesvin's head twitched, startled by Wheel's directness. "If you'd only do me the favor of bringing your findings to Qorv or Eojil. If you came to visit more, you'd know that Qorv had another litter this year—five more mouths to feed. And Eojil's hands won't last forever . . ."

Wheel cut in again as Jesvin took a breath. "I know, but I'll never be able to pay you back if we don't land some bigger finds. We need leads, and Uwen has always come through for us." Wheel had other reasons to go to Uwen, but Jesvin was high on the list of people who didn't need to know them.

"And yet you never seem to find what you're looking for. How long have Max and Lahra been chasing those dreams? How long have you spent ferrying them around chasing scraps? Come home and work for me—you'll wipe away that debt in no time. Safer work, spare money for upgrades . . ."

The *Kettle* had been through so much, and it'd be good to be able to take it easy for a while . . .

Jesvin ran one arm's feathers across Wheel's face. She was

repulsed and soothed at the same time, her wires crossing, blood aflame. "You've never gotten a real shot at a stable life," Jesvin said. "And I regret not being able to convince you to settle down. I could have tried harder, but you're so independent, I didn't want to make the decision for you. It's always better if those you love come back of their own accord."

Something inside Wheel burst like a pipe. She'd almost lost her nerve there for a moment, almost bought into the dream of a life as a house pilot for Jesvin. But it wasn't about her, wasn't even about Max and Lahra. There was more to be done in the world than living off of Jesvin's blood money.

Wheel stood, forcing Jesvin back a step. "You don't love me. You just want your money. And you'll get it, but on my schedule."

So much for avoiding back talk.

Jesvin's feathers puffed up, the gold crest on her head adding another thirteen centimeters to her height. That display used to be terrifying. But Wheel had grown too old and too hard to be pushed around like this anymore.

"Such ungratefulness!" Jesvin chirped. "How many times have I given you safe harbor? How many times have I extended your credit for just one more repair, just one more refueling?"

Wheel matched Jesvin's threat display, her nanites pumping adrenaline through her body. "You buy up every garage and engineer shop you can find. You use prices and schedules like weapons to keep people aboard the Wreck so you can bleed them for more money from your flophouses and restaurants. You've got half the Wreck convinced you're a guardian goddess and the other half terrified to say even one critical thing about you."

Seeing her moment, Wheel turned and walked out of the room, her blood boiling.

Jesvin called after Wheel. But she didn't order the guards to stop the Atlan, so it was all bluster.

Wheel berated herself as she left. *Should have kept my temper*, she thought. *There's too much at stake to get sidetracked by her saccharine garbage.*

Wheel pinged the *Kettle* to contact Max and Lahra, see how much money they could scrape together from Uwen's fees and anything else to throw in Jesvin's face. Buy them some time.

Because Jesvin would remember this. And she didn't take slights lightly.

CHAPTER SEVEN

LAHRA

ONE REFRESHINGLY CALM DINNER later, Lahra and Max returned to Uwen's shop. A pair of Rellix dithered over which of the three mangled perches they wanted to get for their daughter's nursery. Oh, for life to be so simple.

They left the other couple to their consideration and walked back to find the proprietor.

Uwen emerged from his office to wave them in. He closed the door behind them and studied the camera as he returned to his desk. "They're fine. Those two have been here for an hour every day for the last week. First clutch of eggs—they're all nerves." He paused. "I have good news."

The Illhari activated a holographic projector. It sputtered, image flickering in the air for a moment before it shorted out. Uwen kicked the projector, adjusted the lens, then kicked it once more.

That did it. A star sector lit up the air before him, with three locations highlighted.

"I see three viable sites," Uwen said. "But that's being generous. One is likely already raided. When I cross-referenced the coordinates with my deal log, I found some acquisitions from a year ago that match. The second is dangerous—right along a Vsenk patrol route. The third, though? Promising."

Uwen zoomed the projection in to reveal a diffuse mass of asteroids in what used to be the home system of the Atlan.

"There will be lots of patrols at the edge of the system, but once you get past those, it should be easy going."

Max stared at the map, wide-eyed. "This debris belt is huge. Where is the site?"

"Those asteroids are what's left of Yua after the devastation. The temple sections appear to be mostly clustered together. Lucky. You'll need to pick through the various portions to find your way to the artifacts. But the location and the poor condition of the temple makes it less likely to have already been picked over."

They'd never gone this far into the Forbidden Sectors before. Cut off from ship traffic by the Vsenk, most believed the Forbidden Sectors contained test sites, shipyards, and other secrets the Empire wanted to keep from their subjects.

"What is the party line justification for Yua's system to be included in the Forbidden Sectors?" Max asked.

"Hazardous materials. Which there most certainly are. Wreckage of a half-dozen formerly inhabited worlds. Very dangerous. I can't force you to go, but I think the risk will be worth it, yes. Definitely. Probably. Yes, you should go. If you want to."

Max walked around the display, scratching his chin. Lahra thought through approach routes, the availability of cover, likely places to hide from patrols to fool sensors. But evaluating the likely claims at each site would fall to Max.

When Uwen pulled up the second site, Max shook his head.

"Yeah, we've already been to this one."

"Yes, last year. But a deeper analysis of your recordings, cross-referenced with some sources of mine, tells me that there is a hidden sub-chamber, untouched. I will give you the directions needed. Worth a shot."

The last site was likely also picked over, but they hadn't been there yet. It felt like a bit of wishful thinking, Uwen picking at straws to give them a better chance of success.

They could try the obvious site first, then skirt around to loop in on the place they'd visited before, and then try the temple at Yua if it was absolutely necessary. Ascending level of danger. Bribing a patrol to go about your business was one thing, but breaching the Forbidden Sectors was very different. That level of crime landed you in hard labor camps far from civilization. And once you were tagged for those offenses, you couldn't just lay low.

Max sighed. "It couldn't be easy, could it?"

Uwen turned off the projector. "All the easy sites have been picked over so long ago they're just space dust by now. But to the bold go the credits."

"As long as they live to spend them." Lahra handed over a datapad. "Give us the coordinates and we'll head off to see what we can do."

"Not staying?"

"We're barely scraping by as-is. We need to get moving. We don't know how Jesvin will take to Wheel's visit. And the bribe we handed over to the patrol boat only buys us goodwill for so long."

"Wish we were on Illhar," Uwen said. "The Vsenk there give us enough latitude to conduct our business. They know they'll make it up in taxes thanks to the Special Economic Zone. Rare program, not too many planets as lucky as Illhar. Only lasts as long as Qerol's faction—the Bright Suns—retains its influence. Been hearing rumbles about some changes, a more aggressive faction pushing to change policy across warp space. Might become much harder to make a living outside of the Imperial eye."

"They can't be everywhere at once," Max said. "Wheel is good, maybe the best I've flown with. We'll keep flying."

Uwen nodded, plugging a cable into the datapad to transfer the files. "I've already sent you the credits. Should take care of your ship. Will have to. Otherwise you might as well be jumping into the void wearing nothing but a space-suit. No good."

Lahra smiled. "It's not that bad, assuming you don't need to be out for long."

Max shook his head at her. "Yes, but your suit is one-of-a-kind. The rest of us are stuck with the equivalent of garbage bags held together with duct tape."

"That's why I do the fighting and you focus on reading ancient texts and avoiding traps."

Max turned to the Illhari. "Thanks, Uwen. We'll be back as soon as we can, and hopefully with something new and amazing."

Lahra smiled. "And expensive."

CHAPTER EIGHT
WHEEL

THE LOVEBIRDS CAME BACK with smiles and purpose, and Wheel didn't feel at all like joining in the fun.

Max stopped when he saw Wheel in the hold. "How was the visit with Jesvin?"

Wheel crossed her arms. "Terrible. You have good news?"

"Three potential sites. I think we could really make some progress here."

"How much did you get from Uwen?" Wheel asked, holding a figure in her head of the amount that would appease Jesvin.

Lahra looked to Max. "Five thousand."

Wheel shook her head. Once you paid for food and fuel, the remainder would barely put a dent in the debt they'd racked up. "Not good. Jesvin's not my biggest fan right now. Which of course she expresses with love and 'concern.' She thinks I should come home and fly for her. That my life would be simpler without the two of you. She can take a dive out an airlock, but unless we come back with some major loot for her fences, I think we're going to have trouble."

Max smiled. "Then we'll just have to get lucky this time.

I'm sorry you had to go kiss the ring. Jesvin's as cloying as a skunk's stink. You have to wash her off."

"Speaking of which, I'll be in my room. We've got a spot in the departure queue, but it'll be an hour before we even think about firing up the engines."

"Don't you want to decide where we're going first?" Max called as she retired to her bunk.

She'd deal with that later.

Wheel cooled herself down with an Atlan ambient album, made for manual deep-space flight. Repetitive but engaging, soothing but demanding. It helped her shrug off worry and dial in to the focus she needed to keep the three of them on track.

Get the artifacts, get paid, keep going, until the time is right. Then she would make her move.

***

Wheel looked at Uwen's map and notations, tablets spread out on Max's working table in the cargo hold.

"These leads are garbage," she pronounced. She tapped one of the dots on the map. "This is right off of an Imperial patrol route. No way we'd have the time to do anything more than a flyby."

"And this one is a tomb we searched two years ago," Lahra added. "The one with the laser grid, if I recall."

Max nodded. "That place had been picked clean already. But Uwen swears there's a sub-chamber off of the second room. And he told us how he thinks we can access it. It's close, right? Worth a try at least."

"Sure. But I'm not taking us to Yua. If I wanted to go there, I would have done it decades ago."

Yua, which held the most promising lead, was a shattered planet deep in the Forbidden Sectors, a.k.a. the Old Atlan home system. The Devastation was used not once but twice in that system, detonated mantle and crust shredding space stations and holdings on other planets until a second world was detonated, since the Vsenk had yet to meet a case of over-kill they didn't like.

She'd given that system a wide berth her whole life. Those were the Old Atlan. She had to focus on the future. At best, the past was good for salvage. At worst, it was a noose around your neck.

"I've got no interest in having my ancestors' failures rubbed in my face any more than they already are in this job. Plus, if we so much as get spotted out there, it's new tags and licenses for the ship or we're scrapped."

"We can hit the old tomb, peep at the site on the patrol route."

Max started, "We need the mon—"

"I know we do. Which is why, if the first two sites are a bust, then maybe, just maybe, I'll think about taking us to the Forbidden Sectors."

***

The first site was a bust, after all. Max and Lahra spent four hours turning over Uwen's sub-chamber, but they still came back empty-handed.

"I guess we could go into the rubble business. Start a trend. Fortresses constructed from hand-picked rubble—each one unique, lovingly reclaimed from heritage religious sites." Max's joking kept their spirits up as they made their way to the second site. Wheel tweaked the settings and poured the energy that usually powered their shields into sensors to be able to detect Imperial patrol ships as far out as possible as they followed the coordinates to close in on the location by the patrol route.

Good thing, as there were two ships flying nearly in tandem, piercing a dust cloud just as Wheel's scanners unfolded.

"Contact. Two ships, extreme sensor range. I'm going to take cover in the shadow of this moon."

She waited there for an hour to see what the ships would do. Instead of continuing on along the trade route, the ships just circled.

Wheel ran the coordinates again to be sure. Yep. These ships were patrolling the moon that held Uwen's second site.

She shook her head. "Don't know why, but these patrol ships aren't on the normal route."

"That's good, yes?" Lahra asked.

"Not remotely. They're guarding the site."

"Ah."

"We can wait them out, right?" Max asked. "The Empire is unlikely to allot two ships to protect a tomb for long."

Lahra pointed to the waiting moon. "Unless there's something there other than the tomb."

"Or the Empire is doing something with the tomb," Max offered.

Lahra crossed her arms. "Why now, though?"

"Good question." Wheel looked closer at the sensor data, scanning for a facility on the moon, any kind of comms signal or energy trace. "Max, wanna come up here and scan this place with me? Lahra, probably good to check the weapons again, in case we have to punch our way out of here."

The lovebirds' footfalls echoed throughout the ship, every vibration reaching her through her connection to the Kettle.

Max slid into the chair beside Wheel and got to work. "No radiation trace that I can find, and no signals coming off the moon. Might be local, faint enough that I can't pick them up from this distance."

Wheel scanned her radar. "And I'm not getting any closer with those things on alert."

"How long do we want to give this?"

"I'm used to waiting," Lahra called from the gunnery station.

Wheel grumbled, "I don't want to spend all day here. Every time they circle the moon, there's another chance we show up on their scanners through some random crap happenstance."

Max pinched the bridge of his nose. "We need results. We need some kind of step forward. It's been six months with nothing but scraps." His voice hid it, but Wheel could read the worry on his face. It wasn't just that they were scraping by. Max's empathetic nature meant he knew that she didn't want to go to Yua, that he was torn between their desperation and trying not to push Wheel beyond her limits. Since they'd started flying together, Max and Lahra had continually pushed themselves and her, asking her to go farther out, to be more daring in their searches for answers. So far, she'd gone with it. But they were approaching limits. Her limits, or maybe theirs. Much longer, and maybe the lovebirds would move on, maybe hire someone even more desperate for money, somebody who'd get them killed.

And for all their bickering or annoying cuteness, Wheel had gotten fond of the lovebirds. The way they looked at each other, the way they chirped back and forth, bantering like two live wires as they flitted about her ship. She didn't want to lose them.

Four hours later, another ship hit the *Kettle*'s sensors.

"Picking up a ship. Cruiser-sized." Most cruisers were about ten times the size of the *Kettle*. Big enough to field a squadron of escort fighters. This one was bulkier than the patrol ship, but barely sported any armaments.

"Imperial?" Lahra called up the hallway to the cockpit.

"Not remotely," Wheel said. "Freelance. I'd bet they're here for the same reason we are. But they haven't avoided the patrol."

The treasure-hunter ship burned hard, making a break for the surface, probably trying to outrace the patrol boats. The signal coming off their engines told her they couldn't keep that up for long.

The patrol ships changed course to intercept, guns laying into the cruiser.

The cruiser started shaking, rattling itself apart and

evaporating under the patrol ships' fire.

"They're going to ram!" Wheel shouted, more befuddled than scared. Lahra and Max were with her in the cockpit then, their breathing another stream of data behind the river that was her connection with the *Kettle*.

These mercs were ridiculous. Was a possible payday worth losing their lives? Their ship? Yeah, it was a piece of crap, but you love your ship, no matter how ugly it is.

The patrol ships committed to its vector, blocking off the moon.

But where the cruiser should have turned, instead it exploded.

"The hell?!" Wheel shouted. "Get to the guns!" Lahra stomped out of the cockpit. Beside her, Max strapped in. In fights, he'd work the sensor suite or help with spot repairs, leaving Wheel to pilot and Lahra to the guns. As the explosion cleared—the heat signatures fading and the radar resolving back into sensible blips and blobs—Wheel got the trick.

The cruiser was a shell. A battering ram. The raiders had launched an escape ship to make a break for the surface in a freighter no larger than the *Kettle*. Clever. Ridiculous, but clever.

One of the Imperial patrol ships was hurt, bad, but they still outgunned the raiders by no small margin. Lasers and missiles hammered into the freighter even as the patrol boat listed uncontrollably, sinking into the planet's gravity, explosions rippling across the ship. Its partner tried to cover, but it looked bad.

"They're both going to blow!" Max said.

Wheel pulled up projections on one of the screens. "As long as the Imps have the engines to avoid a permanent decaying orbit, they'll pull through." The screen showed the most likely response from the patrol ship, saving them from crashing to the planet.

A moment later, lasers from the undamaged patrol ship

sheared the freighter in two, leaving the damaged patrol boat to fire its engines and push through a freshly formed field of spaceship debris and slow to a stop next to its pristine companion.

The fires receded, and the *Kettle*'s sensors painted Wheel the picture of little worker bee drones buzzing about the ship, patching up breaches, activating emergency force fields, and retrieving spaced crew. Most of them wouldn't have been wearing suits.

"They'll make it. And you know what that means . . ."

"Backup," Lahra added over the comms.

"No way of sneaking around through the debris?"

"I mean, nothing's impossible, especially for my baby here," Wheel said. "But possible is a damn sight short of smart."

They drifted in cover for several hours on autopilot while Wheel retreated to her bunk with music and a firm desire to not face her own bullshit about the home system.

If they went back, Jesvin would scrap the *Kettle* to pay off their debt. No ship, no passengers, no more work from Cog or anyone. She'd end up a bound pilot on someone else's ship at best and conscripted by the Vsenk at worst.

She was not going to let Jesvin win, wasn't going to let the lovebirds down. And she sure as the void was not going to lose her ship.

She stormed out of her bunk and set the course before she could lose her nerve. Once it was set, she couldn't let herself weasel out.

"Next stop, Yua. Ancients protect us or something."

That night Wheel found a bottle of aged liquor in her bunk. One she knew Max and Lahra had been saving. Max had affixed a note with a single phrase:

"Thank you."

She popped the cork and set about drowning her fears about repeating her ancestors' mistakes.

CHAPTER NINE

MAX

MAX WALKER CREPT DOWN the hallway of a living tomb. This site was . . . interesting. According to Wheel's account of Atlan history, Yua was one of the first places destroyed by the Vsenk's planet-killer known as the Devastation.

The system once held six planets, two inhabited by the Atlan, along with another three moons. Now there was no terrestrial body left in the system larger than a capital ship. If you didn't know the history, you'd write the system off as just another big asteroid cluster.

The formerly-inhabited moon of Yua was now broken into hundreds of pieces, the temple a disassembled puzzle exposed to the vacuum of space. Some sections were larger, with several rooms intact from floor to ceiling. Others contained a single room or a hallway with one, two, or three sides exposed to the nothing. They had to hop from fragment to fragment to progress through the tomb—easy for Lahra with her suit's thrusters, less so for Max and his more basic EVA suit.

It was more complicated than any site he'd worked in on Earth by several orders of magnitude, and he couldn't be happier.

Atlan ruins like this never quite died, not for a long, long time. And though the moon had been shattered centuries ago, the temple puttered along, biotech systems on standby mode, conserving energy picked up by solar arrays on the roof and exterior walls. As soon as Max set foot on each fragment of the temple, circuitry flickered to life, casting the hall in emergency lighting. Bioluminescence flowed from mechanical veins in the walls, tiny life forms with cilia cables and reproductive ports passing on data, chugging along like they'd just been napping when the temple had to have been silent and still for a thousand years.

Lahra's chem-torch was almost too much. It was a soldier's light, strong enough for precision rifle fire at fifty paces.

Max just needed enough illumination to not run into things and to read the glyphs on the wall. It was always best to work through a site using the lighting it would have had when in use—you could sometimes catch things with more light, but then you'd have a harder time imagining what it was like for the original creators or inhabitants. When Max walked a site, he tried to see it as they would have, rather than as an outsider. To understand more than to investigate.

Atlan tombs were densely packed with legends, biographies, schematics, and more. Atlan were quintessential tinkerers. They experimented with everything, especially themselves.

These Atlan weren't the modern mechanics and warp-jockeys like Wheel. This tomb dated to the era when the Atlan held nothing back, when the galaxy was their laboratory. The Atlan that had discovered how to access warp space, the ones that terraformed worlds. The Atlan that crossed the universe and left a teleporter behind, which led him to this galaxy, this world, this moment.

Max stopped every few meters just to dip the toes of his attention into the threads of narrative. With just those tiny samplings, he'd found a dozen new accounts. Three that straight-up contradicted Vsenk doctrine.

Lahra broke his reverie. "We need to hurry, love." Her voice came through the short-wave, but even muffled by her suit, he could make out the loving impatience.

Max's default mode was set to stop and smell the corpses. Lahra's was set to hurry up and fight. They were, after all, technically thieves trespassing in sectors forbidden to all but the Vsenk command.

Those folks didn't care about Max and Lahra's mission. When you got caught with something expensive and dusty, people tended to bring out the knives first and ask questions—well, never. It was a big leap from his old life on Earth as a linguistic archaeology post-doc. He'd grown up wanting to have adventures on digs, and boy did life over-deliver in the weirdest possible fashion. A long-shot expedition to learn more about Linear C, a.k.a. "Maybe the language of Atlantis?" ended when he stepped on a disc that looked just like the ones lining the floor here, and poof, he was teleported from Earth to an abandoned temple on the border moon of Almey.

A trio of Atlans found him, took him for a concussed Yaea, and the rest was weird, amazing, scary history. Somehow, the legends of Atlantis on Earth had something to do with the Atlan (ancient outpost, downed ship turned colony, or something else), and what humans called Linear C was their basic script. He learned Atlan and, with the trio's help, found his footing. Not long after that, he and Lahra found each other.

"There's just so much here. And if we go too fast, we might miss something critical. Ancient Atlan tombs have all had a through line that tells the story of the site. Once I can isolate it, we'll be able to speed up."

"Read faster, then." He didn't need to see her face to make out the smile.

Max scanned the walls for signs of the through line story. Larger circuit-glyphs, a tighter rhyming structure, anything. Lahra would barb him gently about it, but this was his territory, just as bar brawls and collapsing bridges and anything involving swords, guns, or punching was hers.

Max picked the different stories apart, searching for the thread left by the Atlan Ariadne to lead true seekers down the correct path to the tomb's treasured relics.

And so it was. The last of the Atlan Republic Tale-keepers, witnesses of the Devastation. Hear us . . .

"There you are." Max jumped, the suit carrying him up to the roof of the room. He scanned the script, which arced forward along the roof in a single line, leading them forward.

Lahra headed to the next door. "Tell me where to turn. This place gives me the shivers. Walking among ghosts invites bad fate."

"Atlan don't die, they just upload. That's what Wheel says."

Lahra readied her greatsword, the blue orb at the pommel bright with a full charge after their last solar storm. "Data or spirit, they're all ghosts. Broken memories on loop, filled with regret."

"So you're saying I shouldn't start dancing my way through the tomb."

"Not recommended. I've never met a ghost that could take a joke."

"How many ghosts have you met?"

"Not counting the spirits of my ancestors calling me to restore Genos?"

"Since you've said they're metaphorical ghosts, no. Just the spooky ones in tombs."

"Three, then. But do not dismiss the ancestors so easily."

Max ignored the terrifying intimation that ghosts were real in this galaxy and turned to meet Lahra's gaze. "Sorry, just joking around. I mean, Wheel likes my jokes. That has to count for something."

"Wheel laughs at catastrophic engine failure."

Lahra plunged her sword into the slit joining a pair of double doors. She hauled on one side, cracking the door.

Dust and air whooshed out from the next room as pressure equalized.

"Who knows, maybe the Old Atlan were more chummy. Humor is evolutionarily adaptive. Releases stress."

"Yammering, however, is maladaptive. It reveals your position to predators."

"Only predator I can see here is two-meters tall, gorgeous, and wielding a Genae beat-stick."

"Do not call my sword of station a beat-stick. And save your pleasantries for our bunk."

"I can never tell if you mean that seriously. Your deadpan is legit."

"You're speaking Terran again."

"Yeah, I know."

They stepped into a new room, and Max held his arms out, stopping Lahra before she could advance. Like most of the other sections of the tomb they'd seen so far, this room still had power, solar cells on the roof fueling the circuitry woven into the stone. Even the Devastation couldn't totally erase the past. Max wondered what it'd take to pull enough samples to re-create such solar technology. He could imagine a hundred ways to use that level of resilience and system redundancy without even trying.

The room contained four pillars in a square, each with dim lights coursing up from the floor, sigil-laden panels on the top. The stone and steel panels at the floor were dusty, remnants of millennia-old biological material partially preserved by the room's hard seal. And on the far side of the room, instead of a wall there was a gash like a wound, crumbled debris and other chunks of the shattered planet floating nearby.

"This room's trapped. See the slits in the walls?"

Lahra nodded. "What is our course of ingress?"

Max studied the room, looked at the patterns of the slits, the composition of the stone below. The ur-narrative looped from the roof down to the floor.

Max squatted and pulled the magazine of pebbles from his belt. You could never have too many pebbles.

He lobbed a stone through the air, waiting for the trap to spring. The stone ricocheted off a waist-high pillar. Three brown-yellow metal darts shot from the walls, two from the right and one from the left.

He skipped another pebble along the stone tiles.

Nothing.

A third he bounced off the steel panels, blue and yellow channels of light connecting the panels like circuitry.

Another volley of darts chased the pebble, knocking it to one side.

"Got it. Stay on the stone, and keep low."

"Understood." Lahra crouched, adjusting her sword so it hung horizontally across her back.

"I finally get you to play limbo, and all it takes is a forbidden alien tomb."

"This may not be the time for jests," Lahra said as she advanced. Anytime there was danger, Lahra insisted on taking lead. It helped that her encounter suit doubled as ship-grade armor, and that some of her battle songs could create force fields out of nothing. Pretty handy.

Max followed, walking on all fours, limbs spread to keep his body low. His hand slipped, one of the stones slick with undifferentiated bio-mass. He flattened on the ground, his elbow brushing a lit panel.

"Crap!" he said, pushing off and launching forward as the darts leapt from the walls.

Lahra moved at a blur. Her sword lashed out, broad blade blocking the darts coming from the right. She hauled him forward, shielding his other side with her body. He saw several darts bounce off her armor as she pulled the both of them to the large stone panel at the far side of the room.

Out in the starry night, something moved against the

void. Something familiar.

"Are those what I think they are?"

"No. They're candy-bearing elves from your North Pole, heralding the arrival of your bearded frivolity god. Yes. Erreki. But they're far off. If they don't spot us, don't register the threat . . ."

At that moment, one of the shapes turned, grew thin instead of long. And then set off his parallax vision.

Or said more plainly, the Erreki started coming right at them.

"Get back, love." Lahra grabbed her greatsword in both hands, one on the hilt, the other above the guard. The sword came alive with blue light, electricity dancing across the blade as she aimed. She waited as the Erreki approached.

Closer.

And even closer.

Contrary to the movie slogan, there was sound in the vacuum, it just dissipated very fast. But when the sound was an ear-splitting *ZOT!* from a meter and a half away, you heard it.

The bolt lashed out and turned the Erreki into barbeque.

"We're not stopping to bring that in, right?"

"When have I ever gone out of my way for less-than-prime-grade meat?" Lahra asked, chuckling.

"Well, there was that time with Ducchu whelps on Hunbas-3."

"You were a liter down on blood and thinner than a power cable."

"Technicalities."

Lahra set the banter aside. "Where next?"

Max looked to the walls, tracing each thread stanza by stanza. One spoke of a great darkness gestating-compiling, the other thread spoke of darkness rising from within their own core. The second line's alliterative structure was off, too glaring a mistake to be an accident, and not matching any historical trend. That meant they needed to . . .

"Go left?"

Lahra gestured out into the void. "Left is out there."

"So it is."

"Where the Erreki are swarming. Where I just roasted one of their own. Where their radar will ping back from dead relatives in mere moments."

"I never said this would be easy." After a second, he started again. "Plus, if this were easy, you'd complain about being bored."

"Your people were not trained for battle as mine were. We have needs."

Lahra walked onto the wall and stood at the threshold, a mere handspan from the open void. "Out there, then. Which fragment, do you wager?" She gestured at the options with her sword.

Max blinked and called up the digital zoom in his view-mask to get a closer look.

There were four different asteroids nearby, each with some amount of temple fragment. He tried to find a match for dimensions of the room around him, or the patterns of breakage in the rock. Or, ideally, the one farthest from the Erreki.

No such luck. But he did have his best guess, a larger asteroid spinning counter-clockwise with an opening that fit the room they were leaving.

"Third from the left, looks like."

"It had to be the one that takes us straight through the Erreki."

"Just our luck."

"You have plenty of luck. You hired me, and I've been keeping you from getting yourself killed ever since."

"And I keep you from walking into death traps. It works out."

She swung the greatsword around to her back, where the cross guard locked onto a hard-point in her armor, specially designed for the guardians of her line.

"Ready to go?" she asked.

Max checked his gauges and boosters. Battery nearly full, O_2 solid. "We could have Wheel pick us up."

"The Erreki will swarm. Our options appear to be as such: either we pick our way around them or Wheel wastes battery on scattering them and we fight our way through an angry swarm. What would you prefer?"

"We could take the other pathway, which is almost certainly littered with traps, and hope it loops around?"

"The short way it is." Lahra leapt from the edge, boosters guiding her up and to the left, bearing for the nearest asteroid. "We will go rock-to-rock and evade them. With skill and patience, we can cross without incurring the wrath of the school."

Max followed her path, one eye locked on the school of Erreki prowling in the distance. One of them went wide, then made for its barbequed school-mate.

"They've twigged."

"Just one of them. Keep moving." Lahra leapt off a planetoid with all four limbs, straightening into a dart shooting through space.

Max followed, failing to look as cool as he veered off-target. Moving rock-to-rock was hard when they spun and slipped, so it was all he could do to keep the planetary fragments between him and the ever-more-agitated school of shark-mantis hybrids.

Erreki weren't proper hybrids. Near as he could tell, they had no actual DNA in common with the Terran creatures, but damned if his brain's taxonomical system could read those things as anything but shark-mantids. They had chitinous shells, switchblade foreclaws, fins that rode solar winds like ocean currents, and rows of jagged teeth for shearing and grinding whatever biomass they could get a hold of.

A head jerked toward him as he leapt from an asteroid. It

tracked him as he soared forward.

"I think they've seen us."

"I'll be the one to determine that. Keep moving and stay out of sight."

The benefits of being married to a bodyguard, he thought with a smile on his lips.

And then the Erreki surged, and Lahra shouted, "Move!"

CHAPTER TEN

LAHRA

Lahra Kevain read the battlefield. Twelve agitated Erreki, a scattered field of asteroids, and her only ally at hand a lovable but combat-unsteady man from the other end of the universe.

But she had her sword and her songs. Grabbing the hilt, she pulled the blade free of its magnetic lock and took it in both hands, drawing a bead on the nearest Erreki.

Lahra called up the comms as she bounded to the next rock. "Wheel, we may need evac on the afterburn." And with that, she began singing "Markswoman's Meditation," which would grant her focus and far-sight.

Behind her and to the left, Max continued to scramble on, bouncing like a child still finding his void-legs. He'd gotten better over the years, but he was a child of atmosphere, not the void.

As her ancestors had been children of atmosphere too, before the destruction of Genos.

The Erreki probed forward as she finished the first verse, crescendo building. The beasts moved as a school, a mass of shimmering scales catching light from the distant sun.

She stared down the Erreki as they converged. She bellowed the chorus, "Come, foe, show your steel. Only death will you find here!"

"Your comm is on," Max said.

"I know."

"You're doing the creepy death-bringer thing again."

"It is a song of the Oathsworn."

Lahra jumped back, keeping her focus on the Erreki as she resumed the song. It was possible to speak words not of the song in the moments between lines, but it required great focus. A focus she had worked hard to cultivate to be able to give orders while maintaining the power of her battle songs.

The Erreki fought as a school, but none of them wanted to die. They held fast as she bounced between meteorites and rubble from the temple, firing as she went. She docked her sword again to move faster, bounding off each asteroid on all fours like a Vebaarn.

She tossed a small rock at the school to disrupt them, then crawled around to leap from a piece of rubble. "Keep going," she told Max. "Try to stay out of sight. They'll turn away soon, but if you make yourself a target . . ."

"Only target I feel like being is yours."

Lahra scoffed. "Not your best, love."

"Terror is not conducive to making jokes off the top of my head."

"So noted."

The radar in the upper left of her heads-up display showed Max moving on.

Ahead, Max bounced from meteoroid to rubble, scrambling and flailing but always moving in mostly the right direction.

Ten years ago, if a seer had told Lahra that she would marry an archaeologist from a species she'd never heard of and end up cavorting about the galaxy in search of ancient artifacts, she would have laughed them off the station. But desperate times made for strange shipmates.

Even if her sworn duty—her true mission—seemed many lightyears away, almost beyond hope, she'd learned that there were many ways to fulfill her duty, and some of them let her find joy along the way.

And despair was the vanguard of failure, so she would not yield. Even if the path to restore the Genae was long and full of strange detours.

"Get inside the tomb and signal me when you're secure," she said over their comms.

"That would be great, but they're onto me."

Lahra bounced from rock to rock, making for her gentle, brilliant, and sometimes aggravating husband. The Erreki had gone wide around her to close on Max directly. Clever.

"Keep the rocks between you and them," she said out of habit.

"Doing my best. But they've got my scent. Or whatever they hunt with. Infrared, right? Or is that the Xuaf-li?"

Lahra hurtled from asteroid to asteroid, tracking Max and the Erreki by radar. She came in behind them, forcing the swarm to choose between prey and predator. "Both." She drew her sword and fired a bolt of lightning, catching a creature's spinning tail. It spasmed in pain and turned to face her.

The Erreki raced forward, jaws distended, teeth catching the reflected light from the nearest star. Lahra waited, waited, then sheared three of them in half with a single perfect cut. The swarm scattered.

Satisfied, she called up her comms. "My moon?"

"I'm fine. And—" he paused, "—now I'm in the tomb." She looked up to see him scanning the roof of the temple fragment.

Lahra locked the sword back onto her suit and hopped forward, joining him in the temple fragment. Light filled the room, bouncing off bass reliefs, intricate stonework, and the ritual implements of the ancient Atlan.

How strange for the Atlan to have changed so much. These ruins felt like they belonged to an entirely different species.

"Are you having fun yet?" Max asked.

"Barely worth the use of my blade. This is all dust and debris to me."

Max shook his head. "Dust and debris. But hey, maybe there will be some traps ahead. That's exciting, right?"

She grinned. "The best kind of puzzle. Without risk, without a chance of consequence, puzzles are nothing but mental self-satisfaction."

"This is why I can never get a game night going. That and the fact that Cruji still can't roll dice."

"That you expect Cruji to do anything other than smile and eat is a puzzle all its own."

"He always has nice things to say about you." Max walked into the room, tracing a finger along a wall.

CHAPTER ELEVEN

MAX

THE STORY BRANCHED AGAIN, and Max dismissed the version where the imagery became all organic, abandoning the preferred hybridity of the Atlan.

"This way." He pointed to the other path, where the leitmotif continued forward, looping around the nucleus CPU circle at the center of the room. Stone and patterns arced around the center left blank to honor the core of all life and technology.

"How much further, do you think? That many dead Erreki will attract scavengers. And not just the little ones."

"Atlan tombs usually have a prime number of rooms. Given the size of what we've seen before, I'd bet another three or four to get to the main chamber, as long as we don't take a wrong turn and have to go through a decoy path."

Approaching the doorway, Max stopped, eyes panning over the runes. They spelled something on a spiral, ur-narrative curving from the roof into the door itself. It told of trials faced by the Atlan as they balanced the desire to both foster knowledge and control its flow in order to protect themselves.

"Puzzle ahead." It was an educated guess, based on other Atlan sites he'd researched over the past few years. Each one told him a bit more about what they were like before the Devastation, another piece in the puzzle that could lead him home. If anyone on this side of the universe knew how to reverse the phenomenon that had dropped him here, it was the ancient Atlan.

Max traced the story and pushed on a panel with the sigil for balance. The door shook, then receded, folding in on itself, the spiral unspooling in the opposite direction to reveal a spherical room.

Max zoomed his suit's camera. "That's different."

The room was a geodesic dome with a hundred sides. Each side was marked with a symbol.

"What is this, love?" Lahra's voice was less curious than annoyed.

"Probably a death trap, if we do it wrong." He drew the tablet from his pack and used the eye-gesture UI to scan through the digitized texts he'd 'liberated' from a previous site. "Just a minute . . ." He skimmed one of the sections he'd highlighted for quick reference. Yes. The story sphere. A living trap-chronicle. "Tell the room the right story, and the door appears. Get it wrong and the room turns you into pancakes."

"Those tiles are barely 15 centimeters in diameter."

"If what you mean by that is 'Max, you are not nearly nimble enough to do this right. You tell me which tiles to hit and I'll do it,' I agree completely."

"Let the chronicle show that you were the one to volunteer that plan." Max heard the warmth in her voice.

"We each have our strengths."

"Were you not here, I'd have merely tried to blow up walls until I found something I could haul away and have interpreted. This way seems more efficient."

Max scanned the room, looking for the sigil that opened every story, the Atlan equivalent to "Once Upon a Time," though it translated more closely to "And so it was." Finding it, he pointed, piping his video to the viewscreen in Lahra's helmet.

Lahra jumped, firing tiny bursts from her suit's thrusters. A booted foot depressed on the tile, which came to life with light in circuit-veins.

The next part of an ancient Atlan story would be the invocation of the machine god Xef. "Up and to your left," he said, sending the sigil from his computer over.

Lahra bounced around the sphere, hitting the small plates with precision as the story unfolded. Soon, he had to supplement his view with hers, to find the tiles not visible from the safety of the threshold.

"How are you always so certain of these things?" she asked. "There are as many stories as there are stars in the sky."

"It's like how you know what sword style someone trained in by the way they hold their blade? Or what song goes with what occasion? Repetition brings familiarity, there are structures and formulae. Especially for ancient Atlan. And I'm getting a handle on the style of this tomb's builders. Now the one ten to your right and two up, that looks like a Drell with their limbs retracted."

Max held the story in his head and then shot out his hand, though she wasn't looking. "No! I was wrong. It's the one next to it, the four triangles."

Lahra twisted in mid-flight, reaching out to hit the other panel, pushing against it to avoid crashing into the wall and spoiling the process. Her thrusters kicked on, spinning her in place until she could regain her equilibrium.

They resumed the tale. Five tiles later, the whole room filled with light, and Max cheered. A door opened, revealing a small square chamber beyond. He sprang forward, diving across the open space. But he missed the corner of the door he was aiming for. Lahra grabbed his foot and spared him the indignity of crashing into the far wall.

"Thanks."

"No need to rush ahead. As you say, patience is the best guard position."

"See, I knew that putting that into fighting language would make it stick."

A tender hand on the faceplate of his suit. "You have your moments." The kind of moments that had built their relationship. Expeditions and escapes, comfort and commiseration.

"Let's hope a few more of them," he said. "The next trap or puzzle isn't likely to be as easy."

"Standing and talking is easy. Precise zero-G maneuvering in a contained space is much less so."

"But we made it."

"We always make it. Our fates do not end here. I will see the Genae restored, and you will find your way back to Earth."

Max's mood soured.

That's what it always came down to. He'd go off to his home, she to hers. After seven years, were they any closer to either of their goals? They were becoming a lot more like grail quests than anything that seemed real anymore. And if either of them got what they wanted, what happened to their marriage?

The two of them talked about their goals, but never the repercussions. Avoiding the topic had created an accretion disk orbiting their lives, always in view, its gravity causing tides of worry and always-deferred fear.

That's Future Max's problem.

He turned his focus to the script on the wall. The tale picked up near his foot, and he traced it into the next room, which was shaped like the letter 'T.'

He picked out a sigil to start, and Lahra activated it, then three more. When Max stepped into the room, the doorway behind them slammed shut. And then the walls started closing in from both sides.

"Oh, that's not good."

CHAPTER TWELVE

LAHRA

L AHRA DREW HER BLADE and jammed it into the wall behind them, trying to pry the door back open.

She pulled, fired her thrusters, and leaned her entire body weight into the blade. It did not budge.

There were songs for this, but she doubted that even then could she open the door. They would need another solution.

Retrieving her blade, Lahra watched the walls close in. But this was not a simple crusher trap, with two flat surfaces pressing in. Each wall expanded with geometric patterns piling on atop the other, building toward the center while the wall filled out in similar patterns below.

"What ridiculous hazard is this?" She pointed her sword at the pyramid growing out from the nearest wall.

Max hopped forward and touched the pattern. And it moved.

"Why did it move? We've very little time for study. We must act."

"Maybe it's a variation on the last puzzle."

Max's hands moved at a blur, his movements confident when dealing with puzzles and traps. He'd grown up with digital games and tactile puzzles for their own sake, she with swords and military strategy. How different their childhoods had been.

Lahra had learned to handle a blade before she came up to her mother's thigh. Lessons of letters came from songs about the many brigades in the Genae military. Colors from heraldry. Among the last of their kind, her mother had pre-served the ways of the Genae Royal Guards, certain they'd find the lost heir.

Max pushed an elbow-shaped piece over and then up to fit into another part of the puzzle. They clicked together, and several pieces below receded.

The excitement in Max's voice was palpable. "Try to make the top layer pieces fit together."

Lahra put her sword away and set to work. Her moth-er had raised her on pattern-matching games, but they were always in terms of finding poisons, matching the faces of known assailants to faces in the crowd. Everything folded back into her supposed purpose, to defend nobles long since dead. In her travels, Lahra had met a handful of Genae sol-diers, numerous servants and merchants, and a single priest. But no nobles.

Max was no Genae, but he was her charge. And a child's puzzle would not be the end of them.

She worked as fast as she could. For minutes that seemed like hours, they moved pieces together, stemming the tide of new blocks as they emerged from the walls.

"What is the endgame?" she asked.

"I . . . don't know."

As traps went, crushing walls were unoriginal but very effective. That this one was distinct did nothing to reduce its inevitable lethality.

"We cannot continue forever, love. Eventually we will be overwhelmed. There must be a solution, a win condition. What would your Atlan ancients see as the completion of such a task? Something from their stories."

Max's nerves were beginning to fray, his eyes casting about the room for a solution. "I. Well, maybe. No. What if..."

"You're thinking out-loud again."

"Well, usually I have time to figure things out like this and don't have to also be working with my hands and worrying about my wife and maybe dying because I wasn't smart enough to figure something out ahead of time and asking us to come and do something ridiculous and dangerous when we could have been raiding much simpler and less out-of-the-way tombs!"

He was caught in the gravity of spiraling fear. Lahra gripped Max by the shoulders, steadying him. She looked through his bowl helmet, his brown skin ashen and worried, and held his attention. "Focus, love."

Max took a long breath, then turned to the tower and resumed working, sliding blocks together. She returned to her own pyramid, which grew closer and closer to its opposite.

Another long minute later, Max spoke, "What if we win by losing?"

What folly is this now? she thought. But she said only, "Explain."

"There's an Atlan saying about arguments. They're thesis and antithesis—though they don't say it like that. Point and counterpoint are two towers built to overshadow one another. And sometimes synthesis isn't about one tower overshadowing the other, but about building a bridge between the two. What if we move the blocks so that the towers lock together?"

Lahra looked at Max's pyramid and her own. They were misaligned—their peaks would pass one another before they touched. She moved the blocks, stemming the growth below and directing it to stack toward Max's tower. And Max did the same, steering his toward hers.

Two dozen moves later, the two towers grew toward one another, and Max's breathing was fast, but regular. Controlled stress. The panic had passed.

"Almost there." Max pulled a block up and let it rise toward the peak Lahra had formed. She locked in another piece to keep the pyramid from growing off-center and waited as the two pieces merged together.

Click.

The room shook, then went still. The towers lit as the tiles had in the previous puzzle. They thinned to a single-block wide, all of the others pulling away. They piled in on themselves, then receded into the wall, revealing an open door.

Not a crushing trap at all. Or a puzzle disguised as one to throw off invaders. Lahra filed the memory away to review and keep in mind the next time. Learn to see the use of expectations as a feint.

Lahra took Max's hand and squeezed, hoping to pass her confidence to him, that he would see the strength he had, the strength she saw in him. Not of blades or physical might, but perseverance and wit.

They would need all that strength and more if the challenges continued to escalate.

"We press on," she said. "New treasures and wisdom await."

CHAPTER THIRTEEN

MAX

MAX AND LAHRA PICKED their way through three more chambers, each with its own puzzle.

One was a word game, a story, and a video game proportions puzzle all in one. That one took a good thirty minutes to sort out.

As Max got to his feet, the four-cylinder puzzle complete, Wheel's voice cut back into their comms. "We've got incoming." Her signal was a bit fuzzy with all of the debris in the area.

"What is it?" Lahra asked.

"You don't want to know, which means you already know."

Max sighed. "Imperials? Already?"

"Just one ship. But its markings say there's a noble on board."

"Shit," Max and Lahra said in unison. The Vsenk nobles were one-alien wrecking balls, each capable of taking apart a neighborhood-sized ship on their own.

"What's your ETA?" There was no crackling in the signal, but Wheel's voice was distorted, its dial-up-modem undertone drowning out the organic side. That meant she was worried.

"We're close. Can you evade them and pull around for pickup?"

"I can try anything. The question is whether I'll survive."

Lahra's voice was rich with pride. "Your best will be sufficient. It always is."

"Thanks for the vote of confidence. And hurry up with the thieving."

The door led into a double-wide chamber with two pedestals and a tall altar holding a metallic vessel, chrome and silver, blue lights running along the sides, a system in equilibrium. The vessel was three meters wide, two meters tall, and six meters long. What container needed to be that big?

On the pedestals were two smaller rectangular devices with intricate carvings of Old Atlan heroes on all sides, save one with a screen. Each were a half-meter long and about twenty centimeters wide and tall. They looked somewhere between ancient and primordial. Max stepped carefully across the room, wary of traps, and looked at the smaller devices.

Max tilted his head, confused. "So, I have no idea what these are."

Lahra paced around the room in her soldiery way, checking the corners. "If they're here, they're likely important, no. But are they trapped?"

"Good question." Max walked around the pedestal, studying the construction of the device. He turned and took in the story told in the walls and ceiling of the tomb, tracing the tale to its conclusion.

"Faster, love."

The story told of the Atlans reaching out to the ends of known space, connecting hundreds of species with their network of warp field generators. This network of devices circumscribing the reach of warp travel became the boundaries of their empire. But there was no mention of the Vsenk that took over and inherited that empire.

He looked for the interface that would summon the

gestalt. The tomb had been in remarkably good condition despite the fragmentation. Maybe this place would provide answers where the others had not.

"We need to hurry. What do we take?" Lahra asked.

"I need more time. There's so much here!" The video alone would prompt a bidding war among Uwen's buyers, plus whatever he could get for the vessel and the rectangular devices. Max could easily spend a month picking through and cataloging this site. Get them all the way out of debt and well on the way to reversing the Atlan trick that had brought him here.

But they couldn't do all of that at once.

He heard an echo of his thesis advisor's voice during his first dig as a grad student. "Break it into doable chunks; prioritize. This stuff isn't going anywhere."

Max instructed his scanner to snap panoramic pictures as quickly as possible. The tactical cameras on Lahra's suit took video to accompany the pictures.

With Atlan tombs, being able to touch everything was better, but with Vsenk inbound, burglars couldn't be choosers. They'd grab the lot of them and sort it all out in transit using the pictures and video for context. And if he couldn't identify the artifacts, then maybe Uwen could.

"Get the vessel on lifters, I'll grab these things." He opened the comms. "Wheel, we need an exit, now! Zoom in on our location. We'll meet you halfway. There's an open section where the temple broke. Got it?"

Max inspected the small artifacts on the pedestals. Didn't look like they were trapped. He held his breath and snatched one artifact, then the other, making his way to the door. They were heavier than expected, maybe ten kilos each, but they cradled well and didn't slow him down. Lahra had the vessel floating with the lifters and nudged it out into the hallway.

"On our way!"

"That's great," Wheel said, "because I'm getting orders to

power down and submit to a search."

Fuck. Dammit. Every time we get lucky it flips all the way around. Panic bloomed in his mind and he shoved it back, trying to focus. "How far out are they?"

"A few minutes. Weapons range before that."

"They'd rather catch you and fine you to the nearest sun and back." Max rushed back through the tomb as Lahra shoved and directed the vessel. These three artifacts were by far the biggest finds. Probably. Except for the hundred little things he could be missing by having to rush. Archaeology wasn't supposed to be rushed, it wasn't a smash-and-grab. But they were desperate, and this wasn't anything like what he'd trained for back home.

He turned the corner and saw the stern of the *Kettle* through the open hallway, stars around the edges. Wheel held the ship steady. Ish.

Lahra moved with power and grace, pushing the vessel double-time.

"I see you. Opening the hold." Wheel spoke through gritted teeth, digital reverb punching through. "I've got fighters inbound."

Max held both of the smaller devices under one arm, crossing the hallway at a run. He leapt up into the hold, lowering the devices to the ground as the ship's gravity took hold. He could swear he heard the pursuit ships already, but that was just fear taking form to mess with him.

"We're in!" he shouted on the comms.

A volley of laser fire battered their shields, knocking Max off his feet.

Wheel cursed like a possessed modem as she guided the *Kettle* through a desperate dance of spins and dodges to break the Imperials' firing solution.

Lahra gave him a hand up, and together they lifted the vessel onto the *Kettle*.

In real gravity, they'd never be able to move the thing.

But the hold was set to half-gravity—a fact for which he was incredibly grateful in the split second as they hauled the several-ton artifact into the hold.

"Let's go!" Max pulled up the straps, tossing one over to Lahra so they could secure the vessel in place.

A summer storm downpour of laser fire rocked the ship, splattering against its shield like a violent aurora borealis. The ship lurched, sending Max hurtling into the back wall of the hold. The world spun. The ship's thrusters spiked, the vibration shaking his teeth like he was back on a turbulent flight to visit his great-uncle in Tennessee.

Lahra crossed the hold and helped Max to his feet. Then she bounded her way to the flight deck.

Max reset his mag-boots and strapped in. He wasn't allowed on the flight deck during fights anymore.

You brownout the weapons systems while trying to overclock the ship's codex to expedite a translation ONE TIME... he thought, strapping into the workstation to start analyzing their haul.

Wheel spoke through the ship's PA. "What did you take? I thought the Imperials at that second site were pissed, but this is worse. The haul better be worth it."

Laser fire pounded the shields like golf-ball-sized hail "Keep us alive for a few minutes and I'll tell you."

Lahra passed him in a hurry, making for the ladder. "You focus on the dusty artifacts, we'll handle the not dying."

"Division of labor. The key to any successful marriage!" The sarcasm in Wheel's voice was thick as molasses. But the modem tones had receded, which gave Max some small comfort. "You in the gun battery yet, L?"

"Weapons hot! Bring us around."

Max set to work deciphering the first of the two smaller devices, trying to shut out the thoughts of imminent doom.

So basically, it was a Tuesday.

CHAPTER FOURTEEN

WHEEL

SHUTTLING THE LOVEBIRDS AROUND was becoming incredibly hazardous. She'd already had to navigate the asteroid belt of planetary debris from the long since shattered remains of her ancestors' homes, and it turned out that was just the warm-up.

Wheel leaned the *Kettle* into a turn, diving and weaving right to avoid the latest volley from the Vsenk forces. "When this is over, we need to talk about hazard pay!"

"Fly now, bargain later," Lahra responded over comms, her voice level. The Genae was as unflappable as a twice-blasted rock.

Still steering and dodging, Wheel partitioned off a part of her attention to start a warp jump to get them a ride out of this system. The rest of her attention stayed on navigating the debris. She led the *Kettle* through spins and dives, staying two steps ahead of the slower, clumsier ship. If the *Kettle* was stationary, it'd take less than a minute to jump to warp. But right now, staying still would only qualify them for a non-stop ride to oblivion.

Vsenk lasers battered the *Kettle*'s shields, knocking the

ship into a lateral spin. Wheel poured on the throttle and leaned into the spin to reclaim control.

That'd push back the warp timer again.

If she could just make it to the sensor umbra of that larger fragment of the broken world, they might be able to get clear.

Outside, the Imperial forces fanned out, trying to corral the *Kettle* back toward their main ship.

"Sorry, kids, no such luck." Wheel sent the ship into another spin. The *Kettle* arced between planetoids, forcing the fighters to match her reckless level of maneuvering. They wouldn't be able to keep up with her *and* flank her. Not unless they went all the way around this miniature asteroid field and managed to catch her on the other side.

Which, if she had to be honest, was not going to happen. Wheel had a thousand years of festering Atlan grudge against Vsenk on the line.

One of the fighters zipped by, and a volley of fire hit the shields before Lahra blew the thing to pieces. Another fighter twitched and dodged right, sending it straight into an asteroid. Shields were holding. For now.

Lahra's voice grew louder, her battle song echoing throughout the ship.

One fighter left, plus the pursuit ship.

Whenever Imperials were involved, there was a big, scary variable that hung in the air like a jury-rigged regulator box: *Where's the Vsenk?*

Tensing, Wheel pulled the ship out of the debris field and looped back around to the left, heading for her escape vector, the warp drive nearly ready.

Some Atlans who flew on the wrong side of the law kept their warp field generators spooled up nearly all the time, but they were the same kind of Atlans who didn't mind the risk of a spontaneous implosion when their field hit an antimatter bubble. That was the wrong kind of reckless. Wheel played the margins like Erreki surfed solar winds: she knew what risks to take, and she got paid.

As long as her partners didn't get her killed.

"Feel like using some more of that dead-shot Genae training, eh?" Wheel asked.

"Feel like telling me how you're going to evade so I can aim worth a Terran damn?"

"Am I supposed to be insulted?" Max asked over the comms.

"Yes!" said Wheel.

"No," countered Lahra.

Something popped onto the *Kettle*'s radar. Small, but moving fast.

"Vsenk noble, incoming!"

There was a reason the Vsenk were the rulers of the galaxy. The Vsenk ranged from four to six meters tall, and they could live and fight in the vacuum of space for hours. A Vsenk could slap on a rocket pack and scattergun and take apart thirty heavy infantry without breaking a sweat. Also, they didn't sweat.

And now there was one bearing down on them, coming in hot.

"Hold on to your asses, kids. This is about to get uglier than the useless sack of feathers you call a pet."

In his battle-secure crate at the rear of the cockpit, Cruji, their brightly-colored feathered and tentacled mascot, purred.

Wheel pushed the engines past the redline, well into the danger zone she railed against so often.

Stuck between possible implosion and the business end of a Vsenk scattergun, she'd take her chances with the engine.

CHAPTER FIFTEEN

LAHRA

SITTING IN THE LUMPY chair with growing tears in the cushion, Lahra belted "Dancing at the Edge of the Black," a gunner's song designed to help improve aim, reflexes, and to maintain optimal firing patterns in a dogfight. She'd picked the song up from another member of the soldier caste back when she was a mercenary.

Lahra spaced outbursts of fire to avoid overheating. Run the guns too hot and it would tax the engines and the warp core. And Lahra did not wish to undermine the systems that could get them out of this death trap.

Trespassing in the Forbidden Sectors was punishable by up to twenty years of Grade-X heavy labor on a mining colony. And they were gender-segregated into a binary, so not only would she have to break herself and Wheel out, then she'd have to go and rescue Max, too. Far too much bother.

As the Terran saying went—that was more easily spoken than accomplished.

At the other end of the flight deck, Wheel shouted a litany of curses. Her arms were buried deep in the control console, flying the ship through direct neural interface in the manner of her people. They didn't have the songs, but even a novice Atlan pilot had a better connection with ships and machinery than a Genae veteran.

Without an Atlan at the helm, the Imperials would have taken them minutes ago.

But Lahra fought as if there would be no rescue, as if the engines would fail and everything was on her. Her mother had raised her to make use of allies, but to assume that they would always fall short. Halra trained her daughter knowing that one day she could be the only thing between a restored queen and certain death.

It made things incredibly simple, really. Triumph alone or die.

And so Lahra kept singing, kept firing. The song told the tale of a lone Genae ship cutting a path through the Hijan Honeycomb with a dozen enemies at their back. The ship wove through the lethal maze of ship-killing ionic radiation, wrecking foe after foe. Some versions made it into a drinking song.

That part would have to wait until they were clear.

Lahra destroyed one of the remaining fighters, only to see the Vsenk noble soar through the debris, wielding a scattergun as big as Lahra.

Bellowing the chorus, she opened fire on the noble with both cannons, weaving a killing field with the bursts in time to the song.

The Vsenk dodged to the side, moving nimbly through her laser fire. The *Kettle*'s turrets were made to target machinery, not the living. And no arms dealer with any sense would design weapons specifically to kill Vsenk. The Imperium's control was too tight, especially on weapons manufacturing.

The privileges of rule meant that in a galaxy of dangers, countless weapons from a dozen species, none were made to adequately threaten the Vsenk.

At least, none made today. Her people had fought the

Vsenk to a standstill.

Until the Devastation.

Lahra kept firing, leading the Vsenk, then firing wider, trying to force them to back off.

Nothing worked, and the Vsenk's seven-limbed form closed, scattergun pummeling the *Kettle*'s shields.

"They're on us!" she shouted to Wheel between verses.

Wheel pitched the *Kettle* into a sharp dive. Lahra listened to discern whether they'd thrown off their pursuer.

Her heart sank at the rending of the scattergun blasts piercing the shields and gouging the hull. The Vsenk would tear the ship apart, one piece at a time. And that was if they didn't get inside.

A stabilizer blew, then a sensor array. Then the shields gave out entirely.

Lahra unbuckled herself from the gunner's chair. "We need to warp, now!"

"Not ready!"

The thrusters cut out, the ship coasting. Lahra leapt from the gun battery, heading for the hold. "That was—"

"Yep. The engines. Noble's coming around to the hold. I haven't seen one this ticked off since my last stint in the Shadow-Cells. Whatever it was you took, it must be important."

Lahra dove through the ladder chute, flipping in mid-air. Landing hard, she redirected that energy into a leap, unlocking her sword as she went.

She reactivated the EVA function on her battle suit, watching as the Vsenk ripped a hole in their hold. The noble peeled two-meter slivers of the hull back like a child peeling fruit. Air rushed out of the room, pulling Lahra off her feet, sending paper and tools flying. The emergency force field activated to keep the atmosphere in, but it couldn't keep the Vsenk out. Detritus hit the floor like hail as the Vsenk clawed inside. Max scrambled to pack away his desk, yellow stun gun shaking on its hook where she'd placed it for just such an occasion.

The noble's coloration was orange and yellow—a male, and not a large one. Not quite five meters tall, with two arms that held a massive gun while the others folded steel to make itself an entrance. The powerful Vsenk arms tapered gradually to comparatively small fingers for fine motor control, which were some of the species' few vulnerabilities. The Vsenk had an exoskeleton, their chitin stronger than the *Kettle*'s hull. The Vsenk had already pulled most of his body inside, skull-like face and glowing gold eyes glaring at Max and the Atlan artifacts. Once he was inside he'd fill a third of the cargo bay by himself, stooping somewhat in the hold only barely taller than he was.

The Vsenk had conquered the galaxy through ruthless aggression, intimidation, and personal might. They'd brought Lahra's people to their knees, scattered her ancestors to the solar winds. One noble could destroy a small battleship with nothing more than a thruster pack and a scattergun. Lahra had seen Vsenk before, but only at a distance. She'd thought long about how she might try to fight one, but facing the noble in person, all of that confidence crumbled, and she came to understand how they'd conquered the galaxy, how they'd defeated even her people. They were terror and power made real. Every movement of his arms could crush steel, every step could propel him ten meters.

He'd come for them, pierced the ship's defenses, and she was the only person standing in his way. The Vsenk stepped forward, arms poised to strike like vipers, his attention on the Atlan artifacts by Max.

You can't have him, she thought, as she began the first verse of "Yuxi at the Pass," her favorite song for one-on-one combat. It also doubled as a drinking song, best performed with a large drum as accompaniment. Her sword would have to suffice.

She passed a charge into her blade. The room flashed

white for a moment as the weapon fired.

But this was a Vsenk. The noble shrugged off the blow and stooped forward, clawing at Max and the smaller devices. The force field couldn't operate at the same time as the gravity, leaving Max to half-dive, half-float out of the way.

Max snatched one of the smaller devices, climbing across his workstation toward the other. "A little help!" he cried, diving through zero-G to evade the noble.

While the Vsenk's attention was elsewhere, Lahra leapt and slashed at the Noble. She belted the tale of Yuxi, a guard who stopped the rebel princess Ifah at the Widow's Pass. The song granted her strength, speed, and above all else, the stamina needed to hold a chokepoint against all comers.

The Vsenk parried with the scattergun, the weapon as long as Lahra was tall. She spun the blade back and then around, cutting at the Vsenk's limb. The charged blade cracked the noble's exoskeleton but didn't draw blood.

Merely attacking a Vsenk was punishable by death.

The Vsenk slapped her with a spare limb, sending her hurtling toward the far end of the hold. Lahra turned into the spin and made herself a spring, absorbing the energy and sending it right back to leap at the noble again. On the comms, she departed from her song to say, "We need to be gone, now."

"With the joyrider?" Wheel asked.

Lahra poured another charge into her blade. "Leave that to me."

She picked up the song, the power of her ancestors filling her with the strength to wreak vengeance upon this monster.

The Vsenk unfurled his limbs, two grabbing the vessel. The other whipped out and grabbed the other smaller artifact.

But he didn't fire on Max to claim the last device. *These artifacts are not to be damaged, then,* she thought.

Lahra slashed at the Vsenk, lightning crackling across

the noble's chitin. She fired her suit's thrusters to arc around to the noble's back and grab hold of its jetpack. She slashed at the Vsenk's neck, just above the pack.

And, as predicted, the giant reared back to claw at her.

The Vsenk lashed out at Lahra, his other limbs holding him inside the ship. The suit took most of the force of the Vsenk's blow.

But it was not just one strike. The Vsenk hit her across the neck, flank, and legs. She grabbed ahold of Max and pushed against the hull of the ship while Max held onto the device.

"Yield, criminals," the noble boomed, his face curled into a sneer. Though the Vsenk, to Lahra's knowledge, did not tend to express positive emotions and were nearly always sneering.

"Get off our boat, Starro," Max said. Then, in his Terran tongue, "I'm wearing the gloves."

He didn't move his hands to show her, but he didn't have to. No Vsenk spoke Terran. Lahra found the tongue point-lessly complicated, but it served well enough in this case.

She charged her sword and tapped the giant artifact, setting it alight with power. Max's rubber gloves turned the charge back onto the device and to the noble.

"Now!" Lahra said, comms on.

Max used his wrist tablet to de-activate the force field, exposing the cargo bay to the void. Wheel hit the thrusters, and the ship lurched forward.

Lahra hit an emergency thruster button on the pack.

Between the charge, the thrusters, the decompression, and the Vsenk's own jetpack turned against it, the noble shot back through the force field and out of the back of the ship, taking the vessel and one of the smaller devices with him.

Lahra clutched Max to her and activated the magnetic locks on her boots, which clicked and locked to the floor of the cargo bay. Max re-activated the force field, and the twice-disrupted room re-scattered to the floor.

Annihilation Aria

They'd lost most of their find. But they would live.

She banished the song from her mind and shouted on the comms, "Get us to warp!"

Out the back of the ship, the Vsenk's form grew small, spinning as he tried to get control of the jetpack again. The artifacts spiraled away, but the patrol ship would be able to scoop them up.

The world around them contracted and then went black as the *Kettle* pierced through to warp space, carrying them beyond the noble's reach.

The Vsenk had claimed two of the three artifacts they'd taken from the tomb. And Vsenk were not the type to leave things unfinished.

79

CHAPTER SIXTEEN

MAX

THE BEST THING ABOUT warp travel was that no one could track you. Not even the Atlan engineers that maintained the massive regulators on the edge of warp space knew how to track a ship once it entered the parallel dimension.

Enter warp space in one part of the galaxy, fly a while, then return to regular space halfway across the system. Max just had to not spend too long thinking about where they really were in transit. But you couldn't stay in warp forever, and the emergency shield wouldn't protect them for long even in warp space.

Lahra riveted sheet metal across the fresh-made hole in the hull, a crude fix that would let them limp back to the Wreck while Max tried to concentrate on the last Atlan device.

He'd thought the Vsenk were terrifying at a distance. But he'd just had one rampaging around their hold, the place where he worked, the place filled with a thousand small memories, and the Vsenk had nearly killed them all.

All of these artifacts. What were they? Throw this last one in a cardboard box and it could have been a toaster, a boombox, maybe a child's toy. It was covered in dense Old Atlan script, full of dated technical language beyond even his knowledge. There was some kind of screen or display or input area on one side, and no discernible way to open or unlock it. He didn't even know how to start identifying its function.

But if a Vsenk noble came after these things directly, they had to be important.

Max just had to figure out how and why.

He reviewed the facts:

I)   This was one of two seemingly-identical devices procured from the heart of an Atlan temple.
 A)   A temple that dated back several centuries, before the Devastation. That was probably relevant.
   1)   A temple that also tried to kill him several times.
   2)   Yes, but they pretty much all do that.
 B)   The circuit patterns on the device don't quite match the dominant style of the temple.
   1)   It could have been built by a different person than the temple architect.
   2)   It could have been a later addition.
     i)   Note to self: Look up the best possible dating for the temple, cross-reference with Atlan architectural survey.
     ii)   Problem: That survey was officially contraband, and all he had were snapshots thirdhand from other sources.

Max scanned back through his codex, looking for the citations on those sources. The codex represented the sum of his accumulated knowledge about this part of the universe, a bulky tablet running a jailbroken version of standard Imperial software and loaded with texts, analysis programs, and every other bit of gray- and black-market archaeological and cultural information he could get his hands on.

But even with all of that, he kept striking out.

The Great Atlan Library—burned in the fall of Yua.

Vrendi's Database of Lost Histories—deleted by Imperial Censors.

The Qix Sisters' Chronicle—confiscated by local police.

Oculus's Archaeological Survey—Oh.

Oh.

The last known copy was rumored to be a part of the Xidd archives, the private collection of Yeddix, the Drell Matriarch.

Outline forgotten, Max tabbed over to pull up the star charts and look for the location of the Drell migration.

There was only one school of Drell in the galaxy, and they took the same path through the star systems to lay their eggs among the Breuu Nebula and then loop around to forage for food, coming around to pick up the babies every twenty years or so.

Yeddix was *old*. Like, around to see the fall of the Atlan Empire old. And her archives were second to none. When you were several kilometers long like the Drell were, you got a bit of autonomy. Last time Imperial forces took on the school, four Drell died . . . along with fifteen ships, thousands of troops, and eleven Vsenk nobles. Almost five percent of the ruling class.

Since then, the Vsenk mostly left the Drell to their own business. Which meant their migration was uninterrupted, as regular as clockwork.

Max took the data from the almanac and pinged the ship's navigation systems, getting back the result in seconds.

The Drell were merely weeks away from the Wreck. Maybe a six-hour warp once they'd set down at their port of call.

This could work. It could actually work.

Max flicked on the comms.

"So, we need an audience with the Drell Matriarch. Anyone have ideas?"

Wheel laughed a full belly laugh, filling the comms for several seconds as Max continued. "Is it really that hard?"

Wheel stopped laughing to say, "Kid, Yeddix's appointments book decades in advance. She's probably the oldest living being in the galaxy. You can't just pull up alongside the school and pop in for some U'uh'ish. What do you need to know?"

"My records show that the only sources that might be able to explain what these things are that we pulled out of the temple probably exist in her archives. And unless I'm mistaken, you don't get into the archives until you get the Matriarch's okay."

Max put his head in his hands, massaging his temples. Why couldn't things be easy just a single time? It'd be so novel!

Lahra set the rivet gun aside, the patch job done for now. "Then we must find another way." She crossed the hold to speak to him directly, her voice resolute. "The Vscnk will be posting a notice of our crimes. Therefore, we must make ourselves scarce, or unload that device as soon as possible."

"I'm not selling something if I don't know what it does! For all I know, this could be a galactic divining rod and point to super warp gates or help you find the Genae heir. I just don't know, and I barely know where to start."

Lahra squeezed his shoulder. Of all the bizarre ports, the infinite stars and endless black, she was his constant. "Breathe."

His world narrowed to her words.

Inhale.

Exhale.

The pressure relieved, slowly, and the world expanded again as the spell passed.

He gave a mild smile, and relaxed, slumping back into his seat.

"Start with what you know."

Max turned back to the device, to his codex, and to the problem at hand. The heaping stack of "Things I Don't

Know" stood tall in his mind, but it wouldn't come tumbling down just yet.

"I believe in you. I always have. Always will." She kissed him on the forehead and traced a line down his jaw with her fingers.

"Except when I'm talking out of my ass."

She grinned. "Of course not then. I can believe in you without believing everything you say. I'm dour, not gullible."

"I'm still waiting to hear some of those Genae jokes."

Lahra shrugged. "They're in the songs."

Max had grown up with music all around him, but he could never pick it up. Languages were one thing—he'd picked up Spanish from the Salvadoran kids down the street, then Greek in high school, a couple more in college.

But music was different.

So, of course he'd end up marrying someone from a civilization where music was the unchallenged cornerstone of their culture.

Max picked the device up in both hands and turned it end over end, twisted and rolled and looked at it from every possible angle, tracking the overlapping sigils and trying to find a foothold, a handhold, anything as a beginning. Every puzzle, every story, every formula had a beginning. And beginnings told you so much. What to expect, the stakes, the language, the priorities.

Beginnings were a key to the first door toward understanding.

And maybe, just maybe, a way home.

CHAPTER SEVENTEEN

LAHRA

Max was still deep in study when their ship popped back into normal space near the Wreck. Lahra left him to his work and took the co-pilot seat beside Wheel.

Even with the pressure from Jesvin, the Wreck had become something close to a home base over the last few years. Close enough to the places they needed to be to do their work, far enough out from the core of the Empire to stay off the radar.

Shadows peeled back from the Wreck as the *Kettle* flew into the line for docking. Wheel chattered back and forth with their port officers, Atlan banter going fast and thick.

Whenever they were walking the Wreck, Max would rattle on about ethnographies and how the place reminded him of a walled city back in his homeland. What sensible city would exist without a wall she could not say, but she knew the Terrans to be strange people, grown impersonal in their wars, rulers using bombardments and proxies to wage war without facing the results of their slaughter.

There were more Genae on the Wreck than nearly any place she'd ever been. But with Jesvin's debt hanging over them it still felt like contested ground.

Still, it was a welcome refuge from the dangers of the fringe.

"We're tenth in line," Wheel said into the comms. "You done solving the mysteries of the universe back there?"

Max responded a few moments later. Wheel must have caught him mid-calculation. "Not quite. But I think I know where to start looking. Can you beam a message to Uwen? I think he'd be interested in taking a look at our hard-fought prize."

Lahra tapped through the comms system to call up Uwen's address. "What do you want to tell him?"

"Let's leave out the part where we almost got spaced by a noble. Just say we got a solid hit. Found something so old even I don't know what it does." Max paused. "No. Cancel that." She could practically hear his smile. "Tell him it's so old that I bet *he* doesn't know what it does."

"But you do not know what it does."

"Yeah, but challenging Uwen will get him excited."

"I shouldn't have to remind you that it is unwise to, as you say, 'pull the tail' with our fence."

"Mmm. And since he has not only a tail but claws, that's not a great idea."

Wheel cut their banter short. "Why don't you get that bull's-eye of an artifact off my ship as soon as we touch down. I'm going to need some serious quality time with my baby to get her in fighting form again. Vsenk brutes."

Lahra sent off the message to Uwen, tamping down Max's challenge and giving a suggested set of times. Before she could deal with Uwen, she would need to stretch her legs and get something to eat. She dealt poorly with the trifling on an empty stomach.

Wheel jumped back from the console as if she'd been struck.

"She took them."

"What?" Lahra asked.

"Message from Ruku. Jesvin's strong-arms beat him into a puddle and took Eihra and the girls. Wrecked the stand. And left a message for us."

***

The three stood around the center console as Wheel played Jesvin's note:

My dear friends,

I have grown tired of your repeated abuse of my trust, despite years of unceasing support and patronage. Even my patience is not without limit, and I am afraid that more drastic measures must now be taken in order to properly convey to you the weight of your obligation. I had hoped that the better parts of your nature would call you to discharge your debt in a timely fashion, but after my last visit from Wheel it became clear to me that too long on the fringes of space had taken from you what little sense of propriety and shame you had left.

Therefore, I am forced to inspire you to higher action in another fashion. I will be hosting darling Eihra and her girls in my apartments for as long as it takes for you to come to your senses and do the right thing in balancing the scales.

I remain dutifully yours,
Jesvin Ker

"Dutifully a fucking monster," Max growled. "What's the play?"

Lahra clenched her hands into fists, rage flowing through her. It was not enough that this harridan assailed them with guilt and shaming and manipulation. Now she had the audacity to endanger innocent lives, to attack Lahra's closest Genae kin in order to reclaim her debt. For Jesvin, lives were just another currency to take and spend. She'd never get her feathers dirty; it was always others that held the blade or the gun. Was there nothing in the galaxy that Jesvin couldn't turn into a chit to spend or a prize to display?

She stood from the seat. "I've had it with that monster."

Wheel looked up from the console, the ship on auto-pilot in the docking queue. "What does that mean?"

"It's time to pluck the strings Jesvin uses to make people dance to her will, turn the Wreck against her, and knock Jesvin from her roost."

Max gestured down to the hold. "We've kind of already got our hands full. But what about artifacts? What about the Vsenk on our tail?"

Lahra should have been excited for the lead. Energized to fight the Imperium. And she was. But family came first. She'd failed to restore the Genae. But here, on the Wreck, she had to protect what little of their people remained. "All in good time. They won't come to the Wreck, not for a while."

"And how long is it going to take to depose Jesvin? I don't think that's the kind of thing you can do in a weekend."

"It will take as long as it takes." Lahra held back her exasperation. Her anger was not his fault, nor Wheel's. They should not be made to suffer its consequences.

"I hate her as much as anyone," Wheel said, "but I'm not signing up for a crusade. The last time someone tried to wage war on Jesvin, the Wreck became a disaster area for months. Two hundred dead. There's no way to go after her on a large scale without innocents getting hurt."

Lahra thought for a moment before responding. "We will be more precise, then. Reach out to Uwen and anyone else you can trust here. We need to know exactly where Eihra and the girls are being kept. And we need some way of repaying Jesvin. Not for the debt, but for the affront and her violation of the Wreck's trust. If we can expose Jesvin, truly expose her, we can shed enough light to banish the shadows and lies she uses to control people."

"Okay . . ." Max said. "Of course we get Eihra and the girls out. But taking Jesvin down? That's a massive job. One that won't get us paid or help us find out what these artifacts are."

Wheel turned back to the console, apparently done with the conversation. "Let's start with Uwen. He'll have contacts and something to say about our findings."

Lahra stared at the growing shape of the Wreck as the *Kettle* pulled in slowly, still behind a half-dozen vessels.

No place other than a ship had ever felt as much like home as the Wreck. But as they returned this time, they returned not to safety and friendship but to uncertainty and danger.

CHAPTER EIGHTEEN

WHEEL

THE LOVEBIRDS WERE OFF to see Uwen, leaving Wheel to patch up the poor, abused *Kettle*. She'd scrapped with Imperials before, but never a noble. She sent out some feelers before she set to work. Any follow-ups could wait a couple of hours while she got the repairs underway.

The biggest priority was the airlock. Wheel lowered what remained of the platform, pulled the rivets out from the emergency sheets Lahra had attached, and cleared the scrap. Walking the perimeter, she checked the stress points, the joints, and looked again for the worst of all niggling problems, metal fatigue. And all the while, her mental repair bill ticked higher and higher. She ran a hand over the jagged edges of the hull. Seeing a Vsenk's handiwork up close sent shivers up her arms. That monster would have torn her entire ship apart piece by piece if she hadn't gotten them out when she did. As is, they were all void-blessed to have survived.

While they were in transit, she could only repair from the inside unless someone went EVA for emergency fixes. Here, Wheel could take her time and do a full walk-around of the ship. Not just to fix current problems but to prevent future ones.

She'd have to write off three whole panels, and the weld job on the fourth would be tricky thanks to the patch she'd made two months ago on a courier run gone bust.

Every time they came back to the Wreck, Wheel made a go at trying to find a garage and parts shop not in Jesvin's pockets. It was a shitty game that got harder every time without any real sense of reward. Bad design.

On the fifth call, she got lucky with a third-rate supplier she'd used once before and regretted it—a Rellix who brokered deals between mechanics and wreckers. They provided spare parts and raw material for mercs and traders, as well as more desperate folks trying to fix up a dead ship just enough to blast off this rock.

Wheel wired the cash for three new panels, wincing at what their lower quality would do to the ship's stability. When they arrived two hours later, she swallowed her pride as she hauled the panels off the delivery cart to get her baby back in space-worthy condition. She got some gossip along the way, rumblings about a power grab on Vsenkos by an aggressive faction within the Empire. Just what they needed.

Four hours later, she was soaked through with sweat, but the job was done.

Just as she put away the rivets and wrenches, a message pinged on the ship's comms.

Wheel encrypted every message she sent by habit, as did most of her people. When you lived under the thumb of an empire full of domineering shitheads like the Vsenk (Terran profanity was so satisfyingly precise), it was just good practice. Her baseline wasn't hard encryption, just a phrase substitution cypher that turned messages into boring family updates. Nothing that would raise the Imps' hackles if one of their data-sniffers decided to pick it out for audit.

So when a call came in with three layers of encoding, Wheel took notice. She hustled through the hold, up the ladder, across and up to the cockpit.

Only one person Wheel knew used that much crypto. Cog was a paranoid old hand, as cranky and brilliant an Atlan as Wheel had ever met. She had good reason, though.

It paid to be careful when you were plotting to bring down an empire. Over a decade ago, Cog and Wheel had been partners working shipping and logistics on Illhar. They took a job with some loose bolts to it, and Wheel investigated. Which led them to a group called the Resurgence, trying to build an insurrection against the Vsenk. They spent two years working with them, arranging import/export, some smuggling runs. It was dangerous, paid for crap, and made Wheel incredibly paranoid that they were going to be caught at any moment.

After a string of bad missions, Wheel packed up the *Kettle* and made for the fringe, leaving the cause . . . and Cog.

Wheel ran the signal through the private decryption systems Cog had provided.

"What's the word?" Wheel asked, walking up to her comms console, broadcasting audio-only to start. The *Kettle* automatically encrypted the message going out, matching Cog's level of protection.

"Figured you might have something for me after your trip to the Forbidden Sectors. Imperial patrols have it out for a ship with your description, they want you bad. It's all over the comms."

Wheel didn't officially think of herself as a member of the Resurgence anymore, but she took jobs for Cog on the regular, connecting the lovebirds with Uwen, who routed useful Atlan tech back to Cog and the others on Illhar. Especially anything with a military application. Best as Wheel could tell, Cog had a dozen or more groups like them out on the edge. Void, maybe all of them were Cog's exes, too. It was a big galaxy.

"Probably, but Jesvin's on our ass. Kidnapped some Genae friends of Lahra's."

"Voiddammit. What does she want?"

Wheel flipped the video on. Cog sat in her garage, arms crossed. She was as sweaty as Wheel this time, so at least she had that going for her. Wheel waved her hands for Cog's benefit, channeling her frustration into the movement. "The money, of course. Money we don't have. Care to float us a loan?"

Wheel and Cog had an arrangement. Cog kept Wheel and the lovebirds in work and the *Kettle* flying when things got really bad. In exchange, Wheel helped Cog build up her little rebellion. Except that even Cog's help hadn't been enough to keep them solvent thanks to a long string of strike-outs in their artifact-hunting.

Cog's expression was sympathetic. "I'm not exactly drowning in cash here. Revolutions are expensive."

"If you want my team to come on board officially, helping us out of this bind would be a great way of making that happen."

Cog went still for a moment. Likely she was sending a message to someone or reviewing some spreadsheet in her cybernetic HUD. "I'll see what I can do. Maybe move some things around in a couple of accounts. I'll message Uwen if I can scrounge some extra funds."

"They're already on their way to see him with their haul. Took it from an Old Atlan tomb, so it's probably stuffy and useless."

"Our ancestors survived long enough for us to get here, Wheel."

Bullshit, she thought, but kept it to herself. "By giving up practically everything and holding on by one finger."

"We can re-hash this argument again next time you come to visit, but I'm not having it now."

They had time, assuming neither of them got killed in their respective dangerous lives. Atlan lifespans were long. Cog's skin had jewel-blue undertones chipped around the eyes, mouth, and where her original meat met her cybernetics. Which was often. Cog's arms, hip, and legs were nearly all mechanical. She'd lost a lot in her struggle, not all of it physical.

The Resurgence had grown since Wheel left. They'd stayed under the radar, gathering supplies, making isolated strikes on supply stations and system patrols. And it worked because they were mostly bankrolled by people making out well thanks to the looser regulations of Illhar's Special Economic Zone.

"Any word from Illhar or the Imperium? We just barely escaped a noble as we were busting out of that system."

Cog laughed. "You could have mentioned that earlier. Or are you that blasé about facing down those monsters?"

"I mean, I didn't have to face it down, not directly. Did a number on the *Kettle*. Had to strip and replace half the cargo hatch." The sight of the ship's patchwork hull, the low-quality steel, the thousand little things that could go wrong, all of it crowded the edges of her attention like malware on an unprotected network.

"Glad you made it out. Patrol ship?"

Wheel nodded. "Void-damned lousy timing. Maybe they had sensor buoys mixed in with the planetary debris. Or those artifacts are a bigger deal than Max thought."

Cog's expression grew bright. She was trying to cheer Wheel up, void take her. "The hotter they are, the more interesting they become, and the more my colleagues will want in."

"Don't get yourself too excited. I'll let you know what Uwen says."

"You could just bring them in, Wheel. I bet Max would love the brainiacs we've got collected here."

That pitch again. Not six months after the lovebirds had come aboard, Cog started asking her to bring them all in, to help her make the Resurgence into something real.

"Not while Eihra and her girls are in chains because of us. Help us fix this and we can get back to working for you out here. They get what they want, and you get what you want. Without me getting screwed over trying to balance in the middle."

"Every era comes to an end, eventually."

A shadow passed over Cog's face. The same one she'd get whenever their complicated past together came up. Rivalry turned to friendship turned to love. Then when it all blew up, they settled into this messy void with microgravity and no sense of direction.

"True enough. But just because you're right doesn't mean you're the one that gets to write the history when it finally happens."

"Not for lack of trying," Cog said. "Take care of yourself, and keep me in the loop."

"And you try not to get yourself killed before I can come and set you straight about our fuckup ancestors, okay?"

"Yeah, the promise of another argument with you is definitely what will keep me alive."

Wheel grinned. "No, that's stubbornness."

Cog rolled her eyes, smiling as she ended the call.

Waves of memories passed through her mind. Good, bad, mixed. She floundered, heart racing. They were in deep this time. Enemies coming at them from all sides, short on friends and resources, and no closer to completing Max and Lahra's missions than they'd been months ago.

Wheel listened to the music of the ship, the flow of power, the streams of data. The tide of worry receded for the moment, leaving her with worries about what was to come.

Back to business. With the hull taken care of, she sat up and set about her normal maintenance and upkeep tasks. If she was busy working, her ears and mind filled with the sounds of drills and data, she wouldn't have the time to worry about their stolen cargo, Jesvin, Cog's revolution, or the Vsenk that could still be on their trail.

CHAPTER NINETEEN

AREK

Arek paced the command deck of the battlecruiser *Vigilance Without Respite*, waiting for his crew to give him some good news.

He'd been waiting for quite some time.

Less than an hour ago, he'd held all three artifacts in his limbs. He had responded quickly, efficiently, with the brutality and prowess worthy of the Vsenk.

Based on the response he received for his initial report, whatever those artifacts were, they were important. He'd been so close to a commendation, perhaps even a promotion out of the fringe.

But no. That Genae throwback had gotten the best of him with little more than some jury-rigging and the help of a clumsy Yaea and a servitor pilot.

"Where. Are. They?" Arek asked. His people were legendary for their rage, but Arek prided himself on being approachable, sometimes even friendly.

In his position, he needed his crew rising to the task as allies, not cowering in fear as sniveling minions.

The ship's XO, Gralo, a nervous Rellix with shimmering

blue and green feathers, gathered herself before speaking. "We've put out the notice to all systems. Their ship will be easy to spot given the damage, Lord Arek."

"Assuming a patrol finds them before they're able to make repairs or replace the ship."

Pilot, the obviously-named Atlan, scoffed. His hands were still buried deep in the console, as one with the ship. "Not likely, Commander. That was an Atlan at the helm, guaranteed. Experienced, judging by how they moved. No Atlan with skills like that will just ditch a ship, pardon my saying."

They all feared him. For good reason. But at times it kept them from maximal efficiency. Hence his efforts toward approachability. "Thank you, Pilot." He turned back to the XO.

"What of the devices?"

Gralo chirped in the affirmative. "The device we can track by trying to match the signature of the one we have here. But the query has to bounce back and forth between the station nodes. As soon as we get a ping, we can warp right there, and we'll be on them with the vengeance of the Imperium."

Arek raised his voice, turning to speak to the whole bridge. "We will find them, we will retrieve the other artifact, and then we will deliver the set safely back to Vsenkos. And when it is done, the records will show that this mission never happened, and we never carried these terrible artifacts in our hold. Officially, they do not exist, and your lives, all of our lives, rely on both our efficiency in reclaiming the other key and our discretion in never thinking of or mentioning them again—Have I made myself clear?" Arek asked, knowing the answer. It was always the same answer.

"Yes, Commander!" the crew called in chorus, voices filling the command deck.

"For the Imperium." Arek stalked over to his office.

"For the Imperium!" they shouted in response.

Always for the Imperium. The Imperium that had judged

him weak, insufficiently callous. The Imperium which had stationed him on the rectum of the galaxy, guarding tombs and ghosts and contraband. His faction was out of power, moderates coalescing around Evam and his hard-liners as they pushed for stricter laws, less cultural tolerance, and higher taxes.

Arek had not seen his wife and daughter for most of a year, and it had been six months before that. Twice a year he could be something more than a low-ranking noble far from home, casting all of his votes through proxy via Qerol, the leader of his reformist faction. He was one of mere thousands of Vsenk in the whole galaxy, but he was as constrained by the Imperium as any. This posting was supposed to be temporary, a way to prove his mettle, to earn the loyalty of those that served under him.

That was three years ago. And there was no end in sight. Unless he could turn this debacle around and make it into an opportunity.

If they'd been an hour earlier on their patrol, he wouldn't have this cluster headache and a ship full of nervous crew. Wouldn't have orders to retrieve the artifacts or count his life forfeit, hanging on the line. All because of a servitor, a throwback, and a peasant.

Heavens help them if another of his people found them first. Those thieves would be little more than a red mist disintegrating into the never void, their ship shredded, their lives erased from history, along with the incompetent noble who had failed to find them.

Better that Arek find them. Better for them all.

And he would find them. This much was clear.

What would happen after that?

Sitting on his stoop, Arek flexed his limbs. Felt the strength that was his birthright, tasted the rage, so rare for him where it flowed freely in his kin.

That . . . he hadn't decided yet.

CHAPTER TWENTY

MAX

THE WRECK WAS A genuine anthropological gold mine in a galaxy where the Empire required historians to be bonded and licensed (Max was neither). There was more material, more wisdom about distinct species living together, more cultural melding and interdependence, than anywhere he'd visited since getting shunted to the other side of the universe. If there was a key to interspecies and interplanetary peace, it would be found from the lessons on the Wreck.

Max and Lahra never stayed long enough for him to do proper fieldwork. Even when they'd lived next to the Bazaar, he'd barely scratched the surface.

But when they did come back, he took notes as best he could to learn everything he could. And if nothing else, it made moving through the Wreck easier—knowing the local dialects of major languages, identifying factional conflicts and which neighborhoods to avoid.

And where to find the best Feoe. It tasted like barbeque but was actually made from mushrooms and a spiced nut sauce and had zero business being as delicious as it was.

When things with Jesvin were less tense, the Wreck was

a great place to live. And there were still moments where light broke through the clouds. They were just less frequent lately.

Max munched on his second Feoe sandwich of the day as they trekked across six kilometers and down a dozen levels on the way to Uwen's shop. The Illhari word translated to "market of what was and what is," which always sounded much more mysterious than "pawn shop."

With his other hand, Max pushed the floating cart. It contained a box, which held a smaller box, which held the ancient Atlan device. With the Imperials on their tail and Jesvin on the hunt, they'd agreed on maximal caution.

He could tell Lahra was on edge, courtesy of her "dare to challenge me and I'll cut you down where you stand" gait, which was close to but perceptibly different from her default, which said "I am somewhat relaxed and you may live if you do not trouble me unduly."

Jesvin had eyes just about everywhere on the Wreck, so there was no chance they'd be able to pass totally undetected. She'd know they were back, but would she make another move, or wait for them to come to her?

Lahra hummed a song under her breath, punctuated by sips of Gaez, a traditional Genae milkshake made with cream and the minced meat of this galaxy's analogue of oysters.

It was no more than the fiftieth weirdest thing he'd learned to eat out here, far far behind Erreki steaks, Juush berries (which were actually living bacterial colonies), and U'uh'ish, which was better enjoyed and not thought about.

The two wove their way through a series of switchbacks, elevators, and labyrinthine pathways until they reached Uwen's storefront.

"Hey there, Uwen, what's good?" Max asked, once again using a saying from back home.

Uwen was nearly shaking with excitement. "How was your hunt? Which site worked out? It was the second one, wasn't it?" He dropped to all fours and scurried forward, rising back up with surprising speed right in front of them, his whiskers twitching, eyes wide.

Lahra had little patience for the Illhari and their endless angling and dealing. So, whenever they visited Uwen, Max took the lead while Lahra restrained her urge to smack the endlessly negotiating merchant.

Max shook his head. "Second one was crawling with Imps. This is from the third. And we almost died getting away with it, so that should tell you right away that it's something incredibly special. So special that I admit I don't even know what this is for."

Max pulled back the tarp on the cart, revealing the smaller device. Lahra lifted the thing with disarming ease, placing it on the Illhari's desk. Uwen wouldn't be able to focus on Eihra and the situation with Jesvin until he'd gotten his paws on the artifact, so Max held that topic back for the moment. He saw the waiting pull on Lahra like a gravity well. She held strong, but the quicker they could get through this, the better.

Uwen put his snout right up to the cart. Lahra peeled back the layers of protection, and Uwen grabbed the device with the zeal of Max's younger cousins exploring their stockings on Christmas morning. Uwen's claw-fingers explored the surface, the contours, the edges and angles.

"Fascinating. This is Old Atlan tech. Very sophisticated." He turned it over as he stared at it. "I'll need to consult my codices."

Uwen set the device down and scurried over to his console, which was wide and low, arranged in a half-circle around a deep reclining chair. "Very interesting. The regulators are all running on a different frequency than I'm used to. Something with a very powerful signal. Some kind of resonance, yes. Very interesting."

Max knew artifacts, but the warp space electrical engineering parts he left to Wheel. And Uwen.

"What do you think? We've got some other business to talk about, too."

No response. The furry technician kept fussing over the devices, head down in contemplation and analysis.

Lahra contained her worry, standing guard in a way he imagined countless generations of her ancestors had done. How many of her predecessors had kept watch over moments of crisis, stood by their charges while their own families were under threat? Max thought about firefighters and EMTs white-knuckling through shifts during hurricanes and tornados, their minds present at work while their hearts were at home trying to shield their loved ones with good thoughts.

Max turned to Lahra while Uwen worked. "You think the Empire will still be looking for us? Seeing a Vsenk up close is always memorable, in the same way that nearly crashing head-first into an asteroid is memorable. But that doesn't mean they think the same way about us."

Lahra crossed her arms. "The Vsenk do not easily forget or forgive. The fact that they still control the galaxy while factions tear at one another for sport speaks to their dangerous strength. That one at least will not easily give up the chase. Wherever we go next, it should be some place not regularly patrolled."

"Not like we make a habit of hanging out in regularly patrolled places."

"Indeed."

There were reasons for that beyond the work that the three of them did. The few Genae that remained were frequent targets of Vsenk prejudice. It was odd for Max, growing up in one of the most segregated cities in the country, to be nearly invisible in this galaxy. He'd been surprised and delighted to discover that the Yaea people, a populous species that worked in technical fields alongside Atlan and administrative roles along Rellix, looked 97% identical to humans. And more specifically, humans from the African diaspora. As long as he kept his hair covered in public and didn't get pressed too much on his invented backstory, he was fine.

Just another face in the crowd. He fit in here but didn't belong. His thoughts returned to Earth. What did his family think? Did the expedition say he was MIA? Did they declare him dead? Some of the memories were getting fuzzy. Names of cousins' partners, lyrics to songs he only half-knew to begin with. And it wasn't getting easier to hang on to Earth even as he searched for a way home.

"I am very sorry, Max-and-Lahra," Uwen said, slamming their names together in the custom that Max had learned was cultural as much as linguistic. "Don't have records complete enough to tell what these devices are meant for. Clearly ancient Atlan, and this one has some transmission capability. From the mapping you provided, large device might be the target of the signal. But nothing more. Cannot say. Would have been much easier if I had all three." Uwen waggled his claws, palm-down, a sign of frustration.

Max took a deep breath, trying to think through the implications. "That's more than I could figure out. Know anyone we could talk to that might know more? Especially why the Vsenk would go ballistic to recover them?"

Every answer spawned a million questions, swarming over his mind like those little locust things that had nearly eaten him whole.

Uwen's whiskers twitched. "I can send some messages to the Illhari collective, call in a few favors to ask around, but that's dangerous, even through my channels. Our governor's faction is in a bad spot with the Empire. My smuggler cousins are bearing down for some tough times. More scrutiny, maybe even a dissolution of the Special Economic Zone."

Every planet in the Empire fell under a Vsenk noble's territory. They got to set policy, and the Illhari had enjoyed many privileges under Governor Zerna and his faction, the Bright Suns, who were more cosmopolitan and permissive.

"Breaking down the SEZ would be massive self-sabotage," Max said. "The Chinese were smart enough to leave Hong Kong well enough alone, and the Vsenk are supposed to be these god-warriors, each one a genius far beyond the other species' capacity."

Lahra gave him that look that said, "Not a useful comparison." Fair. Barely his fault that all of the cultural touchstones from his life before they met were unintelligible out here.

Uwen's whiskers shook with frustration. "That's all propaganda. Most nobles cannot keep up at university without preferential treatment."

Lahra tapped the device. "There's clearly a reason to go after this thing, and the Empire has done reckless, disastrous things to make a point before."

The Devastation, the unspoken words hung in air. The Vsenk had been forced to go all-in to beat the Genae. They absolutely weren't above using overkill for the sake of intimidation.

"So, maybe we don't ask through the Illhari grapevine? I don't want to put your people at risk if things are tough. Keep your heads down if you need to."

"I will make some inquiries. My curiosity has been awakened, and now I simply must know. Will keep me up at night, no sleep. Then I get cranky, and business starts to sink. No, no good. I have to know."

"The only source I could think of that might know more was the Drell Matriarch."

Uwen stopped, brushed his whiskers. "She'd know, of course she would."

Max scratched his chin. "But how can we get an audience sometime this century?"

"Yes, almost certainly hopeless. But she'd remember the era when this was made. Even if you couldn't get an audience, maybe you could consult the archives of her pronouncements. The Migration is not far, you could get there easily. Very easily. There's a Yaea scholar there, has a taste for Xuvian cherries. I'll sell you a bushel. Very cheap. Your best chance to learn more."

Max looked to Lahra, ignoring the mention of the cherries. That was just Uwen trying to move some product. "These devices are hot," she said. "They might be more trouble than they're worth. Especially with what's going on with Jesvin."

"What about Jesvin?" asked Uwen.

"She's taken Eihra and the girls. Said she'd grown tired of us not paying down our debt to her satisfaction. We were going to try to smooth things out once we were done here but didn't want her getting wind of these artifacts."

"I mean, we could just give this thing to her and tip the Imperials," Max deadpanned. "Let Jesvin and the Imps sort things out. It's not like hundreds of innocent people would get hurt along the way."

Lahra narrowed her eyes. Uwen wrung his hands, head tilted to the side.

The joys of cross-species communication.

Max sighed. "That was sarcasm."

Uwen looked at Max and Lahra for a second. Max imagined he was trying to sort out whatever unspoken social context had just passed him by. The Illhari's voice went soft, conspiratorial. "Jesvin is very dangerous. Very well-connected. Hard to move against her. Ruku has some friends who might be brave enough, but what you need is information. I'll ask around. Pay you for the data on these devices, too. Not enough to appease Jesvin I think, but enough to escape if you need, or to make some plans if you're staying."

"That's amazing, thank you." Max couldn't help the relief in his voice. "Did you have anything else about these devices before we go? What about that transmission capability you mentioned? If it's strong enough, do you think they might be designed to communicate beyond warp space? What if this could be the way to get in touch with Earth, or to tune into communications from the surviving Genae? Like your mother's rendezvous point hypothesis, somewhere beyond warp space. I don't think we can let these things go, trouble or not."

Lahra closed her body language, clearly not happy where the conversation was going. "This device could hang around our necks like an energy noose. Strangle us with patrols, bounties, and the fury of the Vsenk. If we wash our hands of it, we can move on to the next site, the next dig. Free Eihra and the girls, pack them up, and we start over somewhere else. Maybe even meet up with the Migration and stay there. They'd have use for a scholar like you, we could continue our research there, protected from Imperial pursuit."

Max shook his head. "But this is our only lead, and it took months of searching to get there. And if the Vsenk want this thing, who will buy it to keep it out of Imperial hands? I'd want to meet those people, for sure." Max asked the question half to Lahra and half to Uwen.

Uwen's whiskers shook. "I know a number of antiquarians. They would take the device on my word. No one of consequence. The more mysterious, the better with these collectors."

"But wouldn't that get them on the Vsenk's radar? I can't put people in danger like that."

"I appreciate your consideration, Max. I can look out for myself. I know how to handle hot goods."

"We've got too many puzzle pieces already for me to throw out a whole box-worth." Max turned to his wife. "We're onto something here, love. I need to see it through to the end."

Lahra studied him in that way she did when he was focused on something, or when they were arguing. It was like she was reading every square centimeter of him for intent, for possibility. He felt naked every time. Sometimes it was incredibly hot. This wasn't one of those times. This time it felt more like she could see straight through him to the future. Her future.

One he wasn't sure would include him.

But she'd built on the confidence he learned from his uncle when he was in kindergarten back in Baltimore. Uncle James, who taught him to commit even when you weren't certain. That earnest mistakes were better than never trying. "A dangerous plan is better than no plan, right?"

Lahra smiled, and stepped forward, running the back of her fingers down his cheek.

"We keep following this path, then. Once Eihra and her daughters are safe."

He took her hand in his and squeezed.

It was settled. Time to outfox a giant bird crime boss and then go see even gianter turtles about ancient alien artifacts.

Awesome.

CHAPTER TWENTY-ONE

LAHRA

GATHERING INFORMATION FROM DOZENS of contradictory sources, each possessing only a sliver of the truth you needed, was no game. And yet, Lahra's mother had played games like this with her as a child, programming simple text-based investigation scenarios to hone her mind. When Lahra had mastered those, her mother had enlisted friends and neighbors as actors, giving them each roles and details for Lahra to interrogate in order to piece together the puzzle.

On the Wreck, these challenges were magnified by the jumbled distribution of people, the plurality of species and micro-cultures that had developed over the city-ship's history, and most notably, the threatening shadow of Jesvin Ker.

Despite Max's numerous charms and connections, as soon as they turned the topic to Jesvin, once-friendly people became nervous and distant, cowed by the stories told in fearful whispers about how Jesvin responded to those that moved against her.

"Oh, I mean, I couldn't say. I don't get above the fortieth tier much—bad knees," said the skinny Yaea who acted as guardian-mentor-boss to a crew of pickpocketing youth.

Max took a moment, rolling his shoulders back. She could read the frustration coming off him in waves, but he kept his calm.

"Jesvin's bad for business. For everyone. She's gone way past the point where anyone here could make a living on their own. Wouldn't you like to see her lick her wounds for a while? To not be in everyone's business all the time?"

The Yaea looked back and forth, checking for listening ears and prying eyes. The light painted their face poorly. Whoever designed the ship hadn't been thinking of favorable lighting, just function and visibility. Some areas had been re-done with new lamps and brighter bulbs, mostly markets and artistic districts, but here in the poorer levels, people made due.

"Yeah, maybe I know someone who saw Jesvin's people hauling those Genae away. But don't let it get traced back to me. Have enough going on without getting on Jesvin's bad side. Two levels down, find Brisn. And don't come back around, okay?" They gave the chin nod common in the Yaea, a confirmation-seeking gesture.

Max matched the chin nod. "I'm sorry to bother you. Thanks for your time." He gave a quick wink, then turned to walk away.

They balanced between pushing people to be brave and giving them the space to deny helping anyone move against Jesvin. It was a careful dance, and one that Max excelled at.

Brisn led them to Oyi. Oyi was missing, but her friend Qizi had heard that some of Jesvin's people drank at this one bar to let off steam.

And so on. Across the next few hours, they spoke to another dozen people across half the ship and pieced together the following picture:

Two Yaea and two Rellix had broken into Eihra's apartment late in the night and dragged all three of them out, stunned and bound. They traveled up two levels and disappeared with the hostages into an outpost of Jesvin's in Feather Hole, a low-traffic neighborhood she controlled with a great deal of local support. Jesvin poured money into development and social programs as a way of buying people's loyalty and maintaining her image. In those neighborhoods, she was as a goddess—untouchable, infallible. She did just enough to earn people's loyalty, though never enough to actually make permanent change. The needy became just more tally marks in her campaign to get the entire city-ship under her wings.

It would present a substantial challenge.

Max and Lahra discussed the options at a busy café that served the sex workers and others that worked the least-populous, least-compensated third shift. The café was located in one of the least Jesvin-friendly neighborhoods called Boxtown. And even better, it was run and patronized by people that had run afoul of Jesvin's machinations. Boxtown had once been the bulk storage part of the ship, wide open spaces that had been filled with ramshackle pre-fab houses and other shoddy designs. Bereft, orphaned, outcast, or hunted, the Boxtowners made a new family together, looking after one another as best they could.

Lahra and Max had never fallen this far, even during the hard times before working with Wheel. She'd commanded good rates doing guard work, and his combination of linguistic and academic capabilities were in high demand on a cosmopolitan ship far enough from Imperial eyes to have somewhat free speech and association. But even then, she'd worried. What if she was injured and couldn't work? What if the jobs dried up? There were only a few Genae on the Wreck, and Max didn't actually have a Yaea clan to call on. Even with Wheel they were short on family and allies.

"As long as we can get to the outpost, I know you can take care of whoever they have inside." Max had a cone filled with sugar suns in front of him, which he always called "donut holes." He continued, "I think the problem is more how do we do that and get out fast enough that Jesvin's people can't deploy enough bodies or weapons that it becomes a real problem."

Lahra smiled at Max's estimation of her capabilities. He'd told her that back home, men were coercively socialized to be strong, emotionless, violent protectors, and women to be empathetic, gentle nurturers. He'd rejected that binary at home and rejoiced in escaping it in her galaxy. He'd never balked at her capabilities, never tried to compete with her or degrade her. If he had, they'd have been done years ago.

Instead, he treated her skills and abilities as a given without expecting her to fight his battles for him, even though she would gladly do so. He was her charge but also her partner, which required some re-negotiation of how she'd been raised. Genae soldiers were servants, even when they were life-bound with their charge as the royal guards had been with the queens. But Max did not ask nor expect her to play that role. Instead, he wanted an equal partner, a contrast rather than a support.

"I'm most concerned with collateral damage. If we cut a swath through the neighborhood, innocents will suffer, and we'll likely rally Jesvin's supporters against us even more than we will just by defying her openly. Which calls for a surprise, a deception, or some other method that will let us arrive and depart quickly."

"Wait." Max swiped through options on his tablet until it displayed a schematic of the Wreck. "Feather Hole is only a hundred meters from the hull of the ship. If we could find an old airlock, or a maintenance hatch, Wheel could pull the Kettle around the outside of the Wreck and we could come in and out through the hull. Change our approach and exit vectors, maybe let us get out of the area fast enough to beat an escape."

Lahra nodded, heart growing warm with approval of her husband's bold strategizing. "Unconventional. And very dangerous. We'd escape Feather Hole rapidly, but then we'd be subject to nearby ships loyal to Jesvin, and we'd have to return Eihra and the girls to their homes, exposing us to another round of attacks. Promising, if fraught."

"I don't see a way for your cousins to stay on the Wreck. Not unless we take down Jesvin entirely."

He was right. She'd been trying to think of a way to restore the uneasy equilibrium they'd enjoyed before—in Jesvin's sights but not under fire. But even if they bought Jesvin off for the whole sum, she'd find another way to torture them, to extract favors. Kidnap another group of friends, run Uwen out of business, threaten Ruku and the people of the bazaar, or something else.

The Wreck was no longer their home. It had become a battleground, enemy territory. They could rescue the prisoners and escape, wage covert or open war, but they could not pretend that things were as they had been.

Lahra talked through Max's idea, laying out the questions that came to her automatically but would be worth discussing together. "If we take this route you suggest, we'll need to know how many ships and guns Jesvin has access to. Avoiding a fight within the Wreck will not save us if they tear the *Kettle* to pieces."

Max paced as he thought. His brilliance was focused on other disciplines, but his mind was sharp wherever it was put to use. "Right. So it might be safer, but we don't know yet. And that'd take a whole other round of research and finding informants. The EVA route is slower but might be safer. Or we come up with a way of getting in and out through the Wreck without setting off Jesvin's alarms. Which sounds better to you? The research and people stuff I can do, but there's too much strategy and tactics in this for me."

Lahra pressed her hands into her palms and hummed "The Tactician's Repose" to help her focus.

A stealthy approach with concealment over invisibility could deliver the best results, but concealment on the way out would be four times as difficult with the others in tow.

The straight-forward, and likely aggressive, approach would require fighting an entire neighborhood. More if she wasn't fast. It would be very difficult to protect Eihra, the girls, and Max and make their way out. For that plan, they'd need backup or at least a distraction. Maybe a vehicle to get out of the neighborhood quickly.

"Do you think we could arrange to get a transport deposited into Feather Hole to use for an escape?"

Max cocked his head to the side, considering. "Maybe, but it sounded like Jesvin's people kept a pretty close eye on everything that went on around there. We wouldn't have much time."

"I could commandeer a transport coming into the neighborhood, take their uniform, and use it for an escape."

Max's pursed lips told her that he was dubious about this plan.

"Maybe someone else should do the intrusion and deception part?"

"And by someone you mean yourself?"

Max shrugged. "I make an alright spy." He popped another spherical confection in his mouth.

"I do wish you'd come with copies of those films you speak of. They sound amusingly absurd."

"Especially the ones with the extra lives and the moon lasers. Just let me finish these and I'm good to go." Max gestured to the spheres. "They're so much like donut holes it's kind of unnerving."

Lahra laughed. Soon they'd be facing overwhelming odds in a hostile territory, but his concern was finishing a snack that reminded him of Terra.

What a strange and wonderful man she'd found, and what an unexpected life.

Now she had to make sure that Eihra and the girls got to live free and find their own unexpected wonders.

CHAPTER TWENTY-TWO

MAX

MAX HADN'T BEEN THE type to run hustles on people back home. His family took good care of him, which included instilling a well-placed fear about ending up in the police's sights.

"BPD is bad enough if you haven't done anything," his Aunt Deanna often said. "You don't want to give them a single reason to go after you even harder."

His aunt's words rang in his mind as he drove the water truck through the streets of Feather Hole, trying to look inconspicuous. He imagined Lahra, hunched over in the storage container between sloshing water tanks, waiting for his signal. His job in this part was more precarious, but hers was just as uncomfortable, squeezed into a box small enough that it'd be cramped for Max.

The trunk floated by beefy enforcers on corners and reedy lookouts. He kept a poker face and nodded at those who looked at him, driving casually until he was stopped at an intersection by a trio of toughs led by a broad-shouldered Rellix with a three-meter wingspan and bright plumage of an unmated male.

Max nodded to the Rellix and put his hand on his chin in the traditional Yaea greeting.

The Rellix shouldered the Atlan youth aside. "You're new. What happened to Vic?"

"Vic got called in-house to be Xifo's driver. I'm Cal."

The Rellix looked him up and down, head darting in short bursts of movement like Terran birds.

"What have you got today?"

Max shrugged. "Just some fresh water. I have a bit up here if you or your friends want some." He held up a small jug with a tap on the front.

The Rellix passed, but his Atlan companion stepped up. They were young by their look—gray skin, still almost silver. They produced a mug with a handle in the shape of half a gear. Max filled it up with as much folksy charm as he could muster. "Heard that the boss is working folks pretty hard down here. How are you holding up?"

The Atlan took a long drink. "These hours are killer. Don't even get to plug into anything. Makes me twitchy. They won't even tell us who they have holed up in the warehouse back there."

The Rellix shouldered the Atlan out of the way. "Ignore them. Just be on the lookout for anyone who might be snooping around looking for them."

"Always." Max brought his fingers to his chin again, and the toughs stepped back to let him go.

The truck hovered on, and Max exhaled, releasing the tension in his neck and shoulders.

He continued down the street then turned into the alley that terminated at the warehouse. Armed guards held up a hand to stop him. He waited with his hands on the wheel, focusing on his breathing. A real driver would be nervous here, but not that nervous.

Two Yaea with rifles approached the truck. Max handed over the truck's manifest, doctored to account for Lahra's presence, and waited, trying to look bored.

The guards raised the same point about Vic, and Max repeated his lie about the transfer.

"Boss hardly lets Xifo out anymore," said one guard, a burly woman with bright orange eyeshadow. "Why do they need a driver?"

Gulp. Their intelligence hadn't covered that.

Fortunately, Max was used to improvising.

"You haven't heard? Vic had a few warrants pop up. Since the Imps have been sniffing around, she wanted to get him off the street without leaving a trail for the patrols."

The Yaea cocked her head to the side. "Huh. Not surprising. Vic always liked to brag on what he did before joining up." She waved him forward to turn the truck around and start unloading.

Max knocked twice on the front wall of the container, giving Lahra the signal.

A few of the guards helped Max unload the boxes. Or maybe they were staff. It was hard to tell the difference, as they were all well-built and carried themselves with the ready confidence of experienced criminals.

Max kept up the chatter as best he could while they moved the boxes inside a Vsenk-height opening to a storage area, goods broken up by category—food, water, small arms, medicine, credits to be laundered, clean credits, and so on. It was hard to turn his anthropology fieldwork skills off, so as they hauled the boxes, Max listened for dialect differences, inside jokes, and power relationships. He filed the information away in case they ran across these people again, or in case something went wrong on the way out and Max had to run a hustle on them to create the opportunity for an escape.

When the unloading was done, Max asked, "Anybody want to grab a drink?"

Two of the younger, junior muscle seemed interested, but the bossy Rellix in charge wasn't having it.

"Jesvin gives us the good stuff. You want to relax, take a load off outside and pass this around." She handed the nearest junior a flash and sent them off.

"Thanks for the help. I'm supposed to wait here until the next shipment out is ready."

The Rellix chirped in confusion. "What shipment?"

Max's heart dropped. How could they not be moving some kind of product through this place? The guns, the meds . . .

He forced a shrug, trying to recover. "Dispatcher didn't tell me what it was. I don't ask questions."

"Why don't you come inside and have a talk with Xej." One of the Rellix's wings drifted toward her club.

He had a split-second to decide what to do. Try to keep bluffing his way through. Or go loud.

Just as he was coming up with the next lie, one of the crates exploded.

CHAPTER TWENTY-THREE

LAHRA

PERHAPS MAX MIGHT HAVE been able to talk his way out. He was clever and charming. But perhaps he would fail. He could fail and be carted off to Jesvin and make their already difficult rescue mission even more perilous.

So instead, she decided to, as Max would say, "go loud."

He had performed admirably, but the time for talking had passed. Lahra prepared her blade as she watched the Rellix question Max through the video link.

Lahra braced the blade, pointing at the far corner of the crate. The shot blasted the corner off the refactored plastic, enough for her to tear her way free of the container.

Three of them in sight, who knows how many more elsewhere in the building.

She could handle the rest later. As "Ivhra's Last Stand" went, you can only fight what you can reach.

Lahra swung her greatsword through the Rellix and watched her crumple onto the ground. Another life fed to the mill of Jesvin's ambitions.

"With me!" she yelled to Max and waved him over. "Watch the exits." A guard across the room was reaching for an alarm. Her shot knocked them into the wall with a sickening thud and Lahra turned to face the third guard.

But they were gone, running out the exit. For reinforcements, maybe.

This was not going remotely according to plan.

Lahra dashed for the door and confirmed that the guard she'd blasted was in fact unconscious.

"We'll go room-by-room. Stay close." She could not hope to protect Max if he was out of reach, if Jesvin's toughs got ahold of him, if they came at an unlikely angle.

A thousand things could go wrong. But that was life. And others were counting on them.

Max gave a smile that said: "don't worry about me," as if that were possible. "I remember the score. Three paces back—close enough that you can reach me if you need to, far enough that you can swing the sword."

And so they went. Max kept close, pointing out guards and cameras so that Lahra could dispatch their foes with maximum efficiency.

Seven guards and three rooms later, they found Eihra and the girls.

Her cousins were being kept in a small makeshift apartment bounded on all sides by clear plastic walls. Like a zoo.

As Lahra stepped into the room, she was knocked from her feet by a scattergun blast.

She scrambled, looking for her assailant. A small Yaea stood three paces back from the door, concealed by shadow. They'd heard her coming.

But even if they knew she was coming, one scattergun blast would not break her armor. This was unfortunate for the guard.

Once they were dealt with, Max walked in, saying, "Where's the door?"

There was a flurry of activity inside the apartment-pen. Eihra shouted, her words muted by the cage but not her gestures, and she led them around to a corner.

There was nothing there. At first. Max moved his head, then smiled.

"Had to catch it in the glare. There's a keypad."

Lahra turned to face the exits while Max worked.

"Reinforcements will converge on us at any moment."

Lahra grabbed the scattergun from the guard and trained it on the door, sword leaning on her shoulder.

They came soon enough.

Lahra sang the battle songs of her people as a neighborhood's worth of street toughs poured through the door. Big and small they came, bearing guns and swords and clubs, screaming or deathly silent.

They were insufficient.

"I am Lahra Kevain, daughter of Halra, daughter of Aytra!" she sang, filling in her lineage at the beginning of "The Oathsworn," the oldest and most foundational song of her caste.

A lanky Atlan caught her at the shoulder with small arms fire. She turned with the force of the blow and felled a Yaea with an elbow.

Three Illhari tried to tackle her and bring her down, so she slammed one's head into another. Then threw a round-house kick that picked the Illhari off the ground, smashing them into a Rellix.

"Got it!" Max shouted. There was a hiss, and on her heads-up display, Lahra saw her cousins scrambling through the door.

"Now we leave!" Lahra started a new verse as she waded through the crowd.

If the guards did not come faster and smarter, this could work.

The wall closest to her exploded. Lahra stumbled back but kept her footing. Smoke and dust would have obscured the vision of a lesser protector, but her suit's thermal optics were intact.

Four attackers emerged through the hole, but these were not common toughs. They were armored in sleek, flexible lacquered plasteel and bore guns and blades. They moved as one, tossing pairs of stun grenades as they began to flank.

Lahra fired the scattergun at the group to foul their maneuver. Then shouldered the gun and swung her sword at the first stun grenade, knocking it back into the group as the two detonated.

The other grenade knocked Lahra back with the force of a Vsenk backhand. She picked a spot on the wall and focused, refusing to let the grenade break her focus. Her ancestors were with her in song, and she would not falter.

"Stick together!" Lahra shouted to Max and her cousins, planting the sword on the ground. She pushed herself to her feet.

The quartet fired as they advanced, trying to create a killing field. Lahra grabbed the scattergun again to fire in the direction of one pair while she charged the ones close to Max and her cousins.

The battle was joined, sword-to-sword, point-blank fire, maneuvering and shouting from all directions.

Jesvin's elites were good. Very good. They knew the weaker parts of her armor, forcing her to use her sword more for defense, always keeping it between her and one of the elites while she fought hand-to-hand with the other. They were skilled, but they were not Genae. She had survived an attack by a Vsenk noble, if only just.

She disabled one killer's arm, then broke the other's knee. She cracked their helmets together and turned to the other pair.

Max was trying to hold them back with a pistol.

Lahra spent the last of her blade's charge fouling a kill-shot from one of the elites. One turned to face Lahra while the other pursued her cousins. That choice would be their downfall. Lahra lunged with the sword, and the killer dodged. Lahra knocked them off-balance as she pulled the blade back and up to block their counter.

This one was faster than the others, moving like quicksilver. And their blows bit hard. Augments, perhaps.

The quicksilver killer caught at her side, her arm, and across her ribs before Lahra felled them with an overhead swing.

But it had taken longer than it should have. The last killer stood over Max, Eihra, and the girls. They had a gun trained on Max. He was bleeding from the side, one of the killer's rounds having pierced his concealed armor. The girls were crying, Eihra singing a lullaby to try to calm them.

The killer sidestepped and saw Lahra, drawing another gun and firing in her direction.

Lahra dove away from the fire.

They were too far to charge. The blade was spent. They could fire on her charges at any time.

So Lahra used one of her rare maneuvers, one that was too ostentatious and wasteful to be properly efficient.

But that was a problem with expert fighters. They played the numbers, trained to deal with the optimal strategies.

Truthfully, what warrior would throw an almost two-meter-long sword like a disc?

Lahra tossed her sword of station in a tight spin, belting "The Schemes of Bihri," a song of a diminutive Genae trickster born into the soldier caste. Taunted by her caste-mates, she grew wise and defeated her enemies with savvy. It was a complicated song demanding vocal dexterity and intense concentration. Without the song's power, this maneuver would have no chance of succeeding. But it granted incredible flexibility, each verse speaking of one of Bihri's feats and enabling the singer to echo her abilities.

The world slowed as Lahra took in the scene.

Max shouted "Down!", covering the Genae.

The sword arced toward the killer, who fired again at Lahra and the non-combatants as they dove out of the way. The sword whirred past the guard, missing by several meters.

And that was where the true power of "The Schemes of Bihri" came into play.

Lahra segued into the third verse, which sang of the time Bihri had turned a bent sword into a boomerang, her soul calling it to curve back toward her when she threw it. The power of the song connected her soul to her blade and the sword spun to return, point-first. The unorthodox strike pierced the guard through the middle.

They dropped to the ground, and the fight was done.

Until the next wave arrived, she thought.

Lahra wobbled to her feet, suit gone slick with blood.

"Lead them out," Lahra said. "I will be right behind you." She put a foot on the last killer and retrieved her blade.

Max was bleeding too. The wound was minor, but he was not nearly as used to being shot.

Eihra and Max leaned on one another as they shuffled out of the warehouse.

If Jesvin had more fighters in the neighborhood, they chose not to breach the warehouse. Wise.

They walked back through the trail of combat and piled into the truck Max had driven.

"Will you be capable of driving?" Lahra asked.

"Let me," Eihra said. "We just have to get out of Jesvin's territory, yes?"

Lahra took the second seat in the cab while Max and Eihra's daughters climbed into the back. They even pulled one of the cartons back up the ramp to give themselves cover.

Eihra pushed the truck to its limit, tearing through the street, dodging between vehicles with practiced ease. The truck rattled and whined but held.

"Where did you learn to drive like this?" Lahra asked, holding herself in place.

"Remember how I told you the stand was my retirement? I was a courier for Ngri. Until Jesvin had him killed. Hold on, I'll have to take this one hard."

She had kept this secret from Lahra, perhaps from her daughters as well. Ngri had been ruthless, but he was honest and took care of his people.

Eihra made an aggressive turn, slamming into a parked vehicle and then racing down a street. She pointed them toward a transit tube that arced across the gash in the Wreck to another neighborhood. Toward the *Kettle*.

"There!" Eihra pointed down the street. Jesvin's people had erected a blockade made of overturned vehicles, trash bins, and a food cart. Behind the blockade stood five armed guards.

Max's voice was strained, shot through with worry. "Can you get through? Around?"

If only. Lahra thought through a dozen angles of attack for ramming, and nothing looked promising. "We don't have the mass to punch through."

An angle of attack presented itself. Ludicrous, but the best option. Lahra gave instructions to Eihra. "Prepare for hard turns. Right, then left." Then she climbed out the window and onto the cab of the truck.

"What are you doing?" Eihra shouted.

"Keep driving!"

The guards opened fire as they approached. Lahra blocked as many as she could with the blade, covering herself and Eihra. These weapons weren't strong enough to pierce her armor, but the truck's front view glass shattered under the fire.

Eihra did not yield. Their people were strong—from servant to noble, priest and soldier to merchant—all tough, all capable.

Some of the guards backed off as the truck hurtled toward the barricade. Good. Fewer in the way.

"Right!" she shouted as she leaned over the side of the cab and stabbed her greatsword through the cheap steel of the street. Lahra screamed as she held onto both sword and truck, causing the truck to whip a quarter circle almost instantly.

Pain flooded her mind as wounds and muscles alike tore with exertion.

But she was not done.

She wrenched the sword from the ground, then spun and stabbed down on the other side, calling, "Left!"

Eihra guided the truck through another impossible turn.

The guards were not fast enough to respond. Instead, they watched, struck silent by the Genaes' display of prowess.

Lahra removed her blade once more and looked back on the guards. They fired pitifully at the truck as they made their escape.

Her charges safe, she crawled back into the cab and passed out.

CHAPTER TWENTY-FOUR

WHEEL

THE LOVERS CAME BACK from their mission on the Wreck with three passengers, a smoking ruin of a truck, and a clinic's worth of injuries. About what she expected.

"What in the name of the void did you do to that vehicle?" Wheel asked as the merchant Genae helped Max and Lahra up the ramp of the *Kettle*.

Eihra was pale, from terror or exhaustion or both. "They saved us."

"It was just like the songs," exclaimed one of the girls. "Better than any of Lahra's stories!"

Wheel looked to the double doors of the dock. "Were you followed?"

"I don't think so," Eihra said. "We need to attend to the wounds, but Vlera can help you with the ship." Eihra gestured to the smaller girl.

She wore orange silks and a gray beaded necklace, her eyes a bright silver. "I've been studying. And I learn quickly."

Wheel shook her head as she helped get the lovers laid out on workstations to start first aid. These kids lived like they were immortal. She remembered those days. Remembered visiting hospitals to see friends who discovered that they were all too mortal.

Once she was sure that neither of them was going to die, Wheel left the pair in Eihra's hands and scaled the ladders to the cockpit.

As the *Kettle* floated away from the Wreck, their departure gave her a view of the bizarre mishmash tech-biome. The place was as Atlan as you could be without being built entirely by her people. The people that originally crewed the ship had adapted, not in bits and pieces, but with their entire being. They took what they had and made a new life, a new purpose. They changed for themselves, not to appease someone else. The founders of the city-ship deserved praise for that, though she couldn't be blamed if their ramshackle safety protocols made her blood circuits run cold.

She burned the place into her memory as they left. With what they'd pulled, there was a good chance they'd never see the Wreck again. Not without an army.

***

The next day, both Max and Lahra were back on their feet. Lahra first, despite her more significant injuries. It wasn't the first time she'd bounced back from injuries that would lay up an Atlan or Yaea for a week.

But Terrans were surprisingly tough as well. Max said it was because his species started as pursuit predators.

When they were both up and fit for company, Wheel called a meeting.

The three passengers sat on the other side of the galley table with her and the lovebirds. It was the most crowded the ship had been since Wheel's ill-advised job transporting five-dozen Molja to a resort planet.

Max pitched the idea of traveling to the Drell Migration with care and qualifiers, trying to make her feel included in the process, to not treat her as the glorified cargo pilot she sometimes felt like.

"You don't need to sell me on this, kid. I love it."

Lahra cocked her head to the side in surprise, then winced, leaning on the table for support. Max reached out to her to give comfort, which then made *him* wince. It was both cute and painful to watch.

Wheel sat back in her chair. "I've always wanted to fly through the Great Migration. Catch solar winds with the largest sentient beings in the galaxy. I can't do anything about the waiting list. But even looking through the public archives, I bet you could pull up some juicy leads."

Eihra piped up, voice wavering in the company of the legends from Lahra's stories. "You can drop us off there. I've known more than a few families that left the Wreck for the Migration. We've got the skills to earn our keep, and I picked up a bit of payback from that warehouse." Eihra slapped a pile of credit sticks on the table with a wide smile. "Plus, there will be plenty of opportunities for Vlera and Yldri to learn their trades."

Lahra looked worried. "The Migration isn't so far away that Jesvin couldn't get to you."

Vlera put on a brave face for the group. "There are a million things that could kill us out here. It's a miracle we got out of that warehouse. Your miracle. Our people should be dead, but we're still here. We're not going to live our life governed by fear."

Some kid, Wheel thought. "Hard to argue with that. Navigation data says that the Migration is two short jumps away unless we want to wait a day or two and catch them after the next turn."

Max piped in. "Waiting sounds like a bad idea. The more time we spend in warp space, unable to be tracked, the better."

He learned fast. "Spoken like a true outlaw."

***

Warp space was blissfully empty. Wheel's people had legends of creatures in the void, traded in stories in bars across the galaxy, but Wheel'd never heard a story that approached airtight. Even the Atlan knew relatively little about warp space, just that it was a parallel dimension, proportionally smaller than normal space, and that it was not good to linger in longer than necessary. Whether that was because of the legends or some other forgotten danger, she didn't know.

She dropped out of warp space to set the second jump. Sensors showed no Imperials, no other ships at all. They were on the far end of a trade route between the Wreck and several agrarian planets, so there was always some risk.

The console chirped while she was plotting the second jump. The message shot up her veins and hit her mind like a splash of fresh water after a long day.

Wheel flipped on the comms. "Response from the Migration. Congratulations, kids, we have an appointment in 25 years."

"Did they give us petitioner status for landing in Xidd?" Max asked, his voice echoing inside her head.

"If not," Lahra added, "we'll need to do quite a lot of retrofitting this ship to pass as a Drell."

She wasn't serious. Was she? Genae weren't the easiest to read.

Don't get distracted, she told herself. "One, you are not doing anything to my beautiful ship. And two, we have petitioner status. The Drell stay out of the Imperium's way. But we can't count on them standing up for us."

"We repelled the Imperials once," Lahra said. "And fighting an enemy that's behaving because they're on neutral ground is very different from fighting them out in the void. We will have more options, and they fewer."

As Wheel fed the warp jump data to the *Kettle*'s navigation systems, Cruji whined in his cage.

"Someone comfort the little beastie?" she asked.

A minute later, Max climbed into the cockpit and opened the Molja's crate. The creature grabbed both sides of the open crate and slingshotted himself at Max's face, feathered tentacles wrapping around his head and shoulders. Cruji had orange and purple feathers on semi-translucent yellow skin. And that was tame coloring for a Molja. Cruji had been a runt, born two tentacles short on the cargo mission to the resort planet. He was destined for the biomass recycler before Wheel rescued him. He was the one Molja she'd not hated during that long, noisy trip, so it worked out.

Max laughed and gasped, and Cruji's excited chirping softened to a purr.

"Might as well feed him while you're at it."

"I love that he lives in the cockpit with you, but you never think to feed him or clean up his crate."

An old argument. "I'm working here. The two of you are passengers. Earn your keep!" She chuckled and turned back to the console.

This division of caretaking labor made perfect sense to Wheel, but the Terran and Genae had yet to be convinced. Something about proximity and ownership and the fact that Cruji's suckers could drain Max's blood, but not Wheel's.

Excuses, all of them.

"Time to jump. Everybody find a seat."

"So am I supposed to feed Cruji, or find a seat?"

"Prove yourself to be a higher form of life and do both."

"If we were really passengers, you'd have to treat us a hell of a lot more politely."

Wheel threw a lever in the console, locked the thrusters, and put the systems on standby for a smoother jump. "You just keep on thinking that, kid. Make sure the actual passengers are sorted."

A half-minute of shuffling and clasping later, they gave the all-clear.

"In three, two, one." Wheel exerted her will, and the *Kettle* jumped sideways, cutting into warp space, the parallel dimension her ancestors had discovered. The Atlan built hundreds of satellites across a dozen galaxies to circumscribe a quadrant of space. Within that territory, ships with the right drive could pierce the barrier between those dimensions to speed up their travel by several orders of magnitude.

Fortunately for her, the only people who could properly operate the warp drives were the Atlan. It was the way her ancestors had guaranteed themselves a future when the Vsenk destroyed the Old Atlan Empire. They'd closed ranks, disappeared scabs, and consolidated enough to establish the tradition which made her and her people indispensable.

"Stable jump. We'll be in warp space for four hours this first jump, then I'll recalibrate to adjust for the Migration's drift on solar winds."

Wheel leaned back, giving herself a few minutes' rest to disengage and let the ship do its business.

And given the likely warrant on their heads from Imperials plus the one from Jesvin, warp space was the one place where they were truly safe.

Hours later, Wheel woke to the sound of something pounding on the hull.

CHAPTER TWENTY-FIVE

LAHRA

"**W**HAT IN THE NINE heavens is that sound?" Lahra asked.

The ship lurched again.

Lahra made for the hold, where her sword was fixed to the back of her armor. The suit was incredibly tough, but she hadn't had the time to sing it back to whole, and even then, it took several minutes to properly attire herself. There was no time.

The sword, however, came off with a simple click.

She was hurt, unarmored, and facing an unknown threat.

Warp space was supposed to be safe.

Nowhere is ever completely safe. Her mother's words echoed in her mind. Being raised by a paranoid perfectionist had left its marks.

She called up again toward the bridge. "Wheel, what is happening?"

Wheel did not often wear a look of panic, and seeing it now, Lahra's heart sank. "I . . . I don't know!" The pilot looked back to her instruments, as if searching for a hidden truth.

Those were not the sort of words often uttered by Wheel.

The Atlan had been around the galaxy several times and had an answer or a quick comeback for everything.

Lahra activated the ship-wide comms. "Max, get up! Something's wrong."

Max's response was slow, shaky. He'd been sleeping. "This is a dream, right?"

"I'm afraid not," Wheel said, joining in. "Something is hitting the ship. And we're in warp space."

"Now I know I'm dreaming."

"Throw on some pants and get out here."

"What about Eihra and the girls?"

"They should stay in their bunks. I did not save them only to see them hurt now."

Lahra pulled up diagnostics on the console at the near end of the hold. The *Kettle* had a dozen full consoles built into the walls, designed to make it easy to operate the ship from anywhere.

"Proximity sensors are showing three distinct silhouettes. Maybe now would be a time to trot out some of those Atlan legends about creatures in the warp Max keeps asking you about?"

The sound of thumping came through the comms. It seemed that Wheel was attempting percussive maintenance. "This shouldn't be. Hull integrity is down twenty percent, already. Let's just hope they don't find the weld points on the hold."

"Can you tell me anything about these legendary creatures?" Lahra asked.

The digital undertones of Wheel's voice grew stronger, bringing with them buzzing sounds from somewhere both near and far. "There's a hundred conflicting accounts. They're twenty-meter-long electrified beasts, or they're great hairy creatures with five arms. The only thing the accounts have in common is that they're attracted to warp drives."

"But if we turn off the warp drive, we'll never be able to

get back into normal space," Max said.

"That's the grit in the oil." There was worry in Wheel's voice. Another uncommon occurrence.

Lahra put on her war voice. "Whatever comes, we will face it. I need you both in fine form. Max, prepare the emergency hull sealant."

The pounding stopped.

Lahra scanned the hold, checking the corners, steadying herself with her mag boots in a wide stance.

Max clambered down the hallway and the second ladder to the hold, wearing pants but no shirt, the emergency lighting playing across the lean curves of his muscles, bandages a reminder of their all-too-recent injuries. He held the nozzle and canister for the sealant, looking for breaches. "Is it gone?"

"I think that unlikely."

A sound like docking clamps cut through the hull, and Lahra saw two sets of four depressions, several meters apart, formed in the hastily-applied steel patches on the door of the hold.

A moment later, the sound of drilling rang throughout the hold, centered on the space between the two sets of depressions.

"How long until we can jump out of warp space?" Max asked.

"Not soon enough!" Wheel said. "We switch back now, and we'll be right in the middle of an Imperial patrol lane."

The drilling intensified.

"It's breaking through!" Lahra called. While she'd not had the time to sing her armor whole, there had been time to recharge the sword's gem.

A bone-colored drill pierced through the plate. It was contoured with natural spirals, not artificial spikes like she'd seen on industrial drills on mining asteroids.

Air rushed out of the cargo hold, whipping papers past her face, but Max reacted quickly, activating the force field, creating a demi-sphere on the outside of the hull to hold in the atmosphere.

But that system was far less robust in warp space due to physics even Wheel seemed to find elusive. It might not be able to hold several small fields across several points on the ship. Not for long.

"What the hell is that!" Max scrambled away from the creature. A beat later, he seemed to remember and reached for the stun gun Lahra had stowed in his workstation for just this type of situation. He held the stun gun out in a shaky stance, letting her take the lead.

Lahra kept her voice level. "Soon to be dead." Curiosity was the purview of a scholar. She only needed to know two things: how this being attacked, and how she could kill it. Though, given how nothing was supposed to be able to live in the void, even she felt the pull to know more.

Instead of a battle song, Lahra found herself singing an exploration song she'd learned from Eihra. It spoke of a traveler in the deep and the strange creatures they met. She shifted it down an octave to fit her voice, and so the song sounded just a bit off.

Lahra stepped forward and thrust at the drill, testing its strength. She spared her sword's charge, uninterested in discharging a bolt of electricity throughout the interior of the ship.

The blade and drill met, and the drill stopped for a moment, then resumed, the indentations on each side growing deeper, but Lahra refused to yield. The hull gave way, revealing translucent and white claw-feet gripping it.

Lahra cut at the feet, shearing off the tips. Pale blood-ichor splashed from the wounds, and the drill shook.

"Whatever it is, it can be wounded."

Lahra felt a brief bliss of relief that the battle would not be more than she could handle while wounded.

Then, the pounding multiplied. Four more sets of

indentations pressed into the hold, as more of the drill-thing attached itself to the hull.

Or other parts of the same being, she thought.

The first drill pressed forward, folding back the steel. The claws retracted, and the drill-being punched through the hold, flying into the ship.

The thing was translucent, like its claws, the innards of a digestive tract showing. It was a tube-shaped beast as long as she was tall, but fully half of its size was the natural drill. One set of gripping claws remained arcing around the drill-beak, and it had three antennae, spaced equally in a circle around the body.

Lahra stepped aside as the drill shot through the air and cut at its body using only her arms and shoulders, not her entire body. Small motions. Efficiency. She would fight to protect her body as best she could, until the situation demanded more.

The thing slowed in the air, and her sword caught the drill section, glancing off again.

Two more drills picked up.

"These things are going to shred the ship!" Max grabbed ahold of the bolted-down work desk. "The force field is going to give out any time . . ."

"Steady, love. It will be but a moment."

Lahra's facade of calm was shaken when yet more pounding started up on the port side of the hold. She dropped the explorer's tune and switched to a battle-brawl, a call-and-response contest of warriors sharing their exploits.

The drill-thing bounced off the backside of the hold, claw-feet adjusting. The drill shot forward once more, making its way toward Max's workstation, where the Atlan device rested in a secure clamp. The creature wailed, its antennae glowing like the lights of lure-fish.

Gauging its movement, Lahra sidestepped into its path and cut at the first drill-thing. This time, her blade cut into the rear of the creature, tearing it nearly in two. It folded in on itself, hissing.

"Patching the hull!" Max moved forward, spraying quick-forming foam that grabbed hold of the shorn steel and formed a lattice to cover the breach.

And then another drill pierced the steel.

Max dashed for the new breach. "If we wait until they break through, there won't be anything left of the hull to make the jump back to normal space."

"Agreed." Lahra was breathing hard. She was not fully recovered. But she would not let it show. "Wheel, I'm going to electrify the hull. Just long enough to shake these things. Can you work with that?"

"You're going to what?"

"If I spent the time putting on my suit to meet them in the void, too many will break through for us to handle at once. But if I electrify the hull, it may shock them off the ship long enough for us to lose them if you go for a hard burn. Our passengers are well-insulated in the cabin, and we're all wearing boots, yes?"

"If you crisp my instrument board with this . . ." Wheel said with the annoyance of an empty threat. She was resigned to the plan as well.

"Find something to insulate yourself," she told Max. With a step, she swung her blade flat-first, like a paddle, pushing one of the drill-heads back out of the ship.

"I still think this is a dream," Max muttered from his workstation as he grabbed the rubber gloves he'd worn during the Vsenk attack.

"All ready?" Lahra asked as the drills continued to tear through the weakened hull.

"Ready!" came Wheel's voice over comms.

"Ready!" Max echoed, gloved hands hanging onto the side of the ladder, his feet tucked up under him.

Lahra released the grav-lock on her boots and began

floating toward the top of the hold. She drew deeply of the sword's charge and unleashed a massive bolt of electricity. White-blue arcs of energy shot across the room.

More hissing, and the drills writhed, smoking, and receded. The pounding stopped.

"Seal the holes, quickly!" Lahra called. "Maximum burn as soon as possible!"

The engines picked up, hurtling Max toward the hull. The hissing sounds grew distant.

Max cried out in panic but landed with feet braced to receive his impact. He filled up the other holes with sealant. "Hull patch secure!"

"Everyone operational?" Wheel asked.

A door opened down the hall, showing Eihra looking frazzled but unhurt. "What happened?"

"Nothing of note. We're safe."

Lahra was unharmed but dissatisfied. Thought them safe, removed her suit to recover, and they'd been caught off guard. "It's my fault that we had to endanger the ship. If I'd stayed ready, I could have met them on their own terms."

"By going EVA in warp space?" Max said. "While injured? You don't have to throw yourself at every situation like you're just a weapon, love. We'll be okay." Love and frustration poured off of him.

She raised a hand to his face. He stepped into it and held her hands in both of his, caressing her calloused fingers. She leaned in to kiss his forehead, then spoke. "I will not apologize for embracing danger to protect those I love."

Max shook his head. "I appreciate that, but running EVA in the void is—I can't." He looked up and away as he called, "Wheel, help me out here?"

"I'm not playing judge right now," came Wheel's reply over the ship's speakers. The digital undertone to her voice had faded, but only partly. "Busy fixing the ship. Re-booting secondary systems now. There'll be a bit of a shudder."

The engine beneath them spooled up, whirring sounds growing in pitch and frequency. There was a lurch, a whine, and cursing from the cockpit.

The ship could not find its song, too shaken by the trauma.

"Come on, baby. Just a little shock. We'll get you all patched up soon, I promise. I know these people we're flying with are trouble, but you're tougher than this." The emergency lights flickered, and then faded, replaced by the usual dull yellows of the *Kettle*'s interior lighting.

Joyous laughter came over the comms, followed by the sound of switches, panels, and the modulating metallic sounds of Wheel resuming her position connecting with the ship. "That's my girl." Her voice was thick with relief.

Lahra and Max put the hold back in order with assistance from Eihra and her daughters. Then the two scaled up toward the cockpit, where Wheel was running diagnostics, still talking to the ship in soothing tones.

"Hey, Wheel. Next time you trade stories with another Atlan, looks like you'll be drinking for free."

Wheel gestured to the worse-for-wear control console. "Great. That'll pay for about one one-hundredth of the cost it'll take to repair the ship for the third time in as many weeks."

"Savings is savings," Max shrugged. A moment later he said, "I'm going to make something to eat."

CHAPTER TWENTY-SIX

MAX

THE SHIP MADE IT back out of warp space and into the next jump with only a moderate amount of cursing from Wheel. It hadn't been two days since their last fix-up, and already the repair bill was mounting.

Returning to the Wreck would be walking into enemy territory, which cut off most of the repair shops Wheel could trust to do right by the *Kettle*.

And they still didn't have any real sense of what those devices were, or what the payday at the end would be.

Max's mind jumped to terrible eventualities, strains that could push them past their breaking point.

A few more scrapes like the one they'd just escaped and the *Kettle* would be grounded. And then Lahra would end up taking a bodyguard position on some port, he'd have to take work on doing translation or research in an underground scholar's den. Either of those could get them embroiled in local politics . . . which went great for them on the Wreck.

Better that they shake the Imperium's tail and get back to the real work.

Max took notes about the drill-head beasts, including

biological samples from the corpse of the one Lahra had cleaved. That at least would fetch a keen price from scholars as a curiosity, even if they couldn't convince the buyers that it came from warp space.

Hours later, the *Kettle* dropped into normal space a second time. The viewscreen filled with a binary star system and traces of a solar windstream. Micro-meteors and other bits of space dust caught the light and traced a path through the stars.

And in the distance, a hundred floating figures swimming their way through space.

The Drell Migration.

As the *Kettle* approached, Max saw well enough to tell the great space turtles apart. Of course, they weren't technically turtles, but they had great curved shells, flippers, green skin, and they could retract their heads into their shells. Close enough for his internal monologue.

Max resisted the urge to press his face up against the screen like the glass at an aquarium. Even the babies were the size of a single-story home. Most were over thirty meters long and ten meters tall from the underside of their shells to the ridged tops. The larger ones, about twenty of the hundred, were hundreds of meters long, with metallic structures attached to the peaks and valleys of their shells. The shells themselves made up a wide color palette, oranges and greens and yellows mixed in with browns and grays. Small ships buzzed around the edges like flies on a herd of cows. The Migration was a living flying space archipelago, and it was amazing.

And at the head, the Matriarch Yeddix. She was big, almost impossibly big, easily five times the size of her next-largest kin. Yeddix had an entire city on her shell—called Xidd, or "place of refuge"—that held recordings of her memories, including prior consultations. Her archives were the envy of any scholar, not least because they dated back to the earliest times in Imperial history.

And before, though the Drell didn't advertise that part.

The Imperium asserted that they'd always held power. That they had made the other species to serve the Vsenk, and that the stars themselves had crafted the Vsenk to rule the void.

Propaganda, all of it. Any scholar worth their salt knew that the ancient Atlan pre-dated the Vsenk. As did many of the people Max talked to, when they trusted him enough to not sell them out. Families and communities had their own secret histories telling of the Atlan Empire that came before.

But say as much on a public channel, or in the earshot of any officer of the Imperium, and it was a one-way trip to a prison colony.

Charming dictators, the Vsenk. Made the tyrants from Earth look infantile in comparison.

The Vsenk held so closely to lies with seemingly no sense of self-awareness that Max could barely wrap his mind around it.

Wheel opened a comm line. "This is the freighter *Kettle*, hailing the Great Migration. May the solar winds always guide you home."

A Rellix voice answered their hail. "Greetings, freighter *Kettle*. Blessed be the winds that brought you here. What is the purpose of your visit?"

"Archive access. Refugee placement. And repairs," Wheel added. "Transmitting codes now."

Max's mind was blown several times all over again as they approached the Great Migration. The Drell lived for many centuries, and the story of their lives swimming through space played out across their fins, shells, and faces. Any one of them would have seen enough to fill a ten-volume oral history, and that was without any of their individual interests. The Drell were legendary for their studies, each member of the Migration a specialist in a different field. Together, the Drell held more information and memory than several solar systems. The Vsenk could control public history, but the Migration had enough autonomy to keep the fires of knowledge well-tended.

And he was going to meet them. At least one. Probably one of the younger administrators. If he was lucky, maybe he'd live long enough for his consultation to arrive. But for now, the archives would have to be enough. They were running short on money, leads, and options.

Because if they didn't figure the device out soon, his curiosity and insistence on holding onto the artifacts could get them all killed. And he rather liked living. Not that he'd explored other options, but being a ghost sounded like a drag, and he liked having a body too much for that or for the uploaded life. And with that, you were always one bad ion storm away from having your entire existence obliterated.

Max put away the thoughts of all of the terrible ways he could die and returned to his workstation to secure the device in the ship's smuggling hold. Cruji couldn't exactly be counted on for guard duty by himself.

Just one lead. Just one good lead. That's all they needed.

CHAPTER TWENTY-SEVEN

WHEEL

ONCE THE WARP-THINGS WERE taken care of and the *Kettle*'s course confirmed, Wheel was left with the broken-down, bugged-out snarl of her feelings and a glass of Rellixian grain alcohol. The stuff tasted like distilled jet exhaust but doubled as a cleaning solvent, so it was easier to justify in her budget.

They'd gotten one over on Jesvin but lost the Wreck. No more dice games with the grease jockeys in the port district, no more joking with Ruku, no more hours walking the levels and taking in the best the galaxy had to offer outside of tight Imperial control.

But no more Jesvin.

She might continue to send people after them, post bounties, maybe even sell them out to the Imperials, though Jesvin did everything she could to stay off of the Vsenk's radar entirely.

Wheel's mind looped through those thoughts as she downed spiced liquor in the galley. Still not enough. She'd never really faced the lasting impact of Jesvin's abuses, always partitioned it off and filed the memories away in the back of her mind.

She'd have to face those feelings, grapple with the ways that they'd shaped her. But today wasn't that day. The absurd and impossible she could deal with, but not the other thing.

Wheel stood and poured herself another glass.

CHAPTER TWENTY-EIGHT

AREK

THE THIEVES' SHIP HAD reappeared on their sensors for a few hours, then disappeared once more. Arek ordered the *Vigilance Without Respite* to pursue. The navigation team worked overtime crunching the numbers on possible destinations, how long their jumps might be, and more. Arek put out the notice with the ship's information but kept the artifacts out of the notice, per Qerol's instructions.

If word got out that he'd let pre-Imperial artifacts slip through his grasp, he would lose face with his faction, and their already shaky status would be further diminished. Evam and his hard-liners were already putting pressure on the Special Economic Zones, and Arek would not let himself be a liability.

Arek paced on the command deck, arms laced behind him as he stewed. It would be a delicate thing to use Imperial support in tracking these grave robbers without tipping their hand to Evam. If they crossed into another faction's sphere of influence, his connections might not be able to keep accounts from reaching their way to the court.

The stakes escalated. Whatever these things were, Qerol

believed that if Arek secured and retrieved them, it could provide the Bright Suns with the leverage to push for policy changes in the council. The tide would begin to turn, and then he could secure a better posting, spend more time at home . . .

"Commander." The Rellix XO interrupted his hopeful trail of thought. "We've picked up the signal from the errant artifact."

Arek turned, directing the full force of his attention to the feathered XO. "Report."

"It's tracking to a sensor buoy in the trade lane between the Woala binary stars."

"Excellent, Gralo. Chart a course."

"There's more, your lordship."

That was never a good sign. "Yes?"

"Our charts show the signal within the Drell Migration. They've likely docked with the great beasts."

Precisely what he did not need. The great space-beasts were the only creatures in the galaxy that could properly threaten the Imperium, their adults large enough to engage a battlecruiser on even terms. Without a decision from the Grand Melee, a non-aggression, non-interference pact was sacrosanct.

The last time that Vsenk forces and Drell had clashed, the losses had been massive on both sides. At the height of the battle, the Matriarch broke the back of a Lotus-class dreadnaught with a single bite, killing thousands in one stroke.

After that, the two had maintained an uneasy armistice. If the thieves were seeking refuge among the Drell, he would need to be very careful.

"Understood. Lay in a course to intercept the fleet, but at a respectful distance. We will approach per the treaty and wait for the thieves to leave the Migration."

"For the Imperium!" The Rellix shouted, turning back to their console.

"Activating Warp sequence," echoed the pilot's mechanical voice, and the ship tore through the barrier, taking them into warp space.

Arek liked the quiet of warp. It provided respite, time to reflect.

Every step he took toward reclaiming the other key, the fates pushed him two steps to the side. So he would come at them from the corners.

CHAPTER TWENTY-NINE

MAX

THE CITY OF XIDD was hillier than San Francisco. Probably. Max had never actually been to San Francisco, but Xidd seemed to be even more hilly than the version of San Francisco he'd seen on TV.

Rather than a single smooth curve, the Matriarch's shell rose and fell in mounds, square sections creating natural divisions between through-way streets and the foundation of buildings. A system of trains rolled on lines overhead. That left six meters of clearance for pedestrians and small ground vehicles while shuttling dozens of people at a time around the lanes of traffic.

Higher above, a net of satellites generated the bubble-shaped force field that contained Xidd's atmosphere. The technology was older than the Vsenk Empire and was one of the secrets the Drell would not share.

Max and the four Genae rode the shuttle several kilometers from their docking berth to the public archives.

Again, Max found his attention drifting from their mission to the tiny details. Unfamiliar script, subtle differences in municipal design, and most of all, the people. Members of a half-dozen species he'd only heard described walked the shell streets of Xidd. Some would be petitioners and visitors like him. Others, the permanent residents of the Migration— people who had sworn fealty to the Migration to live free from the Imperium.

The Migration wouldn't take just anyone. Petitioning for the chance to swear to the Drell was nearly as hard as getting an appointment with the Matriarch herself. In dark times, he'd considered applying, hoping that he could get in as a scholar, make something of his life even if he could never find a way home. But he'd never leave Lahra behind, and her devotion to finding the heir had never wavered.

Those that made the cut on the Migration could travel the stars for their entire lives, needing never fear the Imperium again. He definitely got the appeal.

The Imperium held so tightly to control that they quashed any dissent. The Vsenk had enough infighting on their own, though they publicly denied it. With the Vsenk, there was always a disjunct between the public record of the Imperium and the private reality.

The first stop was the Office of Welcome, where refugees and would-be scholars made their application for the right to stay in the Migration. The building took up an entire block, and once they got inside, there were a dozen different lines that looped down hallways, up staircases, and back on themselves a dozen times as they led to a wall of stations at the far end of the room.

But this wasn't like the bureaucracy in the movie *Brazil*. The lines and departments here all made sense. There were signs, there were places to sit, and there were attendants everywhere answering questions.

It was everything that a DMV was meant to be and seldom was.

"It's beautiful," Max said.

Eihra chuckled. "Looks like we'll be here all day."

Even here in the heart of Xidd, Lahra was on guard. "But you'll be safe. Raise me on comms if any problems emerge."

Vlera started singing what Max recognized as the song of leaving, the one they sang every time Lahra finally pulled herself away from her cousins.

His wife hugged all three of them in turn.

Tears welled in the corner of her eyes.

Max squeezed his wife's hand. "This isn't goodbye. We'll see them again."

"You never know that. Each leaving could be the last. That's why we have the song."

"And why you have the song of greeting, too."

Lahra wiped the tears from her eyes. Once they were out of the building, she stopped and pulled him in for a kiss. It was a kiss seeking reassurance, for holding on to what you had because you were afraid you might lose it. They'd kissed that kiss many times before, but now he was the one giving reassurance, not seeking it.

"We can do this," Max said when they pulled apart. "We're safer here than almost anywhere."

***

Max and Lahra disembarked the shuttle within view of the archives.

Lahra was on edge, in bodyguard mode since they left Eihra and the girls. Lahra's eyes were always moving, watching the crowds, assessing possible threats, and identifying escape routes.

But just because Lahra was on the lookout didn't mean he shouldn't be. Xidd had its crime like anywhere else. The Drell delegated public safety to their vassal-allies, since most everyone else was tiny by Drell scale. Of the hundreds of sentient species known in and around warp space, only two were larger than three meters tall on average—the Drell and the Vsenk. It made a certain kind of Darwinian sense that they would be the major powers, thanks to their size.

But it wasn't destiny. Nothing lasted forever. Over time, every society changed, expanded or contracted, or re-invented itself. How long would it be before a change like that came to the Vsenk? Would it come from within, from some reformer faction? Or from outside? From some new species or a change in policy by the Drell?

The public archives were built across Yeddix's central ridge spines, the building arcing across the living horizon from the Matriarch's head to her tail.

There were two entrances—one for humanoid-sized beings and a much larger one thirty meters up. A pair of juvenile Drell flew through the larger opening, rumbling voices back and forth with the cadence of kindergartners.

The smaller door opened, letting Max and Lahra in.

"You can still go help Wheel with repairs if you want."

Lahra shook her head. "With the Imperium hunting us, I will not let you travel alone. No matter how tiresome this effort will be."

"I bet they have information about Genos as well."

"We must sing in unison. If our attention is split between these devices, a route to Earth, and finding the location of the last heirs of Genos, then we will not be able to make forward movement on any of them. I will stay, I will assist where I can, and I will watch for the forces of the Imperium."

Lahra had this ability to be devoted but grumpy at the same time. It sometimes made him uncomfortable, to have his wife so ready to stand by even as she was bored to distraction. He'd brought it up, and every time, he ran smack-dab into the cultural norms of her people. Lahra's line had been bodyguards, trained to compartmentalize personal interest away while focusing on the greater good.

Coming up with his mother and aunties in Baltimore, the idea of a woman putting her own happiness to the side to support others wasn't new for him. And because he loved them, he didn't want to ask that of anyone. Seeing people accustomed to being catered to rubbed him the wrong way. He'd spent twenty-plus years watching powerful, vital women struggle with balancing their hopes and dreams, running themselves ragged keeping the household going. They weren't superhuman, just driven. He'd watched his father learn when and where to step up, when to take care of his own bullshit rather than dumping it on one of the women in his life.

And he'd seen the results of trying to put someone else first all the time, in any relationship: parent, child, lover, friend.

He didn't want Lahra to resent him. Resentment was a poison that could kill even the strongest relationship. But this galaxy was so different from his life on Earth that it was easier to set new patterns, new expectations of himself. After they figured out this device, he and Lahra could take a mission that focused on Genos.

The two walked into the archives, and Max's jaw went slack. The room stretched up for dozens of meters, stacks upon stacks arcing toward infinity in all directions. And on the "ground" level, there were dozens of reference desks, attendants, and supplicants. The workers pored over scrolls, tapped away at ancient consoles, and scurried back and forth to the floating pods that traversed the stacks like bees in a hive.

"Daaaamn."

Even Lahra was impressed. "It is truly remarkable. And rather defensible, given the small number of entrance-points. Though once an invader broke past the front line, it would instantly devolve into trench warfare with questionable cover."

"Then let's make sure we get in and out before the Imperium decides to launch an all-out assault." He meant to be sarcastic.

Lahra, of course, pretended to take his words at face value, as she often did to reverse his joke. "Indeed. I doubt they've laid in provisions for a siege of that severity. I will find us an optimal bunker site."

***

They checked in and were assigned an attendant, a carousel for reading, and a floating pod for browsing. These were just the public archives, so it was a research free-for-all.

After spending several minutes grabbing everything in sight like a kid in a candy store, the overwhelming options hit like a battering ram.

The archives' search algorithms were strong for text queries, but garbage for visual. Max fed the pictures he'd taken into the search engine and came back with a series of vague thirdhand accounts. He spent an hour massaging the search systems, trying to hit the right keywords to find some archaeological texts which might have references to more specific writings in their bibliographies. All the basic texts he already knew.

But if these devices had been easily findable, they probably wouldn't have been squirreled away in the Forbidden System on a shattered world. These were full-on esoterica. But to what end?

Lahra helped where she could, holding numbers in her mind to cross-reference. Lahra was savvier than he in many ways, but she didn't have the passion for this type of research. Her inclinations were more practical. She could rattle off the critical stats and relative merits of a dozen shipboard and hand-held weapons or maintain a defensive position for hours, but in the archives, she felt the tedium very keenly.

Once he'd exhausted his search capabilities, Max returned to the attendant for a reference consult.

Their attendant, Neellaaoo, was a Jeehnn—like sapient amphibious jellyfish but bright orange. They'd emerged from their planets' oceans and taken to the stars, both curious and cautious. They tended to move slowly in all matters, figuratively and literally, as in floating sloth speed at the pace of floating sloths. The Jeehnn majority religious scripture had a saying, "Nothing of worth was accomplished in haste."

Unsurprisingly, they weren't great at warfare. Strategy, sure, but nothing that required reflexes and twitch speed. But they made fabulous scholars, able to hold a massive amount of information in their minds at once, and to evaluate data from several different perspectives simultaneously. Having a Jeehnn on your side was like having an entire research team.

Neellaaoo said, "If you were able to bring the devices here, we could run an internal three-dimensional scan. But I understand your caution in not wanting to travel the streets with an artifact of that . . . unique provenance." Jeehnn spoke about one-fourth the speed that Lahra did, who chose her words carefully and did not rush except when they were in a fight.

Max kept himself from cutting them off, even though he got the point. The Jeehnn was clearly trying to talk around the circumstances that had led to their possession of the artifacts while subtly displaying their displeasure. Max blew right by their intimations and continued.

"I provided a scan, but it's only external—can't read past the outer layer. But the real problem is that there's just no frame of reference. I submitted scans I took in the tomb, and we're getting nothing on the ping-back. Have you ever run into something like this? It's like there is a big hole around the information we're looking for."

The tips of Neellaaoo's tentacles twirled in a fashion Max couldn't help but associate with the "thinking" cursor on an Earth computer.

"Perhaps there is, in fact, a hole around the information. When a situation such as this arises, the most common explanation is that the information is held in the Matriarch's private archives, from recordings of her consultations. If that is the case, there is little more we can do for you here."

Max looked over to Lahra. Her face said both "I'm sorry" and "It is as I estimated."

He slumped in his chair, then massaged his temples.

"Let's check through the searches just one more time, if you don't mind." But it was pointless. He'd already suspected the information would be privately held, but there was no way they could stay out of the Imperium's sights for twenty-five years with forbidden tech.

Which meant that their options were: fence it to Uwen or space it like a bag of Cruji's droppings.

They ran the searches one more time, to the expected results.

"I need a drink," Max said, finally, and Lahra led him from the archives in search of a nearby bar.

CHAPTER THIRTY

LAHRA

THERE WERE MANY FACETS to her calling. A great bodyguard not only protected the physical safety of their charge but also looked after their emotional and spiritual well-being.

It was the latter two that now occupied Lahra's attention. Max sipped at his third drink, rambling his way through a bout of self-pity. Max was her charge and her partner. At times he supported her, at other times she supported him. He made her laugh, challenged her linear approach to all problems, and kept life from ever becoming boring. It was an odd pairing, but lately, Lahra could not imagine life any other way.

Lahra and Max sat in a corner booth at a small bar very close to the archives. It had low ceilings and a plurality of seating, which made it a nightmare for security. There was little room to maneuver and too many vectors of attack for an assailant.

Fortunately, the patrons were mostly as morose and sluggish as Max. A few were on the opposite end of the emotional spectrum, celebrating some triumph or discovery in the archives, messily drunk in their elation.

Max's glass hit the bar with the clinking of ice against glass against cheap steel. Third drink down. They were both still recovering from their injuries on the Wreck, but this was not the most appropriate form of pain medication.

Wheel was back at the *Kettle*, hard at work trying to make the ship space-worthy again. Max was one drink away from becoming a sack of dead weight. He'd be done with that drink before Wheel's repairs were done.

After a long moment of deliberation, Lahra spoke. "We should return to the ship."

Max looked at his empty drinks, at the bar, and back to Lahra. "I'm afraid. I think we finally got in over our heads."

It was wise to name one's fear. An unnamed fear was protean, it fed on your unwillingness to face it head-on. "I know. We still have options. We could use a courier to get the artifacts to Uwen or have him come here and take them off our hands. We could return to our quests. Or take some paying jobs for a while, let the Imperials forget us."

Max nodded emphatically, his motions exaggerated by his inebriation.

Lahra settled their tab, leaving enough of a tip to keep them in the bartender's good graces should Imperials or bounty hunters come sniffing. It wouldn't stop the barkeep from selling them out for the right price, but it would likely increase that price. A calculated expenditure of resources.

"Move out," she said, looping one of Max's arms up and over her shoulder so she could support him.

Max wavered but followed, matching his steps to hers as best he could.

Xidd was a city of all hours. Lights gleamed, transit vehicles arced across the curved horizon. She watched the skies for Imperial ships, watched the streets for patrols or furtive glances. Danger wore many faces.

Max hummed lyrics from Terran songs as they walked,

shifting between keys seemingly at random. He grew slightly more lucid as they changed locations from a place of drunkenness to one of sights and sounds. His attention was split between a hundred stimuli, but it meant he was not caught in a loop of his worry.

Lahra hummed along with him as best as she could, carrying the tune as she carried him physically. Genae were rare, but a Genae hauling a drunken charge was about the most inconspicuous they could be given the circumstances. Just a Yaea scholar and his hired bodyguard, winding their way through the streets on their way back home after a long day of searching. Not star-hopping tomb raiders on the run from the Imperium.

Several blocks from the *Kettle*'s berth, their luck ran dry.

An Imperial patrol, polished armor and oversized carbines cutting their way through the crowds.

"Imperials," she whispered. Max stood up straight, then wavered. "How do we get around them?"

Lahra scanned the streets, her head moving slowly. Sharp movements would draw attention. This patrol might not be looking specifically for them. So as long as she and Max did not stand out, they might be able to get by. As casually as possible, Lahra turned them back to the way they came.

"There's a shuttle station one block back. We'll take it past the patrols and get underway."

So began the game of Verch and Thahl. Losing a tail was one of the first skills she'd learned as a child. It was just Verch and Thahl at first, a game named for animals from their long-lost homeworld. Her mother used play as a mask for the foundational skills of her caste.

One was the loping Verch, sniffing and hunting. The other was the scurrying Thahl, smaller and faster, trying to make its way back to its den.

They doubled back, took a left, and then cut through an alley beside another bar, taking a break in the shadows.

Lahra took Max's chin in her hand and drew him in for a gentle kiss, both distraction and gentle reassurance. They would fade into the background for a minute while the crowds passed them by. Max made happy sounds, and she ran a hand down his chin. "Just for a moment, love. The danger is not yet past."

"Good evasion."

"I know."

Max's forehead rested on her chin. She leaned in, cheek against his sweaty head-wrap. *You cannot have him,* she told the universe. *If we are to be adrift on the solar winds, let us have these moments at least.*

They disentangled, and she squeezed his hand. "Can you walk unassisted?"

Max blinked, clarity seeping back in. "Adrenaline is a hell of a sobriety booster."

"Indeed. Follow me."

And then they were off again. Lahra set their pace at a fast walk. They were people with somewhere to be, but not fugitives on the run. Unobtrusiveness wasn't just about speed—it came from gait, carriage, attitude. She dashed off a quick message to Eihra as they walked, the signal beaming out from her suit.

"Keep your head down. Imperials."

The patrol passed through an intersection heading the other direction, and her worry softened from fortissimo to forte. The shuttle station was painted to match the mottled greens and yellows of a Drell's fin. They joined the two-dozen petitioners, workers, and tourists filing through the turnstiles and scaling the escalators to the shuttle platform. She led them through the crowd and took up a position with minimum visibility from the street, between a pillar and a sitting station.

Several minutes passed, crowds shifting, announcements droning from the speakers about upcoming service changes and delays of trains elsewhere in the city.

A shuttle rolled along the rails, three segments long. Its head slowed to a stop four meters to their left. The crowd parted to let them out. Too quickly. She caught nervous glances, whispered complaints.

And then spotted a gleaming black helmet. Another patrol.

"This way." She grabbed Max by the hand and turned on her heels. The shuttle was only one story up, and she'd pegged a waste canister on the far side of the station. The Drell liked to combine public services for convenience—transit maintenance and waste management side-by-side.

"Halt!" called one of the Imperial troops. *Void,* she thought, containing her frustration. She'd moved too fast.

The crowd noises changed from worried civilians to terrified civilians, which meant that their crowd cover was gone. The soldiers would have a clean shot very soon.

She dropped her pace to put herself between Max and the guards, counting on her armor to absorb the first few shots.

As they approached the edge of the platform, she shouted, "Jump into the waste container!"

"This is going to suck," Max muttered as he half-jumped, half-fell from the platform, arms flailing. Lahra checked the rear camera in her suit, showing the patrol charging after them in three rows of three, weapons raised. A tall Rellix officer stood in the back, feathered arm-wing raised in their direction.

"Do not let them escape!"

Confirming that Max had landed safely and there was room for her in the waste container, Lahra jumped, turned, drew her sword, and fired two bursts at the guards. They dropped as she fell into the muck with a whump-splorch.

It was disgusting, a mix of refuse, biological waste, and more. But it broke the landing. Lahra flipped her blade and hooked the cross guard over the container's edge, pulling herself to one side, then up and over. She offered a hand to Max, and they jumped down and into the street.

"Run as fast as you can. Straight back to the ship. And call Wheel, tell her to start the launch sequence."

"Run. Ship. Wheel. Got it." Max fumbled with his comms while sprinting, wincing as he went.

The Imperial forces gave chase, not taking the jump but instead climbing down the side of the shuttle station. One of the Imperium's many faults—their training standards were pathetic. They were reliant on the overwhelming power of their fleet and the Vsenk themselves. A quartet of Genae infantry could hold their own against three times the number of Imperials, and the elite troops, with their decades of training and discipline, were hosts unto themselves. That's why her people had fought the Vsenk to a stand-still.

Her mother's voice filled her mind, stories of how their righteous ancestors had stood toe-to-toe against the Empire during the flight from Genos as it shattered under the power of the Devastation.

Here, she had only to fight the underlings. But this was not a last stand, and she was not fighting alone. She had to keep Max safe and get them back to the *Kettle* in time and then escape the Vsenk patrol ships. And keep them off the trail of Eihra and the girls.

They turned a corner, now just a block away from the space port. If the Imperium was here with any strength, there would be squadrons at the ports. But would they know which one? The forces required to cover every one of the Drell ports would be far greater than the Migration's arrangement would permit.

So she thought.

And yet, there they were. Four troops, flanking the door.

And eight still following them from the transit station.

Singing "The Skirmisher's Tale" under her breath, Lahra opened fire with her greatsword. The gem had not fully charged thanks to their misadventures in warp space, so she had little energy remaining. Two more guards went down, the energy cracking their armor and leaving them spasming on the concrete floor of the entranceway.

Before the Devastation, Genae royal guards had dozens of spheres, all charged and on rotation during interplanetary travel, servants on-hand to switch them out at a moment's notice. There were even tales of some legendary spheres that could manifest other effects—moving objects at a distance, controlling flame, and more. All far beyond the scope of the internal effects the songs Lahra had learned could manifest.

But she had only the one sphere and its one power. Her mother's, which was her grandmother's and great-grandmother's, and so on. And she would have to make do.

Lahra switched into a sword-guard, blade out and angled, the rhythm of the song's verse keeping her steady. She launched into the accompanying battle-form, blade sweeping across her body to deflect coming fire.

Ten paces out. The carbines spat death, and she caught them across the broad blade of her sword of station, voice growing louder as she moved into the chorus.

Max tapped his wrist-computer. "I can't raise Wheel. There's just no answer."

"She may have been captured," she said, then returned to her song. She prayed that her cousins would not get caught up in this. At least some of her people should have the chance to live free.

"What do we do now?"

They could go to ground, hide in the streets and alleys of Xidd, the labor houses or the refugee camps. But without access to the ship, they were separated from the artifact and their resources. There would be more troops on the way, especially if the Drell did not object to the investigation.

Options narrowed, the threat of capture closing in on them like a vise. She reached the bridge of "The Skirmisher's Tale."

Time to decide.

"We stay and fight."

The two remaining soldiers lowered their carbines and drew stun sticks. But their crude weapons were barely half the length of her sword. She swung for one soldier's head, and as they parried, she pulled her blade back and then stabbed the other through the midsection. Lahra leapt and kicked, pinning the other to the wall. His armor cracked, eliciting a scream. Then he crumpled to the floor and did not move.

Lahra turned to face the original patrol, blade at the ready. She steadied her breathing. Her energy was waning. Already. The wounds had closed, but she was not yet whole again.

"Open the door and get to our ship. I will hold them here."

"But if they're on the ship?" She heard the console beep and whir as he worked his technological magic. Wheel was of course their best hacker, but Max had been learning quickly. Her method of hacking involved stabbing the computer with her sword, which worked far less often than logic would indicate.

"One foe at a time. Open the gate, and then we will retake the ship."

"I've got a bad feeling about this." His words carried the weight of some Terran reference she did not know.

"So noted, but I feel only the heat of battle."

Four from the larger patrol laid down suppressive fire while the other three flanked. Her blade could not parry bolts across a full half-circle, and they knew it. The Rellix Lieutenant held their pistol out in a way that was more ceremonial than threatening, but they were directing their troops well.

Lahra used the last of the gem's charge to down one of the flankers, then drew a throwing dagger from a compartment in her armor's vambrace. She tossed it between two guards straight at the Rellix.

Lahra re-set to a guard position on instinct. That training saved her life for not the first time as a burst of plasma arced through the air, dissipating on the flat of her blade. Lahra looked up and felt her fragile hope shudder.

It was a Vsenk noble. By the markings, the same one that she'd repelled in their flight from Yua. He leveled his scattergun at her, flight pack keeping him far out of reach of any thrown attack.

Eight-to-two odds, including a Vsenk, and her only ally a half-sober non-combatant. And the routes of escape were few.

This was not a fight they could win. "Got it!" Max said. The sound of sliding doors and moving air confirmed Max's excitement.

And yet, the Rellix officer grinned.

More black-armored troops appeared in the reflection on her blade. They'd already taken the ship.

A muffled voice from behind her said, "Don't. Move."

Worse than ten-to-one odds, and nowhere to run. She could die here if she wanted, join her mother and her ancestors. But she would not give up on Max, on Wheel, or on her people.

Lahra took a steadying breath and flipped her sword in her hands so that it was lying flat in her palms, then lowered it to the ground, her eyes locked on the Rellix officer. Looking a Vsenk in the eyes was punishable by death. Not that they would be spared for what they did. But if there was any chance to survive, it would lie in waiting for the right moment to come.

Beside her, Max was forced to his knees by one of the officers from the ship, "I'm sorry, if I . . ."

"We will get through this, my love. This is not the end."

The Vsenk's voice was a duet of malice and dismissal. "Your fate is no longer yours to control." Then to his crew, "Collar them, search them, and bring them to the *Vigilance Without Respite.*"

As the guards approached, Lahra allowed herself the moment to fantasize about how she would kill the Vsenk. She'd cut off one tentacle at a time. Then the legs. Then she would toss him into a sun. Vsenk were anaerobic, so he'd survive long enough to be roasted into a cinder.

Yes. That would do nicely.

CHAPTER THIRTY-ONE

WHEEL

FIRST, THE IMPERIALS JAMMED her comms, kept her from warning the lovebirds or Fihra's family.

Wheel danced with the Imps for a while, gave as good as she got with electronic countermeasures, proxy spoofs, and viruses. But in the end, the Vsenk just blasted a hole in her freshly-repaired hull and took the ship by force.

That was ten hours ago. After a quick shuttle trip, Wheel, Lahra, and Max boarded a Vsenk patrol cruiser and got a short tour before ending up in three adjacent cells, locked up with force fields.

Wheel stared at the ceiling. "This is fun. Definitely what I had planned for my evening."

Lahra paced in her cell, fuming. There weren't many worse things you could do to a Genae guard than disarm and imprison them away from their charge.

If they'd gotten picked up by a colonial police force, there would be room for bribes, favors, etc. But none of that would fly here. The only hope they'd have would be if the Drell decided to put their foot down and call this arrest the violation of the non-interference pact that it was. But were three random visitors worth testing the strength of that pact?

The *Kettle* was impounded within a patrol ship, and when they couldn't find the artifact, they'd pick her precious girl apart piece by piece.

"Shouldn't have fed the box to that little monster," she thought, not meaning it. They'd learned of Cruji's predilection to steal and hide large objects in an extra stomach when Max's codex had gone missing for a week. Retrieving the device had not been fun, so this was the first time they did it on purpose. And that was beside the question of how he actually hid something that large in his stomach without it showing. While the Imps were attacking her firewalls, she'd set up Cruji with a week's worth of food and stuffed the little irritant in her best smuggling compartment between her room and the lovebirds'.

But if the Vsenk wanted something that bad, the right thing was to keep it from them. And the thought of Imperial flunkies scratching their heads and sensor antennae trying to find her hidden compartments gave her some comfort in this crap-sack situation.

She looked at the cell again, searching for a panel. If they were smart, there wouldn't be anything accessible from the inside.

But Imperial contractors were not renowned for their thoroughness. Most operated within micrometers of regulations, doing the absolute minimum to minimize costs. Which meant cutting corners.

If she could access their wiring, she could crack their security, drop the fields.

But then they'd have to sneak through, and likely have to fight their way out of a heavily-staffed Imperial ship. And pray that she could get the *Kettle* to run despite being tossed and torn apart and void knows what else.

And there was the question of the security cameras she'd spotted on the way in. Every ten paces, panoramic views.

They'd have overlapping fields of view. Nowhere to hide.

Even with a distraction, it'd take her several minutes to pull down the panel and bring the fields down.

Nothing. She had nothing.

"So, what are our options?" Max asked.

Lahra kept up her pacing as she spoke. "I'm imagining the variety of ways I could kill my way through the ship. But as satisfying as the vision is, I cannot see a viable escape plan that ensures all three of us make it to the *Kettle*. Especially considering we don't know where the ship is."

Wheel said, "These ships have two docking bays, so we've got a fifty-fifty chance. But those bays are always crawling with troops and technicians."

Max put his face in his hands. "I should have sold the artifact to Uwen. We'd be halfway across the sector by now, and the Imperium would forget us as soon as the device popped up on the black market."

Lahra stopped pacing to speak. "Perhaps so. But we took another path. Regretting past choices once they have been acknowledged as mistakes does nothing to help our current situation."

"True, but I can't do anything else right now. If force fields could be brought down by quoting Illhari legends at them, then we'd be fine."

A door whooshed open, and Wheel caught the twitchy gait of a Rellix. Four guards followed, all armed with long rifles. Two guards focused on Lahra, the others turned with the Rellix to look at Wheel's cell.

"Atlan. Come with me."

The Rellix tapped several buttons on the console outside the cell, and the rippling force field dropped.

Lahra could probably take the group, but not safely, and certainly not with the two of them in the line of fire. And without access to computer systems, Wheel wasn't much use in a fight.

Wheel stepped forward, steeling herself for the torture to come. Flesh responded to torture, but her cyborg mind could partition the pain away from her consciousness.

But that trick wasn't at all rare. The Imperials doubtless had viruses and data worms for Atlan prisoners, and her internal countermeasures might not be enough. For all she knew, this would be her last day as Wheel. They could hard-wipe her mind and reboot her as one of their many servitors, relegated to maintenance or navigation. Little more than a cybernetic drone.

"See ya later," Wheel said to Max and Lahra. It wouldn't help them for her to show fear. Max was already terrified, and Lahra was a couple of heartbeats from beating her fists to bloody messes on the shields out of frustration. She hadn't been able to out-play the Imperial code-breakers, hadn't gotten them far enough away.

So now she'd pay the price.

***

The guards didn't lead her to a torture cell. Instead, she walked into a room with a three-meter-long table as tall as she was and eight-meter-high ceilings.

This room was built for Vsenk.

They let her idle there for the better part of an hour. Trying to make her bored, fidgety. Learn her ticks through that camera up in the corner. Instead, she spent the time reviewing her mental countermeasures, shoring up her code and building in dummy memory sectors, hoping to make her brain hard enough to hack that they'd just kill her and get it over with. Cog hadn't told her much about the resistance's movements in the past few years, but it was enough to get a whole lot of good people killed. For Cog's sake, for the sake of what they once had, she had to protect them as best she could.

A massive door slid open, revealing a Vsenk noble nearly five meters tall. And that was small for a Vsenk. Wheel pulled herself up in her seat, taking reassurance from the cold metal. It was a far cry from her ship, but it was the closest she'd get to being connected to a computer system without busting out of this impossible situation.

"Atlan. Your ship is carrying contraband from the Forbidden Sector. Your Genae has killed eleven Imperial troops and assaulted a Vsenk noble. You are all marked for death. The only way you can escape this fate is if you comply immediately and completely. Do you understand?"

No pretense, no solicitation, no pandering. Just hardball. *So that's how it's going to be?* Wheel could deal with that. After years of dealing with Jesvin, the Vsenk's bluntness was refreshing. "Oh, I get you. I've got one card left, and as soon as I play it, there's nothing to keep us alive. So right now, you and I are staring at one another across a planetary divide, guns hot and waiting to see who glitches first."

Vsenk eyes glowed, but they were deep-set in the flower-skull head. Made them harder to read. Wheel was being as obstinate as she could manage, and this noble just took it in stride. "Telling us where the artifact lies is the only way for you to survive. Many of my colleagues would have tortured you first. I prefer a smoother approach."

Wheel held her ground, saying nothing more.

The Vsenk waved three arms in concert, one hand chased by two others. Wheel flinched at first, then realized the gesture was maybe supposed to be inviting? "You are a pilot of no small talent. You could find a home for yourself here. The Yaea was clever enough to navigate through the tomb. And we might even be able to put that Genae to use, should she learn to obey. But their fate depends on your cooperation."

Now the pandering? Interesting play. Evaluating the Vsenk's tactics helped her keep her calm. And the soft approach just wouldn't work as well when she knew for absolute sure that it was just another play, feinting right to push her left after the direct method failed.

The longer she held out, the more furious the Vsenk would be. If she was going to give up the last artifact, she had to do it now. This Vsenk wasn't like the stories. More practical than cruel, almost respectable.

She'd been lying before. There was one more gambit she could use. It was a sacrifice play, but it might pay off in the long run. "So, what are those artifacts, and why are they important?"

The Vsenk straightened. That was the big reaction she was hoping for, but she couldn't tell what it meant. It wasn't like she'd spent any time talking to a Vsenk. The closest she'd seen one before was arcing toward the *Kettle* as they burned hard away from the ruined temple on Yua.

The Vsenk said, "You don't know what they are. And yet you cling to the one you've hidden away somewhere?"

He'd taken her bait. She pushed back into bluster, even though it was forced, covering barely contained panic. "It was the cornerstone to an ancient Atlan tomb. It's got to be worth something. We knew that much, didn't need to know more. We've just been looking for a buyer that will pay the exorbitant price we know it should command."

The Vsenk folded several arm-tentacles across his trunk. A smaller door opened, and a Jeehnn hover-walked into the room.

"What is it?" the Vsenk said.

"Sir. There's been an urgent message."

"It can wait."

The soldier looked torn. Jeehnn religious teachings valued patience where the Vsenk's Imperial doctrine demanded quick thinking. "I'm sorry, sir, but . . . It's from the Drell Matriarch. We've been ordered to answer within five minutes or face dissolution of the non-interference pact."

The Vsenk's tentacles twitched. Was that fear?

He turned to Wheel. "It would seem you have some more time to consider my offer. I'm not unreasonable, but my patience is finite." His voice was curt, but she thought she could hear a bit of fear there as well.

And with that, the god-warrior left the room with the Jeehnn, leaving Wheel alone once more.

Wheel exhaled and relaxed. But the question rang loud in her mind: *What the void would the Matriarch want enough to threaten the Vsenk with their pact?*

CHAPTER THIRTY-TWO

AREK

As Arek and the Jeehnn ensign returned to the deck, Arek realized the enormity of the threat backing up the Migration's demands.

Visible on the command deck viewscreen was a three-kilometer-long Drell, twice the size of his own ship. By its head, a satellite. A comms relay, converting Drell speech into and from Imperial Standard.

The pact with the Drell took a pre-emptive strike off the table. Being responsible for breaking the treaty would bring world-ending amounts of disfavor upon his faction in the Imperium, even if it didn't lead to all-out war with the Drell. But he'd be expected to skirt the letter of the treaty while pushing as hard as possible for the Imperium's agenda.

He would have to hear them out.

Arek approached the window, looking the Drell in the eye. "Give me a direct line."

A Yaea comms officer said, "The line is open, Your Righteousness."

"Greetings, Drell messenger. This is Arek of the House of Ojh, commander of the cruiser *Vigilance Without Respite*. I stand prepared for your message."

The Drell's voice rumbled across the comms. "Matriarch Yeddix bids you greeting, Arek of the House of Ojh, and to your crew of the cruiser *Vigilance Without Respite.* You have in your custody a Genae named Lahra Kevain, daughter of Halra. The Matriarch requires her presence. She has an appointment."

Dying Suns, Arek thought, keeping his sharp words back from the communication line. The Matriarch's appointments were booked decades in advance. And one of the specific stipulations of the non-interference pact was that the Imperium would not detain, waylay, or pursue a petitioner from their appointment with the Matriarch.

And precedent established over the centuries demanded that courtesy be extended to a petitioner's crew and ship, precedent that he could violate only with great cunning or great boldness.

He had them in his grasp, had the final artifact back safe, if not directly in possession. He could order the ship dismantled in order to retrieve the artifact before the prisoners were granted safe passage, but that too would court rebuke.

But if he refused to release them entirely . . . they could scarcely afford it, even without the squabbling over the Illhari. The Drell would lose the war, but the cost and the burden of guilt would crush his faction's standing for centuries.

No result was optimal. So he would work at the edges as best he could to show his ferocity, his loyalty, and his judgment.

"Understood. We will release the petitioner into your care, per the terms of the agreement between our people. Of course, her companions and ship must remain in our custody." Maybe he could feign ignorance and the Drell would leave the Genae's companions in his custody.

The Drell's eyes narrowed, their head tilting slightly to the side. "Thank you, Arek of the House of Ojh. Allow me to clarify. When we invite a petitioner to Yeddix, they become for that time a member of the Migration. They are family. And only that petitioner may decide who counts as their family. I understand that Vsenk culture is different, but this is a place where our traditions must be respected."

A riposte and an insult along with it. He could lash out, could double down. He could even arrange an "accident" for the Yaea or the Atlan on the way to their ship. But what would it gain him? Without the artifact, it would be nothing but petty revenge that would poison the Drell against the Vsenk in any future encounters, costing his faction greatly in standing.

He would double the crew searching the ship, return the Genae and her entourage as slowly as possible. And hope that he could represent his actions well before the watchful eye of the Grand Melee.

"The Genae and her companions will be returned to their ship as quickly as possible, out of respect for your traditions. May the solar winds always guide you home. Cruiser *Vigilance Without Respite* out," he said, giving the traditional farewell-blessing of the Drell.

Arek turned to his staff. "Double the search crews on the ship. Release the prisoners and escort them back as slowly as you can. They are not to be harmed . . . much."

He paused for a moment. "And when their ship has departed, drop back to just within sensor range of the Migration. We will intercept the ship as they depart from their appointment." The protection of the Drell ended with the formal close of the appointment. The Drell could not protest that. Patience would win out.

He turned to the bridge crew, holding their attention. "Am I understood?"

The entire room bellowed, "For the Imperium!"

Arek answered the line, though his mind was dark with worry. He was so close. Victory and shame were equally visible, each waiting on the horizon.

CHAPTER THIRTY-THREE

WHEEL

WHEEL EXPECTED DEATH EVERY step of the way back to the *Kettle*. Especially after the roughhousing they got as the soldiers put the mag-cuffs back on for their walk. Forget what the soldiers said, she knew it was a trap. When they removed the three from their cells, escorted by a half-dozen guards on each side, she expected a firing squad. Turn after turn she expected the worst.

And there were a lot of turns. She wasn't totally read in on the internal layout of Imperial cruisers, but she was pretty sure it hadn't taken this long to get from the ship to their cells.

But in the end, after switchbacks and elevators and long walks down soldier-filled corridors and a gauntlet of death stares, eventually, a set of doors opened onto a landing bay. And at the far end, her baby. She had really thought that she'd never see the *Kettle* again. That she'd waste away or get executed during an escape, that the ship she'd poured her life into would be ripped apart for scrap. Their too-hot-for-comfort cargo lost for good. But Cruji was still within his cage, stomach still bloated with the artifact.

The *Vigilance Without Respite* didn't even follow the *Kettle* as it flew in formation with a two-kilometer-long Drell, communicating through the relay.

"Your appointment has come due, Lahra Kevain. I trust you have your question?"

Lahra toggled the comms off and turned to Max. "Is this one of your jests, love? Did you make an appointment in truth, find some way to shave the time off? I never made an appointment with the Matriarch."

Max shook his head.

Lahra looked to Wheel, who shrugged. "Whatever it is, we'll take it, right?"

The Genae activated the comms again. "I am ready."

CHAPTER THIRTY-FOUR

LAHRA

A S THEY FLEW AWAY from the Vsenk ship, Wheel ran system scans to check for Imperial trackers and set Max and Lahra to doing a visual inspection.

But before long at all, they were back among the Drell Migration.

Instead of docking on Yeddix's shell, the Drell passed them off to a far-smaller junior, who then escorted them to the Matriarch's presence. Several ships clustered by her immense head.

"Your consultation is next, Lahra Kevain. Prepare yourself."

Lahra, Max, and Wheel had spent the entire journey discussing what they should ask.

Max wanted to ask about the artifact, hoping that knowing what it did would help them escape the Imperium. And beyond that, she knew that if he were on his own, he would ask how to get home to Earth.

Wheel would just ask how to get away from the Imperium. Always practical.

For herself, Lahra burned to know where she could find

the Genae heir. But based on the lengths the Vsenk had already gone to in finding the *Kettle* and their cargo, the Imperials would not cease their pursuit. And if she led the Vsenk straight to the heir to the throne, without warning them, the Genae would be truly done for.

Max stood by Lahra's side, squeezing her hand. He was perhaps more nervous than she. He was just a bystander, a witness to this moment that would doubtless shape the destiny of at least one member of the crew, and as many as millions, depending on the results.

Wheel leaned into the command console, down to her elbows, running comms as well as sensors. "I can't be sure, but I think there are Vsenk ships out there, still. They probably think I can't detect them, but what they don't know about proxy sensor repeaters could fill one of their boxy-ass carriers."

The comms came to life. A gentle, melodic voice said, "Petitioner Lahra Kevain. Your time has come. You are in the presence of the Matriarch."

Yeddix's head moved, and the *Kettle*'s viewscreen filled with the sight of one massive eye. They were too close to see the Matriarch's entire face, but even the attention of one eye was almost overpowering.

The next voice was impossibly deep, and yet still somehow audible to her ears. "Greetings, Lahra Kevain. I wish I could have spoken with your mother, but now you inherit her appointment. How fitting that the time for our meeting has come up now, when it is needed. The stars and their workings are an eternal mystery."

Lahra looked to Max. His expression said, "Something is going on." She agreed, thought she read conspiracy in the Matriarch's tone. Had she gotten wind of what was happening to them and moved up the appointment, or was this another stratagem, some move by the Drell against the Imperium?

But it was obvious why her mother had made an appointment—she'd talked about the Drell and their memory but never connected it to the quest for the lost heir. Halra Kevain was not one to hold out needless hope, nor foster it in others, likely why she had withheld the information. If Halra had lived to see Lahra's twentieth cycle, perhaps she would have revealed the rest of her plans. But her life had been cut short by an unlucky rifle-bolt on what should have been a simple escort mission.

Lahra had never had the chance to say goodbye. Now, more than a decade later, her mother was still pursuing her family's quest.

And so Lahra would honor that memory.

I'm sorry, love, she thought.

"Thank you, great Matriarch. I am ready with my question."

"Ask, and be it within my power to answer, I will do so."

Lahra took a long breath, looking straight ahead at Yeddix's massive eye.

"Where do I go to find the rightful heir to the throne of Genos?"

The great eye blinked.

"The Imperial ships are coming closer," Wheel whispered. "Just out of weapons range."

Lahra muted the mic. "How long do they have to give us after we get the answer?"

"I don't know. We ask the escort when she's answered? I get the sense that interrupting the oldest living being in the galaxy would be a bad idea."

Lahra glanced to her side. Max was silent. She saw the hurt and disappointment in his eyes. They had too many mysteries to solve, and one chance. She chose her own quest over every other, and she would face the consequences.

The Matriarch's voice rang out, "Go to Genos."

Lahra froze. Impossible. Genos was dead. The survivors

fled centuries ago.

"What? How?"

"You have your answer, Lahra Kevain," Yeddix said. "Much will be revealed when you visit your homeworld. More than you suspect."

Lahra stumbled through her response. "Thank you, Matriarch Yeddix."

Max jumped in. "I apologize for the intrusion, Matriarch, but we are hounded by Imperial forces. I have reason to believe that they might break the spirit if not the letter of the non-interference pact. If it is within your heart to grant us safe passage to Genos, we have many secrets we could trade, to enrich your already vast stores of knowledge."

Bold. Too bold. But clever.

"I know of the Vsenk that seek you, and why. You carry a dangerous burden." Yeddix's eye moved again, and her voice grew far louder. "Kenoa, you have longed to visit Genos."

Another resonant voice, not nearly as deep, echoed through space and bounced through the translator and relay.

"Yes, grandmother. If you would see wisdom in granting me leave to visit the planet's remains, it would bring me great joy to see it with my own eyes and add to the record."

"If you are to visit Genos, you will need one of their people to show you the way. Lahra Kevain, would you do us the favor of accompanying my granddaughter to your homeworld and granting her what assistance you can in learning the history of your people?"

Lahra looked to Max. He was tearing up. But his expression was one of relief, the sorrow wiped away and forgotten. They'd been hounded halfway across known space by gangsters and tyrants, and finally, they were catching a break.

Wheel muted the comms. "Void. This might just work."

Lahra nodded and re-activated them. "I would be honored, Matriarch. Kenoa, you have my sword and my pledge to accompany you to Genos. I will share what I know of my people as we visit the homeworld together." She took a breath, deciding to press her luck. If the Matriarch was truly an ally, a benefactor, Lahra could do no less. "I have a favor to ask in return. My sister-cousin Eihra, daughter of Xheri, came with her family recently to your city of Xidd, and I would ask that you do what you can to keep them safe."

Yeddix blinked. "It is done. May the solar winds guide you home."

"Thank you, Matriarch."

The functionary came back on the line.

"Kenoa awaits. Are you ready to—"

The signal cut off.

Wheel spat a string of curses. "We're being jammed. It's the Vsenk ship. I can't raise anyone else."

The voice of a Rellix filled their cockpit. "Freighter *Kettle*, this is the cruiser *Vigilance Without Respite*. Your business with the Drell is concluded, and you will return to Imperium custody immediately."

Wheel leaned into the comms. "I'm sorry, Cruiser *Vigilance Without Respite*. As part of the appointment, we've accepted a commission from the Matriarch herself to escort Kenoa of the Drell Migration on a mission and are honor-bound to see it through." Wheel's grin was as wide and pleased as Lahra had ever seen. "If you would like to explain to the Matriarch how you're interfering with one of her children, I would invite you to take it up with her."

Lahra wished she could be aboard the *Vigilance Without Respite* to see the look on the Vsenk's face as he realized that he'd been outmaneuvered. Again. The Imperials could try to pick them up after Genos, but that was tomorrow's problem.

Her mind still spun with questions. Did Yeddix have this all planned out before she even asked her question? Were appointments actually heritable, or had the Matriarch learned of Lahra and the vessel somehow and used them as a lever with which to move the flow of destiny? Would she have volunteered Kenoa if Max had not asked? She'd gotten an answer to a question she'd been asking her whole life, though it made no sense and raised a hundred more. And now they were positioned to escape certain death through the generosity of the oldest creature in existence.

Rather than sinking in the storm of questions, she called up thoughts of her mother, *I will find the heir, mother. I will see our people's glory restored and your memory honored.*

"Signal jam is lifted," Wheel said. "Kenoa, we are ready to depart. Lead the way."

The *Kettle* pulled back and turned, revealing a much smaller Drell, maybe half a kilometer long. Kenoa had a brighter shell, more reds and yellows in her coloring than the greens and browns of the Matriarch.

"Let us depart, then." The Drell turned end-over-end and began swimming away from the Migration, leading them out of the Imperials' grasp.

"The Drell don't use warp space, so how long will it take us to get to Genos?" Max asked.

Figures scrolled across Wheel's eyes, then down and through the console and back. "Twenty days."

"We'll need to arrange a re-supply stop before we arrive at Genos," Max said. "I can't believe it, Lahra. What do you think is there? If it's like the tombs in the forbidden sector, maybe the Devastation left behind some signature, some trail, or maybe there's a coded message." He was swallowed up by excitement, adrenaline from their near-escape channeling into his archaeologist's curiosity.

"I'll check the charts and figure out our options." Wheel waved them out. "Now you two get out of here, I have piloting to do."

Max followed Lahra out of the cockpit, nearly vibrating with excitement. "I'll need to consult my library, look for a baseline of data on accounts of the Devastation and Genos. And spend the rest of the time reading the epics. Though I might need your help reading through fast enough to get to the best parts."

This was Max's way of reaching out, an olive branch, telling her he wasn't pulling away after what she'd done. And it was her world, after all. But right now, she needed to calm her mind.

She paused in the hall by their bunks. "I will join you soon. I need time to reflect, and to focus."

"You mean get sweaty and hit inanimate objects?"

"Yes."

Max floated up to kiss her on the cheek. "When you're done, you know where to find me."

Finding Max was not in question. Lahra worried instead about what else she might find at Genos. It was a barren, broken shell of a planet, shattered by the Devastation. The atmosphere was gone, the cities destroyed; any survivors of the war had long since conducted their exodus and search for a new life in the margins.

But the Matriarch would not send them to Genos for no reason.

The choice she'd seen as far off, perhaps never to be faced, was now on an intercept course. Genos might be the last time that her path and Max's pointed in the same direction.

She was not ready for that moment. She prepared for a hundred scenarios and a hundred more, from what she'd do if a stowaway tried to take the *Kettle* to how she'd bring war to Vsenkos itself.

Here, she had no plan of engagement, only a rising tide of fear and a shaky bulwark of hope.

CHAPTER THIRTY-FIVE

MAX

THE PASSAGE TO GENOS was the longest journey through normal space Max had taken in quite some time. Without jumps, they merely chugged along, occasionally lashing to Kenoa's back in order to preserve fuel when they had to work around or maneuver through gravity wells.

They needed the time. To recover, to think, and for Max to get his head on straight.

He might never get home. But if he could reunite Lahra with her people, this bizarre accident that had landed him far beyond the reach of human imagination—the time he'd spent here—it would all be worth it.

Even if her beautiful future didn't include him. That's what love was, after all, wanting only the best for someone, your own happiness be damned.

Fuck.

He put down his tablet and took another walk around the hold. This defeatist martyr shit was not helping. They would face this together, and he hoped that when the time came, he'd act out of love and not selfishness. Or that he wouldn't have to choose.

Cruji tugged on his pant leg, as if the little creature sensed Max's worry. Cats and dogs would do that back on Earth, comfort people when they were flipping out, so why not a Molja? Just because he looked more like a squid-starfish than a dog didn't mean he couldn't have the same sensitivity.

The Molja had vomited forth the small artifact yesterday, several days after they'd given up on getting him to regurgitate the thing. It was still gross, but not as gross as having to pump his stomach.

Max sat with Cruji, caressing the creature's neck ridge. It cooed with satisfaction as he tried to focus on work and not the hundred-ton freighter of fate barreling his way through warp space.

***

Nine days into the journey, the *Kettle* stopped at a small station to re-supply and re-fuel. Only Wheel left the ship, Max and Lahra staying behind. Max was busy cramming on Genae history and linguistics, Lahra watching the sensors for signs of Imperial vessels.

Kenoa told them that following a Drell on a research voyage would be yet another affront to the non-interference pact. If the Vsenk were following them, it would be a passive tracking, ships spreading out along possible paths and keeping out of sensor range, retreating when they got a signal. Max imagined a loose net of patrol ships, like a pride of lions watching a wounded gazelle from the tall grass. Not that he'd ever seen a lion outside of *National Geographic* featurettes or the Baltimore Zoo.

Lahra was restless. She'd spent most of each day working out, practicing forms, and rehearsing her battle songs. And when he tried to help her wind down, she was prickly. She said little during meals, didn't respond to his friendly banter bait, and seemed like her mind was light-years away. Which, of course, it was.

Would he be any less shaken up if they were just hours

from some hypothetical destroyed Earth colony that could lead him back home? Or if he'd just learned that it even existed? *"There are Terrans on Chiros-3 after all! Too bad you never bothered visiting earlier because everyone says that the whole planet smells like rotten eggs!"*

Lahra was so rock-solid ninety-nine times out of a hundred that seeing her this wound up had him legitimately worried.

Or maybe that was because of the Genae, and the idea that he might lose her to them.

He was stuck in a Zeno's paradox of fear. The closer they got to something, the more Lahra pulled away.

Cruji still wanted him around, thankfully. He made for a cute, if needy and disruptive, research partner, rolling around and climbing Max like a jungle gym, cooing and probing along the way.

Three days later, the *Kettle* and Kenoa finally reached the Genos system; Max was ready to get out and push just so they could get there faster.

Max and Lahra joined Wheel on the bridge once Genos came into high-resolution sensor-range.

The shattered planet was still miniscule in the viewscreen, but the *Kettle*'s sensors painted a more detailed picture.

Genos's water had all evaporated away, the atmosphere dispersed with the planet's destruction. Unlike Yua and the other worlds in the Old Atlan home system, Genos was relatively intact, broken into four or so large sections and a few dozen smaller ones. Where Yua had been detonated from the inside, Genos looked more like someone had taken a gigantic jackhammer to it just long enough for it to lose hold of its atmosphere and then waited for it to die.

Lahra's expression was split between fascination and terror. Max squeezed her hand. No response. She was in her own head.

They got closer, and Max took in the scene himself. He'd heard the accounts, official from the Vsenk and unofficial from Lahra, the story passed down through her mother's line.

Nothing compared to the reality. Genos had been a highly-urbanized planet, like if a third of the Earth's surface were urban sprawl. Pieces of skyscrapers floated alongside the broken hulls of spaceships. Crafted stone and steel, fragments and ruins worn down by micro-meteors over hundreds of years.

"I had never known that so much remained of Genos," Kenoa said over her comm relay. "More here was preserved than on other Devastation sites. I wonder why?"

"My people build things to last," Lahra said. "But given what happened to Yua, Genos seems to be in remarkable condition."

"I wonder how much is left of the capital city?" Max asked.

"The Vsenk bombarded Aeno for weeks before the Devastation. I doubt that much is left. But I will see it for myself."

"Debris is starting to get thicker. Kenoa, can you make a path?"

"Of course. Follow in my wake."

Kenoa took the lead, carving a path for the *Kettle* to pass without having its shields pummeled by the centuries-old ruins of what had been the Genae's home.

Max fed their sensor data back to his workstation, trying to capture information about the patterns of destruction along the fault lines of the Devastation. Information about the Vsenk's secret weapon was highly regulated, and there was no solid data on how it really worked.

Kenoa and the *Kettle* passed through the main clusters of debris and approached what would have been the outer atmosphere of the planet.

"Sensors are showing several structures relatively intact on this larger land mass." Wheel pushed scans to the other panels for Max and Lahra to see.

"That must be the capital. Even after the bombardment,

after the Devastation and centuries of decay, it's still there."

Lahra reached out to the window, as if she could touch it from this distance. Drawn like a moth to the flame. "Take us in."

CHAPTER THIRTY-SIX

LAHRA

THE BROKEN STUB OF the Royal Spire guided them to the center of the city like the spool of thread gifted to the hero in the maze from Max's old Terran story. Kenoa followed the *Kettle* into what would have been low orbit, then into the ruins of the city itself. Kenoa stopped a hundred meters up, just beyond a bramble of towers and building fragments.

"This is as far as I can go. Take this sensor buoy with you. I would see what has become of the capital through your eyes."

"You'll be right there with us," Max said.

Lahra knew he was trying to stay positive, even as they flew through yet another dead world. It was almost endearing how much he tried to make the best of situations, to frame this painful memory of her people's loss in terms of discovery and hope for their future. That he could be so hopeful despite what his people faced back on Earth ... it was remarkable.

She wished she could be more hopeful. But the loss she'd held at bay now flooded over her like solar radiation through a shattered shield. She had no defenses; she felt every moment, every sight on the viewscreen, every sound picked up by the sensors.

I should have been born here, she thought. *I should have lived, fought, loved, and died here. My mother should be buried here.*

She wanted to curl up and cry and at the same time throw herself outside to touch, just once, the world that should have been hers.

But those were fantasies, shadows of another life in another time. Genos was dead, but the Genae persisted.

Max put a hand on her arm and she pulled him in, pressed him against her, a life raft in the darkness of fear.

She would press on, delve deeper, and learn the truth.

If only mother could be here to see this, she thought at last.

"Take us down, Wheel. The guards' entrance should be to the rear, where the western hill would have looked over the ocean." She recited the directions from memory. Her mother had drilled her on that and a hundred other details from home that she herself had only ever learned by rote. So much of her memory of Genos was nearly mythology. But it was all real. It was all here.

She scanned the spire below them, finally spotting a place for the *Kettle.* "The docking clamp there. Is it still functional?"

"Let's find out. Coming down for a docking attempt."

"This is where I find something to hold on to." Max reached for the rail at the far side of the cockpit.

Lahra stood. The ship shuddered as it touched down. As it touched Genos.

She rode out the rough landing, then darted down to the hold.

"EVA gear. Meet me outside when you're ready."

Lahra could not wait one more minute to set foot on Genos. She wondered how many other Genae had come here since the fall, had made it past the Imperial patrols. But no stories of those returns survived in the diaspora. She might be the first. Or maybe just the latest to come and perish, caught by unexploded munitions trapped within the rubble or lost to sorrow.

Lahra hit the panel to seal the interior door of the hold, leaving Max atmospheric pressure to change into his space suit. She retrieved her sword of station, re-attached the power sphere, and donned her armor's helmet, setting it to EVA mode.

I'm home, she thought, opening the outer hold. *Now for answers.*

Her people's songs spoke of a vibrant planet, proud cities with massive parks suspended above buildings to provide shade and grow crops, shining transit lines arcing to the horizon, and ambitious inventions. Foliage intertwined with buildings and adorning roofs—artifice and nature in concert—threaded through Genae life in beautiful harmony.

Now, all was withered and decayed.

She walked out onto the platform and stopped by the docking clamp.

For my mother, she thought, and stepped onto Genos.

CHAPTER THIRTY-SEVEN

MAX

MAX HAD WALKED THROUGH more tombs than he could count, but this was different. Jumping from stone to hull to stone through the long-dead ruins of Genos felt more like going home to meet a girlfriend's family.

Except they're all ghosts and the house is a ruin, he thought. So, pretty messed up. And just as stressful.

Much of the city was still recognizable as such, if long ago given to the entropy of the void of space. Many buildings were intact, their top floors turned into tiny asteroid clusters. A thirty-meter-long tip of one broken tower stabbed through the heart of a broader building, like a staked vampire.

The ruins told the story of warfare, disaster, and decay. Picking out which was which wasn't always easy, but it was exactly the right kind of challenge for Max. He kept silent, leaving Lahra to take the lead. She'd been overwhelmed since they first got sight of Genos. Before that, even. His usually even-tempered wife was a barely controlled tempest. And the best thing he could think to do was bear witness and be there for her.

He never strayed more than a few meters from her as they

floated and climbed across the debris. When she stopped, he stopped. They would lock in grav boots to walk along a building or the street, then bound through the void to another block, another building, another wreck.

"Which way from here?" he asked.

Lahra scanned the broken horizon. "Left. Up and over the barracks. The palace should be beyond. Then we find the back doors."

Kenoa's voice filled his ears. "How do you know which way to go, friend Lahra?"

"My mother sang me the songs that taught our line the secrets of the palace. So that I would know how to use the building itself as a weapon when the time came to reclaim Genos."

Max held shakily to a small asteroid connecting two larger sections of the planet. "I'm glad she did. I don't think that the Imperials would leave us alone for that long."

"Your worry seems warranted. We will be expedient." She sounded so far away, buttoned up, all business and no warmth. Based on what he knew about Lahra, it was a defense mechanism, holding on tighter to avoid overflowing with emotions.

Kenoa's voice came over comms. "The middle-sized buildings appear to have fared the best. Large enough to be well-built, but not so large to be targets for bombardment. Fascinating. Were those buildings older? Newer?"

Lahra looked embarrassed. "I don't know. I would need to study them more closely."

"I think the middle-sized buildings are older. But that depends on whether the Genae changed their construction materials, and if so, when." Max continued thinking aloud as they bounded over debris. The horizon reset every time he landed on a fragment large enough for his brain to call it "down," leaving him disoriented enough that he took it slow. Very slow.

Too slow for Lahra. Of course she'd be rushed, would want to get answers as fast as possible.

There she went again, disappearing over the lip of the barracks.

"Wait up, love!"

"Hurry." The word came out strained.

"Doing what I can!" Max scurried over the broken outer walls of the barracks, avoiding jagged chunks of rock, and bounded into sight of the palace. He wanted to banter, to relieve the tension and occupy the worrying part of his mind with wordplay. But he knew that Lahra wasn't in the mood for it. There was nothing but her questions, her need to know, and the obstacles between her and the answers.

CHAPTER THIRTY-EIGHT

LAHRA

THE TOP HALF OF the palace was obliterated. Lahra and Max picked their way through shattered rubble for twenty minutes until they found a door at ground level. Her ancestor's song had told of a different door. Perhaps the wreckage had shifted over the years. Or others had come on their own search, their own reckoning with the Genae's past.

A semicircular arch cupped a three-meter-tall layered steel door. Max failed to brace properly and landed hard against the wall. But he made it. She'd been engrossed by the door, by the promise it held, hadn't even noticed him coming in.

She'd put Genos and her mission into the distance, assumed it was so far-off it might as well be impossible.

But now she was here, and she didn't have to wait.

Lahra traced her gloved hands across the door, searching for the code pattern. She leaned in, face just a breath away, only her visor between her and the door.

There. They were so faint, worn down over the years. There, the seal of her caste from her mother's books, and inside it, the circular banner of her family.

She evaluated the door, looking for a control panel or a

secret switch.

Two spheres popped out of the wall above the doorway. Lahra pushed Max back, covering him with her body as red lasers swept across her, top to bottom.

Like the Atlan, the Genae used solar panels built into the sides of buildings, and so the palace still had some power even after hundreds of years.

"What was that?" Max asked.

The spheres receded, returning to the door without a trace.

The door shook, then slid open like the wings of a beetle taking flight.

"Genetic scanner."

"Ah."

If it had scanned Max, she'd need to apply an override code. 'Terran' was not a species known to the Genae, and the results of such an error would have been lethal.

"Since it scanned only me on the first pass, my presence should continue to open the door, even with you here."

"Should? This won't, like, activate traps or something because I'm not Genae?"

"We hosted honored visitors. Never Terrans, but I hope that the scanners won't trigger a lethal response once we pass initial clearance."

"Good to know. You first?" Cheer and hope were back in his voice.

His chem-torch would light the world, and the brightness of his spirit kept the shadows of doubt at bay.

"I knew there was a reason I kept you around," Lahra said.

"I thought that was my distractingly charming good looks?"

Lahra cracked the barest hint of a smile. "That's the reason why I let you talk."

Max was the light beyond the shadow, the curiosity that

kept boredom at bay. He was the best kind of trouble, and there was no one alive she would rather have with her on this journey home.

If her mother or grandmother still lived, she would wish to share this moment with them, would sing together as they witnessed the history they'd only learned of from afar.

Max chuckled, tapping through several commands on his wrist panel. "Feed coming through okay for you, Kenoa?"

The Drell's voice rumbled in their ears. "Perfectly. I will keep watch. May the winds carry you to your destination and safely back."

"I'll keep transmitting as long as I can. Don't know how quickly the signal will degrade once we get inside."

"Are you ready?" Lahra asked, as much for herself as her mate. She could only step into the palace the first time once. And given how her life was, once might be all she got.

Max gave the Terran thumbs-up. "Let's go."

Lahra turned the lights on from her helmet and walked inside, grav boots locking onto the floor.

Even now, after centuries of decay, the palace was magnificent. Spared from the void, the walls were filled with color. Purples and golds in concert, swirling across the walls and ceiling. Tile mosaics honoring the gods, telling the story of how the castes were created to design a society in perfect harmony. In another timeline, one where the Genae had felled the Vsenk or reached an armistice, she would have grown up in these halls. Living with pride, surrounded by the colors and the textured beauty of the castes singing in harmony.

As she walked through the hall, the walls sang the story of her people. Pieces of her life, her soul, snapped into place as the recorded chorus filled her ears.

"This is magnificent!" Max said. "The remaining records were so incomplete. It only makes sense in three dimensions, with the audio, like a movie that plays out by optical illusions as you walk. Amazing!"

Max viewed it as a scholar, she as a wayward daughter. But it was still a tomb. Tombs could yield great wisdom.

But wisdom could not raise the dead.

Her mother's songs echoed in her mind as she led them down the hallways. The patterns on the wall gave directions that only one of her caste could read. Being here touched a part of her she'd known was empty but never expected to fill. It was right. Or more right, if not complete. More like proper footing after a lifetime on unsteady ground.

"The throne room is this way."

They scaled down two levels and a kilometer across, judging by the metrics scrolling across her heads-up display.

Kenoa's voice crackled through their comms. "Truly, this palace is a marvel of the stars, unlike any other. To have lost such beauty, such precision. I weep for your loss, friend Lahra."

"Thank you," she said. "But if your grandmother is to be believed, what was lost may yet be re-made. We're approaching the throne room."

The throne room itself was thirty meters tall, just as wide, and a hundred meters long. It served as court, council, ceremonial center, and feast hall. Her people were nothing if not efficient.

Lahra's mind filled in the shattered remains with rows of chairs, tables, tapestries, carpets, and more. She imagined the thousands of lives that would have come and gone through the room over the ages.

But now, it was a dusty, broken shell. The great throne of Genos had a cannon-hole through the middle.

"This is where Queen Selai barely survived an assassination attempt," she said, hand hovering just above the throne. It was not for her to touch, even empty and battle-worn. "A traitor from my own caste, who sold out her people to the Imperium for a promise of riches. But she was caught and executed before she could enjoy the spoils of her betrayal. After that failed attempt, the Vsenk grew desperate, throwing everything and anything they had at the Genae—bombardment, ground invasions, and finally, the Devastation."

She should be proud that it took the greatest weapon in the galaxy to kill her people. But pride alone could not sustain anyone, not even a Genae.

Max chattered, filling the air with his marvel and speculation about the faded remnants of tapestries, the mosaic floor, and the throne itself.

"Do not touch it. It is forbidden," Lahra warned. "Also, the throne was protected by a dozen failsafe systems designed by my ancestors. They might have outlived the planet. The solar circuits were built to survive nearly anything, and all power in the palace flows through this room."

Max pulled back his curious hand. "I'll just observe from here, then."

"That would be wise." Lahra approached the throne again, imagined what it would be like to stand beside it, to serve the royalty as she'd been meant to.

If she had to get the Empress out, down to the bunker, where would she go? Lahra drew her sword, sense memory helping her imagine a battle playing out in the throne room, Vsenk forces led by a noble charging across the expansive space. Angles of attack, defensive formations. She thought through an attack the way Max would talk through the construction and design of a burial chamber, hypotheticals and inferences.

The guards would assemble with the queen and make a fighting retreat. The first place to check would be behind the dais of the throne.

"Behind the throne. Check for switches, or more of those sensors."

Max nodded and hopped down from the dais, setting to work.

She guided him through the patterns, but he found nothing.

Then she looked back to the three exits at the rear of the throne room. They'd come through the one on the far side, cutting in at the corner. That left one at the middle and one on the opposite side. Genae followed the laws of symmetry, so she made her way to the door directly behind the throne, twenty paces back.

"Let's try this way," she said, pointing to the doorway.

"I see a wall."

"The pattern." Lahra pointed to the inward-turned spiral braid pattern. "It signifies digging deeper for contemplation."

"Stairwell?" Max asked.

Lahra stood before the panel, looking for the seams.

Another pair of cameras emerged, scanning her.

"Well look at that." Max beamed. "How do you like being the cultural expert with all the cool knowledge?"

She gave a small smile of acknowledgment. She appreciated the gesture but could not pause for celebration when the answers were at her fingertips.

The four corners receded to reveal a square door, three meters on each side.

"It's an amusing change of pace."

Max gestured with the hand holding the chem-torch, inviting her forward and lighting the way. "In that case, I will enjoy being a hanger-on and light-man while it lasts."

The door led to a stairwell, spiraling down in a tight circle wide enough for two soldiers shoulder-to-shoulder or one fighting with a blade. Here, one of her long-dead cousins could hold off enemies, spending their life's blood to buy the royals time to reach the fallback position and reinforce. As a child she'd dreamed of a glorious death like that. Since then she'd come to expect more of life even as she'd found new people to fight for.

Lahra took the stairs three at a time, just this side of a controlled fall. She was so close, now. She didn't know what to expect, but the palace was welcoming her, guiding her.

Fifty meters. One hundred. Two hundred meters down, and their signal from Kenoa was gone, nothing but static.

The stairwell ended, emptying into a fifty-meter-long hallway, three meters wide.

A killing field. The hall climbed ten meters on a steep grade, giving the defenders the high ground against an oncoming charge.

"Your people don't screw around when it comes to defensive measures."

"Not in the least. If the Vsenk had managed to break through our fleet and our army, we would have clogged the hallways with their dead before they could touch the queen."

Finally, they reached the doors to the royal shelter. They were three meters thick and weighed fifty tons each. They could repel tactical nukes, assuming the seals held.

Lahra approached, and the doors responded. They slid open, each to its side.

They were not greeted by darkness.

Nor another stairwell.

Instead, a squadron of four Genae, their greatswords drawn and sighted, wearing full suits of armor.

They said only, "Halt."

Max looked to Lahra, but she could not move, could not think. She was trapped inside an impossibility, the sight before her shattering her reality.

How?

CHAPTER THIRTY-NINE

MAX

THE GENAE LED MAX and Lahra across a short hallway to another door. Air hissed out as the door expanded. Atmosphere.

The guards tapped their armor, and the helmets folded back into it. Max went to remove his, stopping when a guard shoved a blade in his face.

Touchy.

They were led down another hallway, this one lit by sconces every few meters where the wall joined the ceiling. They reminded Max of the LED trail of lights on the floor of an airplane.

In a polite, air steward-y voice, he imagined: "In the event of an emergency, follow the path of lights you are instructed to follow by the Genae soldiers that shouldn't be here."

Every time Max opened his mouth, one or more of the Genae gave him a hard stare and pointed their blades directly at his forehead.

So it wasn't the time for talking. At least not yet. They walked in silence while he sent text messages to Lahra using the retinal cursor in his helmet.

"Who are these people? Scavengers? Other questors?"

Lahra glanced at him through the visor of her helmet. She looked shaken. *"I do not know. Let me do the talking,"* came her text response.

Their captors led them at last to another reinforced door, which swung open to reveal a wide room about a hundred meters across.

Inside was another set of guards.

And behind them, dozens and dozens of other Genae. Some were dressed in guard's armor; some in simpler, neutral-colored clothes; others in layered vestments; and several in elaborate robes with shoulder adornments and coronets. For the first time ever, Max saw all five of the Genae castes in one place—nobles and priests as well as soldiers, servants, and merchants. Their skin tones ranged from sky blue to royal blue to aquamarine to blues with jewel tones and more.

He'd read all of the books on Genae history and culture he could find, buying up military records, sumptuary guides for approved fabrics and dyes by caste, and more.

But how were they still alive? Had they been here the whole time? How did that even work?

Max looked around the room, trying to put the pieces together.

Down one hallway, he saw a hydroponics station, a sea of green leaves and stems half-obscured by mist.

Two servants and a merchant emerged from a hallway marked with biohazard signs, in heated conversation. An emergency power source, perhaps? Lahra did say their power grid was built to last. Or maybe the room beyond just contained centuries' worth of waste.

He had a million questions, each one spawning two more as soon as they came to mind. Lahra kept her gaze steady, scanning the room. He recognized that look as the front of calm she put up in dangerous situations. If he didn't know her as well, he'd assume she was unfazed. She was fazed, but he could still count on her if things went bad.

The Genae led Max and Lahra to the center of the room, had them kneel, and took Lahra's weapon from her. Max saw her swallow her protest.

One of the nobles approached, a tall, thin woman with a haunted look, the cracks of wrinkles at the edge of her eyes.

"Why have you come?" Her voice was a rich alto, the Genae language flowing from her like a waterfall. Max scanned through his memory, thinking which actress she reminded him of. *Not the most important thing right now,* he told himself. But he'd never seen someone wield their force of will quite that way. Not without a weapon in hand.

Lahra stood tall, shoulders back, head held high. She answered in Genae. "I seek the restoration of our people. The crowning of the true heir. Matriarch Yeddix of the Drell told me I would find answers here. And so I have. But now I have more questions."

The noble narrowed her eyes. "We will ask, and you will answer. Firstly, who are you?" Lahra flinched at the noble's dressing down. Barely. But since this discovery of surviving Genae felt like the floor was moving underneath Max, and he knew Lahra was feeling it even more, he hung on every change in her expression, half like a life raft and half like waiting to see if someone falls so you can catch them.

"I am Lahra Kevain, daughter of Halra, daughter of Aytra. My blade shows my lineage." She gestured with her chin to the sword held by one of the guards.

The noble pointed at Max. "Who is this?"

"He is Max, son of Danielle. He is my spouse."

The noble narrowed her eyes. Not a fan of cross-species marriage, apparently. "Take him away," she said. "I will question our lost cousin further."

Two of the guards grabbed Max and started hauling him away. He dashed off a quick message to Lahra, asking her to not fight. Not yet. They had to get answers.

As they led him away, Max took the opportunity to commit as much of the secret refuge to memory as he could. Numbers, technology, designs, food, schedules. He didn't have Lahra's training for tactical analysis, but if he framed it in terms of a living site, it was easier to take in and not panic about what they were going to do to the two of them.

So much of this rested on Lahra's shoulders. If they were going to come out of this alive, it'd be because of her.

They'd come to this planet looking for answers and ended up in a whole new world of uncertainty.

CHAPTER FORTY

LAHRA

LAHRA WATCHED AS THEY marched her husband out of sight. He put on a brave face, told her not to fight, but she could read his expressions at a hundred meters. Her mind played out a dozen different escape plans, but they all ended with the two of them tossed out into the void around Genos.

If they hurt Max . . .

Spilling Genae blood was forbidden. There were special exceptions from the throne, or if the killer could make a strong enough case before her family. Countless songs focused on a Genae caught between loyalties, trying to justify sororicide to herself and to her family.

She'd tried to find Genae community on the Wreck, found Genae spaces where she could, but none of that—not the songs, the drills, none of it—prepared her for this. All at once she had fallen deep into the hierarchy like she'd never known.

She had pledged her bond to Max, and if her people didn't respect the bond, did they have the right to be considered her kin? But she should not be hasty.

"What do you want from me?" she asked the noble.

"We must ascertain whether you are a spy for the Imperium or some other faction. If you are a true and loyal Genae, you will be welcomed back into the fold and we will find a purpose for you."

The presumption. But they had every reason to be suspicious. How many others could have found the castle in the past centuries? What had these Genae done already to keep themselves secret? Lahra kept her voice level, swallowing her anger. "I have a purpose. It is the purpose, the only purpose for my caste. I seek the lost heir."

"Many have sought the heir," the noble said. "Each generation, we sent our best and brightest to the rendezvous coordinates, where a surviving heir would have gone after the loss of their homeworld. None have returned. We stopped fifty years ago; there is no help in the void. If there is an heir, she will come home eventually, and we will join her. For now, we ensure the survival of our people."

A shudder passed over Lahra. "You call this survival?" She gestured to the room. "Thirty-thousand-square meters and no plan?"

"Do not raise your voice to me, Yevoh," the noble said, using the word for "down-caste." It hit Lahra like a slap to the face. These were the first nobles she'd met. She was supposed to be deferent. Attentive. But that deference was given in acknowledgment of good judgment and leadership derived from the queen's wisdom. There was no queen, and these distant cousins had not yet proven their wisdom in doing anything more than surviving.

"I have been out in the stars, lived among dozens of other species. They barely remember us. Our people have become mercenaries, drifting on solar winds. There are enough here to start a proper colony, to call back the hundreds of us out in the stars. You've hidden in the shadows. Now is the time to step back into the light."

"Remember your place, Yevoh. You protect. We lead."

The noble turned and stormed off, crisp steps echoing with resentment.

How did our ancestors get anything done with leaders this obtuse? Lahra wondered. Had these Genae fallen that far? Or were her people always this obstinate and hidebound? She'd only interacted with other soldiers, merchants, and servant-caste Genae. Most of her people didn't talk about the past this way. They focused only on the now, on what they could control. The Genae here seemed haunted by their past, afraid to build a future.

An attendant flanked by two guards approached. One held her sword.

"I am Maure," said the attendant. "I'll be checking your lineage claims. Please present your arm for a blood sample."

One of the guards produced a silver stick. Lahra opened the medical port in her amour, and they took the sample. Another first. Her mother told her that Genae were known by names and lineage. Lying was out of the question, since even after the Devastation, the Genae that remained kept good enough track to be able to tell a claim that was out-of-tune.

"Tell me about your mother," Maure said. "Everything you know about your lineage, back to the Devastation. We will consult the ancestral records."

Lahra recounted her full post-Devastation ancestry, dating back to Viehra Kevain. Viehra had escaped from the siege on Genos with her charge, a minor noble who quit the fight, abandoning her family militia unit.

"Viehra Kevain stayed loyal even when the baronet abandoned her people, quitting the battle above Genos. The baronet died three years later. With no charge to protect, no heir to inherit that bond, Viehra set her sights on restoring the royal line. She taught her daughter the songs, and her granddaughter, and so on for seven generations, leading to me."

Maure continued asking about Lahra's travels among the stars in exhaustive detail. Every member of every species she'd talked to, every planet she'd visited, every relationship, and so on.

"How did you meet this Max, son of Danielle?"

Lahra crossed her arms, leaning back. "That story is our own and need not be shared. We met, we joined forces for a shared mission, and we fell in love."

"Your cooperation is essential."

Obstinance would not help her move things along, but some lines should not be crossed, even to placate an obstinate foe that might become an ally. "There is nothing in the story of how Max and I met, or the progress of our relationship, that is essential from a tactical or strategic perspective."

"That is for leadership to decide, not you."

Lahra began to clench her fists. She stopped herself, laying them against her sides in a proper ready position. "Then let them decide. If they wish to press me, they can explain how it benefits the Genae to violate my privacy to serve a leadership that will not lead."

Maure moved on to other topics. Perhaps an hour later, another attendant returned with a report. Maure scanned it, then nodded. "Your bloodline claim was validated. We'll analyze your report, and when the nobles have made their decision as to whether you can be trusted, we will call on you." Judging by Maure's expression, what the attendant really wanted was for Lahra to be thrown out the airlock.

The feeling was mutual. Is this what it was like for her ancestors before the Devastation? Treated as so much meat to be ordered around according to the whims of the nobility? Where were the songs about that? Were they another casualty of the diaspora, or had they never been permitted? Did guards complain about power-hungry nobles throwing away lives the way Max's people did? Or was there something wrong with her—had she spent too much time outside the chorus of her people? Could the Genae ever be what they were, or was the chorus a lie, too?

Then they took her to a cell. Max was inside. He beamed like it was their wedding day all over.

Lahra grabbed hold and did not let go of him for a long time.

She was finally home. Then why did it feel like anything but?

CHAPTER FORTY-ONE

WHEEL

HUNDREDS OF KILOMETERS ABOVE the ruins of Genos, Wheel and the *Kettle* sat in the gravity shadow of the fragmented planet.

Wheel leaned back in the pilot's seat. Cruji snorfled at her hip, tentacle-arm probing into one of her pants' many pockets, looking for treats.

She reached down and pulled the little nuisance up into her lap as the ship decoded an incoming message. The Molja cooed his approval, wrapping tight around her leg and waist.

The message wasn't from Kenoa.

This signal was triple-encrypted.

Which meant it came from Cog.

Exerting her will, Wheel pulled back the final layer of encryption. Cog appeared on the *Kettle*'s viewscreen.

"Hey there, wanderer," she said.

"How are you doing, rabble-rouser?"

Cog looked even more tired than last time. The fight was taking its toll, and quickly. Atlan could live more than a hundred years. But both women lived hard, burning their lifespans like booster fuel.

"People are nervous, Wheel. There are rumblings out of Vsenkos. Dozens of ships have returned from deep space over the last few days. Rumor says there's going to be a Grand Melee."

Wheel's whole body shuddered as one. "Void take us. There hasn't been one of those in what, four years?"

"Sounds about right."

Because the Vsenk were violent fucks, when their leadership couldn't agree, all the nobles with the status to vote in their ruling council jumped into a sandpit and beat the crap out of one another until either only one faction was left standing or someone conceded.

It was an utterly terrible way to govern. But it was incredibly Vsenk. Might makes right was their entire thing.

"Any word on why they called it?" Wheel asked.

"Not yet. Some of the folks think it's because they're onto us, but that's just the paranoids. We know Imperial Intelligence's capabilities, and we've stayed clear of their probes and plants."

"So let's assume it's not the Imps getting on our trail. What else could it be?"

Cog rolled her eyes. "Who the void knows. One Vsenk looked funny at another one's brother."

"For ragging on their intelligence, you're not giving me a whole lot."

She shrugged. "I'd guess it's something about trade and production quotas. That's what they've been fighting over mostly the past few years, pushing back and forth on ways to bleed more money out of us commoners. Maybe something about the last failed expedition beyond warp space. But that's my best guess."

"So you're sure it's not about the mystery box my lovebirds found?"

Cog's brave facade cracked. "Void, maybe. But how important could it be if it was just stuffed in some broken temple in the ass-end of the system?"

"That's for Max and his brainy-people to figure out. Just keep your sensors active. If the Vsenk are getting riled up, right when we're getting ready . . ."

"I hear you."

"Anything else I should know about?" Wheel asked.

"There's a data packet attached. Nothing else urgent. Just get to Illhar as soon as you have something solid on the mystery box. I don't like the idea of you out and bouncing around between systems while the Vsenk are losing their shit."

A gloating grin took shape, thinking of Cog getting upset about her welfare. "I didn't know you still cared."

"I like that ship. And your little Molja monstrosity is cute." Cog pointed at Cruji. "May the stars guide you home."

"And you," Wheel answered. Wheel hugged Cruji, keeping still as the little beast stuck a tentacle up her nose. He was worried. Damned thing could read emotional states better than most sapients.

She prided herself on many things, but she wasn't the sort who was good at processing her own feelings. Feelings got you killed. Instincts and skill were the way to go.

Wheel checked the comms and saw the follow-up data packet. She set the computer to decrypt and got up for a walk, Cruji still in-arms.

Hurry up, you two . . .

CHAPTER FORTY-TWO

LAHRA

THE NEXT MORNING, ANOTHER member of the soldier caste came to retrieve Lahra from her room with Max. They'd spent the evening sharing information, speculating on what the Genae would do to them, and trying to get a signal to Wheel. And some other things. For maintaining morale. The room was inevitably being watched. *Let them watch,* she'd thought.

The guard, Nevrau, was of a height with her, with darker blue skin and jewel undertones.

"You've been given probationary status. You will be watched closely. If you serve well, perhaps you will be trusted."

She didn't need their trust. Just answers. Lahra had already faced censure and suspicion for marrying out of her species. But that they mistrusted her for keeping faith, for daring to keep any part of her life to herself?

Who were these people? Were they even Genae anymore? Or had her mother songs been a beautiful lie for her, one that masked the dissonance of their people's past? And did they expect her to stay, now? Would she be required to take duty rotations with the rest, to just fall into their centuries-long holding pattern?

Being back among her people, she felt out of place, like she'd lost part of what made her Genae.

Or was it that the survivors had lost something? When your world died, how did you say who was or wasn't honoring its memory? Isolation or adaptation—the choice lay bare before her. One here with the sisterhood, one path moving forward with Max; one was familiar but felt like an abandonment of her duty. The other was what she been raised to pursue but felt nothing like she'd expected.

Nevrau walked Lahra through the compound with efficiency and no warmth. "This is our barracks and testing ground." A long room with rows of bunks and a slightly padded floor at the end, wall lined with training weapons and gymnasium equipment, most of it well-worn.

Genae equipment was made to last, but this bunker strained the craft of her people. Did they have absolutely no contact with the outside world? Had that stopped with their expeditions? Did they have no merchant-craftspeople to make new tools?

These were the questions she wanted to ask, but instead she chose a more tactful route. "Everything here is in remarkably good shape. Do you bring in supplies?"

"We are self-sufficient. This facility was designed to protect a royal heir and her household for hundreds of years if needed, with fusion generators, waste reclamation, material refactors. We added solar panels to the jagged end of the crust shortly after the Devastation." Nevrau pointed to her left, which Lahra thought of as North—the same direction they'd come in, or the far side of the facility.

Refactors. That explained the same-ness, the lack of innovation. "Your engineers do the crown proud," she said, continuing to flatter. None of these Genae had been off-planet. Most had likely never been beyond the halls where she and Max were captured. She thought about a life like that and despaired.

Nevrau nodded. "They are sufficient. For the most part."

The tour continued. The runner lights flickered several times as they passed through a back hall. She glanced at Nevrau for a reaction, but the other Genae gave her nothing. Lahra filed away the detail to consider later. Once out of the hallway, Nevrau showed Lahra the hydroponics bay, the material refactors, and finally, their archives.

Scanning the shelves of books and lines and consoles, the lines of artifacts and tapestries, Lahra said, "My husband would wrestle a full-grown La-ta-reh to get access to these. Can we get him approved? He will not do well if kept locked away in those chambers."

"If he is monitored by a scholar, I think it might be arranged. He is literate?"

"He reads more languages than I do. Several more. And he's visited over a dozen major Atlan ruins."

"They might find that interesting," Nevrau deadpanned.

And Max thinks me to be emotionally flat, she thought. Her caste wasn't known for their warmth or affection, but all Genae had passions. What they felt in private did not always show in their work. Duty came first.

"Who is your charge?" Lahra asked in the formula of her caste.

"Noble Ahlair. You haven't met her. She is ill. Bedridden. She may take some months to die."

"I'm sorry. I hope her passing will be painless."

"It won't be." Nevrau's voice softened. "But thank you."

Nevrau led Lahra through the rest of the complex, save for the nobles' wing, which looked like it comprised a full third of the total size of the facility.

"This concludes our tour. Here is your schedule. The scholars wish to glean as much information about current events and recent history as is possible. Your . . ." Nevrau's face scrunched up, "charge is expected to attend, as well.

When your obligations to the crown are discharged, you may pursue your own inquiries. Come to the door of the noble wing at 20:00. The nobles will then provide further instructions. You are dismissed."

Nevrau turned and walked toward the nobles' quarters, leaving Lahra by the door of her shared chambers with Max.

She opened the door, and Max was lying on the bed, his legs up on the wall. He did this during long bouts of reading and thinking—shifting every few minutes, each position more ridiculous and less sustainable than the one before. This one told her he'd probably been plotting or processing the whole time she was gone.

The door closed behind her. "I hope you appreciate now that I am much more fun than my cousins."

"You're not lying. Most of them look at me like I'm wasting their air. I liked it better when I got to leave that look behind on Earth."

The social dynamics of Earth had never quite made sense to her, but why would they? The Genae were one species with several castes. Humanity had a different history, different biology (not that different, thankfully), and different environments. They were all one species. But they had still managed to create so many divisions to fight over.

Max had speculated several times that if humanity ever met other species writ large, it would probably only form another layer of conflict and division.

But here, amongst the stars, he was taken to be just another Yaea, one of many million.

Lahra reviewed the sights she'd seen, the things she'd heard from Nevrau. "Being here reminds me of the Fhrea. I'd never really understood them before, living apart from my people."

The Fhrea tradition of songs were all meant to be inter-caste critiques, all told through allusion. The use of truth and their common ancestry to remind the Genae of the beauty and essential nature of each caste, of their people as one organism—the queen the brain, the soldiers the sword hand, attendants the eyes, and so on.

"Maybe we can catch a show before we head out." Max's eyes lit up with mischief.

"We've already given them a show; it's only fair we get to see one in return." She took another half-step forward and took his face in her hands. She kissed him slowly, reveling in having time just for them, away from questions, from expectations, from the future.

"Speaking of giving them a show . . ." Max tossed his shirt over the camera in the corner just below the ceiling. Then he matched her, wrapping arms around her back, one up, one down. She wished to turn every fiber of her attention to sensation, but a niggling hook of duty pulled at her.

She stepped back. "We are expected."

Max smiled, incorrigible. "They can wait."

So be it.

CHAPTER FORTY-THREE

WHEEL

WHEEL WAS TIRED OF waiting. Kenoa had flown up to low orbit to join her, so she'd spent most of the day talking to a destroyer-sized turtle while a barely-sentient tentacle-beast tried to stick its limbs up her nose.

"How long should we wait before going in after them?" Kenoa asked. "I will not be able to enter the palace, but . . ."

"You're presuming I could. Lahra said that the Genae had genetic locks on their doorways, so how would I get in?"

"Do you not have items of Lahra's on-board that would carry her genetic signature?"

"Depends on how the locks work." Wheel stood to check. She wired Kenoa's speaker-drone into her earpiece and slid down the railing, headed for Max and Lahra's bunk.

"She better forgive me for the intrusion. You'd hope 'I rummaged around your dresser so I could come in and rescue you' would fly as an excuse, but you haven't known Lahra as long as I have. I mean, she'd complain for a while, but also be grateful for the rescue. And then resent needing to be rescued."

"I believe she will understand. The drive to preserve life is pre-eminent in all moral species."

Wheel rooted through piles of gear and random crap, looking for something acceptably fresh. "Tell that to the Vsenk."

After a beat, Kenoa said, "I would not classify them as a moral species."

"I think their compassion just extends about as far as their noses."

"They don't have noses."

"I thought they were just internal? Take in air for stimuli, not for breathing. Then they sort the stimuli."

"I wouldn't call their perceptive sacs noses."

Wheel shrugged with her elbows. "That's fair. But you get the idea. They only care about the in-group. Vsenk mothers probably love their babies, but an Atlan baby, or a Yaea? Not so much."

Wheel picked out a shirt Lahra had worn recently while exercising. To her disgust and delight, it was still damp. She proceeded directly to the ship's lab at Max's workstation and squeezed the garment onto a slide, producing a few drops of sweat, and set the scanner.

She walked back up to the cockpit to check the sensors while the scanner processed the genetic material and fabricated. Still nothing from the lovebirds.

Most of an hour later, it was done. These finger caps used Lahra's fingertips and a thin sheen of oils based on her genetic signature. More than enough for the job. The tech she was using had only been perfected in the last 30 years, so there was no way the centuries old Genae biometric security was advanced enough to detect the fraud.

Hopefully.

She printed up a set of backups, then returned to the cockpit.

"I'm taking the ship down. Follow me in?"

"As far as I can. I came to witness, and the story is far

from over."

"Oh, I'm betting we're right in the middle of it, no end on the horizon."

"Horizons in space are a difficult thing." Kenoa paused. "That was an idiom, yes?"

"You got it. Watch the debris. Here we go."

Wheel punched the engine, and the *Kettle* and the Drell descended toward the ruins of Genos.

Genos was in bigger chunks than Yua had been, which made navigating easier. Up to a point. Soon Wheel found herself steering the ship through the narrow space between spinning chunks of city half a kilometer across. She left Kenoa in low orbit, keeping in touch through the relay.

Following the path Kenoa had relayed from Max and Lahra, she spotted the palace and plotted a course down to land and see if she could hack and or fake her way inside to see what had become of the lovebirds.

A pair of automated cannons pivoted up and took aim at her ship.

Voiddammit. Wheel pushed the *Kettle* into an evasive dive. Lahra always said the Genae built things to last. Of course the point defense cannons would still be active. It was just her luck. Built to protect the Genae and now they were keeping the friend of one of the last living members of the species from helping.

A third cannon from the side of the palace came to life and clipped the *Kettle*, sending her spinning.

Space this, I'll have to pull out and find another way in, she thought, furious at the Genae for taking exactly the wrong lesson from the Old Atlan in building their weaponry to outlive their civilization.

CHAPTER FORTY-FOUR

MAX

THE GUARDS LED MAX and Lahra through the noble wing.

Even in hiding, the nobles maintained their standards of living as best they could. And why wouldn't they? The nobles represented the Genae at their most refined, their most glorious. Without a queen, the job of inspiring the people fell to the nobility.

The guards led them to what looked like a conference room. It was lushly appointed, tapestries and instruments finely displayed on all walls, but he didn't have time to browse.

Three nobles sat on one side of the table. The guards seated Max and Lahra on the other. Max noticed that his and Lahra's seats were lower than the nobles'. *This is some subconscious power play bullshit,* he thought. It was straight out of an intergalactic MBA program.

Max took a steadying breath. Nothing to worry about. Just a pleasant conversation with reclusive nobles certain of their superiority, surrounded by armed guards and hundreds of other people suspicious of him largely because of what he looked like. It was almost like being back home.

The noble on the right spoke. Her hair was the least ornate of the three, a single braided strand around the line where a hat would sit. "I am Palrae. This is my aunt, Mirai"—the woman gestured to the Genae on the opposite side, a middle-aged woman with three-layered hair—"my mother, Lejoh,"—Lejoh sat in the middle, clearly the oldest and of highest-status, judging by the braided masterwork that was her hair. Palrae continued. "You are required to answer further questions. Once you answer satisfactorily, we will determine how you will be used."

Everything about this woman's language and bearing set off alarm bells in Max's head.

"We understand," Lahra said, her voice clear, strong.

Lahra went first, filling in her life's story, tracing her family's ancestry back to the destruction of Genos, even though she'd already told it to another of the Genae earlier. Lahra told the rough outline of how they met, how he hired her to get his feet under him. How they fell in love. Lahra wasn't exactly effusive with emotion around strangers, but hearing her tell the story of their romance got him a bit choked up, which was highly uncomfortable given the steel-eyed Genae staring them down the whole time. Not quite as fun as telling the "How Did You Meet?" story to extended family.

Max reached out and squeezed Lahra's hand as she continued. She summarized their adventures together. However, she left out the three artifacts they'd recovered from Yua.

Lying, even by omission, was a form of defiance. Lahra had spoken more than a few times about the absolute obedience required by the nobility—all were required to uphold the hierarchy, the divine chorus of the castes. His heart warmed, and then instantly sank. What would the nobles do if they found out that she was lying to them?

The only way out was through.

Next, it was his turn.

When they asked his story, he answered with the first

verse of the *Fresh Prince* theme.

None of them got the joke, but it wasn't for them. It was for him. To help him calm down.

With a smile on his lips, he switched to the real story.

They dismissed his claims to be from an unknown planet from beyond warp space, asked questions about Earth thinking they were being clever and forcing him into revealing his lies.

So he started talking in English. Lahra joined him. They went back and forth, talking about how frustrating these nobles were.

"I'm hungry," he said in English. "Think they'll feed us anytime soon?"

"That's probably enough taunting the people who are holding us captive."

Palrae said, "Stop. We accept that you speak a tongue unknown to us. Please continue in a proper language."

Max switched back to Genae, grinning.

He told his version of how he and Lahra met, as well as a greatest-hits version of the Atlan sites they'd visited, the artifacts they'd found (not including the ones Uwen had paid extra for them to tell no one about or the ones Lahra had omitted), and then skipped ahead to their visit to the Drell and being pointed at Genos.

These people didn't need to know about their apparently valuable finds. All they'd do was demand Lahra hand them over. That was if there were any chance of the two of them getting off the planet for the rest of their lives.

Mirai, the aunt, spoke up. "You're leaving something out. Perhaps we did not make ourselves clear."

Max exhaled a long breath rather than lashing out in frustration. "Do you want to hear what I had for lunch every day along the way? Fair warning, it's mostly algae soup. I guess I could give you recommendations for where to find good Genae food on the Wreck."

Lahra gave him a look that suggested he lay off the snark. "We told you everything important. Greater minutia will not serve the Genae."

Finally, the elder Lejoh spoke. "We've intercepted broadcasts from the Vsenk about fugitives matching your description exactly. Would you care to explain?"

Lahra's face sank. She'd made the call to protect Max and Wheel, and they'd called her bluff. She affected a shrug. "The work we do is illegal. Of course the Vsenk would have us in their files."

Lejoh narrowed her eyes. "They also described your crimes. Theft of valuable artifacts from the forbidden sectors. From Yua, shattered by the debris from the first Devastation."

Fuck, Max thought. They'd known the whole time.

The noble continued. "Those artifacts could contain information about the Vsenk's weapon. You will share everything that you've learned of Kelmai."

"What's a Kelmai?" Max asked. As soon as he spoke, he regretted it. Confirming or buying into anything they said was tantamount to admitting that they'd been deceitful.

Lejoh cocked her head, slightly. "I see. Niece, bring me the Record." Max could hear the capitalization in her tone.

"Sister . . ." the elder said.

"Trust me. This serves the crown."

The youngest noble stood and walked out of the room with uncanny grace.

Max looked to Lahra, the *"what's going on?"* question as clear on his face as he could manage.

She shrugged. It was a gesture so unlike the Genae here. It was half the Terran gesture he'd taught her and half the Atlan elbow shrug.

Palrae returned with a massive hard-bound book, ten centimeters thick and as long as the noble's arms. She set it on the table between them, spinning it around to face Max and Lahra. She opened the book and paged ahead to the final third. She opened to a page with Genae calligraphy as well as illuminated images of a heavily-augmented Atlan standing astride a shattered world.

Palrae pointed to the Atlan. "This is Kelmai. This is the source of the Devastation. Kelmai is not just a weapon. He was an Atlan."

Max could read Genae, just not quickly. Their writing was all set to music, and he had to slow down to pace it out correctly so that the structures made by the timing worked out.

Max's voice shook as he asked, "Can you read this for me?"

Lahra scanned the page. Just as she was about to start, Lejoh spoke.

"It is forbidden for outsiders to know the Record."

Mirai shook her head. "The royal line is broken, sister. We've sent and lost countless soldier-cousins since the fall, and now we've all but abandoned the notion that the crown can be restored. But if the Vsenk seek to use Kelmai again, I will not stand by and let another people suffer as we have. Do you want another dead planet, another shattered people on your conscience? Because I do not."

The elder exhaled a long sigh. "Proceed."

Palrae resumed. "Kelmai was an Atlan engineer of the highest renown. He endlessly tinkered with life, especially himself. He made himself immortal, unaging, and terrifyingly powerful. He pushed the Atlan to war, to conquest. He created the Vsenk as his elite troops, but the greatest among them desired more power. The Vsenk turned against him, using devices created by other Atlan, and took control of his mind and body."

Max had suspected that the official histories were missing some details of the old empire's fall, but this was far wilder than he had imagined. He looked to Lahra. Her eyes were wide, too. He squeezed her hand as Palrae spoke.

"The Vsenk then turned on the Atlan, using Kelmai's control over gravitic forces to destroy entire worlds. He reversed Atal's gravitational field, stripping it of atmosphere, shunting its oceans, and cracking the core and mantle open from the inside. The debris hurtled across the system, shredding satellites and space stations, even causing chaos in a neighboring system. And then, the Vsenk did it again, in the same system. This time on Refuge, the first planet colonized by the Atlan. The system was reduced to rubble, a half-dozen planets and moons rendered to nothing.

"After his rampage, the Atlan who had created the vessel and keys recaptured Kelmai and locked him away, hiding him from the Vsenk."

"Then what destroyed Genos?" Max asked.

"When Kelmai disappeared after the Devastation annihilated the Atlan worlds, the Vsenk spent centuries trying to replicate his power. And when their efforts to suppress us in the revolution failed, they brought their weapon to bear. It was a pale imitation of Kelmai."

The puzzle clicked into place. "Which is why the destruction on Genos was so much less—buildings more intact. It cracked Genos open more than exploded it."

"Your mate is not without wisdom," Lejoh said to Lahra.

Max leaned back in his chair, mind running through the implications. They'd stumbled onto the greatest archaeological and historical find in this entire galaxy, and he'd thought it was, what, just another tomb? He'd been close to fencing it and moving on. *Oh, here's the Ark of the Covenant. I need rent money, off you go.*

He pulled himself back to the moment. "So, this was one person? One Atlan destroyed every planet in that system? How? And how did the Vsenk erase that much history? How are the Genae the only ones that remember? Why is this galaxy so fucked up?" Max's voice rose with frustration and fear as he spoke.

Lahra said, "The Vsenk have had centuries to purge the Atlan Empire from memory. They've stolen away artifacts, censured planets, controlled education." She was keeping her cool, but he could see the anger in her eyes. The Genae had been hiding here keeping a secret from the galaxy for centuries and seemed totally disinterested in the idea that other planets could meet Genos's fate. He didn't have to imagine hard to know how frustrated she must be.

Mirai turned toward her sister. "Our refusal to forget the universe before their rise was part of why Genos was destroyed."

"I just assumed they weren't that good at erasing history," Max offered. "Considering how much we've found over the years. This is wild. I mean, if I'd known that's what the vessel was, I could have run tests. I need to get back to my workstation." He stood, and the Genae guard took a half-step forward.

"I mean, if our gracious hosts permit. While this history is known to you, the Vsenk have succeeded in suppressing it in the modern Empire. We need to tell the rest of the galaxy."

"Sit," Lejoh ordered.

Lahra reached out a hand and helped Max back to his seat. Her eyes said, *"Patience, love."*

They talked more, Mirai walking them through the text, through the scant details they had.

"People need to know about this," Max said. "They deserve to know the true nature of the Devastation. Also, how can they control him? If they betrayed Kelmai, why doesn't unleashing him lead to their destruction? I need a full translation. Everything you have. We can stop them before they can use him on another planet."

Mirai began to speak, but Lejoh cut her off. "You will return to your chambers. There, you will be informed of your fates."

Max reached for the book for one last look. He was met

with the tips of several blades. He backed away, hands up. "Sorry, sorry."

Lahra stood and snaked her arm through Max's elbow. "Thank you, bright ones." And then she started for the door.

"But the—"

"Please, love. I can already tell you'll need hours to process what they said. We have time. Wheel can wait."

CHAPTER FORTY-FIVE

AREK

AREK STOMPED DOWN THE gangplank and set foot on Vsenkos for the first time in almost a year. He took in the rose-red sky, the mighty stems of the nobles' towers, the vast gardens. All the wealth of the Empire passed through Vsenkos, and much of it never left.

He'd been out-maneuvered by the Drell, not once, but twice. So when the message came from Qerol, he expected a dressing down, not delight at Arek's retrieval of two of the minor artifacts and an order to return to homeworld. His duty rotation lasted another year, so this was a blessed reprieve.

Assuming he got to spend any time at home. All he wanted to do was see his wife and daughter, but duty came first.

A Rellix attendant jumped into pace with him. She was small, with blue-gray feathers.

"Your Excellency, I am Tra-el. The artifacts arrived safely?"

"They're all on-board. Have them brought to Qerol's chambers under guard."

"Of course, Your Excellency. Qerol and the others are

awaiting you in the faction chambers before the opening of the floor."

"How long do I have?"

"The gavel will be struck at the high sun." But that would be on-planet time, not the ship-board clock they used.

"How long is that? As you can see, I've just landed." Another Vsenk might be more cross with the Rellix, but he was not other Vsenk.

"My apologies. You have an hour, Excellency."

Crowds of Rellix, Yaca, and other members of the minor species parted before him like the wake of a star-cutter. Arek took the datapad offered to him. The Rellix had prepared a schedule and a precis for the council meeting. A half-dozen mundane items that were required to keep the government moving. Appropriations bills, official declarations of holidays honoring the glorious Vsenk history, and another inane attempt to outlaw ancestor worship on the border planets despite a consensus ruling dictating that polytheistic folk practice was permissible as long as Vsenk were honored as the high gods and the taxes were paid on time.

In other words—tedium. The real debate had yet to be officially announced.

The meetings of the Great Council of the Vsenk were held in a coliseum within the Imperial Palace. The palace was like a many-limbed tree, wings reaching out like tentacles, each holding the chambers of a group of Vsenk nobles when they were in session. The core chambers and coliseum occupied the trunk, where the entire nobility came together to rule.

The faction chambers were all, by necessity, smaller than their permanent chambers, and were yet another privilege that the Vsenk fought over. Who had what view of the suns as they set, who occupied the highest quarters, who had private elevators, and so on.

Other species thought the Vsenk petty, and they were not

wrong. But when your entire species numbered only in the thousands, what might seem like minor movements in status and hierarchy for another species had huge repercussions for the Vsenk. His people reproduced slowly—conception was rare, and gestation lasted a decade. His wife's one child already put them in the top third of fertility for their people. While the vassal species were plentiful, the Vsenk struggled to grow. Most decades, as many died in the field or Grand Melees as were born.

When you were at the top, there was nowhere to go but down. And every Vsenk was taught to view themselves at the top. Though only a quarter of Vsenk were counted as nobility, even a Vsenk commoner was as nobility when compared to the lesser peoples.

But Arek knew that he had a long way to go. He'd been fighting an uphill battle his whole life, struggling against his family's low station, his diminutive size, and his unease with cruelty.

And so, as he stepped into the quarters of Qerol's faction, his faction, he stood tall, prepared to fight for everything he could get. These artifacts were important—enough that ambition and hope sparked in his heart. The sparks were small, fragile, but they could be stoked into a great flame . . . if he could seize the opportunity.

Qerol caught his eye immediately, the broad-shouldered Vsenk holding court. He was surrounded by allies and sycophants, other nobles in his faction milling about in groups and on their own. Some read datapads, some ate and drank as vassal attendants strapped armor to them. Each noble's armor was unique, adorned with house and faction colors as well as depictions of their individual glory.

Qerol threw two of his arms open in a gesture of greeting. "Arek! Returned from the Forbidden Sectors with our winning play."

Arek matched the gesture, and the two embraced. Qerol

stood two meters taller than Arek, one of the largest Vsenk alive. Legends said their ancestors were ten meters tall and could tear through a Dreadnaught with their bare claws, though Arek suspected those tales were as embellished as the rest of the history his people propagated. But Qerol's strength and loyalty were no lies.

Arek spoke in a soft voice. "What are those artifacts? And the others are all wearing armor. Do we expect this to come to blows?"

Qerol crossed one set of arms. "I do. Evam has drummed up some nonsense about a revolutionary group on Illhar. He has convinced his faction that it demands immediate intervention."

Illhar was one of their worlds, overseen by Qerol and his faction, the Bright Suns. The Special Economic Zone had been Qerol's idea—give the Illhari more flexibility, more economic autonomy . . . as long as they still paid their taxes. The results had filled the Bright Suns' coffers. He'd received no word of insurrection in the latest reports from the governor.

"What evidence does Evam have of this insurrection?"

Qerol waved the question off as irrelevant. "Suspicion and paranoia. Tight-beam messages in code, alluding to gathering supplies. No confessions, no suspects." Qerol continued, beaming, "But we have something much better than a scapegoat. That vessel you found contains nothing less than Kelmai the Devastation."

Arek recoiled. *The creator-tyrant, the last ruler of the Atlan.* He'd had Kelmai in his possession this whole time? The thought chilled him to the core.

"I thought the traitor Atlan destroyed the capsule?"

Qerol mirrored Arek's expression of surprise. "It seems not! The first Vsenk spent untold hours searching for the vessel and the keys, but the Atlan hid them away from us after their betrayal. With his power in our possession, nobles will flock to our side, and the question of Illhar will be irrelevant."

No wonder Qerol had been so adamant about secrecy and fanaticism in chasing down the last device. The Devastation was so powerful that the truth of his nature had been hidden from the lesser species along with the Old Atlan Empire. If none knew of Kelmai, then none could seek him out even after the Vsenk abandoned the search.

But clearly, these thieves he'd found had been luckier than his own ancestors.

"If he's pushing this hard, don't you think there's more to it?"

"He's fearmongering. Wants to undermine the Special Economic Zone. Can't stand that we're bringing all of that money into the Empire and luring young nobles away from his faction."

"Nothing good will come of this."

"And that's why we're wearing armor."

"What of the third artifact? Can the thieves use it to interfere?"

"That will require more explaining than I have time for. It would have been far better if you retrieved all three, but you've done well. Now make yourself ready."

Arek had thought himself endangered, his precarious position even more at risk by dint of being in the right place at the wrong time, a large but secret responsibility dropped on him by Qerol and the Bright Suns. But to judge Qerol's mood, Arek was a rising star now. He tried his best to internalize that pride, to hold himself high in the faction that had always felt barely in reach.

Qerol returned to the core of the Bright Suns, leaving Arek to eat a quick meal. Several other Bright Suns stopped by to say hello and congratulate him on his find.

He was not used to being the subject of praise by his own people, and it sat uneasily with him. His armor arrived via courier minutes before the opening gavel, and Rellix attendants were still tying down straps as he walked with the

Bright Suns into the great chamber.

The chamber of the Great Council was a huge dome sloping overhead, over one hundred and fifty meters tall at its apex. The dome was covered in stained glass murals depicting great victories across the generations, from the emergence of the Vsenk from the Galactic Void to conquering the galaxy and wiping clear all traces of resistance. The first time he'd seen the roof, he'd been younger than his daughter, visiting with his clutch from school. As a child, he'd dreamed of joining the great heroes, of his own story added to the living memory of his people.

The ground level was divided into two sections, an amphitheater with space for just over two hundred Vsenk and a great sandy plain. Whoever had the floor would stand upon the plain and address the assembled nobles.

Thanks to his low status and de facto exile on patrol duty, Arek had attended precious few sessions of the court, mostly voting through proxies to support motions by Qeiol and the Bright Suns.

In every meeting of the Court, there was the threat of violence, that a faction would take the floor and that which could not be resolved with rhetoric and bargaining would be solved with combat—a Grand Melee.

He could not know what would come of that day, but he stood with his allies, his friends, prepared for whatever kind of combat the day might yield.

CHAPTER FORTY-SIX

LAHRA

A PAIR OF GUARDS WOKE them late into the night and led them from their cell in hushed tones.

Max was twitchy, full of questions and the need for information. But they wouldn't be allowed to leave without permission from the nobles, so there was no reason to try to defer their meeting.

The guards took them into a set of chambers that were substantially more lavish than the common areas, the barracks, and the small room she and Max had been afforded.

Seated in a dark corner was Mirai, this time without her sister and niece. She stood and walked toward them.

"My sister is invested in keeping our people safe, but I will not forsake our vengeance, nor our responsibility to the galaxy. Tell me everything of your discovery of Kelmai and I may be able to help you."

Max looked doubtful. But for a noble to be this direct and to take responsibility . . . it gave Lahra hope that there might be something to salvage here. And least she wouldn't have to dance around niceties with Mirai.

Lahra nodded. "Of course, bright noble. We found his

vessel and several other devices in the tomb on the fragments of Yua. Not knowing what they were, we tried to extract them but were intercepted by Vsenk ships. We escaped with one of the smaller devices but lost the vessel and the other device."

"Lost to who?"

"The Vsenk."

"That does not bode well for the galaxy." Mirai spoke as calmly as if she'd been told someone burnt her toast.

Max's body language screamed "No shit!", "It sure fucking does!" or another equally exasperated Terran sentiment. He had the grace to not say it out loud. Instead, he managed a diplomatic, "Let us borrow the books that speak of Kelmai's rise and fall, so we might spread the news to others and prevent other planets from meeting Genos's fate."

"I imagine you might. These texts are essential for the survival of our people. And as my sister said, it is forbidden for outsiders to read the Record."

"Then make us a copy," Max said. "I need to study that book, but we don't have time. We need to get the information out there."

Lahra said, "Queen Biara declared war on the Vsenk because of their atrocities on Pejlo. Our people could have stood aside, watched as others suffered. But that is not who we are. Genos died because our queen could not bear to let that evil go un-checked, because our ancestors refused to subscribe to the Vsenk's warped history. I am but a guard, and raised away from our people, but I do not see how cowardice honors Queen Biara's memory."

Mirai's eyes flashed with indignation. "You will not speak with such presumption, Yevoh. I have been lenient with you due to the special circumstances of your upbringing, but you will sing your part and no other. If you are granted access to the Record, it will be an act of grace meant only for your eyes. And you will be grateful if you are so honored."

Lahra was trying to help them, and still the noble sought to keep her in her place. Perhaps she'd over-estimated Mirai's judgment. But a direct challenge would not help.

Max, ever the diplomat, struck just the right chord. "With apologies, brightness, this is bigger than any one species." Max followed custom even as he spoke out of turn. "This is about finishing what Queen Biara started. It's about stopping the Vsenk, removing their doomsday weapon. Without the Devastation as a deterrent, the Vsenk are beatable. And if the Vsenk are gone, then you can stop hiding. Your people can ride the stars once more."

Mirai did not speak for some time. Lahra could see the battles playing out in the noble's mind. At last, she said, "On your lineage, swear to not reveal us to any off-worlder."

Gladly, Lahra thought.

Lahra sang "The Soldier's Oath." Each caste had one song that most centrally defined their role in Genae society. Hers was a driving, resolute song to a march-like beat. She sang of duty, of prowess, of loyalty. She'd sung it to Max on their wedding day, formalizing him as her charge (something else she'd skipped in her account to the nobles, as it was blasphemy). She sang it again to show her dedication, listing the names of her ancestors to the fifth generation, calling on their memory to bind her to her duty and guide her to victory.

Mirai nodded. "Then I give you my leave to go."

Max and Lahra exchanged a confused look. "Your sister will not stop us?"

"Without a clear heir, we have learned to share power. She agreed to let me deal with the two of you. But you will have to go quickly, in case she changes her mind and presses the issue. Tell the other worlds of Kelmai the Destroyer. Stop him if you can. And then return to help us escape from this tomb. My attendants will see to your departure."

Lahra kneeled in a full bow, then stood and turned to leave.

The guards returned them to their quarters. Lahra's armor and Max's suit were neatly arrayed on the bed, along with their other belongings.

They dressed as quickly as they could.

A crowd awaited them on their way out. Genae peeked out from chambers and workstations, all eyes on them as four guards escorted the pair out the entrance to the hidden colony.

One of Mirai's attendants intercepted them on the way out. She bumped into one of the guards and immediately begged forgiveness, waving a hand before her face to indicate her regret and repentance.

Only thanks to her training as a guard and her experience as a mercenary did Lahra notice the attendant's other hand slip something into Max's bag while the guards' attention was on her "clumsiness."

"Out of the way!" the guard said, and she jumped away, prostrating herself and apologizing.

Whatever she'd given them, Lahra hoped it was worth the ongoing censure she'd face for not just disrupting a guard, but for then making a scene out of her apology.

The guards led them out the airlock, then down the long hallway and all the way out to the last genetic lock, where the other guards had first intercepted them. Before she'd known any of this was still there. Before she learned that the largest remaining colony of her people were mostly paranoids with cabin fever.

Outside the entranceway, Lahra said, "Keep walking. We need to get back to Wheel as quickly as possible."

Max failed to contain his frustration, gesturing with wide, sharp movements as he spoke. "I can't believe it. Just tossing us out, with nothing. No help, no resources, just 'thanks for visiting our secret underground colony where we've been hiding from the universe for hundreds of years. Oh, that pesky Empire is about to use a super-weapon? Too bad. You were rude.'"

He stopped to fume. "Come the fuck on."

Lahra kept her voice level, though she had to speak through gritted teeth to do so. He was not the only one angry at the situation, but matching his energy would not help talk him down. "Keep walking, love."

"I'm still on my indignation bender here. I'll try to get it worked out by the time we get back to the ship, but no promises. I may need to stew a bit longer."

"You do whatever you feel you must to get by. But I think you'll like the surprise."

Max raised an eyebrow. She answered only with a smile.

CHAPTER FORTY-SEVEN

MAX

"THIS IS AMAZING!" MAX exclaimed as the Record unfolded on his screens. "How did you do this?"

"I didn't do anything. Remember when that attendant stumbled into us on the way out?"

"She slipped me the drive?"

Lahra gave a knowing grin.

Max paged through the documents. Illustrations. Annotations. It was all here. That entire book, detailing the rise and fall of Kelmai, the creation of the Vsenk and their betrayal. Everything.

This data would bust the lies the Vsenk had been peddling for centuries wide open for all to see, not to just whisper about in the shadows. If only he could get it broadcast in the clear.

But first, the vessel. And Kelmai.

"I still need to figure out what the smaller devices do." Max placed a hand on the artifact. It was still a little sticky from its time in Cruji's impossibly large gullet.

"What are you two prattling on about?" Wheel said. She had come down to check on them and instead met well-hidden sentry cannons in the rocks surrounding the palace. After a ten-minute stand-off, Wheel had peeled off. The pair had emerged from a back entrance a few hours later and met her just outside the cannons' firing range. And told her that they weren't just automated turrets.

The standoff with those cannons would make its way to the elder noble. There would be consequences for Mirai's decision to release them, greater still if the other nobles discovered the attendant's copying of the Record for Max. Now it was up to the three of them to make Mirai's defiance worth the fallout.

Max drew in a sharp breath, taking in the text. "It's—I mean—do you realize how big this is?"

Lahra stood by, hands crossed. This was her standard position when he was talking his way through some finding or another. Present, supportive, but calm.

Wheel came clomping across the ship to join them. Live on a ship long enough with people and you learn their walks. He knew Lahra's the best, since Wheel spent nearly all of her time in the cockpit, but even so, he knew this walk. This walk told Max that she had something to say.

"What's up?" Max asked. He'd blown right by Wheel's "I need to say something" before to tell her about the Genae colony, and this time, he'd try letting her go first. This data wasn't going anywhere, though the ship should be.

Wheel slid down the rails, hitting the deck of the cargo hold with her stompy boots. "That's new," she said, gesturing to the display showing the book.

"We had an eventful trip."

Wheel snorted, "Yeah, you were gone long enough. We came looking but couldn't get in. Not without massive damage. Figured you might have objected."

Lahra cocked her head to one side, like she was listening for or feeling something. "The ship is leaving orbit. Where are we headed?" Those guard senses of hers were eerie.

"Illhar," Wheel said. "Meeting up with a friend. She's got a job for us."

Lahra crossed her arms, brows narrowed. "What job?"

Wheel hiked a thumb up toward the middle deck. "It's a big one. You probably want to sit down."

Lahra looked to Max, then past him to the display. "We have a great deal to tell you; I'm not sure another job is possible at this time."

Max gestured to the screen. "Yeah, we're kind of in the middle of something and are probably still on the Vsenk's radar. You sure we have time to stop and talk it out?"

Wheel smiled. "Don't worry about the Vsenk. For a minute, anyway. Kenoa will cover for us. And you'll want to take this job. I have some friends there that are very interested in that big mystery box we stole from Yua."

"But all we have left is one of the little ones."

"They'll buy the information. Whatever you've got."

"That's the thing, Wheel. It's much bigger than I thought," Max said. "And I've got a big pile of how and why here to sort through."

He turned and pointed to the display, swiping through the interface to get back to the spread that Lejoh had first shown him, with the illuminated image of Kelmai.

Max told her about Kelmai, about the origins of the Vsenk and the true nature of the Devastation. Wheel responded at intervals with a litany of creative swearing.

"How the voiding fuck didn't I know about this?" Wheel asked. "Did all of my people just stick their heads in their warp drives and hope the thing would blow over?"

Max shrugged, "I don't know. Maybe the reports were lost in the diaspora or the Vsenk crackdown. Maybe only the Genae kept records. It'd make sense for the Vsenk to want to obscure what the Devastation really is, to keep it mysterious, un-beatable. The only deterrent better than a planet-killer is a completely mysterious planet-killer."

Wheel's fingers twitched the way they did when she was eager to be back in the pilot's chair. "Tell me you know how to turn it off."

"That's the part I haven't figured out yet. I've just barely scratched the surface of this material."

She nodded at the screen. "And where'd you get this, anyway?"

"This one's yours, love," Max said to Lahra. "I need to get to reading."

While Max scanned the Genae Record, Lahra filled Wheel in on their trip to the surface, the Genae, and the scholar's reveal about the Devastation.

Wheel took a long breath. "Okay, now we really need to jet for Illhar."

"Who's the client?" Max asked.

The Atlan grinned. "We're going to tell all of this to some friends of mine, and then they're going to ask if you'd like to help start a revolution."

Max's jaw dropped. "What?"

He didn't like the knowing smile on their pilot's face. She continued. "These jobs we've been pulling, raiding tombs, searching for artifacts, they don't pay on their own. Uwen, Tarla, the other fences we work with? Most of them are part of a rebellion faction. They give me jobs, you two retrieve important weird stuff, analyze it for your quests, and then we sell it. But where does it go after that? It goes to the movement. And right now, we're needed on Illhar. Word from my friend Cog is that the Vsenk are meeting right now to fight over something, and we're guessing it might be us."

Lahra huffed in disapproval. Which rated pretty high on her scale of emoting. "We're in enough trouble already with the Vsenk on our heels, and now you want us to oppose them directly. We've only survived so far because we've stayed on the periphery."

Wheel shrugged. "Realistically, we're already in the shit.

You assaulted a Vsenk noble. There's no going back. All those artifacts we sold to Uwen? They went to the Resurgence. You've already been in this fight for years; you just didn't know it. But now it's time to come in from the fringe."

Max could barely believe what he was hearing. "You haven't taken a stand for anything other than equipment upgrades since we've met you. Now you're telling me that you've been a freedom fighter all along?"

"And you bought it. Cog and I don't just go way back— we used to be in this together. I got fed up, came out to the fringe to make my own way, but I never lost touch with my old friends. This Kelmai thing, though, it's too big to just sit out. Didn't tell you two until now because I thought maybe I wouldn't need to. That maybe you'd find what you were looking for and could go be happy. But we're all in the meteor shower now. Only way out is through."

Max took a half-step forward, closing in on Wheel. "What else were you lying to us about? 'Hi Max and Lahra, this huge facet of your life and how I acted around you was bullshit, now let's go have an adventure!'"

The ship's comms buzzed. Max's wrist-screen showed a message from Kenoa.

"We can't tell Kenoa. I've been told to keep the Drell out of this," Wheel said.

Lahra scoffed. "Why? They can take on Vsenk battle-ships one-to-one."

"And that's why we need them to hold off. They're a— what is your gambling term?" Wheel asked.

"Ace in the hole?"

"Yeah, sure. That one. They're not a part of the right-now plan. But you two are. So if you're not game, then . . ." Wheel stopped. "Then we've got a problem. Because this ship is going to Illhar to try to stop the Vsenk and the Devastation."

So it was going to be like that.

He looked to Lahra. Her head bobbed side to side in a

gesture of resignation. She said, "We're already anathema. If the Vsenk catch us again, we'll never see the stars through anything but a projected screen in a prison cell. The Imperium is already our enemy. When your enemy has overwhelming numbers, you need allies."

"But we're not soldiers."

Lahra cut Max a look.

"Okay, I'm not a soldier. And how does fighting this war help us get home?" Even the Wreck seemed impossibly far away now, with Jesvin and the Vsenk and the cabin-fever-stressed Genae.

The Wreck was home, until it wasn't. The *Kettle* was home, but not the endgame. Lahra had gone home, and it was nothing like he expected. Would it be the same if he got back to Earth somehow?

Wheel put her hands together, like she was beseeching them or praying to some machine god. "It'll be a lot easier to explore a galaxy not overrun by tyrants. And with the Vsenk off our backs, we can kick Jesvin off her roost."

Max pointed a finger back at his screen. "I'm not going to stop until I've figured this puzzle out. And when I do, we should be wherever we need to be to keep the Vsenk from unleashing Kelmai. So if your people can put this knowledge to good use, then yeah, I'll give them a shot."

Max returned to the manuscript, and Lahra went to the bridge, following Wheel.

Okay, Max. Now you not only have to process all of this information and figure out how the smaller artifacts work, you have to do so fast enough to help overthrow a galaxy-spanning empire before billions of lives are lost in a bloody revolution. Stay cool.

CHAPTER FORTY-EIGHT

AREK

THE COUNCIL CHAMBERS WERE both welcoming and terrifying. Over a millennium of history had been determined by the battles fought in this room.

That said history was fabricated didn't matter. The glass dome above tinted the light of the system's suns yellow, orange, purple, and more. The ceiling mural depicted the story of the Vsenk's emergence from the void to bring order to the galaxy, a reminder that despite their differences, they shared a common history. The room was divided length-wise down the middle, one side comprised of seats that scaled halfway toward the ceiling, the other a field of packed dirt that had feasted on the blood of his kind at times of greatest crisis.

Arek was humbled each time he stepped into this room. He'd battled and scraped and bled to hold on to the right to be here, to maintain his family's hard-fought title. And today, with the vessel in the hands of his faction, he entered the chamber with a view of a brighter future—status, security, and a way home.

Over two hundred Vsenk filled the room, including the assembled nobles, assistants, and the Honor Guard, who stood watch over the sacred space.

It sounded like every single member of the nobility was talking at once.

Dozens yelled back and forth, posturing, slandering, throwing blame around like a ball in one of the lesser species' bloodless sports.

They went silent when Qerol entered the chamber with their prize.

The vessel containing the weapon lay atop a floating board tended by four Yaea vassals. A fifth vassal followed, carrying the smaller artifact.

"To all assembled, I bring you news of blessed victory," Qerol said, four of his arms gesturing to the vessel. "We spent centuries re-creating the power of the Devastation, and now we have the means to bring the original to bear once again. Thanks to the tireless efforts of my good friend Arek!"

Qerol grabbed Arek and pulled him close as dozens of his peers applauded. A swelling of pride he'd never known outside his wedding and the birth of his daughter filled him, all the sweeter for being unexpected. He'd resigned himself to drudgery in all things save the haven of home, and now his peers and superiors cheered him as a hero. And not just those from the Bright Suns—members of minor factions and neutral nobles joined in the chorus.

He had barely begun to internalize the moment when Evam stood and turned to the assembled crowd. A hard-liner voice within the majority faction, Evam was renowned for his stubbornness. "That is indeed fine news, and it could not come at a better time." Evam wielded a great deal of influence in his faction, the Stalwarts, and beyond. When he spoke, the applause died down and he took the floor. "My agents have received numerous reports that track terrorists and dissidents to the Illhari Co-operative. Qerol is so focused on counting his profits and grand-standing with ancient technology that he cannot see what is right in front of his face. This Special

Economic Zone is nothing more than dereliction of duty and enabling treason against our great Empire! I move we rescind the special permissions, lock down the planet, and conduct a thorough investigation! With the Devastation in our possession once more, we have the tools needed to snuff out this insurrection."

Qerol shot right back. "Your agents will say what you want them to say. Bring us evidence! That is how the Grand Melee operates, not on supposition and jealousy. You would bankrupt a planet on hunches and rumors?"

"Do not impugn Evam's agents," said Lhrai, another Stalwart hard liner. Arek had never in his memory heard Lhrai pass up the chance to sling insults, to pile on when the blades were out. "His spies are loyal, wise, and true, unlike your friend Arek, who cannot be bothered to attend to a simple duty such as patrolling the forbidden sectors. How can we even trust your judgment if your choice in friends is so poor?"

Qerol boomed back, trying to beat off the counter-attacks. "I ask for evidence; you respond only with baseless insults and slander. So I will judge your arguments like I judge your rhetoric—pointless. Facile. This council requires evidence to act, not mere paranoia!"

Evam grinned. "And you have given us the means to eradicate this insurrection before it can spread. It has been too long since the vassal states felt our power firsthand."

Arek followed up, trying to wield the power he'd held just moments ago that already felt distant. He'd retrieved an epoch-defining weapon only to have his foes lay a claim to it immediately. "You would destroy an entire planet based on rumors and conjecture? Bring us these agents, let us speak to them ourselves. If you are so confident in them, surely they can convince us themselves?"

"I have provided my agents' reports. If you doubt them, you doubt me." Evam's data was in the precis Arek had speed-read on the way to the Great Council. It was enough to merit an investigation, yes. But not a full lockdown. Especially when such a move could only ever result in the dissolution of the Illhari Special Economic Zone, and the Bright Suns' financial stability with it. Evam was seeking two victories with one blow.

"I doubt you, I most certainly do," Qerol said.

Arek cheered on his friend, as did the rest of the faction. They were in the minority, but far from alone. Several circumspect moderates joined the Bright Suns' chorus. More than he'd thought from the reports he'd read on the way in. Bringing the vessel had swung the balance of power. But would it be enough?

Tyrae, the day's moderator, called for a vote.

More than eighty called for the lockdown. Qerol and his fifty voted no, and another twenty abstained, mostly moderates.

Not nearly enough to meet the two-thirds majority required for decisive action. Evam could move forward with an investigation, the way it should be done.

"I call for a Grand Melee!" Evam boomed.

As expected. Qerol, Evam, and the others knew where the factions stood, would have spent days courting moderates and trading favors. Qerol and the Bright Suns had the vessel; Evam had his sources and the story of an insurrection.

But where would those moderates stand in the Melee? If the battle went to Evam, his faction could force Qerol to hand over the vessel to be used by the military.

The nobles filtered down from the amphitheater section to the sandy field. Attendants appeared with shields and the shock-spears that were the customary weapon of the Grand Melee. Fatalities happened but were discouraged. The Vsenk had never been a populous race, and their young took many years to mature. A Vsenk lost to infighting diminished the power of the host. And yet, more Vsenk had died in Grand Melees the past century than in any other manner. Another price paid for aggression and inflexibility.

Once called, a Grand Melee continued until only one stance-faction remained or a deal was brokered on the field. Some Grand Melees were fought to the last, others brokered very quickly, and some went in cycles. Skirmish, negotiating, another skirmish, and so on.

"Gather together, friends." Qerol called in the faction to huddle up. Their old friend Jxari was off by the moderates, trying her best to enlist their help.

"Even with allies, we'll be out-numbered, so we should stick to the corner and make them come to us. Until we yield, they have not won the point. Arek, I want you on the corner."

Corner positions were crucial. If either flank failed, their formation would collapse. Qerol was placing a great deal of trust in him, especially after being so publicly shamed for his unfavorable posting on border patrol.

Qerol laid out the rest of the formation, just as Jxari returned, fifteen of the moderates with her. Another cluster remained apart, staying in their seats. They would not fight for any side.

"You have our spears, Qerol," said Glora, a strong voice among the moderates. If they were to broker a deal with Evam's faction, Glora would be a great asset in doing such.

"And you have my thanks. We would have you running harassment. When they close in on us, shoot out to flank, draw their attention away so they cannot just line up and lay siege. If they charge you first, fall back to join us in the corner."

Glora and her unit of moderates took up position on the left side, in position to leap out and take the flank as Qerol's forces closed.

"Are you ready?" Evam bellowed.

"We are!" Qerol answered.

An attendant standing in the amphitheater section, away from the field of battle, blew the ancient horn, a polished and painted Vsenk skull, signaling the beginning of the Grand Melee. The Honor Guard stood by to prevent any from fleeing the field.

Evam's massive bloc advanced, spears forward, in full formation. Their line was solid, veterans all across the front. They'd hit hard.

"Form up!" Qerol shouted. Arek slid behind several compatriots, most half a meter or more taller than he. Given his size disadvantage, he was diligent in his weapons practice and had more field combat experience than most. He set his shoulder a centimeter's width from the high stone walls at the far end of the field and took his stance. Kneeling, shield braced on the ground, he locked his spear into position to receive a charge.

"I've got you," said Ylvela, an old patrol comrade. He'd cover the low lines, and she'd strike down any that came too close or focused too much on breaking Arek's resolve and not enough on their own defense.

Shouting filled the room, and as the units clashed, they kicked up a sand cloud on the field. The cloud obscured Arek's vision, cutting off his sight of Glora and her unit on the other flank.

Evam's forces advanced at a charge, a scarred but unfamiliar Vsenk bearing down on Arek and Ylvela. Arek focused on parrying their spears away, leaving Ylvela with an advantage in attacking. It reminded Arek of the wrestling exercise they'd played in the military. Keep a hold of your opponent's weapon or arm, then position your body or theirs so your free arm could land a blow. Only here, it was two people fighting as one.

Ylvela landed a blow to the attacker's shoulder and they fell back. She lashed out at their neighbor, landing a blow to the side of the head. Two down in an instant. Arek levered up and under the next attacker's shield, providing an opening for his friend.

They resisted wave after wave in several minutes of hard fighting. One, two, three different times, Evam's faction closed. The third time, they didn't even bother striking, they just crushed in, trying to break the defensive formation. Arek choked up on his spear and worked the angles to blunt their assault.

But it wasn't enough.

The line broke in the third push, and Arek was forced back. He got to his feet and started fighting side-by-side with Ylvela, trying to keep Evam's faction from taking the corner encircling their forces.

Spears flashed, shields roared with the sound of steel on steel, and the battle became an all-out brawl.

Arek took a blow to the leg and collapsed to one knee. Ylvela stepped forward to cover him and took two stabs in quick succession, convulsing and dropping back. Arek lashed out with his free limbs to block the follow-up shots, but there were too many. He felled two more opponents as they pressed forward, then took another blow. And another. He went down, and the fight passed him by.

When he woke from the shocks, the battle was over. Evam and a few of his faction were still on their feet. Medics filled the field, tending to the nobles.

Three Vsenk were critically wounded. He doubted that they would all live to see the new year. Arek wobbled to his feet, then helped Ylvela up as she came to.

In the lull after the melee, Ylvela said, "I suppose I shouldn't be surprised. But it was good to fight side-by-side once more. You've picked up some new tricks."

Arek allowed himself a brief grin, grateful for the recognition, small consolation though it might be. "Border patrol is not exactly the most demanding duty. I've had the time to practice."

Ylvela stayed to talk for a few minutes, but once the worst of the injuries were addressed, the Vsenk returned to their seats.

Evam had the floor. "As the victor of the Grand Melee, I dictate that the council will dissolve the Illhari Special Economic Zone. Furthermore, we will institute a planetary blockade to prevent terrorists and dissidents from escaping. Qerol, you will lead the investigation into the dissidents, as this is your territory and your responsibility. And if you find the traitors, as I know you will, then. The Devastation."

As per custom, the price of losing a Grand Melee was far worse than a minority faction relenting to majority rule. Now Qerol could not win. If the investigation did turn up this rumored terrorist faction, his victory would be Evam's victory. And if he failed, he'd still be a failure.

The only way forward was to aggressively prosecute the investigation. To root out any insurrection should it exist and remove it so decisively that there was no need to destroy Illhar and the Bright Sun's coffers along with it.

And so, that is what Arek would do.

There was more shouting and dissention, the grumblings of the defeated. But Qerol was silent. He knew what had to be done.

The counsel was adjourned, and Arek joined Qerol back in his chambers to plan their next move.

And to drink. Few painkillers were as effective for Vsenk as strong drink and rich food.

Then, they would turn this setback into an opportunity.

CHAPTER FORTY-NINE

WHEEL

A S THE *KETTLE* WOVE its way out of the wreckage of
Genos, Wheel partitioned her attention. Part of her
mind flew the ship, part coded a decoy copy of the ship's
transponders, and another wiped their transit logs and did
general cleanup of their data trail to throw off the Vsenk.
Having a cybernetic brain was pretty handy.

Kenoa had agreed to accompany a relay decoy with a copy
of the *Kettle*'s transponder to lead the Imperials off their trail
while the *Kettle* jumped through warp space. They knew the
Imperials were out there watching, but if the *Kettle*'s signal
never disappeared, the patrol would follow Kenoa for a while
before realizing that they'd been duped. Kenoa could just
rejoin the migration, safe from interference by the Imperials.

"Thank you for your assistance and your insight," Max
said for the group.

Kenoa spun in approval and affection, looking far too
cute for a being so gigantic. "You are very welcome. It has
been a great honor to accompany you and bear witness to a
tragic wonder of history. Especially when that visit seems to
have born some fruit."

The three of them had considered asking Kenoa to enlist the Migration to extract the Genae but had decided against it, not without investigating other options. They danced around details when explaining why Max and Lahra had been down there for so long, but the Drell could read between the lines that something was up.

"Please give our thanks to the Matriarch. We hope to visit you again under better terms."

"Of course. Max, Lahra, Wheel, may the solar winds be always at your back."

Wheel answered for them this time. "And yours as well. Until next time."

Kenoa bowed and turned, her translator/speaker beside her as well as the decoy buoy, programmed to follow the Drell at a consistent distance to look like the *Kettle* flying in echelon.

Cog would be able to get the *Kettle* through Illhari customs for landing, but the less work that her friend had to do, the better.

Max spent the trip poking through his book. Lahra cleaned her sword and checked their weapons and ammo stores.

It was a blissfully normal trip.

Right until they came out of warp space.

Illhar's orbit was crowded on an average day. The planet's fortunes had risen since the comparatively permissive Vsenk faction that controlled this planet entered it into a pilot program for a system of Special Economic Zones with lessened economic restrictions.

But as the *Kettle* (now flying as the *Gray Dart*, thanks to Wheel's friends on Illhar) emerged from warp space, the first thing that pinged Wheel's radar, aside from the planet itself, was the Vsenk destroyer parked in upper orbit.

"Voiddammit!" Her voice was shot through with the static of fear. "Lahra. Cannons. Now!" she shouted, boosted by the ship's PA.

"What's going on?" Lahra answered. Wheel could hear her already on the move.

"We've got a Vsenk destroyer just outside gun range, parked in orbit. They're here already."

"How did they know we'd be coming?"

"Not sure they did. Haven't gotten any indication they're turning. They are controlling traffic heading down to the planet, though. Reaching out to Cog now."

Wheel sent a tight-beam, triple-encrypted message to Cog, shouting, "How the fuck do we get to you now?"

Lahra's voice echoed through the comms. "In position. Let me know if I should go weapons-hot."

"Not yet. Don't want to tip them off. First, we try the spoofed credentials. If those don't work, then we burn our way out of here."

"I wonder if Cruji will like the taste of that artifact better this time." Max didn't look excited to find out.

"Make it fast, kid." Wheel turned back to the controls.

Cog's response came within minutes, well before the *Kettle*'s spot in the queue. "Just play it cool. I got your transponder data and added it to the priority docking list. They should wave you through."

The next twenty minutes were as tense as any Wheel had seen outside of proper combat. At any moment, the Vsenk could open fire, and they'd have to pull another fast escape.

Lahra paced, Max cradled Cruji, and Wheel had to remind herself to breathe. A minute passed, then another. Then ten more.

Ships stopped, some were boarded, some not.

But the hammer never fell. Their codes were accepted, and the Vsenk ship cleared them for landing. Max grumbled for a few minutes before he and Lahra set about coaxing Cruji into regurgitating the device.

Fortunately, Wheel had more important things to do.

She brought the ship down through the atmosphere to a docking berth in the capital city of Aahar, where Cog would be meeting them to secure the smaller artifact and evaluate whether the Atlan Resurgence could trust Max and Lahra. Wheel had vouched for them all she could, provided histories and medical records, but no one got to join the Resurgence proper without a full interview.

As Wheel lowered the cargo hatch, she asked Max, "Everything secure?"

"As I can make it. If anyone can track that thing through six layers of steel, then good on them."

"Let's hope it's enough."

The hatch opened, letting in the bright light of mid-day in Axhara. Her eyes dilated to account for Illhar's sun, revealing a half-dozen junior Atlan, Yaea, and Illhari bustling back and forth on the docks in coveralls. Re-fueling, making repairs, and more. They all looked rushed, working too fast for too long. Probably something to do with that destroyer parked in orbit.

When Wheel left the Resurgence years ago, it had been maybe a thousand people strong across a dozen planets. Now, from what Cog said, it was many times that, with ships, secret militias, and some real firepower.

And behind the youngsters stood the woman herself: Cog. Hands on her hips, as grease-stained as ever. She kept up her cover by running a mechanist's shop near the docks. The building housed a Resurgence field base in the basement, but the cover business was legitimate. Cog looked better in coveralls and grease than most Atlan did dressed in the robes of the ancients.

And she wore a smile that said, "I knew you'd be back." She'd won this round. "You look like you haven't showered in weeks!" she said.

"Says the woman who bathes in engine grease!"

"It's lubricant. Good enough for engines; good enough

for me."

Wheel grabbed Cog and held her tight.

Wheel spoke almost without realizing. "I missed you."

Cog answered at a whisper. "Maybe next time you'll come and visit without me needing to throw up the panic signal."

"Maybe." Wheel stepped aside to gesture to the lovebirds, "This is Lahra and Max. Lahra and Max, my old friend Cog."

Cog winked at the pair, cybernetic eye irising closed and then open. "Not that old. Nice to meet you, finally. Let's get moving. There's a lot to be done back at the shop, and it would have been better if you'd gotten here three days ago."

"Is that how long that destroyer has been in orbit?" Lahra asked.

Cog nodded.

Max looked back to the ship. "Will the *Kettle* be safe here? This spaceport has to have imperial patrols coming and going all the time. And that Vsenk has to be livid after we slipped his grasp for the second time."

"Safe as anywhere." Cog gestured to the engineers zipping back and forth with fuel, repair kits, and various cables. "These are all my people. She'll be fine."

Max looked to Wheel. *Don't worry, kid,* she thought. "If Cog says a ship is safe, it's safe. And if not, I'll take it out of her rusted hide."

That got a smile from the older Atlan. Max still looked worried. Lahra was already in sentry mode and scanning the crowds.

They walked from the docks to Cog's machine shop. The neighborhood consisted of squat Illhari buildings all around, with jagged spikes of Vsenk barracks and checkpoints jutting up from the mostly level skyline of two- and three-story buildings stretching across the valley. Illhari came up living in burrows; they weren't much for heights.

Illhari, Yaea, Rellix, and members of other rarer species

passed by, mostly dock workers in blue overalls, some travelers dressed in clothes from a dozen worlds.

But no Vsenk. This planet's Vsenk were more hands-off. Or they used to be. The Empire was tightening their grip with the destroyer in orbit. But according to Cog's last update—arriving as they jumped into Illhari space—the real crackdown hadn't landed yet.

It wouldn't be long. In all likelihood, there would be a dozen or more Vsenk in Axhara alone. Each at the head of an entire division of soldiers. More patrols, more inspections, more investigations. Which meant an unprecedented level of scrutiny on every single thing that members of the Resurgence did in public.

Had life ever been simple? Wheel wanted to think that it was so, that maybe there was a time to think back to and remember with fondness. The Resurgence was founded on the hope that there was a better alternative to the Empire, self-rule with a chance of peace between worlds, lessons from the past before the Vsenk, applied for the future. But that past was as much a myth to Wheel as Genos had been to Lahra.

And look how that ended up. Live your whole life hoping for something, and when you finally got it, it let you down. Even worse, it was ridiculous and sad.

But Cog believed in that future.

And Wheel believed in Cog.

Inside, the machine shop looked like it always had—hectic, disorganized, but highly efficient. Atlan and Illhari technicians performed the everyday repairs that kept the lights on. The Atlan in the shop displayed some of the more elaborate cybernetics Wheel had seen: here a trio of tentacle-like manipulator arms arcing out from one Atlan's back to hold an engine, there a pair of what looked like siblings with anti-grav repulsors for feet, skating through the air ten feet up to re-wire a transport.

The Resurgence's real work was done below, but Wheel

had nothing but respect for the people hacking it out day by day in the shop. They kept everything running so that when the time came, people were ready. Ready to survive the war, to get out if they needed to, and to stand and fight.

Max dawdled a bit, taking in the sights. Lahra coughed, and he hurried to catch up with Wheel and Cog as they stood at the entrance of a freight elevator.

Downstairs, the elevator opened onto an office room, still part of the facade.

Cog walked them past a rickety metal shelf filled with tools, bits, and assorted pieces to an equally-cluttered office. Sitting inside was a beefy Atlan man, one arm ending not in a hand but a plasma torch.

"Wheel, you come with me. Regulator Brace here will interview the lovebirds."

Max chuckled, rolling his eyes. Probably wasn't wild about the nickname even without her sharing it with Cog. It was hardly the worst of his problems, given the size of the job they had to do.

The Regulator nodded, offering a hand to shake.

Regulator, Alternator, Motivator. The Resurgence's positions were all mechanically oriented, inspired by Atlan naming traditions. The whole movement was one big machine. Everyone had a role, a job to do. Many coming together to achieve what any one of them could only dream of doing alone.

"This again?" Max asked as Cog departed. He had to be getting tired of sharing his life's story with strangers.

Wheel took the shielded container holding the smaller Atlan artifact and patted Max on the shoulder. "Buckle up, Earth-man. The quicker you tell Brace what he needs to know, the sooner you can get in on the fun."

"Fun. Sure, this will—" Max's line cut off as the door closed behind them.

CHAPTER FIFTY

LAHRA

THIS WAS THEIR THIRD interrogation in a single month, so at least they were prepared. Lahra and Max ran through their histories, their antipathy toward the Vsenk, and the general details of the vessel they'd found on the broken Atlan world.

Brace took it all in, doubtless recording through that telescoping eye of his. Maybe even piping it directly in to the Resurgence commanders or whoever would be listening nearby. The Atlan was formidable, with obvious armor plating, muscular augmentation, and a bracer that Lahra suspected expanded into a shield or battering ram.

Max was not pleased at having to once again explain his history to a disbelieving audience.

"I told you. Earth. It's on the other side of the universe, in the Sol system in the Milky Way. Your ancestors called it the Clouded Eye. I got here through some unknown Old Atlan transportation tech. From what I can tell, they had some kind of limited presence on my planet, though they were only ever a legend to my people. So no, I'm not Yaea, and I don't have an opinion on the Triumvirate's history of unchallenged loyalty to the Vsenk. I'm here. I'm challenging loyalty. I challenge it all the damn time. So can you clear us already? I have work to do."

Brace was not impressed. "These things take time. Can't just let anyone stroll in, you know."

He leaned against the wall, and Lahra felt a story coming. "My uncle was a rebel, back before the Illhari and Atlan groups joined up. He was a renowned holo-technician. He'd hide fugitives in his private theater. Someone sold him out, and the Vsenk strung him up in the city square with a twenty-centimeter chunk torn out of his chest. And beside him, three fugitives they found in his care. The others went quick, but my uncle's nanites were good. Too good." Brace's voice faltered. "It cannibalized every little bit of muscle and fat to keep him alive. By the fifth day, he was just a husk. I put him out of his misery. I was ten."

Lahra watched as tears welled up in the Atlan's eyes, pain echoing across his face. He'd been fighting his whole life, just as she had.

"Given that, I think you'll understand my caution," Brace said.

"I hear you." Max met emotion with emotion, his voice soft. "My people, where I come from? We lost uncles and sisters and cousins the same way. We dared to live free and we paid the price."

Brace nodded. Max took a seat and dove back into the Genae text on Kelmai and the Vsenk.

Lahra waited. She'd handed over the sword, but even unarmed, with Brace's armaments, she was fairly certain she could get them out of this base. Up to the mechanist's floor, at least. If the alarm were already sounded, she figured that about a third would try to stop them . . .

Her mind raced down the hole of brainstorming escape routes, back-up plans, and more.

She could no more readily keep herself from planning for

the worst than Max could resist reading any voided thing put in front of his face.

Several minutes later, Brace cocked his head to the side, the way Wheel did when she was processing incoming data. He stood, reaching for her sword. Lahra tensed, ready to fight, but the big Atlan handed the blade to her, handle-first. "You're cleared. Provisionally. Follow me."

Brace led them back through the shop to an oddly-shaped corner not visible from the front door. It was a dead-end, another shelf filled with junk. He sorted through the pieces in a studied fashion.

It wasn't junk. It was a pass-sequence.

The shelf and wall behind it swung open, revealing an elevator. They entered, and Brace hit a button sending the elevator car down.

Ten meters later, the door opened. Brace waved them in. "Welcome to the Resurgence."

Before them was a war council. Star charts and system maps on the walls, touchscreen tables with plans and data flowing up into holo-projections, and dozens of Atlan, Illhari, and others huddled in small groups. Messengers and low-ranking attendants dashed back and forth, handing off tablets and hand-written notes. Lahra took it in all at once, picking out weaknesses, assumptions, and organizational style like huge gulps of air after being held underwater.

She'd need to learn fast if they were going to be able to make a difference. Max had his role figured out. So beyond protecting him and Wheel, it was up to Lahra to find a role for herself. With Vsenk attention at its height, her ability to conduct covert ops would be needed but pushed to its limit.

Wheel waved them over, and as Cog stepped to the side, she revealed a familiar furry face.

"Uwen!" Max threw his arms open to receive a fuzzy hug.

The Illhari rubbed his whiskers in delight as he approached to embrace Max. "My favorite treasure hunters!

Glad you're here. Wreck became a mess after you left. Jesvin's wrath turned dozens of groups against her, became pitched battle. Had to leave. The secrecy was tiring, anyway." Uwen pulled back from the hug and asked, "Wonder now if you wish you'd just given me the artifact the first time around?"

"How bad was it? Do we need to send people?" Lahra asked.

"We're needed here. The Wreck will survive. Jesvin cannot fight them all at once. Not for long."

At the mention of the Wreck, Lahra flashed back through most of a decade of memories. The sound of Eihra's family singing songs of welcome. The taste of U'uh'ish, the warmth of Max's hand on hers alongside the rattling of old pipes through the lower levels. The Wreck was lost to them as a home, but maybe they could save this place.

Max chimed in. "Did Wheel tell you what we've found out?"

Uwen was beside himself with excitement, whiskers and claws vibrating. "Why do you think I'm here? After years suffering on the fringe, I could be sleeping off the afternoon with wine and zardogh flutes, and yet I am here. Have you cracked the code on this thing yet?" He pointed to the artifact.

"Not yet," Max said. "But I'm not sure how much I can do with only one of them. Near as I can tell, they were identical. The way they were displayed with the vessel . . ."

Wheel gave Uwen a chiding look. "You two can go into archaeologist warp space soon enough. I need to get him and Lahra briefed."

Uwen brushed his whiskers and turned back to speak with Cog.

Wheel led them around the room, unpacking and expanding on the assumptions and guesses Lahra had made. The Resurgence had two thousand members on Illhar, and another five thousand scattered throughout warp space. The crowd here was mostly Atlan and Illhari with some Yaea and

Rellix, as well as small numbers of other species. Their fleet was barely fifty ships, only ten of them worth mentioning in battle. They'd be able to challenge one, maybe two Vsenk battleships in open combat, but they were gearing up for guerrilla strikes on trade routes and patrols.

Illhar had been chosen as their base due to the permissive economic and trade policies, but now they were preparing to re-locate, assuming plans could be made to sneak through the blockade.

Everything about the Resurgence said: "getting there, but not ready." They didn't have the numbers, the resources, or the ships to challenge the Vsenk outright. Especially as the Vsenk were closing in on their base of operations.

"You're screwed," Lahra said, employing one of Max's favorite Terran euphemisms after Wheel completed her overview. "There's no way this force can stop the Devastation."

Wheel gave the Atlan elbow shrug. "Maybe. But not yet. Possibilities haven't all collapsed. And we've got some tricks to pull out when we need them. Can't tell you about those yet, but what you see isn't all of what we've got. We have to convince the high-ups to bring you in on the rest; they're nervous about someone getting so much clearance so quickly. Took me years of doing favors for Cog before I got read back in above a provisional level. We'll get there. But for now, we need to figure out how to operate with this crackdown."

Max looked around the room. "You do that. I need access to a proper workstation if I'm going to crack the artifact."

Wheel picked Uwen out of the crowd, confirming that he hadn't run off to tinker with something. "Figuring out how to stop Kelmai has to be priority one. I'll try to make that the case. Go do your thing with Uwen. Lahra and I will talk weapons, logistics—you know, actual fun stuff."

Max smiled, leaning in to kiss Lahra on the cheek. She raised a hand to his face, caressed his cheek as she let it fall, then let him go.

Lahra straightened and turned back to Wheel. "Tell me about your system of runners and what you know about the imperial patrols."

Wheel activated a touchscreen table and raised both hands. Blue holo-projections resolved into an isometric view of Axhara.

"What do you need to know?"

CHAPTER FIFTY-ONE

AREK

Arek had only one evening to himself before the *Vigilance Without Respite* was to disembark for Illhar. Almost punishingly short, it was still better than being sent back to orbit immediately.

For the time being, he was home.

His daughter Moara climbed all over him, explaining her day and the day before that, though Arek guessed "yesterday" was standing in for every day she could remember.

Arek was still sore and tender from the bruises he'd earned at the Grand Melee. Custom and honor demanded that such wounds were to be worn as badges of pride unless they were life-threatening.

"How was the rim?" Wreva asked, trying to keep his mind off of the coming mission.

"My crew is loyal, diligent, if not exceedingly ambitious or competent. We spend most of our time training, drilling. They're better crew and soldiers than they were when we set out."

"And loyal to you," she added.

"That is the hope. I've not seen any signs of insubordination or duplicity. But work will come back to the fore soon enough. How are things here? How is Moara's class?"

"The other children are cruel, as they always are. She is the lowest-status in the clutch."

As both Arek and Wreva had been when they were young.

Their match had been the best one another's families could do, each only barely a part of the Vsenk nobility. Arek's family were scientists, Wreva's military. But to their great benefit, they'd grown fond of one another, he dared call it tender.

Even among the heights of the Vsenk nobility, there were winners and losers. Arek had long since grown tired of being a loser. But not so tired as to give up hope, or to give in to resentment and hatred.

"When this mission is done, succeed or fail, Qerol will have something else for me. I'll ask for a posting back at home. Perhaps in intelligence. If he's going to make a move on Evam, a smarter move, to get back some breathing room."

"That can wait. I know you don't want to be away. I'm working on it from my side as well. Ygiha says that the academy may need training officers soon. You'd be excellent in that role."

A canny move. She kept surprising him, even ten years into their arranged marriage. The nobility undervalued her capabilities. As he had, at first.

"With no glory to bring to the academy," he said, "I'd likely end up little better than a drill instructor." Arek saw the disappointment in Wreva's eyes. "I'm sorry. Thank you for what you're trying to do. And I am grateful to Ygiha. If she can find me a position here, it almost doesn't matter what it is. Finding this vessel wasn't enough, thanks to Evam's stunt. Perhaps it would be better to just opt out of the status ladder, to try to do the best with what we have."

"We all do our best. Now, let us put tomorrow outside

and cherish what we have of the day."

Arek nodded. He picked up a tablet. "Moara, come here and let your father tell you stories of the forbidden sectors. There are monsters, rebels, heroes, and your favorite: Drell."

"Drell!" his daughter shouted, a mound of toys forgotten. She climbed up into Arek's lap. He wrapped two limbs around Wreva's, using the others to hold his daughter close as he related sanitized and embellished versions of stories from his time on patrols, featuring the traitor Genae, Yaea, and Atlan.

And so, for a few hours, the weight of his worries was forgotten. He was not Commander Arek of the cruiser *Vigilance Without Respite*, runt of his house, failed corner of Qerol's stand against Evam and the Stalwarts.

He was simply Arek, husband and father. He regarded those hours like a chronicler, holding to them desperately. He would need the hope and joy they brought him in the weeks ahead.

CHAPTER FIFTY-TWO

MAX

FIRST, HE TALKED TO Uwen. Then, he and Uwen had to talk to another Illhari. Then the four of them had to talk to an Atlan. The entire day unfolded like that, a run-around that took him back to his post-doctorate days and trying to sell his department on a research expedition. Which, given the fact that it was that expedition that led him to this galaxy, lent the situation a weird sense of cyclicity.

Every time, he had to prove to the Resurgence leaders that the Devastation wasn't a weapon: It was a person. And not just a person, but an Atlan emperor that the Vsenk had erased from history.

Strangely, people accepted that more readily than the notion that the Vsenk had been genetically engineered as elite shock troops.

"But they mature so slowly. Why would you design troops to mature that slowly?" a Yaea merchant asked.

"Well, I'm not a bio-engineer, but Kelmai was, and maybe he had a way to speed up the maturation process so you don't care how long it takes them to mature on their own? But now the Vsenk don't have it, and so they can't replicate what he did."

That got some nods.

After the third person told him he was a void-damned liar, Max got Wheel and Lahra to corroborate his story.

"But they've always been here!" one Illhari exclaimed.

Max was overturning the entire conventional history of this galaxy, so it wasn't much of a surprise that people were flipping out. The fact that this Illhari was so far in denial about the origins of the Empire, even as a member of an anti-Imperial resistance, showed just how strong the Vsenk's control on accepted reality really was.

Max paced the room, working out his frustration as he repeated himself. "They've had centuries to make sure that their propaganda is all anyone grows up with. The older texts show a coalition of planets led by the Atlan before Kelmai and the Vsenk, but until now, I never had any real evidence of where the Vsenk came from, why their archaeological history was so fiercely protected. It's because they don't have anything older than a thousand years ago."

"We need to get this material to our counter-propaganda and media teams," Wheel said, backing Max's play. "It'll take a lot to break the back of their official histories, but we need to get a strong counter-narrative out there. We should also get the story out there of how you fought that Vsenk to a standstill. If they know there is something out there that scares the Vsenk, maybe that helps us in recruiting. Maybe most importantly, we let them know it's acceptable and sensible to question heterodoxy."

Max picked up the thread from Wheel. "And the more people actively challenge the heterodoxy, the easier it is to imagine a world without the Vsenk as the sun and stars."

"We fight on every front we can, each to our ability," Lahra said. "But there's more. Did you tell them about the vessel, the artifacts?"

Max nodded. "That's the next thing. I have one of them,

but there were two. I need help. Engineers, weapon-smiths, archaeologists, especially Atlan. I need to crack the code on how to make this thing work, and figure out what effect it has on Kelmai, or why they were buried with him."

The other Atlan in the group, Wrench, nodded and tapped through a command on his on-board wrist-screen and said into it, "I'm bringing someone down to the Incubator."

The Incubator was another level down. It was cramped, dimly lit, and turned out to be exactly where Max wanted to go.

He was greeted by scholars, engineers, scientists, and philosophers. His people. Nerds.

One, an older Yaea woman with thick glasses and fine gray ridges across her scalp, said, "You're the one with the artifact?"

Max grinned. "You want to see?" He set the case on a table with a thunk. They were far enough down to block signals going in or out, so he opened the case and pulled out the artifact, thinking only a little bit of the massive warehouse at the end of *Raiders*. He saw the brain trust's eyes go wide.

"So, what do you think?"

The Atlan almost jumped forward. "This is amazing. Old Atlan, from right before the fall!"

Max nodded. "I think it's probably actually right after the fall. Or during. We found this with the vessel containing Kelmai, an Atlan warlord."

They were all so excited, two or three of them were talking at any given moment, and proper introductions took ten minutes as people kept looping around to exclaim and wave their arms in excitement or disbelief. He was back in academia, shooting theories and deductions back and forth at lightning speed with a room of equals, each from a different discipline.

An hour passed in the blink of an eye. But they covered ground fast. He related the story of Kelmai's rise and fall, filled them in on everything he'd tried with the smaller artifact so far, and learned the basics of their ongoing projects.

Catalyst, the Atlan, was working on cracking the Vsenk genetic locks on weaponry so that the Resurgence could use the Vsenk's weapons against them. The Rellix philosopher, Professor Chrenae, was the Resurgence's head of propaganda, fitting their R&D into the overall messaging and recruitment approaches, targeting experts in the fields the Resurgence needed most (which, to be fair, were really all of them). The older Yaea woman was named Oyira, and she was working on refining the Resurgence's comms so they could piggyback on Vsenk transmissions to get through the censors. The last member of the brain trust was Uwen's second cousin Usev, a xeno-archaeologist. Usev was more playful than Uwen, but just as forceful in his argumentation.

"We should look at this artifact as part of a turning point," Max said, "a fulcrum on which the Atlan turned. If this was made to create a fall, it'd represent a transition between the Atlan as they were under Kelmai—imperialistic, self-important, but also in crisis thanks to the demagogue they'd hoped to follow to galactic ascendance. How would that transition play out in design?"

"Can I get a copy of that book you mentioned?" Catalyst asked, practically hopping with excitement. "I've never actually seen any records of this. Just the stories my grandmother told me about how the Atlan used to be more than we are, that one day we would evolve again to become more than we've been. I took it to be nothing more than the same kind of long-lost golden age claptrap that every species seems to have, since the Vsenk have always been in charge."

The Genae had asked him not to share the texts. And Mirai would face even more backlash if it got out that he'd broken that trust.

But if he held the book back and they couldn't stop the Devastation, then there wouldn't be anyone left to help the Genae.

He'd been chewing on that reality since they departed Genos. He'd thought through plans where he had to hold back the texts, try to talk people through it. No matter what, he couldn't convince himself it would work if he held back. Was it worth breaking the Genae's trust to save a whole world?

"These were given to me in confidence. I shouldn't be sharing them, but I'm going to do it to give us a fighting chance." Let them call him an oathbreaker. He could skate around the letter of the law in transcribing or paraphrasing, but he'd still be breaking the spirit of the agreement. He could take the blame if it meant saving this world.

"We are very grateful for whatever you can share!"

And so they got to work. Max and company went on like that for several hours before Lahra grabbed him so they could eat dinner and meet the rest of the key staff.

"They'll still be there when we're done. But this can't wait," Lahra said.

It took ten minutes to disentangle himself from the conversational threads, and he couldn't wait to dive back in.

CHAPTER FIFTY-THREE

LAHRA

Hours later, Max was still in his scholar huddle, as were Lahra, Wheel, and seven others around a display table. The others included Uwen, Cog, and other command staff of the Atlan Resurgence.

Another Vsenk battleship had just appeared in orbit.

Yejol, an older Illhari veteran of the Imperial marines with a powerful build, held the room. His silver-white fur nearly glowed in the low lighting. "Our situation becomes direr. With Kelmai in the Vsenk's hands, we don't have much time. The next few hours and days could determine the fate of this galaxy."

"We can't strike now," said Cog. "Armed with only what we have here, we would be wiped out in minutes, and it would take more than a week for our distant allies to make it here, only to get wiped out just as fast as we did."

"Who are these allies?" Lahra asked. When you were organizing a revolution, you took the help you could get. But she needed to know who here was dependable, who was capable.

Yejol beamed, clearly proud of their ranks. "Resurgence

groups from a dozen planets, each fighting in their own way. No one group is enough to challenge the Vsenk in open combat, so for the time being, we operate in planetary cells. When the time comes, they will make themselves known."

"That's vague and not terribly helpful," Wheel said.

This was not the time for sniping comments. Even if she was right. They had to match the leaders' tone and tempo until they earned the trust to strike out on their own.

Lahra jumped in to smooth over Wheel's bluntness, thinking of how Max would do it. "What is the imperial presence like right now?"

Cog's expression turned sour. "This last week it's gone from hands-off to hands-on. Reports from our contacts say we're days away from full martial law—curfews, checkpoints, and more."

"We'll need to get everyone into place and set up encrypted comms before the crackdown," chirped Zekkik, a Rellix with yellow and green feathers, wearing faded urban fatigues. "Oyira is close to rolling out a new encryption, which will make it easier for us to stay in contact with cells elsewhere on Illhar."

Lahra gestured to the room. "What can we do here?"

Yejol looked to Lahra's armor. "You're soldier-caste, yes?"

"I am. Trained in the old ways by my mother."

"Good. Work with Zekkik on our local operations. We'll need to analyze the patrol patterns and determine new messenger routes, as well as sizing up local targets for guerilla strikes."

"If they're here looking for rebels and insurrection like the proclamations say, why should we give them reason to crack down?" Wheel asked.

Uwen puffed himself up to speak for the first time that meeting. "We can't just roll over and let them strangle the economy. We've worked too hard—"

Wheel cut in. "And if you give them cause, they'll destroy

this entire planet."

Yejol huffed, his whiskers shaking. "The Devastation hasn't been used in four hundred years. We won't push back that hard. But we have to show the people that we're not going to be intimidated into silence and inaction."

"You're playing a very dangerous game," Lahra said. "We cannot be too cautious when considering the Devastation. My people made that mistake once, too. And the Devastation on Genos wasn't even Kelmai. It was a lesser copy made by the Vsenk."

A wave of looks and muttering rippled through the meeting. Yejol cut it off. "First, we take the measure of the Vsenk occupation. We value your input, Lahra Kevain, and know that I have no intention of letting my world meet the fate that yours did."

Lahra nodded. The meeting moved on to more hands-on logistics, an overview of which forces and assets they had in play and where. Which projects to rush through before the crackdown could take effect, which were too fragile or visible to do anything but cover up until the occupation was relaxed.

The Resurgence was well-run, partially due to Yejol's experience and Cog's cunning. But one of their biggest assets was inclusion. They embraced different opinions and listened instead of crushing dissent with force. The Resurgence had learned the problems of Vsenk governance and built their operation as not just opposition to the government, but a refutation of its methods and first principles.

Perhaps there was hope, if faint. But the hard truth was that the Resurgence would never win without a major upset or a huge influx of military resources.

When the meeting was done, Lahra traveled downstairs to find Max.

He was deep in conference but noticed her arrival and picked his way through the chattering crowd.

"What's up?" he asked.

"You need to decipher that artifact and figure out how to stop Kelmai. Quickly. I don't think these people fully understand the Vsenk's petulance, or how quickly things move from conflict to destruction."

Max took it in with a long breath, the kind he took when preparing for a great challenge. "I've got help, at least. How long do you think we have?"

"Weeks, if that. Especially if they keep antagonizing the Vsenk. It'll also depend on who leads the occupying force. If it's the faction that controls this planet, we'll have more time. They're less extreme."

Max took a long breath. "Got it. I don't think it'll take that long. But if we have to do something, design an interface, or find a way to get the other one of the two, we could be in trouble."

Lahra shook her head, "We are already in a great deal of trouble. As is this whole planet."

"This isn't Genos, and the people here aren't your paranoid, stuck-up distant cousins."

"Let us hope that you are right and make it so by our actions."

Max reached out for her hand, balled in a fist from worry. "I'll do what I can. We all will." He brought her hand to his lips and kissed it tenderly, his eyes locked on hers. "And you—don't go off and get yourself killed trying to protect these folks from their own ridiculousness, okay?"

Her cheeks grew warm from the touch and the combination of love, worry, and humor in his words.

"Let us continue this debriefing in our chambers."

Max waggled his eyes conspiratorially, and the dam broke, a day of introductions and caution, of hope and frustration. Lahra could not help but laugh at the ludicrous display as she took his hand and they made their way to their room.

CHAPTER FIFTY-FOUR

MAX

THE NEXT MORNING, CATALYST and Oyira were huddled around the Atlan artifact. They'd both speed-read the Genae manuscript, and now they had questions.

So many questions.

Max had Lahra help explain Genae cultural assumptions that emerged from the text, then the group worked well into the night.

His life turned back into research mode for the next week.

Wake up, breakfast, morning briefing on Vsenk activities. Analysis and discussion in the Incubator, lunch provided by the members of the Resurgence who could remember to tie their own shoes and keep people from falling over from overworking. Then more study, write-ups of the day's progress.

Lahra kept him from burning out by insisting that he take dinner away from the Incubator. Out in the city, they watched as each day, the curfew got a little earlier, the patrols got a little more frequent, and the citizens grew a little more nervous.

On the rare times they did go outside, Max took to traveling with full cloaks in the way of the Iwur, the Yaea religious majority, and Lahra covered her armor with robes and cloaks to match. They did their best to blend in. Otherwise their evening dates—which they both needed in order to decompress—would become too dangerous.

They visited neighborhood restaurants, food carts, and open-air markets. Each night, there were fewer people around, and their worries became more pronounced. Rumors flew; people flinched at the glint of lights in the sky or the sound of treaded vehicles as Imperial patrols passed by.

Come each morning, they went back to work. Lahra provided context for the Genae writings, and Max pored over them again and again, talking the material through with the other members of the Incubator.

And then, finally, they cracked the code.

It came down to a pun. Catalyst had been joking about DNA-circuits, and a lightbulb lit in Max's mind.

He pulled up the circuit-story data he'd recorded in the Atlan tomb, reverse-engineered a dozen common phrases, then looked for the wordplay. The Old Atlan word for slumber rhymed with Kelmai's name, but only when you used Old Atlan speech cadence.

Max translated that word into Atlan machine compile, and then 3-D-printed it so he could get the correct hand position.

An hour of try-and-fail with the positioning, working with Catalyst and Oyira, and finally—

They got it.

The artifact unfolded like a mechanical flower in bloom, revealing a display screen, a handle, and a touch interface.

"Oh, damn. That's it. That's it."

The screen flickered on.

The display scrolled through diagnostics and sensor readouts faster than Max could parse the Old Atlan script.

Eventually, it stopped with three lines:

KEY 1: ACTIVE
KEY 2: ACTIVE
VESSEL STATUS: SLUMBER

Max's eyes couldn't be any wider if he were staring at Earth again. Two keys, two devices. This was one of the keys, and they worked independently but maybe together?

"Call a meeting for this afternoon," Catalyst said. "We need to find out where the Vsenk have the other smaller device."

"But first we need to confirm what they do," Max countered. "Do they wake him up? Do they control him? Do they interact with the vessel directly, or do they monitor it?"

"You work on that, I'll report to the others. Don't make any major moves until they've been informed. If we've got leverage on Kelmai, we don't want to play our hand too soon."

"For sure." Max scrolled back up to the beginning of the display and got to working through the BIOS readout. Old Atlan machine compile wasn't in his wheelhouse, so he'd need help to work through the code, especially if they were actually going to throw the switch on this artifact. And assuming that's the thing they'd want to do.

A huge question had just been unraveled, but it'd revealed a dozen more questions. And the situation with the Vsenk wasn't getting any better. Several Resurgence agents had already gone missing, and supplies were starting to dry up.

They weren't ready, but they might have to move soon, regardless.

Which meant he needed to provide answers on the double.

The meeting was called for two hours later, and by then, Max and the Incubator team had parsed out a decent chunk of the interface for the key, though they didn't yet know what commands to issue, or how the key connected to the vessel and to its double.

Max updated the group on everything they had learned so far, "We've still got a lot of questions about how everything fits together. It's still very early on in the research, now that we've got the artifact to open and display an interface. We're moving cautiously, because we don't want to turn it off before we understand what that means."

"Whatever we can be doing to undermine the Vsenk, we should be doing," Yejol said.

Wheel frowned. "But not at the risk of invoking the Empire's full wrath before we know that we have something that can stop them."

"Of course. Whatever you and the others need, you will have it. Removing the Devastation from play must be a priority."

Max pointed to the key. "Right now, what we could really use is intelligence on where the other key and vessel are, and some more people that can read Old Atlan to help brute-force translate the code."

Cog bobbed her head side-to-side. "We don't have anything on the other artifacts. But I can get you people that know Old Atlan. It'll take maybe a day or two to get them here. Lahra, you up for an escort mission?"

"Absolutely."

And that was that. Max went back to work, and Lahra went off with Cog to plan.

It was one thing to run into danger with Lahra. It was another when she did so on her own. Not like she couldn't take care of herself, but he worried. The same imagination that let him unravel puzzles also fed him worst-case scenarios in vivid detail. Especially when Lahra was involved. "Be careful, love," he said as she walked away.

"Obviously," she answered, with affection and strength. No one in this galaxy balanced those two qualities in the same way as Lahra, but no one could be strong all the time without breaking . . .

Once again, Max went down the elevator to the Incubator, to take another whack at the device. But hours into the next round of research and experimentation, his mind kept drifting to his beloved, to the danger she was about to step in once more. This was much more than another evening stroll through the neighborhood.

But they each had their battlefields.

Rather than focusing on the worry about what might happen to his wife out in the city, he threw himself into his work. The better he did in his arena, the more impact her work would have, and the easier he could make her job when the fighting began.

CHAPTER FIFTY-FIVE

AREK

EVERY CITY ON EVERY planet in the Empire had numerous buildings assigned for Imperial oversight. Many went
un-staffed or understaffed, but they were a constant reminder to the ruled that the eyes of their betters were upon them.

The oversight stations on Illhar had run on a skeleton
crew for years, but now, they were bustling.

Arek and his partner-supervisor Bekor stood at a Vsenk-
sized workstation in the main station in Illhar's capital city.

Underneath their three-and-a-half-meter-tall table were
shorter desks and screen stations for the lesser species. Attendants, guards, and soldiers scurried around them, offering
up reports, call requests, and more. The building, set aside
especially for Vsenk oversight, had gone from empty to bustling overnight, and it was beginning to grate on Arek, who
preferred the tidy efficiency and quiet of space.

After more than a year on the border systems in command of his own ship, having a babysitter was more than
tedious. It was insulting, stifling, and likely to end in a brawl.

Bekor was a junior member of Evam's faction, eager to
make her name by riding Arek like a rowdy klarna beast be-

fore it was broken.

But Arek was far smarter than a klarna and knew her game.

So he waged the smiling war, a method Qerol's predecessor Ekraw had popularized decades prior. Arek took advantage of having a so-called partner and shared the load. Read her in on every step of the investigation, asked her opinion, afforded her every courtesy. Doing so implicated her—if they failed, she failed. This meant that two weeks into their assignment, they were operating more like partners and less like prisoner and guard.

Bekor pointed to the holographic map of the city, selecting several nodes of light overlaid on the map.

The table was high for Arek's stature, another reminder of the ways in which he was always an outsider among his people. He worked only with his upper limbs, the lower ones focusing on passing material to and from the attendants below.

Bekor spoke with the certainty of a fanatic. "We're seeing increased movement in the evening and early morning in the dock district, the entertainment towers, and the outlying neighborhoods."

Arek reviewed the numbers to confirm. "Increased compared to the rest of the day, and fewer people are out overall. We have cameras on checkpoints and thoroughfares, as well as double-strength patrols, but we've not picked up any messengers. With the curfew taking effect today, we'll be able to tighten our grip and have a better chance to sort between people going about their business and your hypothetical rebels."

Bekor crossed a second set of limbs. Arek should not antagonize her, but he was getting frustrated by the entire mission. They were one of three lead investigator teams, the others overseeing the investigation in the world's second and third largest cities. The third team also oversaw the smaller forces gathering information in the next five largest cities, whose populations together were less than a tenth of that of the capital. If there was any resistance on Illhar, it would have to flow through those cities. But they were still chasing ghosts. Evam was so certain, but if there was an insurrection on Illhar, they were covering their tracks well.

"We're closer than you think," Bekor declared. "Every day, sources fill the data banks with tips, leads, and more. The analysts are building profiles to enable arrests as soon as the lockdown takes effect."

Arek walked away from the table, ready to head out for their direct oversight of the first post-curfew patrol. "You would know the enforcement side better than I," he said in a peace offering. "I am eager to have the clarity the curfew will provide, and I hope we can move quickly so that any insurrectionists we might find will not have time to react."

"This investigation will take as long as it needs to."

"But if it goes quickly, then Evam will be pleased by our efficiency, and by the way we minimized the disruption to the flow of business. Everyone wins."

"Only if we catch the rebels."

"Assuming they are still here," Arek countered. Bekor had not once acknowledged the fact that he could be right. Stubbornness so powerful that it warped reality was another of the less endearing traits of the Vsenk nobility. In the Empire, only Vsenk truth could apply. But when two of their people argued, those warring world-views played out across every part of their interaction.

The squads were ready. As the senior member of the team, Bekor gave the briefing. And then they set out into the early evening, watched from windows and roofs by scared citizens.

Illhar had always been an Imperial holding, but when Arek and Bekor arrived, it was truly occupied. Now, several weeks later, it was completely locked down. A military vessel could retain this level of discipline almost indefinitely with proper leadership and shift rotation. But the capital city on a planet given leeway and flexibility, home to a species known for their intense social ties and inquisitiveness? Before long, there would not need to be revolutionaries in Axhara for there to be problems with this curfew.

And when they happened, Arek would be ready for them. Ideally showing Bekor that Evam's intelligence had been faulty all along, and her faction leader's grudge was just that—an act of poorly-masked retribution aimed at the most profitable planet in Qerol's territories.

If he could keep himself from scoring points and stick to the mission, he might even come out of this with an ally.

Or, Bekor and Evam could be proven right, and unless Arek could get in front of it and address the terrorists with sufficient zeal, millions could die for the treason of a few. Wasting lives was bad governance, inefficient. An empire without subjects was nothing more than children playing pretend, rulers on a throne of ash.

CHAPTER FIFTY-SIX

LAHRA

THERE WERE FEW GOOD times to have a fight with one's spouse.

Mere hours before departing on a life-threatening mission was one of the worst.

Lahra should have known better than to let her feelings impinge upon her efficiency, but despite what Wheel said, she could not "shut down" her emotions.

She merely controlled them. There were a thousand threats pressing in: the Vsenk, infighting within the Resurgence, and doubtless some agents of Jesvin were searching the galaxy for them as well. But she would face them in the order they appeared.

"If you remove an enemy's weapon before they begin to use it," she'd said in their room, standing by the door, arms crossed, "they will have time to adjust their plan of attack."

Max paced, showing his anger through movement. His voice was level, quiet. "But if you can remove a weapon that destroys entire worlds, don't you want to do that as soon as fucking possible? What if they don't start here? What if they blow up some other planet while we're waiting for the right moment here?"

"This could be the difference between putting off a war and starting it with a decisive victory. This Resurgence needs every advantage it can get, both military and socially. Our intelligence finds it unlikely that the Imperium is preparing to use Kelmai anywhere but here. And the propaganda team made a very clear case for waiting to turn Kelmai on the Vsenk until he is out in the open. Seeing the Vsenk's super-weapon turned against them, and the implications of Kelmai's nature, will cut straight through the spine of the Vsenk's orthodoxy."

Max kept pacing as he talked through his thoughts. "I get the strategic advantage, but there's got to be a more dependable way of doing it. Video footage, release our research, intercept Kelmai before he can do too much damage. If we got the other key, we could shut him down and then wait until the Resurgence is ready to strike. Though maybe then they could just activate their key. We're still trying to figure it out."

"The right time to strike is when you're ready, or when you're left no other option. Controlling the battle is essential."

"But we do have options."

"We feel that we do now, but we can't see the enemy's full intentions. Kelmai is too powerful a symbol, once identified, to leave un-used. And if your reports about the keys are correct, Yejol's plan will devastate the Vsenk occupying force. Maybe their entire fleet."

"And if it doesn't, this entire planet dies, and maybe another half-dozen like it. We have to wait. The report we gave was only preliminary. There are too many unknowns for you all to take up the key like it's just another weapon."

There was power in using the weapon that had destroyed her people against those that had done it. She would not do so lightly. But he knew that.

She rolled her shoulders back, softened her voice. "We

are not the ones who get to make this decision. It impacts millions of other people. And I believe we're both too emotionally invested in this. This argument is not about us."

But Max did not match her action of de-escalation. His focus was turned inward. "But we're the ones having it! If I can't even convince you that this is a terrible idea, why should the others listen to me? If you're not on my side, why should they be?"

Lahra stiffened. "I am always on your side. But that doesn't mean I have to agree with you on all things, especially things greater than the two of us."

It was then, at exactly the wrong time, that Cog knocked on the door to their quarters to collect her for the mission.

She kissed Max goodbye. He kept his arms crossed and did not kiss her back. The hurt on his face wrapped around her like a leaden weight.

It made her slow, and clumsy, and she hated it. But she could not put it out of her mind, even though she knew that she'd been right to try to separate their marriage from the argument.

***

It should have been the work of an hour. Take transit across the city, pick up the translators, and return in time for dinner.

But fate was not with them. A hard curfew came down mere hours before they began the mission, and now they had to adapt.

Cog had floated the notion of waiting until morning, but there would still be checkpoints and patrols. And every hour they waited brought Kelmai closer, Lahra was sure of it.

Her group of three moved down alleys and wove through houses of those sympathetic to the cause. There were far more of those lately—more every day, thanks to the crackdown.

Cog had five small spider drones scouting for the group. They climbed both low and high, ahead and behind, taking footage with tiny cameras. The fifth circled the group, providing coverage from different angles. The video fed to Cog's wrist-screen, keeping the group one step ahead of the Imperial patrols. Whenever a patrol came near, the spider drones transformed into the shapes of discarded scrap, and the trio hid until the drones gave the all-clear.

It was slow going. The journey stretched out for three hours of deliberate routing through lesser-used streets and alleyways. But Cog moved well, knew the city, and kept them safe.

The third member of their crew was an Illhari ex-soldier named Kihyo. He'd done two tours with the Imperial army, then joined the Resurgence after his cousin was executed by the Vsenk for misdemeanor theft. Cog vouched for his loyalty.

They reached the safe house two hours before midnight. It was a single-family dwelling with a basement, carved out over the years by the matriarch of the family, an Illhari named Ocza. She met them at the back door, ushering them inside and immediately down the stairs into the basement through a false back to her pantry.

Very well-designed. An alternate entrance would be better, but Ocza was not a soldier, not a spy. She was a grandmother who had seen this all coming years ago when the Special Economic Zone was first instituted.

Ocza told them the whole thing as she prepared a round of tea. Or, tried. Cog humored the older Illhari for a few minutes, then said, "I'm very sorry, Ocza, but I need to talk to everyone here to tell them the plan. Thank you again for your hospitality."

They sat on cushions and pillows and talked over tea. Lahra preferred stronger brews, but there was a calming effect to sharing a large pot of tea, a symbolic communion that made it clear that they were bound up in the moment together.

Not many Atlan knew the ancient form of their language

and had the technical knowledge to read not just Old Atlan but Programmer Old Atlan. So they had to look beyond the existing members of the rebellion.

Resurgence couriers had passed along the basics of the plan to the three Atlan, but these people were not experienced revolutionaries. They were everyday citizens putting their lives on the line. They needed to be over-prepared so that they had something to hold on to if and when something went wrong.

Cog walked the translators through the plan, then she did it again, more slowly, taking questions. Then she had Axle, one of the Atlans, explain it back to be clear that everything was understood. Axle was very old, with cybernetic replacements for one leg, an arm, both eyes, and half their torso.

Max said that Terrans used replacement limbs sometimes on Earth, but the Atlan did it so commonly that it was barely worth noting within their people. Just another part of getting old. Replace parts as they break down until something breaks down at the wrong time and they can't be brought back from the brink. It meant that many Atlan lived well past a hundred years, like Axle and their companion, Vector, an older woman.

The third Atlan, Prime, was Vector's grandson, a youth barely out of adolescence. He was full of energy but little discipline. Lahra would have to watch him to make sure he didn't do anything brash.

After Axle got the plan right, Cog was satisfied. "Okay, we're good. Now let's get moving before the midnight shift change." The Vsenk were complacent in some ways, but the forces occupying Illhar were smart—they ran six shifts, two active at any time. That way, there were never more than four hours before a shift change, and half of the people on-shift were always fresh.

First, Cog's spider drones spread out to scan the area.

They reported the all-clear with helpful chirps, and the group headed out. They broke into three pairs—Cog and Axle, Kihyo and Prime, Lahra and Vector. They wore their cloaks in several styles to throw off attention and block the rising winds of the Illhari nights. They moved just far enough apart to protect against area attacks, close enough to cover one another.

They moved at a quick walk wherever possible. They had to balance between speed and safety, while also keeping in mind the endurance of their Atlan charges.

Before long, the spider drones alerted Cog of a patrol. Lahra and Cog directed the Atlans to duck behind trash cubes while Kihyo watched their backs.

Once the patrol passed and the all-clear signal came in on Cog's screen, they resumed. Cog moved the spiders out to wider coverage and ordered the fifth to scout ahead.

Cog had programmed them well.

Lahra wondered how much it would cost to procure a pair for her and Max to use when this was all over. Max could write scripts for them to look for patterns and important information on their archaeological expeditions.

Thinking about Max and their fight soured her mood. She renewed her focus, eyes and ears tuned in to the sounds and sights of the city, great and small. The city lights stayed bright throughout the evening to help the Vsenk enforce the curfew.

A third of the way into the trip, they hit their first major snarl. One of the spider drones slipped and fell. The noise attracted a patrol, and Lahra was left with three choices:

1) Flee
2) Face the patrol
3) Change to a new route

Lahra chose option three. She kicked open a door and rushed the group inside.

An office building, empty and dark. Lucky. She pulled

back her cloak and let her chem-light shine, illuminating the room in dull red light.

"Get down and move quick. That hallway there, then find a doorway. Cog, get us a new route."

Cog nodded, and they moved low through the office building, past working pods and computer servers, past conference rooms and break areas. It was mundane, too normal for the impossible times. Rebel fighters sneaking through an office building in the dark while avoiding military patrols during martial law. This was her life now, the space-faring adventures seeming so far away. How long would this last?

She put her questions away and looked to Cog. The Atlan shot her a message on encrypted short-band wireless, proposing a route that avoided the new patrols. Lahra sent back her approval.

Cog led them through the office building, past calendars advertising a company retreat, then a messy break room with posted complaints from some Atlan worker about food missing from the shared fridge.

Cog pushed open the office door and guided the group out into a covered garage, then down and out to the street. A few minutes later, they were back on track.

Or so she thought.

Cog turned a corner and then immediately back-pedaled, waving her arms at Lahra for the group to retreat.

Lahra heard the stomping of boots from down the alley. She counted six soldiers.

And then she heard the Vsenk.

Their luck had run out entirely.

Any Genae-sized species mostly sounded the same in boots as they marched—telling them apart required training and experience. But the Vsenk were totally unmistakable, their footfalls crashing like thunder. Lahra held Vector back with one arm as the group jogged away from the squadron. The elder Atlan had some energy left, but she still moved slowly. Overland evasion wasn't going to cut it. They'd have to find another hideout and detour or fight.

Lahra's sword was too large and conspicuous for a stealth mission. Instead, she bore a small scattergun and a one-handed sword. She adjusted the cloak and drew the scattergun.

"Halt!" came the shout from the squadron.

But the sound of the Vsenk stopped. It wasn't coming from anywhere.

"The Vsenk is flanking us," she said to the group. "Weapons hot, we need to punch our way out."

In a handful of moments, their position had gone from risky to desperate.

She sounded the alarm on her transponder, which would feed directly back to the Resurgence base and then erase itself from her wrist-screen.

The Vsenk squadron rounded the corner. Cog had reached the street, where they'd have room to maneuver but also more space for the Vsenk.

"Way out?" she asked.

"I've got nothing!" was Cog's slightly panicked answer.

As she suspected. But there was a reason she'd volunteered for this mission. "You take them. I'll catch up or see you back at HQ." Lahra had not known that was her decision before she said it, but what else could it be? The mission was more important than one life, and she could fight better on her own than while guarding five people. Especially when she didn't know how most of them moved or how they would react.

"I'll stay, too!" Kihyo said.

"No. You protect them," Lahra shouted as the squadron opened fire. Lahra charged, her suit taking the first few shots without complaint. She fired the scattergun to force them into cover. Then she pulled her cloak off and tossed it to provide concealment for her companions.

Drawing the sword with her off-hand, she shouted, "For

Genos!" and engaged an entire squadron by herself.

The chaos of battle took hold, shouts and blasts and clangs and grunts. The beautifully brutal music of combat. She belted "Yuxi at the Pass" to give her stamina and the heightened awareness needed to fight alone against stacked odds. Every moment she held their attention gave Cog and the others just a bit more breathing room.

These troops were mediocre—no command of small-unit tactics. Their commander, a Yaea, missed his opportunity to call for the squad to re-group. Lahra brought down four of the soldiers before the commander could even draw his dueling blade. She shot the last of his troops point-blank with the scattergun and faced off against the commander.

"Your squad is dead," she said. "Think you'll fare any better?"

"No, but she will," the Yaea commander answered, looking past Lahra's shoulder.

The sound of a jetpack and the settling of a Vsenk's weight in the alley told her all she needed to know.

Lahra launched forward into a lunge, ready to feint, but the commander was so surprised that the original blow struck true. The sword caught the commander in the shoulder. Lahra followed through, ramming the blade in to the hilt, then spun and used the Yaea as cover as the Vsenk advanced. The colorings showed her to be a female, and she stood nearly six meters tall. She wasted no time, her massive scattergun filling the alleyway with plasma fire.

Without her sword of station, Lahra had no real way of penetrating the Vsenk's armor, save turning the Vsenk's own weapon against her.

It was a viable gambit, if difficult. But that had never stopped Lahra before.

Lahra filled in her own name in the part of "Yuxi at the Pass" where Yuxi shouted her lineage, facing a hundred soldiers during a heavy storm. "I am Lahra Kevain, daughter of

Halra, daughter of Aytra. I have fought your kind before and emerged victorious. This will be no different."

The Vsenk smiled and opened fire.

Lahra dove to the side, taking cover behind a trash bin. The scattergun shredded the bin, but Lahra's armor held against the splash-through.

She snapped up from cover to take a shot and refresh her view of the alley.

There was a sewer grate ten paces behind the Vsenk. That was her way out. But first she had to delay the Vsenk long enough that she couldn't follow Lahra's people.

Which meant going toe-to-toe with a god-warrior, armed only with a middling gun and a borrowed sword.

But she was Genae.

Singing the final verse of "Yuxi at the Pass," Lahra rolled out from cover, opening fire.

The scattergun's spray sizzled on the Vsenk's carapace, leaving no mark.

She didn't even blink, Lahra mused. How unfazed the Vsenk was, so confident in her victory.

Overconfidence was a flaw as deadly as a cracked breastplate.

Lahra continued to advance. The Vsenk were so large that infighting with a smaller creature required them to grapple.

And Lahra was possibly the best practitioner of her people's wrestling tradition left alive, even including the survivors on Genos.

She fired the scattergun one more time, pushing the Vsenk back. Then she dropped the gun and swung her sword at the noble's weapon. Two of the Vsenk's tentacle-limbs countered—one high, one low. She dove between them, point-first. The blade deflected off to one side, leaving a welt. Lahra recovered into a crouch, rising with a stab to the noble's trunk. Again, the blow skipped off the carapace, but Lahra kept moving.

She wove in and out of the noble's field of view, constantly circling to limit the Vsenk's use of her extra limbs.

If only her mother could see her then. She was a vessel of the will of her people, their vengeance poured into her and dumped upon the Vsenk in a downpour.

She threw punches, elbows and knees, thrusts and cuts, using all of her limbs in concert to work her way around the Vsenk's arms.

Three times her sword struck true, but only once did it leave a crack in the Vsenk's chitin. With her sword of station, the Vsenk would have already lost the tip of one of her hands.

But the Vsenk and Lahra's greatsword weren't made for tight alleyways like this. That was the other reason Lahra had the chance that she did. In pursuing Lahra, the Vsenk had given up one of her advantages. Which allowed Lahra to prolong the battle.

Most fights were over in moments—a quick assessment, a single volley of blows, a decisive victor. But to protect her allies, keep the Vsenk attention on her and not her companions as they improvised a new route back, Lahra had to drag it out. And that was costly. No fighter could predict and respond to every attack with the perfect counter, no matter the training. Not for long. Not when she had no real way of presenting a credible threat and when the Vsenk could focus on offense.

First, the Vsenk caught her across the shoulder with a swipe of a limb, numbing her arm. Then, several exchanges later, she got a hold of Lahra's leg and squeezed, cracking the armor on her calf.

High on adrenaline, Lahra fought through the injuries, tallying seconds in her mind as the battle unfolded by measuring the length of her battle songs.

When the Vsenk had arrived, she'd re-started her count of the lead time she'd given her friends. Lahra took a blow to the head at 80 seconds, then a barely-blocked thrust to the body at 173. At 200 seconds, she bet that her companions would have the lead they needed, and made one last bargain, accepting a gash across her back to secure her escape route.

Lahra levered the grate open with the sword, then dropped into the sewer, praying that the drop-off wasn't too bad, that she wouldn't land wrong, and that the Vsenk wouldn't be able or interested in tearing up the whole alley to follow her.

She was right, wrong, and right, in that order.

Ten feet down, Lahra hit concrete. But only with one foot. She folded up and tried to roll to minimize the impact, landing hard on her shoulder through five centimeters of cold sludge.

Her leg and shoulder cried out in agony. That pain rippled out and re-ignited the others, her body shuddering.

Lahra looked up, catching the shadow of black against black. A burst of plasma shot down into the sewer, burning the concrete and vaporizing sludge just feet behind her. Despite burning waves of pain, Lahra kept moving, half-roll, half-scuttle, until the Vsenk's cursing faded. Lahra stood, wobbling on her injured leg as she re-activated her suit's light.

The sewer pathway stretched out for more than a kilometer ahead.

She tried to hail Cog via her wrist-screen.

No signal.

That's not good.

As she sang the command for her armor to run a diagnostic, Lahra saw the real problem—one of the times she'd blocked a limb-swipe, her armor had cracked just beyond the screen, damaging the circuitry. Not enough to be obvious during the fight, but more than enough to ruin her comms system.

Which meant that she was on her own. In a strange city, with Imperial forces on her heels. It wouldn't take long for reinforcements to flood the sewers.

And she wasn't getting caught, not again. She got moving once more, taking the first available turn, then the first beyond that. She mapped out the pathway in her mind, laid it on top of the section of the city map she'd committed to memory going into the mission. But the image was fuzzy; she was losing focus. She'd survived three minutes of close combat with a Vsenk noble. Not many could say the same, even among her people.

But the survived portion would only matter if she got back in one piece. If she could tell the tale to Max, if they could settle their argument in a healthy manner.

And push the Vsenk back long enough to get off of the planet.

"Keep going," she told herself. Singing in a soft voice, Lahra recited her lineage to stay focused, all the way back to the chapters of the Genae epics. Minutes later, she'd taken five turns and found an alcove. She could stop and gather her breath before pushing on.

But if she stopped, she might not be able to start again. Instead, she marked the location in her mind and kept going, winding her way to the Resurgence base as best she could manage. Soon enough, she'd find another entrance and see if the way were clear. It might be that she'd need to stay the night in the sewer, dodging patrols, and hope she could keep her wayfinding strong enough to emerge in the district containing the Resurgence HQ.

For now, she just had to keep going. She held an image of Max in her mind, one of her mother, and one of that split-second of fear she'd seen on the noble's face back on the *Kettle* when he realized what Lahra had done with the rocket.

Love, loyalty, and anger fed her. She pushed onward.

CHAPTER FIFTY-SEVEN

WHEEL

WHEEL DIDN'T WANT TO tell Max what had happened. But she had to. It'd be even worse if he heard from someone else. Cog's party was still thirty minutes out, assuming nothing else went wrong. But they'd lost Lahra's signal and could not hail her on comms.

Which meant that Wheel had maybe thirty-three minutes before Max would begin tearing the base up.

This wasn't supposed to happen. This kind of thing *didn't* happen.

One, Lahra rarely left Max's side when things were going to shit, because she was the one keeping him from getting dead. Two, Lahra rarely got in over her head unless all three of them were there together working on making it right.

But things had changed since they got to Illhar, and moping about the way things were had never been Wheel's style.

She paced and processed, considering the options. Max was down in the Incubator—working as hard as he could to put the mission out of his mind, no doubt.

What could she say to inform him without setting him

up to do something ridiculous and self-destructive? Maybe she should let him. He had a right to be worried.

But they also needed him to keep working.

This was the kind of thing she could usually talk to Lahra about, but you couldn't debug code when your hardware was broken.

Instead, she decided to get it over with so she could go back to work instead of worrying.

She found Max and the other brainiacs huddled over the unlocked key.

"Max, got a second?"

"What's up? Is Lahra back?" he asked.

She pulled him a few steps away.

Better to just get right to it. "They ran across an Imperial Patrol. Including a Vsenk." Max's eyes went wide, his body tensing up. She kept going before he could interrupt with a flood of questions. "Lahra sent Cog and the others off to get away, held her ground to keep them occupied. Then we lost contact."

Max put his hands on his face, pacing, but let her continue. "We lost her signal and transponder at the same time— comms team thinks that her wireless radio took damage in the fight. We know where it happened, and scouts are already on the move to re-establish contact. Cog and the others should be here in a few minutes."

Max passed Wheel, heading for the elevator. "I need to be out there with them. I know how she thinks—"

Wheel caught up to the Terran in three long strides. "You know her, but you don't know the city like our scouts do. And after the skirmish, the Imperial activity in the city has doubled. We have to be smart about this. And smart means you here, working on that thing," she said, pointing to the artifact. "Getting ready for the Atlan who can help you crack the code or whatever it is. Make sure that Lahra's choice has meaning, that we all get what she wanted."

Max snapped, "Don't talk about her like she's gone."

"Oh, I have every confidence that she's still out there and kicking ass. But you can't help her by trying to strap on a gun and going off to get yourself killed."

Max didn't respond. Which meant he was going to go do something ridiculous.

CHAPTER FIFTY-EIGHT

MAX

MAX CHARGED OUT OF the elevator, his voice filling the room. "I need a weapon!"

Oyira looked shocked, Catalyst crossed his arms, and both Chrenae and Usev stared at him in confusion.

"I'm serious!" he shouted, growing increasingly frustrated by the room's silence. "Lahra is out there being hunted by the Empire, and I need to do something about it. Catalyst, don't you have some kind of bio-weapon I could use? Something that would let me take a bite out of a Vsenk without having to spend a decade learning to fight? I'll have backup, I just need some good armor or a weapon to balance the scales."

"This is fear and worry speaking," Catalyst said slowly. "You're not a fighter. You go out there and fight, you will die. We need you here. She needs you here. Do the work, have faith, and the others will bring Lahra back."

They were right, but Max wasn't in the mood to be sensible. "I'm sick and tired of being on the sideline every time it comes to a fight," he fumed. "Just because I can't hold a candle to the deadliest woman in the galaxy doesn't mean I can't fight. And if things go bad, I know how to stay out of the way during a battle, thanks to years of being kept out of the way. I can do all of that while using a blaster or bio-laser or whatever."

Catalyst waved to the shelves and workstations. "I'm not exactly drowning in weaponry here, Max. Everything I can and have produced I've handed over to the Resurgence."

Oyira said, "I understand that you're determined to find her. But what if you go and get hurt, and we can't unlock the key because of it? Then millions die, including you and Lahra. Everyone has their fight, their skills. Lahra wouldn't want you to risk your life for her."

Max's shoulders slumped. "She does it for me every day."

Oyira placed a gentle hand on his shoulder. "She chooses to do so. And she's trained for it. She was born to protect. Our people were not made the same way." He hadn't bothered to tell the brain trust where he really came from, though he suspected they already knew—or at least Oyira did—that he wasn't your average Yaea.

Usev waved Max over to the key. "Make yourself useful and come here to check my reasoning on this. I think the source code may be using quantum bases, but only as one of two systems. Very complicated. Chrenae and I are getting bogged down on the hybridity of the programming, and we could use a fresh perspective."

Max flexed his fingers, making a fist and then releasing.

Logically, he knew they were right. But he'd blown up at Lahra, and the thought of leaving it like that, where he'd kept barreling ahead when she was trying to be diplomatic, it just wouldn't do.

But this wasn't Earth. He didn't have to do what was expected of him. Lahra was the fighter: She wanted to fight. Needed to fight. His brain was his weapon.

And that's how he'd convince Wheel and Cog to let him join the rescue effort. Right after he cracked this hybrid machine code on the key. After that, they couldn't advance at more than a crawl until the three Old Atlan-fluent consultants arrived. Finish up here, and then there'd be no reason not to let him join the search, at least on the organizational level.

That settled it. He joined Usev and Chrenae, taking a deep breath and returning his focus to the problem at hand.

***

Three hours later, they'd cracked the machine language, and Max went straight up to plead his case to Wheel. But they were already gone. Wheel, Cog, and several of the Resurgence scouts.

Jgori, a young Illhari who Max recognized as Yejol's assistant, handed Max a datapad. "Wheel left this message for you, Mr. Walker."

It read:

Hey Max,

I know you're fuming. I get it. Never get to go out and have fun with the other self-sacrificing soldier-types. Trust me, it's not really that fun. Seen my fair share of firefights, and if it made sense for me to be downstairs tooling around with you, I would be. Not my scene. I'm more of a "hit it until it works" kind of engineer.

So, to make it easier for you, we left as soon as you went downstairs. We'll bring her back even if I have to tear a half-dozen Vsenk apart with nothing more than a welding torch and a spanner. We'll stay in touch by comms—talk to Jgori and he'll get you set up.

Sorry,
Wheel

Max sighed, handed the datapad back to Jgori, and said, "Okay, take me to the comms station. But first, coffee?"

Jgori nodded. Max filled two mugs, handed one to the young Illhari, and they joined the team huddled around the comms equipment. A real government would have entire buildings dedicated to comms, but in the Resurgence it amounted to a row of consoles and headphones for a variety of head and ear configurations.

"What's happening with the rescue party?" Max asked. A middle-aged Illhari woman raised a hand to shush him for a second, then pulled off an ear of the headphones and lowered her hand.

"They've met up with the original party. Some are headed back with the Atlan. Wheel and the others are looking for Lahra now. They think she may have gone underground, based on the chatter we're hearing from the Imperial forces."

Jgori piped in, "The Vsenk have sent several squadrons into the sewer system. We have public works maps of the system, here. Would you care to help us work out where she might have gone?"

God bless him, Max thought to himself.

"Let me at it," he said, glad to have the work. "But when we have it worked out, I'm going out with the second rescue squad."

Jgori pushed the schematics to the nearest table console. Then they circled an area on the northeast corner of the readout, a maze of tubes and rectangles representing the sewer system under the capital city. "So, based on Cog's report, the Imperials struck here, so we think she started in this area . . ."

CHAPTER FIFTY-NINE

AREK

THE CALL HE'D HOPED to never hear had exploded all over their comms system, and so now he and Bekor were scouring the city with an entire division, trying to close the net on a single Genae soldier-caste fighter.

Citizens cowered behind cordons, looked on with fear from windows and doors and rooftops. The Vsenk had control here, but it was only hard control. Before the crackdown, the Empire had benefited from the Illhari's innovation through influence, with violence held back as a threat. Now the threat had become reality, and there was little more they could do to make the people of this planet comply. Dead citizens couldn't comply, though they couldn't resist, either. And worse, they couldn't pay taxes.

The situation was rocketing directly toward the worst-case scenario he'd feared. An active insurrection, cause for the destruction of Illhar, and with it, both the economic base and credibility of the Bright Suns. Gone with it would be his chances of a settled life on Vsenkos and any hopes for his daughter to live a better life than he had.

They reached the site of the skirmish, blocked off by the

squadron that rushed onto the scene to re-enforce Kulair, the Vsenk captain who had routed the Genae into the sewers.

Arek stomped around the alleyway, replaying the battle in his mind to study the Genae's fighting style. If there was a rebellion, Lahra Kevain could be a part of it, and she might be the very Genae they sought. She and her mate had not professed any revolutionary sentiment, but there was a very thin line between resisting authority and insurrection, and that line had long since been blurred into nothingness by Evam's hard-liners.

Standing just beyond the alley, Bekor said, "Are you quite done? The squadrons in the sewers just checked in and are asking for orders." She was giving him a courtesy by mentioning it, since she could just provide orders herself and cut him out. He was making progress, then.

Arek stepped over the cordon and joined Bekor.

"Repeat your last, lieutenant."

The voice of an Illhari came on the radio. "Commanders, we've covered eight kilometers of sewer pathways here, but the tracks have gone cold. She's skilled, whoever she is, skilled enough to have led us in circles. She's outside this district for sure, that much we can say. But to expand our search, we'll need another three squadrons, or a guess which direction to go."

"Map." Arek beckoned the attendant forward. A slim Rellix with white feathers produced a pop-up hologram with a map of the city. "The port district is the most likely avenue of escape. Any fugitive would try to get out of the city or off-planet, pointless though it would be to try to run the blockade."

Bekor stepped around the map, taking it in from several angles like a predator sizing up their prey. "Send one squad south toward the port. Another will go east toward the major gate bearing for the major sub-cities."

"Understood. Thank you, commanders. Lieutenant Ioyf out."

A squadron of soldiers stood waiting for their next command.

If the Genae were still in the sewers, there would be little he and Bekor could do to engage directly in the search.

"How are the patrols holding up?" Arek asked the Yaea attendant. The Imperium had called in all the off-duty units, and soon enough, they'd start losing efficiency due to fatigue and hunger. The lesser species could not operate for more than half a day without rest. The fugitive would be similarly fatigued, but Kevain or not, this was no ordinary Genae.

"All units have reported in at the top of the hour, as commanded," said the Rellix attendant.

"No, how are they doing? How much longer can they stay on-duty before we'll need to step down the searches and return to the normal six-shift patrol schedule?"

"The soldiers are quite capable. They will continue to search as long as—"

Arek cut the Rellix off. "Don't give me the politick answer. I want the realistic one. Bone-tired soldiers aren't worth anything to us, and there are more problems in this city than one fugitive. We cannot commit the entire garrison to an endless search."

"We can, and we will," Bekor said. "If she is not found in four hours, relieve the two most fatigued shifts. And call down another division from the blockade fleet. That should suffice for reinforcements."

"Understood!" The Rellix saluted. He looked briefly to Arek in what he took to be appreciation, then vanished to execute their will.

"Return to your patrols," Arek told the squadron. "Keep your eyes out for any Genae, as well as anyone else breaking the curfew. The Genae terrorist is your number one priority, but you must also keep the peace."

"Yes, Commander!" came the squadron's reply.

"Go." He waved them off. He needed to speak to Bekor

with no prying ears.

The squadron fell out, moving east to resume their patrol. That left the two of them with just an honor guard of four elites. They could be discreet.

"Strength untempered by reason is brittleness," Arek said to his colleague.

"Mercy in the face of adversity is weakness."

"And spending all of your troops in the opening gambit leaves you with no reserves. If there is a rebellion on this planet, there will be more than a single party of curfew-breakers. We must ascertain what they were intending to do next. If we do not learn to anticipate their potential movements, we will be forced to play defense and always be one step behind."

Bekor nodded only at his last words. "Now you're beginning to act like you actually care about victory."

"I care about stability. And a stable, smart police force knows how to anticipate the actions of criminals."

"Agreed. I'm glad you've come to your senses. We have a Genae, four Atlan, and an Illhari moving through alleys hours after curfew. What does the composition of that group tell you?"

The two walked and continued their discussion, reviewing the material and building profiles of the Genae as well as her colleagues. There were two groups to find and little intelligence to go on. That the patrols hadn't picked up the group of five was both disconcerting as to the effectiveness of the garrison and gave the likelihood that the terrorists had collaborators or allies elsewhere in the city.

"Attendant!" Arek bellowed. The Rellix appeared once more, feathers ruffled. "Give us all of the city's outstanding warrants and details about local cartels. We need to determine what connections these dissidents might have and the neighborhoods where they might find more sympathetic eyes and ears. Then we will be able to both track the terrorists and crack down on local crime syndicates."

Bekor nodded, taking the datapad offered by the Rellix for their consideration. Data streamed in as the group headed south. "We'll have them, and then we can be done with this tiresome investigation and get back to the real governance."

"Every part of it is real," Arek said. "We're holding the lives of millions in our grasp with this investigation. To forget that is to diminish the importance of our custodial duties."

"You can take pride in doting after the lesser species. I have better things to do."

Arek suppressed a sigh. Instead, he extended a limb for the datapad. If she was going to be petulant, there was little point in seeking to change her mind. "If you wish, I can take over the investigation and leave you to whatever it is you'd rather be doing. I'm sure Evam would approve."

Arek looked to his partner-jailer, daring her to quit. Bekor met his glare for a moment, then looked away. "No; no. I will see this through to the end. And then Evam will be informed of your ineptitude."

Evam did not need the truth to view Arek as inept and unworthy. "That will be a great joy for him, I'm sure. Now let's get back to the task before us."

CHAPTER SIXTY

LAHRA

SIX HOURS AFTER THEIR mission had gone astray, Lahra was tired, soaked, and taxed to her limits.

Each time she'd made it to the surface, a patrol drove her back into the sewer within minutes. But those above-ground checks had told her that she was close to the Resurgence base. The problem then was that the entire port district was swarming with patrols.

She'd tried to repair her wrist-screen, but it was no use. Without a power source to fuel the song of repair, the transmitter was dead. And the song would take full light and several minutes of full-voiced singing to work.

Lahra stopped one last time in the dim light of a resting point for public works. Pulling the cord to the transmitter out, she tried to wire it into the short-wave transmitter in her helmet.

Nothing. She didn't have the tools needed to make a new connection.

If Max or Wheel were here, they'd be able to do it. But she wouldn't have let them stay with her, even if it took knocking Max out with a pressure point and having Wheel haul him away on her shoulders.

She'd evaded capture so far. With just a bit more work, she'd be within range of a single sprint to the honeycomb of safe houses and sympathizers by Resurgence HQ.

So painfully close. Close to safety, to Max, and the chance to put things right. To live and fight the next battle.

I've fought two Vsenk and lived, mother, she thought. A feat few could claim, and one she couldn't have imagined even a few years ago working bodyguard odd jobs on the Wreck. *Let me make it just a bit farther so I can do it once more.*

It was not that surprising that a patrol marched into earshot just then, coming from around the corner that was next on her path.

She was exposed there, in the light. She could take refuge in the sewers, try to outrun them, or fight.

Lahra was a Genae royal guard, and she was tired of running. Tired of hiding.

She checked the scattergun, confirming for the third time that it was still functional after her trek through the sewers. She backed up against the wall of the workstation. The walls brightened from black to gray-scale to faded blues as the lights and sounds came nearer.

One squadron, moving slow.

Their commander would have a comm unit. All she had to do was broadcast in the clear on a channel the Resurgence would be monitoring and recording, speak in English so only Max would understand . . .

As the patrol approached, she pushed the plan back until it would be needed to focus on the moment. She waited until the last possible second, then opened fire on the first soldier as they passed into view.

Lahra threw every bit of will and strength she had left into the fight. She shot, punched, kicked, and tackled her way through the unit, demolishing the group before they could react or re-form. The scattergun gave out after two shots. She used the drained weapon as a club on one soldier, kicked another in the groin, grabbed a third to take the gunshot from a fourth, then killed that one with the knife from the bullet-sponge's belt. She shot a Rellix soldier with her own gun and shoved her aside, leaving only the commander, a Yaea.

He screamed into his comm unit for backup.

No respite. No quarter. It would take unrelenting ferocity to win the day and carve out a better tomorrow.

Lahra pounced on him, shoving her elbow into his face so that his head cracked on the polycrete alley floor. She ripped the radio from his hand as she stood, confirming that all five of the others were down or dead. She finished off the unconscious soldiers, whispering a prayer that their gods receive the unlucky souls and forgive her for killing in cold blood. But if any survivors could pick her out of a feed, the Resurgence was done for.

Fortunately, Vsenk were generally terrible at recognizing the faces of the "lesser species." As long as the Vsenk was the only witness, she might be able to evade capture if the Vsenk didn't just arrest every Genae on Illhar. And assuming that her flight and rampage didn't cause the Imperium to accelerate whatever timetable they had for their plan with the zone.

Lahra slotted a knife into the mag-point on her suit and stuffed two pistols into her belt.

Jogging down the alleyway to put space between her and the squadron, she selected a public channel on the radio. She'd need to be above-ground to ensure that the signal got through. Lahra picked the third sewer cover, climbing up and lifting the steel slab to check for patrols. The pink light of dawn crept over the buildings. Curfew would be over soon. But she was far too covered in slime to be inconspicuous.

Lahra squinted at the nearest street sign (which read "Ornved"). Recognizing a local business, she flipped on her radio and spoke in English. "This is Lahra. Corner of the street that rhymes with your favorite side dish from back home, by the pastry shop you found the fifth day we were here. Keeping to the sewers. I love you. See you soon."

She repeated the message twice more and then dropped back into the sewer, replacing the cover. Even the thought that Max might hear her message buoyed her spirits. They had faced countless dangers together, and she knew he was out there, trying to get to her. Doubtless putting himself in danger to do so.

The HQ was almost close enough to make a run for it. But she should be patient, let the Resurgence retrieve her so there would be backup in case of a fight.

Minutes later, the sewer cover slid to the side. Lahra trained a pistol on the opening, ready for another fight.

But what she heard then was as welcome as a hot shower after a long day.

"I miss cornbread almost as much as I missed you."

Lahra lowered the pistol. "Thank the ancestors." She stepped into the light and looked up, where Max hovered in silhouette.

"Hurry!" Wheel said beside him. Lahra practically leapt up the ladder, Max offering her a hand up. As she got to her feet in the alley she found herself completely winded and yet filled with hope. She drank in Max's look of worried relief.

Wheel threw a cloak around Lahra's shoulders and said, "Patrol on our heels. Break into pairs and lose the tail. Good to see you."

Max leaned in to kiss her, and she chuckled. "I'm disgusting," she said.

"Don't care."

The loving couple cover was good for anyone not already primed to suspect them, so she leaned into it. After a short moment, she straightened and took his hand. "Ambling couple. Follow my lead."

"Of course. I'm sorry about before."

"Time for that later. I missed you, too."

They were barely out of the sewer when they ran into another patrol. The Lieutenant barked. "Halt there. Identification."

So close. Five seconds later and they'd have been in the clear.

Lahra looked to Wheel, who sighed. They couldn't all be clocked together.

The lieutenant approached. This one was a Rellix. Short and broad-shouldered, with black feathers.

Lahra whipped her cloak off and tossed it over the lieutenant's head, and then started firing. One day the Imperials might train their officers on how to deal with the cloak trick, but that day hadn't come.

A half-second later, far too late to turn back and change their approach, Lahra heard the sound of a Vsenk's personal rocket pack descending behind them. Not the one they'd fought in space. This one was bigger, over six meters tall.

So close.

"Lahra!" She spun at the sound of her name, and a Resurgence soldier tossed her a bundle. She tore it open to reveal her sword of station.

A smile filled her face as she set the blade into a guard.

Lahra turned and stared down the Vsenk. Not the one that had pursued and then captured them. This one was larger, but he didn't know her techniques.

A smile bloomed on her face as she began to sing, her voice strained from injury and exhaustion. "The Undying" was a composition of Lahra's own family, about a legendary soldier that killed three Vsenk before succumbing to her wounds. It would lend her the energy and strength to face this tyrant and protect those that she loved.

And if I fall, this is as good a place to die as any, she thought. Her husband at her side, fighting among friends.

Plus, if she died, the stench of the sewer wouldn't matter anymore.

Lahra raised her blade and charged.

The Vsenk pulled itself up to its full height.

Lahra unleashed a bolt of electricity from her sword. The energy rippled across the Vsenk's armor and carapace. The Vsenk responded with hot death from his scattergun. But Lahra was already too close for the huge weapon to be effective. The Vsenk tried to track her as she dodged left and rolled under the shot. The heat whipped past her, melting several centimeters of the stone wall off the closest building.

She swung the greatsword in a rising arc, coming up under the Vsenk's five-armed guard. The blade cracked the Vsenk's carapace on one of the limbs, which he whipped back with a roar of pain.

Lahra grinned. "We're just getting started." She crouched low, blade in a high guard. Between her stance and the Vsenk's height, it was almost impossible for the Vsenk to attack her along anything but the highline that she was now covering.

She circled toward the Vsenk's flank, spinning the blade into an overhead cut. The Vsenk batted her blow aside with a free limb and backed up to give himself room.

Looking back over the battle, Lahra saw Wheel, Cog, and the other Resurgence forces mopping up the Imperial squadron. But not without cost. Two of their number were on the ground, wounded. Max watched over the pair as the others fought.

Lahra smiled as Cog turned and fired on their giant foe. Lahra feinted another blow to keep the Vsenk's attention where she needed it—on her and no one else.

The blast wasn't strong enough to crack the Vsenk's carapace, but the force knocked the towering figure off-balance. Lahra unleashed another blast at the Vsenk's upper shoulders. The electricity shot through the Vsenk's body, the scent of singed flesh strong enough to be smelled paces away.

The fight was not quick. It was not clean. Every move, every counter, brought her closer to victory, death, or both.

The Vsenk's skill was not inconsiderable, but he was wholly unused to facing an opponent strong enough to wound him and truly unafraid of his might.

Lahra swung again, anticipated the parry as it came. But instead of letting the blades connect, she pulled the swing short and converted her attack into a lunge.

The crack of the Vsenk's carapace was music to her ears. Lahra unleashed the remainder of the blade's charge, electricity arcing past the carapace and into the Vsenk's gut, tearing through his organs.

The Vsenk screamed once more, voice cracking in pain. Lahra stepped forward and pushed with her whole body, twisting the blade as she went. The rent in the Vsenk's carapace widened, and the warrior-tyrant staggered.

"Go down!" Lahra screamed. The Vsenk complied. They fell through the building, collapsing a wall.

Lahra pulled her sword from the Vsenk's still flailing body.

But he didn't get up.

Death throes, nothing more, she thought. She set the sword down and half-collapsed, the blade holding her aloft.

Her body shook with exhaustion and adrenaline.

Finish it, said her mother's voice.

Lahra stood up straight and turned to Wheel. "Record this."

Wheel's eye irised from gray to red. "You're on."

Lahra looked to the camera. "The Vsenk tell us they are gods. But even gods can die."

Lahra raised the sword and brought it down with both hands on the Vsenk's face, splitting the god-warrior's skull.

All seven limbs lashed out in a death rattle, which knocked her to the side.

Lahra tried to stand, but the energy that had propelled her evaporated as quickly as it had come.

But the battle was done. The Vsenk was dead.

Max and Wheel picked her up, one arm over each shoulder. Someone snapped the blade onto the mag-lock on her armor, and Lahra drifted in and out of consciousness as the group fled to the headquarters.

"If they didn't know we were here before, they do now," Lahra said through the uncontrollable laughter of battle-fog. She'd killed a Vsenk in single combat after a grueling mission and numerous injuries. The songs of her people, the strength of her ancestors, and the fury of her love and conviction had won the day. There would be a tomorrow for her and Max, and for the Resurgence.

Later, they were back inside, and her head was on something soft.

"We're safe. It's okay, you can sleep now." Max's voice was soothing. She reached out, grabbed him, and held tight. At last, she let sleep come.

CHAPTER SIXTY-ONE

AREK

IT WAS A DISASTER.

Arek and Bekor stood at the center of a whirlwind, as they had many days before during the search.

But this one had the air of panic.

A Vsenk was dead. Killed out in the open. For the first time in over a century. Video of Noble Ogair's murder was rippling across the pirate stream channels faster than the technicians could stamp it out.

Arek's quest to contain the situation, to prove Evam wrong, and protect the special economic status of Illhar had utterly failed.

***

Noble Ogair's death at the hands of the Genae was more than enough of a catalyst to provide Evam and his faction the support to order the use of the Devastation. Ogair was Evam's cousin, after all. Distant, but still blood.

And he hadn't been killed by some random Rellix, as if a Rellix could even challenge a Vsenk. No, he'd been killed by a Genae of the royal guard line, the same one they'd been tracking all night. Doubtless it was Kevain, who Arek had been pursuing since Yua. If he'd not let her escape, he could have prevented this entire disaster. They might have rooted out the insurrection with time to spare.

But he could not wind back the flow of time. Instead he had to keep moving forward as the river flooded.

The council's move meant that Arek and Bekor were relieved from their investigation. Instead, they were back in the Axhara command center, tasked with coordinating the multi-stage evacuation of Imperial forces from the planet.

"Three waves," he told the assembled attendants and messengers. "For everyone. No leave approvals. Step down from six shifts to four, then two in the final 24 hours. We're taking three days to do this when it could be done in one, but we need to make it look as natural as possible—keep force out on the streets, maintain a one-to-one ratio of ships coming down to ships going up until the last second. We cannot give the citizens any warning that the Devastation is coming. Some will try to escape regardless, and they will be intercepted and detained. This order comes from the very top."

From Evam.

Bekor dismissed the group. The attendants burst into action, leaving the two Vsenk on their own, save for personal attendants.

Arek had made his opposition to this plan very clear. They had confirmation of a group of terrorists, no more. But the order flowed from the results of the Grand Melee and could not be questioned without compromising the very foundation of their laws.

This extreme action might change some nobles' minds. The aftermath of annihilating a planet might sway some moderates, might sap the conviction of the less-callous members of Evam's Stalwarts. There were many places to go from the precipice of disaster, but few of them brought Arek much hope.

If there truly was a rebellion across the galaxy, and it was not limited to one planet, this genocide would radicalize millions. Even the Imperium's censors could not erase an entire planet. Not quickly, at least.

The Empire could win the battle and create a war. But it wouldn't be the Stalwarts that suffered in wartime. It'd be the Bright Suns, the smaller factions, and the independents, scrambling to create a coalition to minimize the damage while Evam and his die hards fueled the engines of war, desperate for conquest and glory.

Arek put aside worries for the future and turned to his attendant. "Arrests should be conducted as speedily as possible—no need for booking or record-keeping. Just throw them into the jails and get about your business. Paperwork is irrelevant at this point. And allow visitations as long as you can. The poor souls should be at peace before they're taken by the void."

"That's . . . very generous, your Magnificence," the attendant said.

Bekor scoffed. "Too generous. They'll suspect."

"There's no real way to stop what is going to happen. If there's an organized rebellion and not just a handful of murderers, they already know what could be coming. They may be lesser, but they are citizens of the Empire. We promised peace and protection in exchange for loyalty. We are spending their lives for the greater health of the Empire, but they are entitled to some measure of peace before the end."

The attendant put his head down, focusing on the datapad, leaving Arek to a seemingly endless queue of approvals and comms messages to organize the withdrawal.

***

With the evacuation all-but complete, Arek and Bekor accompanied one of the troop transports up to the fleet, where they retrieved the vessel containing Kelmai, as well as the key.

The vessel looked much the same, though it had been polished. Because clearly it was important for the device which housed history's greatest monster to be spotless. Arek supposed it reduced the likelihood of the signal from the key somehow going astray or not being processed correctly.

For the next hour, Head Researcher Vrensi, a high-ranking Vsenk scientist, briefed Bekor and Arek on how to operate the key, what would happen if the other key were used at the same time, and what to do if they were able to recover the remaining device. All the while, Bekor looked at the vessel with the murderous glee of a child receiving her first sword. As another display of Evam's cruelty, Arek would be forced to not only witness the destruction of his faction's greatest holding but be a principal architect of that destruction. With Bekor there to ensure he followed through.

Bekor did not comment on the implications of the Devastation being a person. The Drell were the largest beings in the galaxy, but Vsenk had always prided themselves on being the strongest.

Of course, their highest leadership had always known that to be a lie. Kelmai pre-dated the Imperium, a person turned into a weapon and erased from history.

The process for controlling Kelmai was simple, at least:

While exactly one key was active, Kelmai was awake but controlled. Kelmai would obey the commands of those holding the keys. And if there were conflicting orders, those possessing the vessel could prioritize one set of orders.

They held the vessel and one key, so they had everything they needed to unleash the Devastation.

Arek lodged his complaint—that using the Devastation would radicalize others, that using Kelmai when only one of the keys was in their possession was dangerous to the point of folly, and more.

In response, Bekor shouted reprimands and threats.

So he complied. And sent a message home for Wreva to expect unrest. And to pray for him. If he acquitted himself well in the destruction of Illhar, he might be able to scrape out a retirement to that training position and live with the implications of his actions.

They took a meal while waiting for the next wave of ships to dock and unload troops. Arek and Bekor would be left with just two divisions, just under five hundred troops. They were told that this would be sufficient to hold the capital long enough to begin the Devastation. They would hold their position until the scientists gave them the signal to return to their ships and warp away from the system.

The planet would detonate from the core, and then the pair would be tasked with returning Kelmai to torpor in the vessel.

It was the most preposterous set of orders he'd been given, but he was surrounded by soldiers loyal to Bekor and Evam's faction. No one seemed to want to listen to him as he explained how dangerous it would be to try to track Kelmai down after the planet was destroyed, so his options were few. He could refuse and be tried as a traitor, or he could execute the orders and destroy a world, quite possibly inspiring a galactic war.

This was Evam's true revenge. He'd created a no-win situation for Arek and the Bright Suns. There were no endings that did not serve Evam's extreme agenda.

Arek fumed as the ship descended into orbit. Bekor was nearly vibrating with excitement, speculating on the faces the rebels would make when they realized their doom, their cries as the world exploded.

Once more, Arek felt alone, set aside from his people. If he could not take joy in this destruction, where so many of his peers and superiors did, what did that really mean? Did he have a place in this world, or was he meant to be different?

He'd let Bekor operate the key; he wanted nothing to do with it. It meant that he could focus on defending her from any attackers that might stand in the way of the proclamation.

With luck, the Genae and her people would be there, and he could get revenge before the world died. At least then he could get some satisfaction out of this catastrophe.

CHAPTER SIXTY-TWO

WHEEL

FOR TWO DAYS, WHEEL and the Resurgence gathered
their forces, listened to every encrypted channel they
could crack, and let Lahra recover her strength. Max and the
brain trust worked on translating and analyzing the code
of the key and how to address Kelmai if the Vsenk brought
him to bear. Wheel lost count of how many times Max made
it clear that they'd have no chance without the three Atlan
Lahra and Cog had shepherded through the city.

The Vsenk were constantly moving, ships coming and
going. It was clear from the tension on people's faces that
something big was happening. But what? The civilians' uncertainty made the city as volatile as a redlining engine.

By twilight on the second day after Lahra killed the
Vsenk, their intelligence had yet to report new Imperial
troops arriving. Only leaving. They were pulling out.

That night, Wheel, Cog, and the other leaders debated
the best course of action.

Yejol wanted to run the blockade, fight their way out.
"The only reason to withdraw troops from an occupation is if
you've reached detente or if you're preparing for orbital bom-

bardment. They're going to use the Devastation, and we need to escape before it is ready."

Cog bit back, "Save ourselves and watch a billion people die from our viewscreens? That's not what the Resurgence stands for."

Yejol raised his voice, panic showing through. "The Resurgence will die with Illhar if we cannot get off-world!"

Ignoring the fact that there were Resurgence agents elsewhere. Axhara held the leadership, but even if the worst happened, the Resurgence could rebuild.

"We know what the Devastation is," Wheel said. "It's a person, not an orbital bombardment. With the research we've been doing and the artifact from Yua, we have a chance to intercept Kelmai and keep the planet safe. But not if we run, and definitely not if we try to break the blockade and die in the process."

An explosion shook the building, dust and plaster raining from the ceiling like snow.

Alarms went off and a dozen voices started shouting at once. Reports of cannon fire. Seismic readings.

"It's already started!" someone yelled over the cacophony.

"We need to get out of here," said one of Yejol's assistants.

"No. It's time to fight," Cog said. "Most of the Imperial forces are gone. Now we outnumber them even more. We've bloodied them, shown the Vsenk that they're vulnerable."

An earthquake hit the building. Longer than the shock of the explosion, if only just. Parts fell from shelves, and there was a rolling thunderstorm of sounds from the machine shop, metal on metal on concrete, shouts of worry and pain.

Several Resurgence members panicked, shouting and running for the exits, covering their heads with whatever was available.

Heads turned to Cog. Wheel could see the tide turning. Determination bloomed into hope, which spread like a hotfix across the room. "No more time for planning. We have to drive them off the planet entirely before they can deploy Kelmai," Cog said. "Mobilize everyone. Throw everything we have at them."

Wheel steadied herself on a wall. "Where are these shockwaves coming from?"

A comms tech, a young Yaea, scanned their screens, though they looked like they were about to curl up in a ball from terror. "The city square. Explosions. Seismic readings. All of it."

Cog raised her voice. "You heard them. Broadcast what's happening to the whole system. We do this right, and today will be remembered as the beginning of the end for the Imperium."

The remaining crowd wavered, reeling from the explosions, dodging debris and the sparking of exposed wires. The pounding of feet came up the stairs, revealing Max and Lahra carrying a cart with the assistance of the Incubator brain trust.

As the cart rolled over to the command table, Max said, "The other key has been activated. The display reports that the vessel is open. But we need to get closer for this key to work. I'm guessing within a hundred meters, maybe closer. And we came up with an ace in the hole that just might save our asses if we can't get this key running."

Whatever the trick was, Wheel hoped it would work. They needed it all to work.

Lahra used her battlefield voice, filling the room and cutting through the din. "This is our moment! If we stop Kelmai, we can push the Vsenk off the planet and shake the Imperium's confidence."

Cog smiled. "I rest my case."

The Illhari commander chuffed in disapproval. He spoke not to the group, but to the whole room, trying to win them back. "It's folly. You barely understand the keys and the Devastation. Running the blockade is still the best option. Anyone who cares to take the long view and live to fight another day, come with me."

For a moment, no one moved. People looked between Yejol and Cog.

A schism formed in the room, some moving to Yejol's side, some to Cog's.

Then Wheel stepped up. "Voiddammit all, we need to move! The entire might of the First Vsenk battlefleet is in orbit above the planet right now. If you think you've got better odds running that blockade than you do fighting alongside the Vsenk-killer and me against a division here on-planet, then I've got some long-lost Atlan tech in the back of my freighter to sell you."

Murmurs rippled through the crowd.

"What are you waiting for?" Cog asked. "Send out the call, hit the armory, and find your squads! We form up every ship and truck we have, then we punch a hole through their line and end this voiding occupation today!"

Cheers. Most of the room was with her, though a cluster of maybe a quarter formed up behind Yejol. They were mostly his ex-military buddies and some of the non-combatants.

Wheel and Cog barked orders, breaking people off into units, coordinating groups coming in from the outlying neighborhoods, and relaying orders to the groups already out and about in the city.

Lahra assembled a unit to protect Max and the brain trust. They clustered around the cart holding the key and the equipment they used with it—diagnostics and signal-boosters and whatever else they'd been slapping together since the trio fluent in Old Atlan had arrived to assist with the device.

Wheel made for the *Kettle* with an emergency response squad and some gunners.

She was prepared for a battleground, for chaos. But as the *Kettle* turned the corner into the capital square, the end of the world was already underway.

CHAPTER SIXTY-THREE

LAHRA

USING YEARS OF EXPERIENCE, Lahra took in the scene with a single glance.

The capital square was a wide-open plaza with gardens, small gazebos, sitting areas, and a recessed amphitheater for public events. The square was flanked by five-story buildings. Each was dedicated to a different facet of Illhari life—government, arts, health, and food. She and Max had visited the square once in the time on Illhar before the crackdown, taking in the sights. She'd insisted that he take a break, especially given that they'd had less than a single waking hour to themselves each day for the previous week.

With Kelmai on the rampage, the square was pure chaos. Still blocks away, she heard screaming and gunfire, ships making a break for orbit, and more. The Resurgence was planning for a war, and now a war had come crashing through their airlock. The ground beneath their van shook. Again. That was the third earthquake since they'd set off from the Resurgence HQ.

Their van was a lightly-armored personnel carrier, the modifications all internal to ease inconspicuous use. And that meant it was cramped. Max sat beside her, with the cart holding the key strapped to a hard-point that would otherwise hold light artillery. They all held on as the van jostled, the driver swerving to avoid a crash. Max held his jacket closed, cradling the jammer the brain trust had slapped together based on the frequency the keys used. It was untested, but if it did what it was made for, the device would keep the Vsenk from flipping their key between active and dormant.

Max addressed everyone in the van. "The quakes are in the Genae Record of the fall of the Atlan Empire. They're an indicator of the beginning stages of the Devastation." He shifted, as if struck by a new idea. He produced a piece of paper from his jacket and crumbled it into a ball. "Kelmai created a process that can tap into the gravitic field of a planet. Instead of pulling objects in toward the core"—Max condensed the ball inward—"he reverses the force, tearing the planet apart from the inside." Finally, he tore the ball into three pieces and tossed them into the air.

The shockwave of an explosion rocked the van. Max hit a door hard. He winced, holding an arm. Lahra picked up where he'd left off. "We must stop Kelmai before he can complete the process. Channeling this amount of power is taxing, but the records state that he's capable of killing dozens, hundreds of enemies, even as he amasses power."

"How does Kelmai survive something like that?" one of the Resurgence soldiers asked.

Max nodded. "His control of gravity allows him to create a shield. The world will detonate around him, and only he will remain."

Lahra jumped in. "But if we can find the other key, we can take control of him and stop the destruction entirely."

"There is another option," Oyira said.

Max tilted his head in one of his many nuanced gestures of concern. "It's incredibly risky."

Catalyst said, "Our best reading of the Genae text and

the key's interface says that de-activating both keys will re-lease Kelmai entirely. With one key active, he is awake and capable of using the Devastation but remains under the control of the person holding the keys. If you have the vessel, you can give priority to one of the key's orders over the other."

Max said, "That's why we need the jammer. It seems like it only takes one key to re-activate and control him, so we need to get in range, turn off both keys, and then get to the vessel to take control."

"But as Max said," Oyira added, "this is an untested theory, and the jammer's efficacy is only theoretical based on how it affected our key. We did not have the time nor the circumstances for proper testing. And the stakes are immeasurably high."

They were heading into a war zone out-gunned and under-served in terms of intelligence. But there was no other moral option.

Cog stopped the van. "We get out here. Fighters, watch the corners. Everyone, keep your radios on, listen for comms from evacuation units and from the spotters. There's only one division here running the blockade, but Kelmai or any of the Vsenk can take most people's head off before they can blink. Apply pressure, but keep your distance. They're holding the square to make sure Kelmai can unleash the Devastation. We have to break through or this planet is fragged."

Lahra hoped that her luck against the Vsenk would extend to whatever conflict with Kelmai was necessary. She'd fought and killed one of the god-emperors of the galaxy, but now they were facing the being so powerful that it had taken the entirety of the Vsenk to bring him down.

Lahra was the first out of the van. She led with her sword of station, re-charged by rooftop solar panels courtesy of the power converters in the Resurgence HQ. Not as effective as bathing the globe in the heat of a solar flare, but it'd have to do. She carried a scattergun as her sidearm, plus a trio of knives loaded in her barely-repaired armor.

The van parked a block from the square, near the rear of the Palace of Food, one of the four great towers surrounding the plaza. Crowds fled in all directions, screams and desperate pleas in a dozen languages filling her ears. They did not have the numbers to assist every person individually. Lahra heard Cog's voice repeating something she'd said often the past few days—crisis response dictated a more systemic approach; you couldn't get pulled in a thousand directions at once.

If they stopped Kelmai, they could halt the encore of the Vsenk's Devastation.

Lahra peeked around the corner of the van and saw a unit of Imperial troops trying to keep citizens out of the plaza. They'd started with cordons and a checkpoint, but with the flood of people, they'd just started shooting into the crowd.

"On me!" Lahra shouted, raising her sword to the sky. Her steel banner caught the rays of the rising sun, light rippling across the folded steel.

As expected, the display drew attention from the Imperials. Better they focus on her than the crowd. Lahra sang "Mera Unyielding," which extended the blade's protection out several feet in each direction in a shimmering shield. She brought the sword down and forward, the song-empowered shield intercepting the soldiers' fire as her unit advanced at a charge.

Mera was a unit commander in a battle against impossible odds. The song gave Lahra both strong protection but also bolstered the spirits of those fighting beside her. She hoped it would be enough.

Max and the brain trust would follow them once each section of the street was cleared, until they could get close enough to Kelmai to locate the other key and make their move.

Lahra's unit returned fire, moving from cover to cover. She advanced through the street, waves of terrified citizens parting like the break of water under the prow of a ship. She focused her attention to cut through the shouts, the fires in the distance, the stomping of feet, and the remnants of regular city sounds. Only the battle remained.

"Stop her!" the Imperial commander shouted and pointed directly at their group. The soldiers concentrated fire, and the hail of fire broke through the song's protections. One shot caught her in the shoulder, the other hit her fully-armored leg. She dropped to the side, still three speeder-lengths from the blockade.

Lahra stabbed her blade into the ground, singing louder to fuel what power she could into the song to extend her cover. Then she readied her scattergun. "Cover each other! Stagger your fire to keep them pinned down!"

A second squadron joined the blockade so Lahra's five faced twelve Imperial troopers. The Imperials had high cover and solid lines of sight.

Lahra activated her comms. "Wheel, what do you have near the Palace of Food blockade? We're pinned down outside the square."

"I got you," Wheel said. "Air support is on its way."

Lahra turned her weapon on the enemy, catching two of the soldiers providing suppressive fire. But an Illhari from her own unit took shrapnel from a close shot. He was down, face bleeding, whimpering in pain. Cog and Max rushed to treat the Illhari, but Lahra knew his voice would soon go silent.

Moments later, the thrumming of positioning thrusters and booster jets shook the windows of the buildings above. Reflected in the face of Lahra's blade, the *Kettle* turned a tight corner and opened fire.

Explosions rocked the Imperial checkpoint, bodies and material flying. Lahra ripped the blade out of the street and charged as the smoke cleared. She switched her helmet's visual display to thermal, picking out the handful of troops still moving after the *Kettle*'s attack. Three quick blows from her greatsword felled the remaining troopers, and a pommel strike made short work of the commander.

"Checkpoint cleared," she said into comms. "Cog, advance the brain trust to my location."

Then, to Max, "You were right. We should have come back to the Palace of Food for dinner earlier."

Max's laugh came through the short-wave. "We pull this off, and I bet the Illhari will give us the run of the place. Cater the victory dinner. Hand out some medals."

More Terran chatter. But it meant that Max was tending the flame of his spirit against the storm of battle. They'd need every bit of courage he could muster to win the day.

Lahra scanned the streets. "Watch the corners and snipers up in the office towers. See you soon."

Max reached the checkpoint a little over a minute later, pushing the cart along with Oyira and Catalyst. Cog arrived last, as echelon guard. She wore the face of the joyful warrior, already scuffed and flush from combat. Her left arm had transformed, revealing an integrated energy cannon, still steaming from recent use.

"We'll advance from here, clear you a route into the plaza. Tell us as soon as you get close enough for the key to be usable. We want to know our options as soon as the intel is available."

"Got it," Max said. "We're already reading some gravity disturbances on the sensors."

Catalyst shouted over the sounds of laser fire. "Expect some variances as we approach the plaza. Hate to say it, but Kelmai will likely be more used to them than any of us."

Lahra nodded. "Keep us updated with whatever data you glean from the key or your instruments."

She turned to the four fighters in her squadron and Cog. "The troops are harried, and they move like they've not had enough rest in some time. But they'll be as desperate as we are, so don't count them out. I want every one of you to make it home, so don't go out on your own. Look after one another. Leave the ridiculous heroics to me."

Max gave her a look, part chiding, part worry.

"I have killed a Vsenk, and we know Kelmai's weakness. We're all coming home from this."

"Famous last words," Max muttered under his breath, as if she would not hear them.

She reached out and squeezed his hand. "We're going to make it. I promise you." It was unwise to promise such things. But the blessings of her ancestors had seen her through thus far.

Then she looked to the group. "Let's go."

The Imperials had erected another blockade at the edge of the plaza, this one held by just one unit. They were less focused on suppressing the Resurgence and more on dealing with the yelling and stampeding civilians.

As the Yaea officer bellowed orders, a shadow passed over her, a silhouette back-lit by the morning sun. Definitely not a Vsenk silhouette, but floating a dozen feet in the air, armored. Silver-and-purple waves rolled off of its body.

Kelmai. It could be no one else. He stood five meters tall, but broader than most Vsenk. He was heavily augmented, immense muscles of living steel, armored pauldron shoulders, legs strong enough to leap over buildings, and twenty-centimeter-wide thrusters built into his shoulders and back.

The cybernetics of the modern Atlan were a distant echo of the dread sciences on display in his massive frame. He was still identifiably Atlan, even as his moonstone-gray face glowed purple with gravitic power. His armored body had the look of a scalloped crustacean shell traced with circuitry in intricate patterns.

This was the tyrant Kelmai, usurper of the Old Atlan, creator of the Vsenk, who had terrorized the galaxy for centuries, who had destroyed his own people in an attempt to re-capture his power, his terrifying control. Her whole life had become the flight of an arrow, pointing unquestionably and unerringly toward this moment. She would triumph or die.Millions would feel the ripple of what came of this day and her deeds, along with Max, Cog, and the others.

Kelmai raised his hands, and several of the civilians shot up into the air. As Lahra lifted her gun to open fire on the Atlan warlord, the two soldiers closest to him folded in on themselves, the life going out of them like air from a popped balloon. Kelmai dropped the pair to the floor, and they disintegrated on impact.

Was this how he worked his world-killing power, or was it just cruelty?

Either way, she needed to get Max and the others through to the key.

CHAPTER SIXTY-FOUR

MAX

G ROWING UP AS A nerd and academic, Max had read the Book of Revelation more for what it meant metaphorically than as a checklist of what would happen at the end of the world. But he knew the passages, and he'd read about Ragnarok and other cultures' stories of the end times.

And damned if the scene unfolding in the plaza didn't seem incredibly, terrifyingly familiar.

A dozen ships raced through the air, Imperial fighters versus retrofitted freighters flying for the Resurgence. Wheel gunned down a fair number of fighters and took a hard corner around one of the plaza towers, scraping a rent in the side of the *Kettle*. Max winced out of sympathy.

Another earthquake rippled out from the center of the plaza, knocking him and dozens of others off their feet.

Resurgence ground forces skirmished with another Imperial patrol, while across the plaza, more Imperials corralled citizens behind cordons while dodging purple bursts of energy.

And at the center, a gigantic Atlan with ornate techno-organic armor, throwing purple-silver bursts of gravity around like Zeus with lightning bolts. Kelmai, the living Devastation. Just looking at him was as hard and as painful as staring at the sun. Like Lahra said, their options were victory or death, so there was no room for letting fear paralyze them.

Beneath Kelmai, a pool of crackling purple energy seemed to be seeping into the grass. This would be Kelmai's power reaching to the core of the planet to reverse its gravitational field. The texts weren't clear on how long the process took, so they should just assume the worst and hurry.

Lahra threw back one hand to halt the cart as another earthquake rolled across the field. A gravity bolt tore through a low-flying hovercraft, and Lahra just barely managed to raise her sword in time to deflect the bolt before it could tear through their group.

Max looked down to the key's display, which still read:
VESSEL STATUS: DE-ACTIVATED
KEY 1: OFF
KEY 2: ACTIVE
KELMAI AWAKENED IN AUTAI CONFIGURATION

What Autai Configuration meant, he couldn't say. The Atlan assistance they'd brought in had cracked the majority of the key's code and menus, but not this last part. The best guess they could give him was that Autai shared a root with the word for the steering column of a spaceship. Wheel's name, styled in Old Atlan, would be Aurai, a close cognate.

But what that meant, they couldn't be certain. Max had a guess, and they were about to test his theory out. Not like there were any better plans.

Lahra led them into the cover of a statue in front of the Palace of Food. "See what you can do from here. Lie low while I take care of this squadron."

A small ship crashed into the street thirty meters from them like an exclamation mark on the end of her sentence.

She talked about defying death like it was a stroll down the street. Max returned to working with Oyira and Catalyst.

Watched the data the key was processing. Every variance was another piece of the puzzle.

They knew the command to de-activate the key, but not what range it'd work at. Oyira had clarified that the diagnostic signals and the command signals used different frequencies and different receivers and transmitters. They might be better off using the jammer, but they were so far out past the theoretical that it was hard to find any solid ground to work from.

"How are we looking?" Max asked.

Oyira shook her head. "Still no stable signal. I thought I saw a blip, but it very well could have been interference, given the chaos around us. I'm frankly surprised none of us have died yet, big targets that we are with this thing."

"Maybe don't say things like that that tempt fate?" Cog added, her tone curt. She stood watch, scanning from one side of the plaza to the other.

Less than ten meters away, Lahra carved through the last of the enemy squadron. She shouted in pain, but when Max looked back up, the fighting was over.

Lahra limped back into sight, using her sword as a balance. Max jumped over to offer her a hand, but she waved him away. "I'm fine. Any change?"

"No. We need to get closer."

Lahra narrowed her eyes, scanning the battlefield. "We can move along the building here, use the cover of the walkways. No way I'm taking you through the middle."

The middle of the plaza was disintegrating, chunks of granite-like stone floating in the air, animated by Kelmai's uncanny power.

The Genae book had talked about this. Their theory was that Kelmai had tapped into the warp itself, that he'd become a living gate, able to channel the power of that other dimension. They didn't mention the details, which were even more horrifying than Max had imagined.

Lahra intercepted another squad, meeting steel and blasters with a blade that moved like quicksilver.

Cog's ships roared overhead again, tearing into the Imperial armor. Two more of Lahra's squad were wounded, but the group made it to the corner between the Palace of Food and the Palace of Government.

And there, the key beeped a hope-giving beep.

CONNECTION ESTABLISHED.

"We're in range!" Max shouted over the din.

It was like he'd heard. Kelmai soared in their direction, silver-purple aura shimmering. He was basically a god, and he looked pissed.

"Here goes nothing," Max said, and pushed the surprisingly universal big red button.

VESSEL STATUS: DE-ACTIVATED

KEY 1: OFF

KEY 2: OFF

KELMAI STATUS—NU-AUTOY

"That means 'Unleashed,'" Catalyst's voice shook.

Max reached into his jacket and pushed the button to activate the jammer, thinking, *fingers crossed*. If it worked, the jammer would prevent the Vsenk from re-activating their key to regain direct control.

Just ten meters away now, Kelmai stopped in mid-air.

He spoke in a resonant voice, as metallic as some older Atlan Max had met, but as powerful as any he'd heard.

"What's he saying?" Max asked in Catalyst and Cog's direction.

Catalyst cocked her head to the side. "He asked where he is."

Kelmai turned in place and stopped, looking westward. Max tracked the Atlan's vision and saw a pair of Vsenk wearing jetpacks, strafing the Resurgence line.

"You're on Illhar," Max said in New Atlan, trusting that a world-killing warlord with highly advanced augments would

have a good translation algorithm. Max could read Old Atlan but didn't dare speak it. Especially not if he was trying to
be persuasive. Maybe the most persuasive he'd ever have to
be, with millions of lives on the line.

Kelmai looked at Max, incandescent. But Max wouldn't
look away. Not when so much hung in the balance.

Max tried to keep his voice steady. "You're on Illhar. And
you're being used by the species you created to serve you. The
Vsenk—they betrayed you. Used you as a weapon. Do you
remember destroying Atal and the rest of your homeworlds?"

"Atal?" Kelmai responded with the Old Atlan name
for the planet, which Max had used. He continued in Old
Atlan, but the speakers in Kelmai's suit duplicated the message in Imperial Standard. More evidence that the Vsenk
had co-opted Kelmai's empire. "I had a palace on Atal. Why
would I ever harm it?"

"It's dead. Been dead for a thousand years. The Vsenk
used this"—Max pointed toward the key—"and another just
like it to entrap you. If you don't remember destroying those
worlds, then these keys were used to control you—awake,
but unremembering; not in control of yourself. Your own
creations used you as a weapon to destroy your base of power
and consolidate control over the galaxy. They erased you from
history, forced people to believe that the Vsenk have been the
rulers of warp space since the first people took to the stars."

Max was leaning hard on the Vsenk's role, leaving out the
Atlan that rebelled against him, but it was all to a purpose.

"Blasphemy! Betrayal!" Kelmai shouted, this time in
Imperial Standard. Dude caught on quick. Likely some kind
of technological linguistic adaptation, or good algorithmic
integration.

The difference didn't really matter, so he put that line of
inquiry to the side.

"They brought you here to destroy this planet because
we resisted them." Max gestured to the fighting still raging

across the square and beyond. "Because we dared to talk about the world before their ascendance. They want to keep the galaxy from knowing about your reign."

The last part was an educated guess, aimed directly at Kelmai's pride.

"They will pay for their impertinence!" Kelmai turned to the Vsenk and shot across the plaza like an orbital cannon, knocking his former vassals aside like pinballs.

And just like that, the sun was gone, and he was looking at the world again, not a living god.

And even better, the earthquakes had stopped.

"There." Lahra pointed across the near side of the plaza to a pair of Vsenk locked in battle, their Imperial grunts taking heavy fire from Resurgence forces. One of them held something in their hand, not a weapon.

It was the other key.

Max checked the jammer. Still broadcasting. But there was a lot of disturbance in the area, too many unknowns. "We need to take them out before they realize what's happened and re-activate their key. Who knows how long the jammer will work. While Kelmai is unleashed, we have the advantage. And without the vessel, we don't know how to contain him once the fight is done."

"All I need to know is that if we control both keys, we win the day," Lahra said. "Follow me."

Max split his attention between Kelmai's rampage and the Vsenk emplacement before them. The two Vsenk seemed to be arguing, maybe over what to do with the key.

Lahra and Cog got bogged down in combat by a strafing run by Imperial forces, pushing them back into cover.

But before the Vsenk could work around the jammer to re-activate their key, Kelmai spotted them. He shot across the plaza again, probably close to the speed of sound. Kelmai atomized the Vsenk holding the key, and by the time the dust and smoke cleared, the other Vsenk was nowhere to be seen. Whether they were dead, carried away, or hidden, Max couldn't say.

The key, however, lay on the ground, protected only by a panicked squad of Imperial soldiers. Kelmai shot toward the key but caught a broadside from a Vsenk warship, slamming him to the ground. The warlord's purple aura flared, and he arced across the sky once more, punching straight through the battleship.

"It's coming down!" Cog shouted, pointing to the bisected battleship.

Lahra shouted into her comms. "Get out of the plaza, now!"

Max started sneaking forward, and she added, "That includes us!"

"But what about the key?" he asked the group. "It's right there! Maybe fifty feet away, just sitting there."

Lahra waved her sword at the carnage, frustrated. "It won't be worth a damn if we're all dead. Cover first, key second."

Lahra blew out a window and carved them a pathway toward the rear of the Palace of Society. He was checking to make sure the key's display still showed Kelmai in the unleashed mode when the impact rocked their entire party to the floor. Glass and plastic shattered on every side, dust and smoke rushing in behind the explosion.

Lahra covered Max with her body. A few moments later, he raised his head, and Lahra pushed it back down.

Another massive crash. And a boom beside it. Max's ears rang, popping harder than the time the *Kettle* had crash-landed by a dig site.

Pain. Just pain. That's all he felt. His ears hurt, he was covered in scratches, and he couldn't draw a full breath, lungs full of crap.

Lahra's voice cut through the morass.

And again. "Get up!" She sounded scared.

The rarity of that tone in her voice brought him back. If she were scared, that meant something. Max reached out, found the scalloped folds of her armor. He used that sensation to ground himself, began to rebuild his world around him.

Everything was orange-gray, ash and dust and smoke. Lahra crouched beside him, one hand on his arm, the other holding her sword.

Lahra burst into song. It started strong and loud. "Everyone up! The battle's not yet done!"

The others collected themselves with moans and hisses of pain. Clothes became quick-fix bandages. Max took a long sip from his water bottle, then passed it to a young Yaea fighter. "We can't stay here. It's not safe." His own voice felt like it was coming from a kilometer away.

But Lahra's was clear. "Now we get the key. Keep your eyes peeled for Imperial forces—their escape pods might have saved a few dozen, maybe a hundred. There's no way they had time to brace for Kelmai's strike, but it was a long fall."

The plaza had gone from battlefield to graveyard by the time Max saw the open sky again. The aft of the ship had flopped against the Palace of Art, while the nose of the ship was buried a dozen feet into the ground, looking like a sad excuse for an ostrich with its head in the ground.

Sure enough, they met Imperials in ones and twos, but always shaken or bloodied. Some surrendered, dropping their arms and begging for mercy.

Many did not. Lahra saw to those.

Wheel waved the group forward. "Catalyst, handle the prisoners."

Out of the smoke and ashes, a figure emerged behind the key.

Max recognized this one—he was smaller than the rest of his kind, with the distinctive markings on his face that Max couldn't help but read as a wolf's head. This was the

Vsenk that had boarded the *Kettle* and interrogated them outside the Drell Migration.

And he did not look happy.

CHAPTER SIXTY-FIVE

AREK

AREK'S DATAPAD WAS FILLED with the bloody dead and visions of destruction. Kelmai had demolished the battleship *Unity Is Strength* and the carrier *Great Banner of the Imperium* in high orbit, and then folded, spindled, and mutilated the battleship *Only the Relentless Will Know Glory* in a gravity singularity. In the aftermath of the *Relentless*'s destruction, Kelmai had departed local space.

It was all falling apart, all at once. The facile veneer of control had been stripped away, his people's hubris revealed. They'd tried to harness the power of a living god. Worse, the Vsenk's personal history, their origin myth, had all been lies.

His own people had lied to him. So afraid of the truth that they'd convinced their own descendants of an origin that never happened. They'd been made to fight, to die, but never to rule.

Millennia later, their creator had finally returned to enact vengeance upon his upstart children.

Minutes ago that had felt like hours, they'd lost track of Kelmai as a Resurgence squadron pinned them down from two directions. By the time the traitors were demolished, it was too late.

Kelmai appeared from nowhere, vaporizing Bekor and knocking the key far into the distance. While Arek rushed to recover the device, Kelmai had turned his eye to orbit and cut a swathe through the fleet. Now he was far out of range, rendering the key useless.

Preliminary telemetry was being broadcast in the open, an alarm to any Imperial forces. Kelmai was bound for Vsenkos. His home might have mere hours left. His family. Would the council call for an evacuation? If they did, would Kelmai spare the ships? Or would his people finally pay the ultimate price for their betrayal?

As panic set in, a small party appeared through the smoke. They possessed the other key. Kelmai was far too long-gone to be controlled, not unless he could get on a ship and return to Vsenkos before Kelmai could unleash the Devastation.

"You ready for some payback, asshole?" The Atlan woman he had interrogated on his ship just weeks ago was raising her gun to a firing position.

Every minute cost lives of soldiers and fellow Vsenk. Kelmai's wrath could spell the end of his people.

Survival would take lateral thinking. Entirely un-Vsenk thinking.

Arek did something his people had perhaps never done when faced with one of the lesser species.

He dropped his weapon.

"I do not wish a fight," Arek said. "You've claimed the day. After he killed Bekor, we lost control entirely. Kelmai already destroyed two more ships in low orbit, and we haven't been able to do so much as slow him down. I didn't want this war, but now it's too late for any of us to stop it. Help me stop Kelmai before he destroys my homeworld, and I'll help you lock him up forever. We'll throw away the keys and relegate him to the histories."

The Yaea man took a step forward. "Why should we trust you?"

"A very fine question," added his Genae companion. Even covered in dirt and sweat it was clearly Lahra Kevain, the Vsenk-killer. "And why should we care about Vsenkos?"

He was trying to be reasonable. Showing more humility than any Vsenk ever should. And yet they pressed him. Anger spread like fire across his veins, but he tamped it out. Pride would not save his family, would not save the homeworld. Around them the city burned, even if the sounds of battle had passed.

"I could have killed you when we had you in custody. I did not. I treated you with all of the courtesy of a subject of the Empire. I let you go when the Drell Matriarch called. My faction did not want this fight. We were the ones that encouraged the Illhari's economic innovations. I've seen here, on this planet and in this battle, that Evam's faction has lost all touch with reality. As long as they control the council, there will be nothing but suffering in the galaxy. If Vsenkos is destroyed, the Vsenk remaining will stop at nothing to prosecute their revenge. And eventually, Kelmai will learn of what his fellow Atlans did to bring about his downfall. What do you think he'll do then? There will be no end to his wrath.

"But if you save my world, and let me return home, I can sue for peace. Lessen restrictions and cede some power back to the individual species. We needn't see millions die."

"You're just doing this to save your world," spat the Atlan. Wheel, he remembered; her name was Wheel.

Such impertinence, called a voice in his mind. It was Bekor's. Even dead, her arrogance was rubbing off on him. "Wouldn't you do the same? My wife is there. My daughter. I am not without guilt, but there are thousands of families on Vsenkos, including nearly my entire species. I wager that you would wish the civilians here on Illhar dead no more than I would wish to bury my family."

The Atlan looked to the Genae and the strange Yaea, and they talked in low voices. Arek heard it all, despite their efforts—worry about betrayal, wishing Vsenkos destroyed as a way to assist their rebellion, and more.

Countless trying moments later, Wheel responded. "You give us the other key, and we'll do it."

"And what guarantee do I have that you'll fulfill your bargain?" Arek asked.

The Atlan smiled with ferocity and satisfaction. "You're coming with us. Grab yourself one of those jetpacks. Get us through the Imperial fleet long enough to shut Kelmai down, then we part ways."

Arek ran the numbers, but the reality was that he had no real choice. Not if he wanted to save his planet, his family.

"I will honor the agreement. We will both end the day with what we want—hope for the future."

"Good," Wheel said. "Our ship will be here in minutes. Get us the codes to get out of orbit safely and we'll be on our way."

It was the least-worst result. Even so, if Evam and the Stalwarts found out what he'd done, they'd call for his head. But in that fight, as the Vsenk that saved the homeworld? The battle lines would be drawn very differently.

CHAPTER SIXTY-SIX

WHEEL

LOW ORBIT AROUND ILLHAR was a maelstrom of dead and dying spaceships. Most were Imperial cruisers and carriers, the former occupying fleet. But Wheel spotted several civilian ships dotting the lower orbit as well, those destroyed by the Imperials before Kelmai broke the back of their fleet. There was Yejol's ship among the fallen, broken into a dozen pieces by plasma fire. They'd fucking *told* him how ridiculous it was to run the blockade. And this was the less terrible result from Kelmai's awakening.

Wheel turned from the view and focused on her sensors, trying to pick out Kelmai's signal. A part of her relished the idea of the Vsenk getting their comeuppance, losing their homeworld the way her people had lost theirs . . .

But would he stop with one? Warlords weren't the type to be satisfied with one helping of revenge. Who was to say he wouldn't pick back up where he left off?

The wreckage of three dozen ships brought her back to center. She felt every firing of the *Kettle*'s thrusters, every piece of scrap hitting the ship's hull. She grounded herself in the ship, in the present.

"Such destruction," Lahra said from behind. "The songs told of battles like this, but to see it for myself makes them all seem too cheery, too trite."

She heard someone sit in the chairs at the back of the cockpit. Probably Max, from the sound. "Will we even be able to get close enough to him to use the keys? He listened once, but if we come at him with a ship, what's to keep us from ending up like them?"

"Me." Wheel grinned. "I'll get you where you need to be. Not planning on dying today, Terran. Maybe better spend the trip getting those keys ready than looking at this. I've got it."

In truth she appreciated the company in the face of carnage on such a broad scale, but it was easier to focus alone. Just her and the ship.

Once she cleared the spaceship graveyard, Wheel punched the warp drive and set them on their way to Vsenkos, leaving the wreckage behind. For now. It'd take months if not years to clear the planet's airspace. And even if they won the day, there'd be many other things to do on Illhar that would feel more urgent than orbital cleanup.

Less than an hour after fighting in a war zone, they were flying into the belly of the beast to save it from an even more terrifying threat.

This was not how she'd expected her day to go. Frankly, she'd guessed that she'd end up dead on an Axhara street, a rifle in one hand, Cog's hand in the other. Some preposterous romantic needless death for something bigger than either of them. Maybe victorious, maybe not.

She wasn't expecting the fight to continue, and to have a Vsenk thumping around the cargo hold of her ship, ready to kill them, or maybe, just maybe, to actually hold up his end of the bargain. He had retrieved the vessel on their way off Illhar, which was a good first step.

"Everything okay down there?" Wheel asked on the PA.

Max answered, "No one's dead yet."

"Your ship is pathetic," Arek said. "I cannot fathom how you've managed to survive this long. And you've not even properly repaired it since I was last here, defeated only by—"

Wheel killed the audio feed. She could only take that arrogant tentacled prick for so long at a time. Let Max and Lahra keep him in check.

The *Kettle* would reach the Vsenkos system in just a couple of hours, and she'd need her wits about her to weave through whatever chaos Kelmai was unleashing in Imperial airspace.

Max said that they'd need to get within 50 meters to lock the Atlan warlord into torpor. Which, in space, meant that they basically needed to ram him to have any chance of pulling this off.

Rather than using the *Kettle* as a battering-ram, the plan was for Arek and Lahra to fly out with the keys—Lahra in her suit, Arek with his jetpack—and get close enough to lock him down. Then they'd bring him back in to lock him in the vessel.

Easier said than done. It was a crappy plan, but she didn't see anything better. In space they'd be smaller targets. From the carnage above Illhar, he could bullseye anything freighter-sized or larger without a problem.

What felt like days later, the ship chirped the proximity alarm for Vsenkos.

"Preparing to drop out of warp space!"

"Ready!" came Lahra's response from the cargo bay.

Cruji clung to the side of her chair, twitching nervously. Most of the time, Cruji's empathy was soothing. But now he was as terrified as the rest of them. It was somehow both annoying and reassuring.

"Here we go," Wheel said to the tentacled creature, and dropped the ship out of warp space.

Stars spare us, she thought.

The *Kettle*'s viewscreen filled up with the broad side of a Vsenk battleship.

"Void!" she cursed, sending the *Kettle* into a dive, flying under the battleship's belly.

Extending her senses through the *Kettle*'s systems, she took in the battlefield. Imperial ships flew in every single direction, some in formation, many careening like bugs smoked out of their hive. Plasma, blasters, and missiles nearly obscured the black of space.

Usually, in a battle this size, there were a dozen ships on each side.

Here, it was the entirety of the Vsenk's home fleet arrayed against a single opponent. And they were losing.

Two battleships were already scuttled. One had been bisected like the carrier on Illhar; the other had a core detonation.

Kelmai was a silver-purple blur, arcing from ship to ship, punching through hulls, tearing steel apart with those gravity waves.

"I've got a bead on Kelmai, but he's moving fast," Wheel said. "You'll need to plot an intercept. And Arek, you better hope those passcodes you gave me work, or we'll be cinders before we can even get close." There were still plenty of Imperial ships up and running, laser and missile fire struggling to track the warlord as he rampaged through space.

"I will not betray you," Arek said. "Satisfy your side of the bargain, and I will mine."

"Hold on; this isn't going to be easy." Wheel leaned deeper into the command console. She felt the movement of the ship as if it were her own body, deflected debris skipping off their shields like hail on her jacket. The battlefield stretched out around her like she was seeing it with her own eyes. Even in this voided whirlwind of battle, there was nothing she loved more than being as one with the *Kettle* when her life depended on it.

The battle was pure chaos even without anyone firing on the *Kettle*. Fighters buzzed her trying to cut Kelmai off, so she skidded along the stern of a light cruiser as it pulled an extreme turn trying to get out of Kelmai's grasp.

"Closer! We need to be closer!" Max shouted over the chaos. "The keys are barely even registering his presence!"

Wheel felt the digital reverb of fear sneaking into her voice. "I'm doing the best I can! It's not like he's slowing down. He's bearing for the planet."

Arek's voice came through on the PA. "He's grown tired of toying with the fleet. I've sent a signal to the ships in my faction. They'll help steer Kelmai toward us as best they can. We must act now."

"Agreed," Lahra said.

Wheel asked the *Kettle* to open the hold. "Roger that. Cargo doors released, launch when ready."

"Come back in one piece, okay?" Max said, the comms still on.

Lahra's voice was warm. "You won't be rid of me that easy."

The Vsenk huffed, indifferent to their tender farewell. "Launching."

Wheel watched their signals depart the ship. Now she had to help corral the Atlan warlord so they could put this nightmare to bed.

CHAPTER SIXTY-SEVEN

LAHRA

LAHRA'S JETPACK DIDN'T HAVE near the power of Arek's, but it didn't really matter. Neither of them were able to move at full speed, given the maelstrom of ships, rockets, debris, and other obstructions flying around their field of vision.

Kelmai was still playing with the fleet. He killed ship after ship, each in a slightly different way. Here he perforated the warp drive, causing the ship to implode. There he ripped out the engines and tossed them into a field of fighters.

Each time Kelmai stopped to destroy a ship, Lahra and Arek got closer. Each act of devastation sent shivers running down her back. She'd fought and killed before. But always with good cause, and never with such bloodthirsty delight. She could tell the difference between fighting because one must and fighting to satisfy one's rage, and Kelmai was all rage.

Many of the soldiers dying to the warlord had not been given a choice. Conscripted from their homes, assigned where the Imperium saw fit, sent to die for the ambitions of masters that would never love them, never appreciate them.

It had to stop. Now.

They closed once more, and Arek opened fire with a rifle as long as Max was tall. The Vsenk held the key behind him with one of his limbs. Lahra didn't have the arms to spare, so her key was mag-locked to her back on the hard-point that usually held her sword. The blade's gem was only partially recharged during their hurried race to Vsenkos, so she'd have to make the blasts count.

Kelmai shrugged off the first direct hit, probably thinking it just a stray bolt. The fact that he could shrug off the power of a Vsenk scattergun was scary enough.

What he did next was worse. Kelmai seemed to anticipate the second shot, blurring to the side as Arek fired on full automatic. The Vsenk burned through his magazine, and Kelmai finally took notice. The Atlan blinked forward like an umbral moth, appearing only every few moments, moving quickly through the void.

A beep filled her ears. The key. Max had rigged the output from the key to ping her suit's comms when it was within range. She grabbed the artifact off her shoulder and read the display.

Kelmai shot past the pair in a blur, and suddenly one of Arek's limbs was floating next to him, venting globules of blood as it arced away. Arek curled in on himself like a flower bud, and before Lahra could push the button, the display reported that Kelmai was out of range once more.

"Are you alright?" Lahra asked.

"I will live. Do not stop. We must win, or millions more will die."

Lahra activated her comms. "Wheel, get me radar on Kelmai—he's buzzing us, playing with his food."

"Would if I could, but he's too fast for anything less than a full comm suite to pin down. He's still close, that's all I can tell you."

"Understood." She held the key in one hand, her sword

in the other, and adjusted her jets, flying over to Arek.

"Back-to-back. He comes in, we don't shoot, don't fight, just activate the key. Got it?"

"Agreed."

Kelmai didn't return immediately. He danced around them at the edge of her vision, sometimes passing behind the hull of a broken ship, sometimes silhouetted by the Vsenk system's red sun.

When he finally came, he struck so quickly that she felt the impact at the same time as she heard the beep.

She hammered the button against her chest, but when she read the display, it told her she'd failed. Neither key was active.

And Arek was no longer at her back. He pinwheeled away like he'd been hit by a meteor, his key knocked free by the collision.

Lahra flew after the key, knowing this might be her last chance. Kelmai could claim one key, then come for her to finish the job. And while Arek could survive one fleeting blow from the Atlan warlord, Lahra had no such illusions about her damaged suit's ability to do the same.

"Arek! You still there?"

Nothing. He spiraled away, drawing her attention from the key.

The key first. She could rescue him once this was done. Or not.

Lahra fired her jets as close to random as she could manage, trying to make herself a harder target to hit from long distances.

She reached the key and spun, pulling it into the magnetic hard-point on her suit's back. It clicked into place, and Lahra kept moving, waiting for the next blow to fall. Kelmai's control would have to be greater than hers to pull the maneuvers she'd seen, but that was no reason not to try. Survival was always worth fighting for when you had a greater purpose, when you had people depending on you.

Lahra saw something move against the black out of the corner of her eye and acted on reflex, trusting years of training and generations of instinct passed on from mother to daughter. Today her people would have justice for the destruction of Genos.

The beep sounded a split-second before the button impacted on her suit, and instead of hitting her like an orbital cannon, Kelmai whizzed past her and careened into nearby debris.

One key active. She grabbed the first key between her legs and retrieved the other from her back, activating it as well.

She checked the displays, which both read:

VESSEL STATUS: DE-ACTIVATED

KEY 1: ACTIVE

KEY 2: ACTIVE

KELMAI STATUS: XURAB

That meant dormant, according to the precis Max had passed on from Cog's Old Atlan consultants.

"He's down! Swing by for the pickup! I lost Arek; you'll need to pick his signal out of the noise."

"Fuck him," Wheel said over the comms. "I can't see shit out there. Can barely keep your signal steady."

"We made an agreement. The Vsenk are the betrayers, not I."

"If he kills us all, I'm going to fight my way out of my hell and come haunt you in yours."

"So noted. Max, I'm beaming you the keys' data now, to sync to the vessel."

"Got it," Max said over comms. He sounded relieved. Still worried, because why wouldn't he be, but relieved.

The *Kettle* appeared out of the darkness, but then, behind it, came a Vsenk cruiser, cannons hot.

"Cruiser on my ass," Wheel said. "Find cover!"

Lahra flew to the debris, seeing now in greater detail the mini-crater Kelmai had formed as he crashed, dazed by the key's signal. He wasn't moving.

"I can't shake it!" Wheel said over comms. "They got the thrusters! My maneuvering is shot to shit!"

Lahra gazed up at the *Kettle*, still taking fire even as it dodged and wove through the black. The cruiser was too close. There would be no escape for the *Kettle* this time.

She looked down to the key in her hand, and to Kelmai. There was only one way out. Enslaving a sentient being to fight a battle for her, even one that she had no chance of winning on her own. Shameful. Obedience was only just when it was earned. She'd seen fealty abused on Genos, seen what happened when duty was not rewarded with recognition. She'd seen an unlivable future and could not bear to deprive another of their right to self-control.

But his rampage robbed hundreds—thousands—of their lives. And she would not retain control. She needed him only for a moment, for him to act and then cease his rampage.

And she could not lose Max and Wheel. Not when she had the power to prevent it. Even if it cost her soul.

"Ancestors forgive me." She activated the key in her hand, bringing Kelmai back from his torpor.

The warlord sprung to attention. She'd done it now, so she had to follow through. As best as Max could tell, the holder of the nearest key could give Kelmai commands, so she typed as fast as she could, "Destroy that Vsenk ship and then escort the small freighter back to me. Go."

The enthralled warlord nodded, then disappeared in another of his jumps. Lahra watched as he dismantled the Vsenk cruiser in three tidy passes, killing hundreds at her command.

It happened so fast. No mercy, no hesitation, no consideration.

She took lives in battle, but she felt the weight every time. Kelmai showed no signs of any such consideration.

Lahra had learned to appreciate the beauty of a well-executed plan, the grace of perfection in movement. But this was grotesque. It was slaughter, not battle. And these lives he took by her command, without the ability to deny the order.

"The hell was that?" Wheel asked.

"Come get me now and let's get this over with."

The collared warlord soared alongside the ship on an even arc toward her.

Lahra felt outside herself, observing her actions as a passenger as she boarded the ship, handed the other key to Max. She witnessed herself going through the motions, her mind split by shame and disgust. But she could not shut down, not entirely. It wasn't done.

She ordered Kelmai to get in the vessel, then re-activated her key. Max sealed the vessel, checked it, the keys, and then re-checked them both.

"It's done," Max said.

"Now we get the Vsenk," Lahra added, pushing shame aside to finish the battle.

"I know we made a deal, but . . . his people are out there. They'll find him. We should go now before anyone else catches us."

"No. I did not use the keys and betray the memory of my ancestors to betray them again by breaking my word. Make me a signal relay. I will give it to the Vsenk, then we get out of here and never look back."

Max's eyes went wide, his face pale. "Okay."

"You're both void-damned ridiculous!" Wheel shouted, turning the ship around. But they didn't go into warp space. "One of you come up here and help me with the sensor array. And by one of you, I mean Max. Lahra's the only one that could drag that giant back onto the ship."

By grace of the ancestors, no other ships turned on them the way the light cruiser had. Lahra topped off her oxygen as the *Kettle* tracked Arek down and Max programmed a signal-booster. She went EVA once more and found their Vsenk ally clinging to the remnants of a fighter's wing. He'd lost a great deal of blood, but the Vsenk were famously hard to kill.

"Your people will be able to better care for you than we could," Lahra told him. "We can boost your SOS, make sure they find you."

Arek looked surprised. "You could have left, and none would have known. Even being here and offering help compromises your position. Why would you give up such an advantage?"

"Because we made a deal. We're going to make sure Kelmai never threatens anyone else. And you're going to go home and make your people see reason. With luck, we'll all live long lives and never have to see one another again." Lahra set up the signal booster, tuning it to Arek's SOS. "How does that sound?"

Arek extended a limb to shake. "Your honor does you great credit, Lahra Kevain. Today, you have made a friend in the Imperium. Let us hope that today's carnage is the last such battle for a long time, and that I can convince the Great Council to find a better way forward."

"I wish you luck in moving your people to pursue peace, but I hope we will not cross paths again," Lahra said, jetpack carrying her back to the *Kettle*. It would be wiser to be open, to meet his offer of friendship with the same. But she was too wracked with fear and shame and grief and exhaustion to play the part of diplomat. She was a soldier. And soldiers did not easily lay down swords to embrace their enemies. Their oppressors.

The sensor beacon glowed bright, boosting Arek's signal. A nearby ship would find him in minutes, long before his condition would become critical. The Vsenk were made for space combat, after all. Though it seemed likely that Arek was the only one of their people in centuries who could say that he faced down their maker and lived to tell the tale. That boast should be worth a great deal in his people's war-council.

Max met Lahra in the cargo bay and helped her out of the suit. Not yet. Not quite yet. She held on tight, her heartbeat still racing with the thrill and terror of battle, until she was out of her suit entirely and the *Kettle* was safe in warp space.

"We made it," she said. "We really made it."

"You were amazing. Scary amazing. So. Is it over? We have to take care of the vessel, but what then?" Just being in Max's presence made the fear and shame seem more distant, reminded her why she'd taken control of Kelmai. She'd turned one tyrant on another to save the lives of those she loved and to prevent further bloodshed. Perhaps she could come to live with that decision. With time.

"Then I believe it will be time for us to take a vacation. Somewhere far away from the Empire's eye, but nowhere interesting. I require a week of supremely serene boredom, perhaps on a spa planet."

Max smiled. "I mean, that sounds amazing. There's got to be a spa planet somewhere, right? But with like giant tubs for the Vsenk? Not sure how we're going to pay for it, though."

"I mean, Wheel and Cog can probably smuggle us on, but then we'd need to hold the place hostage to afford the rates they charge."

Lahra laughed. "Compared to what we just lived through, taking hostages would seem a fine respite."

"Maybe we've been criminals too long if we're seriously thinking about knocking over a spa planet so we can afford a vacation. A little more Bonnie and Clyde than I was expecting."

"The logistics can wait for another day, perhaps."

Max looked at her. "Yeah, do you want to lie down? You just fought a self-made god and all."

"Don't condescend to me," she said with a grin. "I've had worse."

"Yeah, but your hands are shaking and you're pale as fuck. You should get some rest."

Lahra looked down at her hands, then nodded. "Very well. But I expect to hear about your spa world heist plan when I wake up."

"As you wish," he said as Lahra climbed into bed. He sat with her, pulling the covers over them.

At last, sleep took her, and worry vaporized into nothingness.

CHAPTER SIXTY-EIGHT

WHEEL

WHAT WAS LEFT OF the Imperial fleet was gone by the time they returned. Wheel flew the *Kettle* through the debris of Kelmai's wrath without incident. The two surveyed the damage to Axhara as the ship came in for a landing at the docks. Lahra was still sleeping. It'd only been a few hours since they left. Fires still burned in the distance, dead still lay in the streets. It would take a long time for Illhar to recover from this, especially without Imperial intervention. Not like they'd be sending aid unless it came with reinforcements and another lockdown. So the best the Illhari could hope for was to be ignored and left to fend for themselves.

"By the void, you're still alive?" Cog said over comms when Wheel patched into Resurgence HQ.

"I always pop back up, don't I?" she answered.

A beat. "I thought maybe this time you wouldn't. But with the day we've had, what the hell do I know?"

"Any word from the Imperium?" Wheel asked.

"Stay calm, remain in your homes. The same repeating message they switched to when they unleashed Kelmai. Rumors from our informants on Vsenkos say some member of the reform faction has called for an emergency council meeting, but that's not until tomorrow. What's Arek say about all this?"

Wheel smiled. "Arek is probably your reformer. We left him in Vsenkos space, down a limb but stable. If he tells them the truth about what happened, the fact that he survived a run-in with Kelmai and helped keep him from destroying the homeworld could go a long way to raising his profile. Assuming the Vsenk react like reasonable sentients."

"So not much hope, then," Cog said.

"We'll see. Docking now. Where do you need us?"

"Take number seven. I'll have someone meet you. Good to have you back."

"Good to be back. I think I'll claim those drinks you owe me tonight."

"You're on."

***

Wheel helped Max carry Lahra down the gangplank into the war-torn capital of Illhar. Last time they touched down they'd been hounded, full of questions, and the lovebirds hadn't even really known what they were getting into with the Resurgence. This time they'd just brokered a deal with a Vsenk and out-smarted a self-made god. Not bad.

They crashed in the quarters the Resurgence had given them, despite some protestations from Max and Lahra that they should help with disaster relief and cleanup. Cog disabused them of those notions and sent them to bed, saying that they could get to work tomorrow.

The next morning, a Rellix youth fetched them from the quarters with a summons from Cog.

"You are to report for an after-action meeting to discuss yesterday's events and set priorities for the day." The Rellix tried her best to sound official despite being maybe the equivalent of thirteen years old.

Except Cog was full of shit. The "after-action meeting"

wasn't a meeting, wasn't prep for a working day.

It was a voiding party. Half of Resurgence HQ was there, the docks turned into a barbeque-wake.

Cog herself stepped out from the crowd, wearing the fanciest clothing Wheel had seen the older Atlan wear in decades. Robes. She never wore robes.

"What the fuck is this?" Wheel said, knowing she had to have the biggest surprised face on, not that she could do anything about it even if she wanted to.

"You saved this world, and then another, though I'm a little iffy as to why that latter one was a good idea. So when folks heard about what you three did, they wanted to do something special."

"What about the relief efforts? Reconstruction?"

"We've got teams out. Hundreds, maybe a thousand people just in Axhara. People will come and go as shifts change over. Everyone here has been working for close to forty hours straight, so we could all use a break."

Max's smile stretched from ear to ear. "This is amazing."

"Thank you, Cog," Lahra added. She was looking a bit less run over, but still wiped out.

Catalyst, Oyira, and the brain trust gathered around Max, all dressed like they'd just stepped out of an academic conference.

Oyira stepped forward. "Thank you. All of you. I honestly did not expect to see this day. The Imperium is reeling, the people have taken to the streets to claim their freedom, and tomorrow has more promise and possibilities than I could have imagined."

Wheel, Max, and Lahra made the rounds, shaking hands, receiving hugs, and listening as Resurgence members and citizens alike heaped praise on them for the better part of two hours. Thankfully, they got to eat and drink along the way, or it would have been intolerable.

Wheel spent most of the afternoon drunk in order to

deal with the overwhelming attention. She disliked being in the spotlight to begin with, and being thanked that ceaselessly made her wish for a shower.

But the party wasn't for the three of them. It was for everyone else. If they were heroes, then this event was for the Resurgence, for the people of Illhar. Wheel didn't fancy being made into a symbol, but right now, people needed symbols. So much was up in the air. Maybe tomorrow the Imperium would be back and bombarding the city from orbit. Or maybe they'd sue for peace. They could say, "We set loose a monster and got kicked in the teeth. Truce?"

Not likely.

But for that moment, there was drinking, food, and laughter, and Wheel played the role people needed of her. That's what Atlans did; they got people where they needed to be.

What felt like days but was really hours later, Max and Lahra split off to the fancy hotel that had been booked for them. Wheel retired to Cog's chambers to celebrate, reminisce, and pick up their messy on-again, off-again affair. Who knew. Maybe this time, it'd stick.

Weirder things had happened.

CHAPTER SIXTY-NINE

AREK

T HE DOCTORS COULD NOT restore his arm. But very
quickly, he found that it helped set him apart. A defor-
mity, but also a badge of honor. He'd already felt himself set
apart from other Vsenk; this just made it more obvious.

Qerol came to visit him the next day for his report before
the Great Council.

Arek could have kept everything to himself. Could have
played the part of the captive, spun a story about how he'd
been overpowered by Kelmai gone rogue, had no memory of
being brought back to Vsenkos.

But he also saw the opportunity. So instead, Arek told
the whole story. Confronting Max and Lahra, Kelmai's turn,
the bargain, how he lost his arm, and Kelmai's return to torpor, taking the dangerous piece out of play.

Qerol had wrapped two arms together, writhing with
frustration. "Why didn't you keep the vessel? We'd have
secreted it away to hold over Evam. In fact, that's what we
should say." He sighed and shook his head as if suddenly resigned. "But it was you who saved Vsenkos, so by right the
choice was yours. If you would let me tell this story, I would

ask that you take command of the faction. And I expect that when this meeting convenes, we will find ourselves with a great deal many more friends."

Arek flashed back to the carnage caused by their creator. The cries of pain, the folding, spindling ships torn apart like crustacean appetizers. Thousands of lives lost because of their hubris. "It is better that Kelmai is off the field. We'd tear ourselves apart fighting over him, given enough time. Right now, I'm glad to be alive. If you're right, then maybe we'll have the leverage to bring Evam to heel, to avoid all-out war."

"Are you sure you don't want more time to recover before the meeting?"

Arek stood and walked toward the door, "I will be fine. We must act now, while the sting of our losses is still fresh."

***

Ahead of the meeting, Arek and Qerol spoke to dozens of nobles, in small groups and individually. Moderates, mostly, but even some of the Stalwarts had come to see them. Most to praise Arek's actions, some to beg for favors, and others merely reading which way the wind was blowing.

Last time he'd entered the Great Council, he was similarly filled with excitement, only to leave utterly deflated.

This time would be different. The Vsenk had suffered a terrible defeat and just barely avoided total annihilation. The Resurgence could press their advantage in any of a hundred ways if they saw fit. A moment of chaos and vulnerability called for sensible, reasonable leadership. Which had to mean Qerol and the Bright Suns.

As Arek walked into the hall of the Grand Melee with his mentor and former leader, nearly half of the room stood and applauded.

Evam, however, did not. The huge Vsenk stared Arek down, hate in his eyes. Arek was now a force to be reckoned with. And while he now had allies from all corners, Evam was far from beaten. The Vsenk's future, and that of the Empire,

373

was anything but settled.

How far would his influence go? And moreover, what did he *want* now that he had real power? He could give it up, settle for the quiet life he'd dreamed of these past years. But now there was the chance to do something more. To move the Vsenk forward. The Resurgence was a real threat, but they could also be an opportunity. Having a visible enemy would rouse Evam's anger, but cracking down now would just foment more rebellion.

The Vsenk had ruled through dominance and cruelty for a thousand years. They'd usurped the monster that was their maker and learned monstrosity from him.

Perhaps it was time to move beyond those lessons into something new. A better Vsenk Empire. Smarter, more calculating. A cold war with the rebels could provide great opportunity, even if peace was never really an option.

CHAPTER SEVENTY

LAHRA

LAHRA AND MAX HAD two whole days to themselves. They spent the first one in bed, recovering from various injuries, ordering food in, and forgetting the world existed.

Forgetting what she'd done.

The second day, they went out to survey the damage and help with the rescue efforts. Max basked in their new-found status as local heroes. But it made Lahra nervous. Anonymity was a security asset. If they stayed on Illhar, especially if they stayed in Axhara, she would need her own bodyguards.

Thankfully, on the third day, they returned to the *Kettle* for one last errand before they went on their way.

There were no Imperial ships to be seen on their way from Illhar to the Drell Migration, now well on the way to the Hulir Nebula.

This time Matriarch Yeddix saw them immediately, thanks to a message relayed through Kenoa. Their traveling companion met them at the edge of the Migration and led them in to meet once more with the largest sentient being in the galaxy.

"You have done well, Lahra, daughter of Halra; Max,

son of Danielle. My grandchild tells me you have something you'd like to hide away."

"Yes, Matriarch." Lahra looked directly at the single giant eye as she spoke. "We thank you for lending us the assistance of your scion, for directing us to Genos, and for receiving us again. We have the vessel containing Kelmai the Devastation, as well as the keys which keep him in torpor. Having seen what Kelmai can do up-close, I believe that there is no benefit to anyone being able to use his power, to hold the threat of Devastation over another."

Lahra shuddered as she spoke, haunted by the memory of seeing Kelmai fold, spindle, and mutilate the Vsenk cruiser at her behest.

"I see," Yeddix said, her voice rumbling as the translator rendered her massive booming calls into New Atlan. "I can take the vessel and keys out of rotation for quite some time. I would have done it long ago, had I known where they were."

"What will you do? How do we know it'll be safe?" Max asked.

"My ways are my own, Max, son of Danielle. I swear on my children that they will be as safe as I can make them. You have your own quests to pursue, and for the gift you have granted the sentients of warp space, I would grant you the peace of mind to pursue them."

"What is she going to do?" Max asked in a low voice, covering the comms.

Wheel chuckled. "She's going to eat them. Her digestive tract takes decades to process food, and her pellets are the size of cruisers. No signal will be able to get in or out."

Max's jaw dropped. "She's going to eat them and hide them in her shit?"

Wheel shrugged, and Lahra laughed.

The Atlan turned the comms back on. "We thank you, Matriarch. May the solar winds always guide you well."

"And you, star-farer."

Max shook his head. "Concealing artifacts in shit? By itself that's not the most bizarre thing I've heard, but at this scale . . ."

Wheel pulled the ship away, chatting with Kenoa on their way out. The younger Drell's next mission would be to the edge of warp space. "I believe you know of which I speak, Wheel."

"What's that?" Lahra asked.

Wheel savored the moment. "That's our next lead. Cog read me in before we left. Those distant allies she was going on about? She told me who they are. It's the Genae."

"We'll need a big ship and a bigger promise to get them out of that bunker before it's too late," Lahra said. "Not unless the queen reborn herself told them."

Wheel smiled. "That's the thing. She wasn't talking about the Genae we met. The Resurgence is in contact with the Genae Queen-in-exile."

"What?!" Lahra's voice shook the walls of the cockpit. Her world started spinning, every part of her torn apart, surprise and hope and guilt in a free-for-all.

Wheel threw her hands up in a defensive posture. "I just heard about it this morning! She made me swear to not tell you until Kelmai was taken care of."

"More!" Lahra seized Wheel by the shoulders. "Tell me everything, now!"

Max crossed his arms, settled onto one hip. He looked nervous.

Wheel continued. "The Genae rallying point is beyond warp space, right? Well, the scouts that the bunker Genae sent didn't die. Most of them actually made it. But the Queen-in-exile has kept them there. The Genae have been building a fleet, preparing to return to warp space to bring down the Empire. And Cog wants us to visit them as the official emissaries of the Resurgence, get them to move up their schedule. That should be enough to convince your shut-in cousins to get a move on."

"How? What?" Lahra's face was hot, and the world spun. "By all the gods, Wheel, if you're jesting—"

"If it's a joke, Cog's the one you should strangle. I've got the coordinates, right here." Wheel pointed to the nav system.

Beyond warp space, past the red eyes of Chiweu. That was the rallying point the Genae had spoken of.

Max offered a hand. "We should maybe sit down?"

She let him lead her to their chambers. She sat, entirely beside herself.

"When we get there, you should do what you need to do. We're a part of this Resurgence now, but that doesn't mean we have to stay with it. I saw how much it hurt to be among those broken and defeated cousins of yours. If the Queen-dom-in-exile is better, if they're what you really want, who you want to be with—"

Lahra shook her head. "That's not what's happening. I just never thought I'd really see the day that the queen would be restored. Being among my people on Genos told me that even though I accepted my mother's quest, took on the duty, it doesn't mean I have to do so blithely. You and I made a vow, Max Walker, that we would honor and love one another. If it comes down to choosing between the people I never knew and the man I know better than anyone, who I love more than the stars and the sky, then I choose you. "

She reached out a hand to him.

"Being Genae shouldn't mean giving up everything I want, everyone I love. I know you want to get home, and I want that for you, too. But when we do find that way home, I hope you'll want me with you. Because we've fought too long, seen strange and terrible things, and every one of them told me that I want you by my side."

Max was struck silent. She couldn't read his face; it moved too quickly from emotion to emotion.

"That might be the most I've ever heard you speak at once except as part of a song."

Lahra cracked a smile.

"Of course I want you to come with me to Earth," Max said. "I just always thought that this was . . . that when push came to shove, maybe you wouldn't choose me. The way you described it, duty for your people is all-consuming. And even if you love me, when the time came, you'd have to choose your people. I always wanted to be more than a bed warmer, but . . ."

Lahra put a hand on his shoulder. "You're far too cold to be a bed warmer. But you're as fine a partner as I could ever have asked for. The galaxy is changing every day. Everything is on a precipice. But the one thing I know more than anything is that I want you by my side, no matter what."

"And you've got me," Max said, tears in his eyes.

She kissed him. Kissed him and shut away the world.

Whatever the future held, she knew they could face it, weather it, and triumph.

Together.

END VOL. 1

ABOUT THE AUTHOR

Michael R. Underwood is an author, podcaster, and publishing professional. His works include the Ree Reyes *Geekomancy* books, the Stabby Award-finalist *Genrenauts* series, and *Born to the Blade*. He's been a bookseller, sales representative, and the North American Sales & Marketing Manager for Angry Robot Books. He is also a co-host on the podcast **Speculate** and a guest host on the Hugo Award-finalist **The Skiffy and Fanty Show**.

When not writing, he geeks out with games, comics, and making pizzas from scratch. Mike lives in Baltimore with his wife, their dog, and an ever-growing library.

ACKNOWLEDGEMENTS

WRITING ANY BOOK IS a journey, but this one has been especially long. *Annihilation Aria* started as a response to a prompt I asked myself in conversation with a colleague all the way back in 2014– "What would it look like to try to write something that made me feel the way the *Guardians Of The Galaxy* movie did?" I wrote a little of it in 2015, then put it aside for *Genrenauts*. Then a bit more before *Born To The Blade* took over my attention. It was my back-burner project for years and went through a number of drafts and iterations before becoming what it is today. It's come a long way from that first spark of an idea over a drink, but if not for that catalyst, this book wouldn't have ever happened.

I'm lucky to have a lot of feedback about the project as it made its way from spark to seed to partial to a short first draft and through a number of revisions. Thanks to everyone that gave their time and insight chatting with me about the novel: Jay Swanson, Beth Cato, A.C. Wise, Gary Kloster, Jason Kimble, and everyone else I chatted with as the book took shape.

I'm very grateful to Sara Megibow for helping the book along its way.

Thank you to Kim-Mei Kirtland for taking it over the finish line to publication, for being a strong advocate and business partner, and for championing the book across the wonderful world of sub-rights.

I'm very grateful to Clarence Young and Maurice Broaddus for their expertise and feedback on ways to better write Max with realism and empathy. Any successes in this are achieved with their help, while any failures are mine.

Writing this book overlapped greatly with my time at Angry Robot, where my colleagues taught me a great deal about storytelling, business, and life. They've all moved on to new projects as have I, but that time means a lot to me and has made me a better writer as well as a smarter businessperson. Thank you.

Thank you to Colin Coyle for believing in the book and giving it a home at Parvus Press. Huge thanks to Kaelyn Considine for the excellent editorial input and for pushing me time and time again because she believed in the book. Thank you to Tom Edwards for the beautiful art, to Jae Steinbacher for the meticulous copy edits, and Rekka Jay for formatting, promotional support, and more.

I'm doing this writing thing full-time now, and it's been a trip and a half. I'm very grateful to all of my Patreon supporters and everyone who has helped me find my footing as I put my writing first in my career. Working from home, I'm especially grateful to friends in the various online communities I've found, helping me figure myself out in this new stage of my life.

At the time I write this, it's a scary time in the world. And things are likely to get worse before they get better. I hope this book has been a break from the storm and/or provided some encouragement to press on. Like Max and Lahra and Wheel, we'll get through this by fighting for what we love and by doing it together.

May 13th, 2020
Baltimore

A WORD FROM PARVUS PRESS

www.ParvusPress.com

THANK YOU FOR CHOOSING a Parvus Press title and for your support of independent publishing.

If you loved ANNIHILATION ARIA, your review on Goodreads or your favorite retailer's website is the best way to support the author. Reviews are the lifeblood of the independent press.

Also, we love to hear from our readers and to know how you enjoyed our books. Reach us on our website, engage with us on Twitter (@ParvusPress) or reach out directly to the publisher via email: colin@parvuspress.com. Yes, that's his real email. We aren't kidding when we say we're dedicated to our readers.

On our website, you can also sign up for our mailing list to win free books, get an early look at upcoming releases, and follow our growing family of authors.

Thanks for being Parvus People,

—The Parvus Press Team

VICK'S VULTURES

UNION EARTH PRIVATEERS

BOOK ONE

BY SCOTT WARREN

PROLOGUE

ATOMIC FIRE BLOSSOMED, WHITING out the rear-facing sensors of the *Dreadstar*. First Prince Tavram scowled as his final Malagath warship disappeared from the battle reader, spent to allow him the opportunity to escape. A regrettable sacrifice, if necessary. Avoidable? Perhaps. Foreseeable? Absolutely not; this convoy was a secret even from the admiralty. Conclusion? Betrayal. The ambush had been swift and perfect. Likewise, the retribution would be equally so, in due time. For now, survival in the next few moments became the paramount task.

The Dirregaunt mastery of ambush was unparalleled within the known galaxy. Their vessels lurked, invisible to the naked eye at this distance, and cooled down to avoid sensor detection. From as far as a hundred thousand kilometers away they fired pre-charged banks of laser batteries, slicing metal and composite before closing to finish the work. The Malagath Prince knew the ships, knew the face of their commander, and knew the battle would not end with his retreat. Dirregaunt considered themselves the greatest of predators, and they would pursue him across the stars.

His helmsman said something, a buzz in his ears as a series of smaller explosions on the screen represented the remaining fighters being cut down by high-wavelength lasers. He lifted a blue, three-fingered hand to the helmsman and the remaining screens blurred as the *Dreadstar's* emergency engine fired, jumping the envoy frigate with her few survivors. His convoy died to provide him time to plot the calculations and activate the engine, generating a mass field outside the ship substantial enough to initiate a space-tear. It was the last jump the *Dreadstar* would ever make. Almost all her engineers were dead and her engines lay damaged beyond repair. His fate and the fate of his crew now rested with whomever chanced upon his distress signal. He prayed to the first stars it would not be Best Wishes.

***

On the bridge of the *Springdawn,* commander Best Wishes tapped his claws together with a mixture of consternation and elation. Technically, he had failed his mission objective. The *Dreadstar* fled, despite several large holes in her hull. The emergency engine was a new addition for which he had not been briefed and it allowed for a space fold to carry the Dreadstar away from battle. Rather than an easy pursuit, Best Wishes would be forced to extrapolate his trajectory based on space-time distortions his sensors read from the emergency engine. But once he followed, he would find the *Dreadstar* hanging limp. The severity of the hull compromises would cause compression shear should the First Prince attempt to accelerate past light speed, leaving the *Dreadstar* stranded wherever they emerged. A failed objective, but an opportunity to continue the hunt.

Best Wishes did not consider himself bloodthirsty. Rather, he carried a grudging respect for the Malagath and relished the opportunity to test himself further. Respect for their military prowess, if not their ideals. The Malagath culture was brutal and cruel and self-serving, antithetical to

Dirregaunt philosophies. Few had more blood on their hands than the Malagath royal family, and the First Prince was the architect of several notable Dirregaunt defeats.

He considered for a moment. His ships had not gone unscathed by the exchange. For whatever else they were, the Malagath were excellent fighters. They managed to destroy two of his frigates and cripple one of his battleships, extrapolating their positions even under fire and lancing them with particle cannons before the Dirregaunt ships began to move.

"Master hailman," he said, "I do not believe we require an entire battle group to pursue a single crippled frigate. Signal the *Surf* and the *High Rain* to return to the staging station."

He turned to his first officer, Modest Bearing, who had been with his command for almost as long as he'd *had* a command. "I should like the science team working immediately. Determine where the First Prince has gone, then plot a route," he ordered. His will carried out, he turned his four eyes back to the viewport where the exhaust residue of the *Dreadstar's* emergency engine expanded in an icy cloud at the edge of their magnification.

"You cannot run from me, First Prince."

CHAPTER ONE
VICK'S VULTURES

THE *CONDOR* PUSHED AWAY from the derelict hulk. There was little of value left aboard the *Morning Spear,* but the Vultures stole it anyway. It was what they called a cold wreck. No signs of life, no hot reactor, and not one of the Big Three. Malagath, Dirregaunt, Kossovoldt; those were the name of the game. Lately, Captain Victoria Marin of the Union Earth Privateers had run as cold as that salvaged wreck tilting out of her ship's forward monitors. Six weeks without good salvage would put her command in the red right fast. Trouble was, word across the Orion Spur said there had been no recent battles between the Big Three or their proxies anywhere within range of her little puddle jumper.

Odd that, since she was in a rough part of the galaxy. Hell, all of humanity was. Earth sat practically dead center in the Orion Spur, a no-man's land providing a bridge of stars directly between the frontiers of the Malagath and Dirregaunt pushing in from the Perseus Arm and the Kossovoldt from the Sagittarius Arm towards the Galactic Core. Right where she would expect them to be fighting. She wouldn't encounter Kossovoldt in this area, a species so prominent that the local galaxy had based a common language off their influence, but the Malagath Empire and Dirregaunt Praetory? You could hardly pull them away from each other's throats in this neck of the woods. They hated each other so much that they rarely left anything big enough to salvage anyway. Half their ships had been in service since before humans put a probe in space, but even the scrap was more valuable than her beloved *Condor.* Yet . . . no battles. Something was going on.

Victoria turned to her navigation officer.

"Huian, take us out of here. Growl Red while you're at it and have him report to the wheelhouse. He better have good news."

"Aye Skipper," said Lieutenant Wong. Victoria scowled behind the young Chinese woman's back as she stood from the captain's chair. Little blue-water puke up-jumped to space duty for being someone's daughter. Nothing against the little shit personally, but Victoria hated her rosters being mucked by political pull. Space was dangerous enough without the added variable of political nepotism.

Ducking through the hatch from the conn she made her way down two ladders, swinging past the galley and entering the officer's mess under the hand carved wooden plaque, labeling the compartment 'The Wheelhouse'. Once inside she made a beeline for the wet stores, snagging a tumbler from the wall on her way. Christ she needed this. As she was pouring the whiskey she heard the swish of the magnetic seal behind her and smelled a body recently freed from an extended vacuum suit vacation. She turned to Red Calhoun, the commander of her marines, still in his armored vacuum suit.

"Christ, Red, you could have at least dressed down. Drink with me."

The big Scotsman squeezed around the table grabbing a glass for himself. "Orders were to report to the wardroom, Vick. 'Sides, I dress down and it gives you an excuse to stare at my ass."

Victoria scoffed. "Don't kid yourself. I've seen what you're pushing. I wouldn't write home about it," she said.

Not entirely true, the marine had good broad shoulders and strong calloused hands. And combat experience was always a plus when serving a tour in her bunk. Not that she would ever tell any of this to Red.

"Anyway," she continued, pouring a few fingers into the second glass. "Anything good?"

There was a static sensation in the air and a change in the tone of the reactor as the *Condor* slid into the superluminal compression of her FTL drives. Outside, the ship began to move back towards the system's star for a horizon jump. Large space-time distortions were needed to enter a horizon jump. The closer to a star, the easier it became. Getting out was another matter, more of an art than a science. The hairs on Victoria's arms stood up, as they had every FTL slide since she had first climbed aboard an interstellar ship. It made her feel chilly, though every doctor she'd seen said it was psychosomatic.

Red washed his throat before answering. "A few high-freq conduits, burnt out core and storage matrixes, identification and effects of a few of the floaters and a functioning UV spectrum laser. Third generation, Tallidox made. Reactor was scuttled, but Aesop pulled some incomplete logs and schematics off a drive. Kid's a wizard with xenotech."

"In other words, garbage," she said.

"In other words . . ." said Red, nodding slowly to himself.

Victoria sighed. "You know what happens if we can't haul in any decent thieving."

"I know, I know. We get to Taru station without collateral and no one will extend us more credit. Ship gets stranded and we have to wait for the *Huxley* to pay down our debt and lend us some fuel."

"And you know I hate owing Jax shit. That cocksucker and his three missing teeth still haven't let me hear the end of it from last time. Never mind when we hauled his ass out of

394

the fire after he got those Graylings on his wake. Don't take to being ransomed, Graylings."

Red chuckled over his glass. "You remember when we pulled him outta what was left of the *Dolphin*? He was grinning so wide I thought his face'd get stuck like that. What'd he get on that haul?"

"Shit, that was the run he made off with the undamaged core manifold what let the third gen Kosso hulks push past 120c wasn't it? Old tech to them, almost ancient really, but we're still figuring it out Earth-side. That's why they gave him the *Huxley*. Shit, 120 times the speed of light? We do that, and we'll be hopping between stars in just a couple days. Without a horizon drive. We're going to go from 40 worlds to 400 before the xenos can blink. Let's see 'em try to push us out of the Orion Spur then."

"That's still a long way off, Vick. How about we start with making it back to human space?"

The two sat in silence for a time before it was interrupted by the mechanical chirp of the growler. Vick picked up the analogue receiver. Ancient tech even so far as humans were concerned, sound powered and nigh infallible the privateer fleet still made use of them for internal communications.

"Wheelhouse, Captain speaking."

"Wheelhouse sensors, Ma'am. We're getting a deliberate distress signal. Encrypted but it's a Malagath Codec. The crypto computer broke it down enough for a location. It's within Horizon range, three rungs up on the azimuth and almost on the way to Taru. Could even be hot, origin is two days old maybe."

"Shit Avery, that's Big Three, why'd you wait so long to tell me?"

"Wanted to confirm it first, Vick. I'll go ahead and kick it over to Huian."

Victoria slammed down the receiver and opened up the command network console in her retinal implants. She watched excitedly as Huian received the information and made the necessary course adjustments to change their Horizon drive destination. She stood up to activate the main circuit and address the crew but found Red had already done it for her, smiling his wide, toothy smile.

"This is the Captain." She grinned back.

"At 1900 hours we detected a distress call within horizon range. It's Big Three, people, maybe even hot. We'll be activating the horizon drive at 2050 hours. General quarters will be at 0230 hours. You know what this means. Rest up if you're not on watch, all drills are on hold. Marin out."

The cheer from the crew was audible through the metal hull of the *Condor* and Victoria couldn't help feeling proud. Even if the cheers were as much for the cancelled damage control drills as for the prospect of hot salvage. Her Vultures were the best privateers in deep space as far as she was concerned. And damn if Earth wasn't getting awful tiny in the rear-view mirror all the way out here.

"Red, you gonna get some sleep before GQ?"

He raised an eyebrow. "You?"

"Now? Shit no. I just hope no one beats us there."

"And I need to debrief my marines, and then brief them back up again, and find time for a shower in there somewhere."

In her current mood Victoria wouldn't mind debriefing one of his marines personally. "Malagath Imperials, what can we expect if there are survivors?" she asked.

"Well if the ship is in good shape we're looking at a tactical Alcubierre drive, high density particle cannons, gravitic seekers."

"Shit. If they were in good shape there'd be no distress call."

"I agree. We manage to board, it gets a little simpler. Toxic atmo is likely, but meaningless to a marine in a vac suit. We're looking at masers and little to no tactical discipline. They haven't had an infantry battle in centuries. The ablative plates should do for the marines and I doubt the Malagath have seen a slug rifle since they went to space."

It was probably true, when humanity first entered the galactic arena they found it packed to the rafters with over a hundred other races; all at uneasy odds with each other, and none of whom still used kinetic weaponry. By and large most had made it about as far as the musket before weaponizing light, heat, accelerated particles, or radiation. Battery and energy production technologies in the galaxy-at-large were an area in which Earth struggled to catch up.

So, now she was headed toward a hulk manned by one of the Big Three. She considered the potential salvage, tapping her fingers on her tumbler. No telling what the Union Earth would do to get their hands on that tech. Or for that matter, what some of the local players might do to keep it out of U.E. hands. Red picked up his helmet and left, leaving her alone with the whiskey. She poured herself another.

***

Best Wishes examined the data brought to him by the science team. For three days they circled the departure point of the *Dreadstar*, attempting to extrapolate the trajectory and likely emergence destinations with what little they knew of the *Dreadstar's* emergency engine. High math. Nigh impossible, he would have thought, but his science team was unparalleled. He thanked the master astrotician and gave the order to his navigator. The *Springdawn* lurched into action, accelerating back towards the distant pinprick of the local star at almost 250 times the speed of light. Best Wishes did not have access to the single-use gravitic generator of the *Dreadstar's* emergency engine. They would have to use the gravity field of the red dwarf to pounce across the stars towards his prey. But he had the scent. It was only a matter of hours now. The Malagath ship fled further in a single jump than the span of most of the lesser empires, but the *Springdawn* could match it. They were both far from any allies.

***

First Prince Tavram huddled in the cold interior of the *Dreadstar* bridge with the nine remaining crew of his original fifty. Habitation control was a luxury they could not afford while emergency power dwindled. The hull breaches exposed the interior of the vessel to the chill of deep space, and with the reactor offline no waste heat was being produced to replace what was lost. Entropy might kill them before ever Best Wishes determined which way they had fled.

"My Prince," a ragged voice called from the sensor display. Tavram turned toward his youngest crewmember, Aurea, a female of only twenty solar cycles. His junior engineer, now his senior engineer. She looked up at him, face illuminated by the display. "A ship has entered the system, it is accelerating towards us."

"Is it the *Springdawn?* Send a signal, let us be done with this one way or another."

"No my prince, it is moving too slowly, I cannot believe it is Dirregaunt. And I am getting very little data, nothing further than confirming that there is something coming. They should be on the optical now but even visually there is nothing."

"Sending the distress call again, short range," another voice rasped. His impromptu communicator. Previously his ship's cook. Everyone's voice was labored; carbons were building up in the ship's atmosphere. Tavram pulled up the optics display on his own console, tuning it to the proper bearing. Aurea had been right, there was nothing. At this range . . . wait, there. A star winked out. Another followed shortly, and then another along the same vector. Soon a profile began to emerge. The ship was matte black, like nothing he recognized. Had they been purposefully flying *between* stars to prevent a visual cue? A predatory tactic. The folds of skin on Tavram's slender throat began to grow moist as the ship's profile hardened. A primal reaction. Fear? No. Caution. Wariness of the unknown.

It was small, perhaps half the size of the *Dreadstar*. Odd lines. No elegance. An ugly craft. He couldn't place it with any of the lesser empires he was familiar with.

In a matter of minutes, the alien ship pulled alongside the *Dreadstar*. While obviously slow to transit, her helmsman handled her beautifully, matching the *Dreadstar's* unstable spin with maneuvering engines. Tavram wondered what the newcomers used to perform the maneuver. Some sort of gravitic adjustors? Subspace repulsors?

The *Dreadstar* jolted with a metallic thump and a spike in the passive electromagnetic sensors. Magnetic locks. Primitive, inefficient, but effective. Two more impacts resonated through the hull and the ship began to vibrate as the view through the forward monitors slowly ceased spinning. Now what? Would they tow the *Dreadstar* back to the system's core and attempt a joined space tear?

He was still postulating when a new sound came from the hull, one that could be mistaken for nothing else. *Footsteps.* Several of the remaining crew looked panicked, and even Tavram sucked in a breath of stale air. *Space walkers,* children's tales to frighten cadets. Creatures who crossed the vacuum to steal souls, who walked in the void. No, this was just an unfamiliar lesser empire, using primitive technology. It must not be . . .

"My prince, the sunward habitat chamber near the foremost hull breach has been . . . compromised. The seal has been forced open, atmosphere is venting."

"By the first stars," uttered a voice.

"Quiet," Tavram ordered. He pulled up the airlock status on his console. The venting had ceased. Had the stress on the ship from the docking caused it? Plausible. The chamber was isolated, in full vacuum now.

The icon for the inner habitation chamber hatch began to flash on his screen. Mechanical failure. *First stars, the spacewalkers were in the ship!* And he could do nothing as he tracked their progress. Nothing except buy himself a few more seconds. He ordered the survivors into position, interposing them between himself and the door. They had no weapons, but they might serve to distract while he got a few shots off. His heart raced, the cartilage in his joints expanded. These were ancient fight-or-flight traits encoded in his genome he'd not felt in years.

Even deathly thin as the atmosphere was, his entire crew's labored breathing was silent. Metallic sounds from the other side of the bulkhead were translating through the metal floor. Tavram could feel the vibrations of the spacewalkers. He fingered the single handheld maser kept on the bridge, and raised it in a ready stance. It was heavy in his hands, burdened with the weight of his lineage's survival. It wouldn't do much good against a serious enemy but the polymer grip was comforting.

Two metal prongs slid through the join in the hatch, startling a cry of alarm from his remaining crew. A mechanical whir, then the prongs began to pry the door open. The device forcing the door open was pulled away. Behind it stood several short, stocky figures. They were matte black like the alien ship had been, except for plating lining their chests and shoulders that was just slightly glossy. Two arms, two legs as evolution had produced on countless worlds as a most efficient design. In their hands they held their primitive xeno weaponry. Long, black, and slim he could not tell if it was some kind of maser like the one he had leveled or perhaps a particle beam. The array of soldiers spread into the room, fingers kept off what must be triggers for the moment. Two of the alien weapons were pointed at him while the rest scanned across his crew looking for additional threats. They found none. Their movement was martial, economical, and precise. No motion was wasted, no part of the bridge unchecked.

Tavram stared through the shaking optics of his maser at

what he thought was the leader, but in truth all eight looked identical. A veteran of several space engagements, he had yet to fire a personal weapon at anyone in his life. As he looked down the gaping tunnel of that alien's weapon he did the only thing he could think to do for any hope of survival. He lowered the maser.

The change in the space walkers was instantaneous. Their deadly muzzles on their weapons lowered, their posture more relaxed, if still tight. The tallest of them reached out and took the maser from his hand. He didn't resist.

"Is there a leader among you?" he asked. The largest stepped forward.

"I am Major Red Calhoun, of the *Condor*."

It spoke in Malagath. His voice was tinny, mechanical, unexpected. Tavram had asked in the common Kossovoldt language, but the alien had answered in his own dialect.

"Space walkers!" cried the engineer from behind Tavram, less in terror and more in amazement. He silenced her with a wave. The First Prince switched back to Malagath.

"What is your empire?" he demanded. Red? Did they often name their warriors after visible spectrum light?

"We are human," it said. Curious. Tavram had never heard of humans, but then he rarely concerned himself with the affairs of the lesser empires. After all, they were little better than animals, and over 1500 had been encountered. Some of them had even been scoured away by the Malagath. Had the emergency engine cause the *Dreadstar to* invade their space? Surely their primitive vessels could not secure a large place in the stars.

"And your intent?" asked Tavram.

The creature turned its head away, muffled sound came through the helmet, perhaps he was communicating over a shortwave communicator.

He turned back. "Our intent is to salvage mechanical technology from your ship, then take your remaining crew aboard the *Condor*," he said.

This was met with wails of anguish behind him, and the creature raised a hand in what he must have thought was a placating gesture. "After which, we intend to return you unharmed to your people, in exchange for what supplies and technology we can barter for you. You will not be harmed in our custody."

Tavram relaxed. He had heard about outfits such as these from the lesser empires. Scavengers who picked the bones of the great battles in hopes of finding any functioning wreckage. Likely these space walkers intended to take anything valuable back to the planet Human to study. Though most were not interested in dealing with survivors, and tended to wait until there were none to move in. Some were even less interested in waiting than others.

"In the interest of self-preservation, human Red, I must inform you that we are being hunted, a Dirregaunt specialist has been tasked with eliminating this ship."

The alien quickly bobbed his head a single time. Curious gesture. "We don't plan to stay long once we get your people aboard. What is the most valuable asset aboard this ship that we can easily remove?"

The first prince gestured to himself. "You are speaking with him, human Red."

Read more in VICK'S VULTURES, available now